The Khan's Mistake

The Fight For Genghis Khan's Throne

By

Diane Wolff

ISBN: 978-1-7346019-1-6
© Copyright 2023 Diane Wolff
All Rights Reserved
Published by Genghis Productions, Port Charlotte, Florida
Publisher: Diane Wolff

Maps and Illustrations: Online

Genghis Khan's Warfare
https://docs.google.com/presentation/d/11i1TD5LxrZAWkWRET6bIe
RUkbueDOXPC/edit?usp=sharing&ouid=106945766984273111328&r
tpof=true&sd=true

Everything You Wanted To Know About Genghis Khan:
https://docs.google.com/presentation/d/11xjrivmm-
mBqfFpMZwedGdN_tol_mKzy/edit?usp=sharing&ouid=1069457669
84273111328&rtpof=true&sd=true

Table of Contents

6

Dedicated to Robert A. F. Thurman and Nena Thurman.

1 The Emperor Summons the Sage

Every year, Liu Wan, the Chinese arrow-maker, made the secret weapon of the Mongol Army, the whistling arrows. Every year, he delivered the arrows to the Master of Weapons.

Every year, Genghis Khan, the man known as The Conqueror, came to the arrow-maker's tent while he worked to listen to the gossip of the military camp.

This was how Genghis Khan heard about the Chinese sage, Master Chang, who lived in a temple in China called the Abode of Clouds and Mists. The Sage, so the arrow-maker said, had lived to the age of 300 years and possessed a magic potion called the Elixir of Immortality.

Genghis Khan had to have it.

The Supreme Khan wore a helmet lined with sable. His eyes were amber. His hair was red. He was tall, six feet. He was a master horseman and had once had a rock hard physique, but he was aging and was not as he was in his youth. His people called him the Man of Iron.

He was the steppe incarnate. He loved mobility, the free open life of the grasslands, the nomad highway. that stretched from one end of the world to the other. He did not like fixed buildings. He preferred the steppes, the movement of The Horde, to civilization.

He wore the same uniform as his men, riding trousers, a belted tunic and soft leather riding boots. He slept in a tent like his men, ate the same meat broth and rode into battle at the head of his army. He knew his commanders' skills and talents. His army was the greatest fighting force in the world. He was indomitable. He never lost a battle. Mobility and strategy were his hallmarks.

The Supreme Khan was known for employing every talent and technique in his world and using knowledge and skill to accomplish great deeds. This was his genius. He used cavalry warfare in the steppe wars. He learned siege warfare in China, the taking of walled cities. He took siege engineers with him when he went to make war in the West.

He had taken an army over the Roof of the World and conquered the Shah of Khwarezm for a breach of his Code of Laws. For this campaign, he mastered desert warfare.

Within a few miles of his military camp, the beautiful old city of Samarkand lay smoldering. He had put it to the torch. The Khan was waiting for the cool weather of autumn to take his army home over the Roof of the World. Genghis Khan's adopted brother Shiki was taking an inventory and packing up the Shah's treasure, hundreds of cartloads, for the ride back to his native pastures.

The Shah had run away and escaped in a boat rather than face Genghis Khan's surprise tactic, taking an army through the desert of Kyzl Kum.

The creation of singing arrows was a closely guarded secret. The whistling terrified the enemy, even the fiercest cavalry.

The light cavalry fired volleys of thousands of arrows to soften up the front ranks. The air came alive. The whistling of thousands of arrows confused enemy archers and spooked enemy horses. The signal flags rose. The heavy cavalry rode in to decimate the enemy. The cavalry formations of Genghis Khan had no equal in the world. He had devised the movements of the wings the army from the Grand Hunt, the greatest spectacle in Asia.

Liu wandered among the tables of his assistants giving them instructions as they sorted and prepared the herbs, measured them, and boiled and strained the secret potions. When the potions cooled, the assistants dipped the cut rice paper into the liquid and wrapped it around the arrows behind the tip, folding the paper so it flared slightly.

9

They sealed the wraps with a spot of specially prepared glue. The Khan came over to the bench to watch.

Liu bent over his table, focused on his task. He made small talk with the Khan. "I have never seen the arrows used in battle. It must be quite a sight."

"It is a magnificent sight. My secret weapon is terror. It is one of my cardinal rules of war. The battlefield is in the mind of the enemy." The Khan sat down again. "Tell me more about the Elixir. I would like to live to be 300 years of age. I have so much left to accomplish."

"What do you have to accomplish, Khan?"

"I must punish the King of Xi Xia. He did not behave as a vassal. The King was insolent to my envoy. He said, 'If Genghis Khan is such a great Khan, how come he needs troops from me for his war against the Shah of Khwarezm?'"

"That was rude!" said the arrow-maker.

"My sentiments exactly. I can't let him get away with a breach of my *Yasa*, my Code of Laws, or my other vassals will test me."

"You are right, sir," said the arrow-maker.

The Supreme Khan said, "I want to complete the conquest of China. The first ruler to put China back together again."

"It has been split since the fall of the Tang. That would be quite an achievement, sir. The Southern Song is rich. You need not worry about the future. You named an heir before you left the homeland. Everyone knows that you named Ogodei as your successor."

"Yes. Ogodei is a diplomat. He has a kind heart and a talent for compromise, but he has weaknesses. He is generous to a fault. He pays the merchants twice what they ask so his name will be remembered in the hearts of the common people. He constantly overspends the stipend he gets from me. He is my son, but I chastise him for being too devoted to pleasure. I need time."

"What about Tolui?" He was referring to Genghis Khan's youngest son by the Empress Bortai.

"His mind works like mine. He likes secret weapons. He's on campaign in Russia with Subudei. He found sorcerers who perform magic with river water and stones. They conjured up a storm in the middle of a battle. The enemy ran away."

"Amazing," said Liu Wan.

"Self-made men are hard men. I created the empire from nothing. My sons will inherit it. That's the difference. They will have everything handed to them. They will forget that they owe it all to me. They will ride Arabians and wear garments of silk and hold the loveliest women in their arms."

"I don't believe that your sons will forget you. You leave the generals to advise them."

"My generals are the greatest commanders in the world, but they are my age and they will die off. Then who will advise them?"

"Tolui is a real talent. He has fought at your side in every campaign."

"You're right about that. Tolui is a solid military man. I left him the greatest part of the army. His task is to back up the reign of Ogodei."

"That was wise, sir."

An assistant placed a rack of finished arrows in the sun to dry. Another assistant picked up the dried arrows with care and placed them in quivers without disturbing the tips.

Genghis Khan told the arrow-maker the story of his youth, how his father had been murdered by the Tatar and his family lost everything. How his father had arranged a marriage for him. How his betrothed, Bortai. had waited for him and brought the dowry that enabled him to rise among the young khans of the steppes.

He promised Bortai that her sons would inherit his empire, for she had been there at the beginning. Before Genghis Khan departed for the West, his wives asked him to make a last will and testament. They wanted to know his wishes in the matter of the succession in case he did not return from the campaign.

He called his personal secretary and his generals and summoned his four sons. The gathering had been a disaster.

No family is immune from the rivalries of children for the love of the father. The eldest son Jochi and the second son Jagadai got into a fistfight. The generals had to separate them. Chancellor Yeh-lu reminded Jagadai to respect their mother, for the fight was about the matter of the kidnapping and the paternity of the eldest.

Genghis Khan passed over the two eldest and named his third son Ogodei as his heir. Ogodei was a peacemaker, but Ogodei drank too much and indulged in a life of pleasure. He loved hunting and the company of his moon-faced mistresses, as he called them.

After the campaign in North China, Genghis Khan thought that he would spend his days hunting and passing time with his wives and concubines. He had no intention of going to war in the West.

Unfortunately, the Shah of Khwarezm murdered his ambassador, a violation of the Code of Genghis Khan, the Yasa. The Shah had to be punished or the reputation of Genghis Khan as the supreme political master of Asia would be destroyed.

So, he took his army over the high mountain passes at the Roof of the World and went to war in the West. He waged a desert campaign full of deceptions. The Shah did not chastise the Khan for entering his territory but put his faith in the walls that surrounded his beautiful cities.

The Shah did not listen to the council of his son Jelaladdin who was a great warrior. The son told his father that the army of Khwarezm was no match for the greatest army in the world, the army of Genghis Khan. The son said the father was making a serious error in judgment, but the father did not listen.

Genghis Khan hired a scout and took an army into a trackless desert called Kyzl Kum. He emerged as a surprise and surrounded the Shah's city of Samarkand, a pincer attack with armies led by his sons. The Shah abandoned his city and ran away.

General Subudei thought the victory was too easy. "Why didn't he stay and fight?" said Subudei.

Genghis Khan took over the Shah's palace. He also took possession of the Shah's harem, but he did not like the veiled women. His fourth wife Gulan was with him. She was younger than he was and she was the love of his life, as much as any woman could compete with his love of war.

His adopted brother Shiki was the Minister of the Treasury. Shiki took an inventory—he could read and write--and loaded up the Shah's treasury. Five hundred black carts would take the treasury back to the homeland.

How did a Khan remain popular and command the loyalty of his troops? The answer was booty. The senior commanders would oversee the distribution to the junior commanders, and they would give out booty all the way down to the soldiers. Every Mongol would be rich.

Genghis Khan recruited Chancellor Yeh-lu after the fall of the Jin Dynasty. Yeh-lu had served the Jin Emperor in the Central Secretariat and he wielded the Seal of State.

After the fall of the dynasty. Genghis Khan summoned him and offered him a post as his personal secretary. He told Yeh-lu, "I am not an educated man, but I surround myself by educated men. You are one of them." Yeh-lu had fully expected to be put to death. He accepted the post.

Yeh-lu knew how to run a government. He designed the government for the Central Asian. It was to be the pattern for all the khanates, from China to Persia and Russia.

The Mongols had no knowledge of administration. Yeh-lu made use of local officials and forms of taxation and left Mongol governors, *darugachi*, to forward the taxes collected from the people of Khwarezm. The revenue would flow to the Supreme Khan's treasury. The governors conscripted troops to serve in the garrison. The arrangement was repeated everywhere in the Empire, including China.

Yeh-lu was a master of the three philosophies of China. He was a Confucian in his public life because he thought Confucianism was the best philosophy for the ordering of the state. He was a Buddhist in his private life because he thought Buddhism was the best philosophy for the ordering of the mind. He considered it his mission to civilize the Supreme Khan. His only mistake was recommending the Daoist sage.

The Chancellor convinced the Khan, who consulted the shamans, to bathe in the river because the men had to overcome their superstition. The men would follow the example of their Khan. They would see that the thunderstorms would not come because the spirits were disturbed. The practice of bathing was the only way to prevent the epidemics of battlefield diseases, cholera and typhoid, said the Chancellor, who was a physician.

"You see," said the Chancellor, "I am civilizing you." The Chancellor persuaded the Khan to cease the slaughtering of survivors after a battle. This was a momentous achievement.

The Supreme Khan had conquered Samarkand and Bukhara, the Shah's walled cities, decorated with beautiful tiles, thriving centers of commerce on the Silk Road. The cities had many skilled artisans and craftsmen. The Mongol homeland had none. He gave orders that 100,000 of these laborers would be moved to the Mongol capital, Khara Khorum, Black Rock--stonemasons, sculptors, potters, metallurgists, saddle-makers, leatherworkers, weavers of carpets. His people would have items of manufacture, where before they had nothing but the products of animal husbandry, tanned hides and beaten felt, and, of course, *koumiz,* the alcoholic drink.

The governors, *darugachi*, would enforce his Code of Laws throughout the empire. His people would build roads and post-stations.

Genghis Khan believed that he was Beloved of Heaven, that he was destined to rule all peoples. It was the will of the Eternal Blue Sky. All his life, he had consulted Speakers to Heaven. He allowed all religions to practice freely within his empire.

He sent for the Muslim imams and mullahs and listened to their explanation of the tenets of their faith. He chastised them for saying that one could only pray facing Mecca. The Eternal Blue Sky was everywhere, he said.

What was this about not eating pork? The Mongols were famously wide eaters. He thought it was ridiculous not to eat boar. He disputed with them, but he let them open the mosques and the schools. He opened the bazaars and trade flourished. After the conquest came trade.

General Subudei was the greatest strategist in the army, after Genghis Khan. He had joined the army as a blacksmith's son and had risen to be the top commander. These two had a meeting of minds. Subudei was essential to the planning and execution of campaigns. Subudei asked for twenty thousand troops and rode across the steppes, the nomad highway, the vast grasslands, in pursuit of the Shah who had escaped in a boat on a river.

Subudei rode with General Jebe and an expeditionary force to Russia where he discovered warriors who fought as mounted archers, the Kipchaks. He defeated them.

Then he discovered Russia's riches. The principalities were small cities walled in timber. The citizens traded in furs and timber on the Volga.

Beyond Russia was the Black Sea, where the merchants from the Italian city-states of Venice and Genoa traded with the Russian traders. They traded luxury goods and foodstuffs to Constantinople, where the ships left for Europe and Africa. Subudei bribed the Europeans to give him intelligence for a future invasion of Europe. He reported to the Supreme Khan that the merchants of Venice and Genoa sold each other out for profit. He promised to wipe out the rival. The Venetians accepted his offer. That is how Marco Polo came to trade in Bukhara, on his way to the palace of Khubilai Khan.

Subudei defeated a coalition of Russian princes at a battle on the River Kalka. The Mongol commanders laid a slab of wood down to use as a table and suffocated the princes beneath while they feasted their victory on top. Then they executed the princes wrapped in carpets while their horses kicked them to death, for it was a crime against The Ancestors to spill the blood of a prince upon the ground. Beyond Russia were the forests of Europe, but the forests were not ideal terrain for Mongol ponies. That was a campaign for a future time.

Subudei received his orders and he returned, leaving a horse depot. After a cavalry ride of 5000 miles, he rejoined the Khan for the ride home.

To Genghis Khan, the world was full of possibilities. Could it be that the Elixir enabled a man to live 300 years? If so, he had to have it.

Master Chang resided in a temple called the Cloud and Mist Retreat, on a mountainside in Hunan. His days were spent lost in contemplation or hiking up the mountainside to gather herbs. He went about his practice undisturbed, contemplating and perfecting his understanding. He instructed students who came to escape the din of the world and find purity in their bodies and minds.

The Master did not teach the superstitions of the common people. The Master had studied the ancient texts and he taught his students the esoteric teaching: the alchemy of transforming the body and the mind into immortality.

From earliest times, the Daoists, the mystics of the Chinese tradition, believed that certain substances--jade, pearl, mother-of-pearl, and cinnabar--taken internally, would promote long life.

The science of transforming the body by means of physical, psychological and mental disciplines returned the practitioner to an original pure state. This was immortality. In his text, "Straight Guide to the Mighty Elixir," Master Chang explained his yoga of immortality.

The Emperor of the Jin state in North China and the Southern Song Emperor had summoned Master Chang to court, but the Master declined their invitations. He had no wish to leave his mountainside. He loved being close to nature.

He told the Jin and Song Imperial Envoys that his movements were controlled by Heaven. "People not steeped in the Dao don't understand. When the time comes, I will go to Court. There is nothing else to say."

Things were different with the Envoy of Genghis Khan. Liu Wan entered the hall of the temple with a retinue of 20 Mongols and presented the Master Chang with a golden tablet in the shape of a tiger's head.

The tablet contained the Great Khan's message: "This man is empowered to act with the same freedom as I myself should exercise had I come in person."

Liu Wan made his pronouncement. "Your name is esteemed throughout the empire. The Emperor has sent me as his Special Envoy across great distances, with the command that no matter how long it takes, I must return with you." A Mongol officer of the guard chimed in and added his speech to convince the Master of the Emperor's urgent desire to see him.

The Master replied, "Wars cause the frontiers to change constantly. You have braved great dangers coming to see me. Thank you."

Liu replied, "My journey took seven months. I had a difficult time tracking you down. Because I act under imperial orders, I have no choice but to exert myself to the utmost. When I finally found out where you were, I wanted to send 10,000 soldiers to escort you, but the officials of the province said it would be improper to do so at the moment--the Mongols and the Jin dynasty are negotiating. A sudden influx of troops might alarm the inhabitants of these eastern provinces. They are just beginning to settle down after the long years of warfare. I followed the advice of the governor and came with only 20 men.

"When we neared I-tu province, I sent two men to inform General Chang Lin of my arrival. The General met me at the city gates with 10,000 men in armor. I told him that I was on my way to visit a sage, Master Chang, and had no need of armored men. The General dispersed his troops and rode with me into town. Once my mission was understood, no one was nervous or afraid in any town we passed."

The Master realized that refusing Genghis Khan was out of the question. He spoke calmly. "I will be ready to travel on the 18th. On that date, please send 15 horsemen to fetch me. In these parts, supplies are difficult to obtain. You and your party had better wait for me in I-tu. I will join you when the ceremonies of the Feast of Lanterns are over."

After the ceremonies, while the Imperial party made arrangements for the westward journey, a message arrived informing Liu Wan that the Supreme Khan had shifted his headquarters further west. Master Chang hesitated and told Liu Wan that perhaps his great age would make him unequal to a journey which involved so much fatigue and exposure. He asked if he could meet Genghis Khan when The Conqueror returned from the Western Campaign.

Something else distressed the Master. He discovered that Liu Wang intended to take with him on this journey all the girls whom he had collected for the Supreme Khan's harem. His Daoist sect had a reputation for extreme asceticism, a spiritual path which would have little appeal to a Mongol Khan since the Mongols were known for their appetites.

The Sage said, "I do not think you ought to expect me to travel with harem girls, even though I am a humble servant of the Khan." He mentioned a story about Confucius. "When the men of Chi offered female musicians as a present to the King of Lu, Confucius quit the state of Lu."

Flustered, Liu Wan sent an urgent message to the Emperor. The Sage included his own message, requesting that the travel arrangements be changed.

As they awaited a response, Master Chang busied himself performing the Ceremonies of the Full Moon. No sooner had he completed the ceremonies than a torrential rain fell, ending a long drought. The local people considered this a great blessing. This enhanced the reputation of the Master.

Word arrived from the Supreme Khan saying that they must make haste and must, on no account, delay their leave-taking. The harem girls were left behind.

19

In September, a member of the Khitan royal house returned from delivering the message. He bore an Imperial Command from Genghis Khan to Master Chang.

The letter praised the Master above the three philosophers and declared that Master Chang's merits were recognized in the remotest corners of the earth. Further, the message said, "Now that your cloud-girt chariot has issued from paradise, the cranes that drew it will carry you pleasantly through the realms of India.

"The way before you, both by land and water, is long, but I trust that the comforts that I shall provide you will not make it seem so long. This reply to your letter will show you how much concern I have. Now that I know you passed safely through the severe heat of autumn, I will not trouble you with further friendly messages."

Genghis Khan's instructed Liu Wan: "Do not allow the Master to over-exert himself or to go too long without food. Make sure that he travels in comfort by easy stages."

The party waited at the Lung-yang temple until the severe weather in the Gobi Desert abated and then they began their long journey. The Emperor's party left on the third of March in excellent weather. A coterie of Daoist friends accompanied the party to the western outskirts of town. The Master completed his farewells and promised to return in three years.

Three years later the master did indeed return to his temple accompanied by Disciple Li. The master carried an edict signed and sealed by Genghis, that Daoist temples in China would no longer be taxed.

There were far fewer Daoist temples than there were Buddhist temples, and the Buddhists were far richer. The edict was to cause a great deal of trouble between Daoists and Buddhists in the future, because the Daoists grew powerful under the imperial patronage and began appropriating Buddhist temples. Daoist and Buddhist students began having pitched battles in the streets of the capital. The result of the master's visit was a matter requiring the intervention of Genghis Khan's grandson, Mongke Khan, an extraordinary ruler.

Disciple Li wrote the story *Travels of an Alchemist* and read the text in the afternoons, under the poplar tree, to the young Daoists.

Master Chang arrived at the Supreme Khan's camp in late spring. The Master's lodging had been arranged. Finally, the moment that Genghis Khan had eagerly anticipated, the teaching, and the delivery of the Elixir, was at hand. The Sage entered the tent of the Khan.

The Conqueror was in an expansive mood. "The sight of you gives me great pleasure. You turned down the invitations of the Emperors of Jin and Song, but have come a far distance to see me."

The Master said simply, "My coming has been the Will of Heaven."

Genghis Khan said that his life too had been dictated by the Will of Heaven. It had been his destiny to conquer many kingdoms.

The Sage agreed. Genghis Khan was eager and asked about the famous Elixir of Long Life that the Master had brought from China.

The Master replied, "I have a means of protecting life, but no elixir that will prolong it."

The Khan let the words penetrate and finally understood that there was no magic potion that he could drink.

Success in war depends on the ability to improvise. Genghis Khan was a master of adaptation. "If your practice prolongs your life, it will prolong mine. I have heard that you are 300 years old. Is this true? If so, I would like to live to be 300 years old."

The Sage explained that the Chinese way of counting years amounted to three in one. He was not 300, but almost 100 years. Genghis Khan was disappointed but admitted that 100 years would be enough for him, although not as good as 300 years.

Nevertheless, the Supreme Khan wished to receive the teachings. On October 1st, the Khan had a pavilion tent erected and sent the women of his retinue away. The Master joined him and the teaching began.

"Dao is the producer of Heaven and the nurturer of Earth. The sun and moon, the stars and planets, demons and spirits, men and things all grow out of The Way. Those who study The Way must learn not to desire the things that other men desire, not to live in the places where other men live. They must do without pleasant sounds and sights and get their pleasure only out of purity and quiet."

The Supreme Khan was a good student and absorbed the profound and simple ideas embodied in the Master's lectures.

Master Chang said, "If the common people, who possess only one wife can ruin themselves by excessive indulgence, what must happen to monarchs, whose palaces are filled with concubines? Things which arouse desire keep the mind filled with disorders. Once such things have been seen, it is hard to exercise self-restraint. I would have you bear this in mind."

The Supreme Khan agreed that this teaching was logical. He did not say whether or not he would remove the women from his harem, which of course, he did not. His young wife wanted to have a second child and was cross about the Master's teaching.

The Master advised the Supreme Khan to avoid alcohol, eat a vegetarian diet and to refrain from hunting at his advanced age.

Genghis Khan was moderate in his drinking, so the first injunction was not a problem. The problem was that he loved hunting. He enjoyed the company of women. He ate meat. He grumbled, but thought the advice was good enough to instruct his men.

The Khan spoke to his troops: "You have heard the holy Immortal discourse three times. Master Chang teaches the art of nurturing the vital spirit. His words have sunk deeply into my heart."

He encouraged his troops to mark them down in their hearts. The Supreme Khan asked that the teachings be engraved in stone steles for the benefit of his people, for uppermost in his mind was the benefit of the Yesse Mongol Ulus, the Great Mongol Nation.

The Supreme Khan followed Master Chang's advice for two months. Then he resumed hunting.

After many audiences, Master Chang asked if he could return to China since he had promised that he would return in three years. This was where the trouble began. The Sage took his leave and again advised the Emperor not to participate in the hunt at his advanced age.

A fall from a horse during a hunt killed the Khan when he was on campaign against the disobedient vassals. Subudei brought the body back to the homeland. The Mongols held a funeral and a shaman performed the horse sacrifice. Tolui was regent for two years while the nobility gathered to ratify the choice of successor of the Supreme Khan.

Chancellor Yeh-lu was sorry that he ever mentioned that the Khan would benefit from studying with the Master.

In return for spiritual advice, the Khan gave Master Chang a political plum: The Daoists were declared to be free from taxation by imperial decree. Chancellor Yeh-lu wrote out the edict and sealed it with the Imperial Seal. The Master took it with him when he returned to China.

Over time, the Daoists grew powerful and they had conflicts with the Buddhists in the capital. They engaged in pitched battles in the streets, confiscated Buddhist temples, and circulated pamphlets claiming that their founder Master Lao was the founder of Buddhism. All of this was to become a problem for Emperor Mongke, the greatest of the heirs of Genghis Khan.

Beyond the Great Wall, which marks the frontier of civilization, beyond even the great Gobi Desert, lies Mongolia, the Land of Blue Sky, the setting of the story of Genghis Khan, who is called by his people Conqueror of the World.

In his youth, the ruler who became Genghis Khan was called Temujin.

His father Yesugei was the ruler of thirteen camping circles, forty thousand white felt tents. The clans made camp with him because he gave them good governance and in return, he received the tithe of one-tenth of their herds from each tent. This was the source of a khan's wealth, the annual tithe of ten per cent of the herds of the Five Snouts—sheep, goats, yak, oxen, horses.

The nobility raised horses, the stubby Mongol war ponies which were known for their endurance and their ability to dig in snow and find grass to eat, even in winter. The commoners raised the other snouts.

The *ulus, native campground*, of Yesugei Khan was in a region called the Altai, the name of the mountain range that bordered the Valley of Two Rivers, the Onon and Kerulen. These native pastures were the most desirable in all of Mongolia, with lush pasture of couch grass for horses and water from two rivers. The world was a nomad highway, but this was home.

The nomads counted wealth as the number of tents, households that followed a khan, and the size of their herds. They did not consider property as wealth, for theirs was a mobile society. The government was wherever the khan was. Yesugei's gift was the organization of camp, the posting of sentries and guards. He also decided law cases and gave penalties to those who wounded others.

The steppe lands, the vast grasslands beyond the Great Wall, were a seething cauldron of tribal warfare in Temujin's youth. Bride theft and horse theft were the most common crimes. Temujin knew this from personal experience. His own mother Oyelun had been kidnapped by his father on her wedding day.

The story went like this. Yesugei had been out hunting with his brother and had seen her riding in the cart of a Mergid youth on her wedding day. (The Mergid were a rival tribe and less civilized than the Blue Mongols). He had been taken with her beauty as though he had been felled by an arrow. He and his brother knew that the youth was too inexperienced to protect his bride.

Yesugei kidnapped her from her young husband on the day of her wedding. At first, she resented him, but she grew to love and accept him. She bore him five children. Temujin was the oldest. His brother Khasar was next. These two were loyal to each other, a formidable pair.

Oyelun was the Storyteller who told him the family lineage and gave them pride in their nobility. As warriors often announced their lineage before battle, this identity meant he was a leader of men. The story of the youth of Temujin is a story of reversal of fortune and overcoming of obstacles, for he did not have an easy inheritance. All of the clans of the steppes watched the son of Yesugei as he began his rise among the young khans of the steppes.

The steppe land swept across the world. Golden waving grasses, stubby green grass, patchy brown grass, stretched from one end of the world to the other, a nomad highway, the grassy heart of the world.

Above. the sky was cobalt blue fading to powdery blue at the edges, stretching in every direction until mountains met the sky in icy peaks. The high mountain ranges scraped in icy peaks against the sky and formed the Roof of the World. At the horizon, powder blue sky turned mauve, orange and magenta, fading into violet when the swift-falling night descended.

In winter the steppes were a frozen arctic landscape. In summer, the steppes were an oven. In winter, the tribes migrated to a campground near Lake Baikal, where the lush forests were full of game and the lake provided fish. The lake was so deep that not even the shamans knew how deep it was. No one had ever been to the bottom.

Grey smoke from the hearth-fire rose up and went out to the sky. The tribes revered *Koko Tengri*, the Eternal Blue Sky. Shamans in camp performed rituals when children were born, healed the sick with herbs, rid visitors to camp of demons as they passed between the cauldrons of boiling oil at the camp entrance. They also performed funerals. They made trips to The Ancestors to learn the will of the Eternal Blue Sky.

The gēr tent was the center of family life. In the center was a hearth fire with a smoke hole at the top of the tent. Over the hearth fire, willow branches formed a circle—smoke from the fire where his mother cooked rose up and escaped through the hole.

On the wall of the yurt were war-bows and swords and dagger-axes, weapons his father captured in battles with the Tatar. In the yurt was a Chinese cabinet which Yesugei had taken as booty and on it was a porcelain bowl from China, bartered from the Ongguds, a Mongol tribe who camped outside the Great Wall.

On the floor of the tent, a carpet that came from the Muslim traders whose camel caravans crossed the Gobi to trade at the Chinese court. These were the men who knew many languages and currency and provided knowledge outside the world of the steppes. Later in life, the Muslim traders would be a valuable source of intelligence on affairs at the court of the Chinese emperor.

His mother had traded sheepskins for hammered copper bowls which had travelled by caravan over the Silk Road from the metalworkers of Afghanistan. The khan's tent was a place of luxury.

The products of the steppes were the products of animal husbandry. They wore clothes of tanned hides. His father drank *koumiz*, fermented mare's milk, churned by the women in his mother's camp. The felt that covered the tent was made by the women every spring at shearing time, wool from the sheep in his father's herds.

In the season of shearing in spring, Oyelun's women pounded the sheep wool into felt for tents. She supervised the women of her camp in the churning of mare's milk, the drying of meat, deer, lamb and goat-meat strips which would sustain them through the winter.

Temujin grew up. His was the boyhood of sons of the nobility.

Temujin was three. He could ride a sheep holding its woolly sides with his knees. He could turn and shoot his bow over the back flanks of the sheep, but to learn how to do it, he had fallen off the sheep many times. He could shoot a bow and arrow well enough to practice on mice.

His father said that Temujin had been born with a clot of blood in his hand and that he was destined to be a great khan. He always knew that one day he would be the lord of forty thousand tents.

An arrow-maker came to the tent to see Temujin's father. Yesugei sat close to the fire inspecting the cypress-wood arrows which the man had brought.

Temujin watched as Yesugei turned the tips over in his hand, feeling the sharp edge and the weight. Yesugei slipped the arrowhead onto the shaft, examining the fit, judging how it would fly and whether it would penetrate deep enough to kill Tatar. The success of the khan's army depended on the quality of their equipment.

His father was pleased with the work and nodded to the arrow-maker, who counted out so many arrows as the khan's tithe. They bartered for the rest, so many flasks of *koumiz*, so much dried venison, one of Yesugei's horses. When the bargain was struck, the man bowed down, touching his head to the carpet, got up and left the tent.

On the migration to the winter campground at Lake Baikal, commoners drove the herds of goats, sheep and yak while the noblemen drove the herds of horses. The caravan of black wagons stretched out over the steppe for miles, advancing slowly. His mother drove the team of a dozen oxen which pulled the black wagons with the big, spoked wheels. Yesugei had a junior wife, Sochigil, as it was the custom for a khan to have as many as four principal wives. Both his father's wives had a household wagon plus wagons for her servants and belongings hitched axle to axle. The eldest female of each household stood in the lead wagon and handled the reins.

At night, when they camped, Temujin listened to the stories of The Ancestors told by his mother. Even the old graybeard storytellers who went around the camp entertaining the Mongols for dinner or for some koumiz or skins or a blanket, said Oyelun was better at telling stories than they were. This was their history. This was their identity.

Temujin lay on his back in his mother's lap while he listened to the wind in her voice, blowing through the tent like the wind blowing through the cattails on the shores of Lake Baikal.

According to the graybeards, the Valley of Two Rivers was the home of Blue Wolf and Yellow Deer. Blue Wolf and Yellow Deer mated and

28

conceived a child who grew up to be a blue man named Borjigin, the original ancestor of the Borjigin clan.

No one knew whether these ancient names signified people or animals. No one knew whether Borjigin had blue skin or painted his body blue. This did not matter. What mattered was the tale, for the tale bore the idea of their people, and the idea was what separated the nobles from the commoners.

Oyelun loved the story of Alan the Fair, the mother of their ancestor. After her husband died, Alan the Fair conceived three sons by a spirit of light who entered her tent in the night. As no one had ever seen any suitors approach her tent, all of the clans accepted the legend. His mother said their tribe was descended from the blue-gray wolf and would always be protected by Heaven. "Remember the stories. They belong to our people, these stories." Temujin was happy listening to her voice, drifting to sleep.

Alan was a wise woman who told her sons never to quarrel. She told her five sons that if they were united, they would be as hard to break as a handful of arrows but if they fought among themselves, they would be as easy to snap as one single arrow.

His brother Khasar was younger, and would be his second in command, totally loyal, the best archer in the steppes. Several years later, a new baby daughter was sleeping in the carved horn cradle made by the reindeer people who lived in the frozen land of Siberia.

His mother had spread a blanket for him far enough away from the hearth-fire so that spraying sparks could not reach him. He lay near the fire watching the coals glow, feeling their warmth on his face.

Temujin grew up with the legends of the Blue Mongols and never tired of the stories. There was a music in the stories. When they reached the winter campground, there would be a hunt and a feast and music and dancing.

Among the Mongols, warriors ate first. When Yesugei had eaten the soup made with strips of dried deer meat and the wild onions and garlic which Oyelun had foraged in the hills and Oyelun saw that he had eaten his fill, she reached for the wooden ladle and filled her bowl and ate, putting extra pieces of deer meat in her bowl because she was pregnant.

29

She moved back from the fire and sat on the goose-down mattress at the side of the tent to suckle her new son, Temuge. The children ate last.

The kettle was suspended on a hook over the fire. Temujin reached for the ladle dipping out the meat that was left, sharing it between them. Khasar was three, chubby-faced and red-cheeked. Already he worshipped his older brother, following him everywhere and imitating everything. Khasar plopped down backwards in front of the fire and ate noisily, chewing the meat as the steaming spicy broth ran down his chin.

All was well with the family. Despite the tribal wars, Temujin's father was prosperous.

Temujin and Khasar worked beside their father at soldier's chores-- polishing riding tackle, repairing boiled leather armor, shield, lance, listening as he consulted with noblemen and soldiers, watching the Master of the Horses break in a new saddle that he had gotten from the Muslim caravan traders who passed through the steppes and traded in the camp of his father.

Yesugei was a man of few words, but he talked to his sons, about horses, their breeding, foaling, breaking and training. Temujin listened as the caravan traders told of the lands beyond the steppes and the stories of the rich and magnificent court of the Golden Emperor of Jin China. His father told him of the Jin's betrayal of the Mongols, and their killing of a Mongol king and switching their protection to the Tatar. *Using barbarians to check barbarians*, the father said. That is how they think. Temujin did not forget.

Temujin and Khasar were five and three, too young to go on the scouting expeditions that were the job of the older Mongol boys who could ride and shoot.

The older boys would ride out from the camp and search for good pasture and report back to the senior soldiers whether there were any scouting parties from other tribes or any soldiers in the area. Temujin and Khasar worked hard at the jobs given to the boys of their age: hunting small game and fishing to provision their tent. When the time came, they would be scouts like the older boys.

Yesugei told them that one of the older boys had seen a band of Tatar nearby. Tomorrow Yesugei and several soldiers would go to see if the band was a hunting party. If so, they would be warned to back off the Borjigin pasture. If not, they would fight.

When Yesugei returned, the camp would migrate north to the forests of Lake Baikal for the winter. When the tribe found good grazing land, the younger boys who could not yet take part in the hunt would take watch. By twos they would take up positions at points along the perimeter of the tribe's campground. They would rest taking turns sleeping in their saddles. They would make sure that no surprise attackers slipped into the camp on a dark night when there was no moon.

A spring snowstorm was raging outside the ger tent, the gusting winds driving snowdrifts against the black wagons. The winter at Lake Baikal had been mild. It was time to migrate back to their native pastures.

Before they left Lake Baikal, Yesugei would organize a Grand Hunt to provision them for the trip north. Temujin had asked to ride with the hunt, but the boys could not take part until they were fifteen. He was eager and he had the skills. He rode his gray gelding as though he were born in a saddle, but he was still too young.

Temujin performed his duties well, rode well, shot well. Inside the tent the family ate the small game--snow hare--that Temujin had brought down with his small light bow. Yesugei chewed the meat off the bones and drank down his broth, He told the boys that on the coming migration. they could assume the duty of riding over the steppes in front of the herds, searching for good pasture, the next camping place for the tribe.

Temujin and Khasar cheered. The baby girl Temulun fell asleep and Oyelun ate. Over the edge of her bowl, she looked at the sons who filled their tent. Temujin was nine; Khasar, seven. And there were two others. It seemed only yesterday that Temujin was born clutching a clot of blood in his hand. His father gave him the name of the Tatar chief he had just defeated in battle. His father said that he was destined.

Soon Temujin would be old enough to join in a Grand Hunt. At sixteen he would be old enough to go to war. At thirteen, his father told him that he would lead the young sons of the clans in a hunt to provision

31

their tents. It was practice for war. He would bond with the other boys. He would command the hunt and feed the clans.

Yesugei gave his sons the assignment of their duties for the migration back to the Valley of Two Rivers. Then he made them a present of fine arrowheads. Every few days the clans would break camp and continue the migration. The boys would ride out in advance of the wagons and search for water and pasture and would report back to the *noyans*, the noblemen who commanded the migration.

Scouting parties of adult males would ride out in advance of the migration to spot enemy scouts or hunting parties for the Mongols were most vulnerable to attack when travelled with women, children, household goods, and herds of livestock.

The Mongols would advance this way until they reached their native campground in the Altai. Once they returned from the winter campground, the women set up the white felt tents. Yesugei organized a great hunt. They would have a feast, for the Mongols loved to celebrate. Everyone would eat to excess the good fresh meat and drink *koumiz*. Musicians would play and people would dance until they wore a ditch into the ground.

The stories were not Temujin's only heritage. Yesugei informed his sons of a great legacy. He had formed a bond greater than all others to the nomad aristocracy.

This was the bond of sworn brother and it was called *anda*. The *anda* bond required that one so sworn should, if necessary, take his *anda's* children into his tent and regard them as his own.

Yesugei had *an anda* whose name was Togril, Lord of the Kereyid. He was the richest and most powerful khan of the steppes. His people were the most civilized and powerful tribe and lived to the southwest, in the valley of the Tola River, where they controlled the trade routes of the Gobi, the Silk Road that passed through the steppes. The valley had good pastures and the herds had clean water from the Tola. The Kereyid had converted to Christianity a century ago. This was the Eastern rite of Christianity, centered in Baghdad, not the Christianity centered in Rome. This conversion was a claim to being more civilized than the shamanists of the steppes.

Togril owed his rule to Yesugei, for Yesugei had saved him in his hour of need. Togril had been rich and powerful but he lost everything when his brother stole the Kereyid clans from him. Deposed and poverty-stricken, Togril was forced to run for his life.

Yesugei responded to Togril's plea and gave him food and shelter and one of his own thick cloaks to protect him from the snow and wind. He also gave Togril an army of Mongol archers and fought beside Togril. The two men punished Togril's brother and took back the Kereyid clans. In return for these favors, they swore the oath that made them brothers.

Togril was the most powerful man in the steppes. Yesugei told Temujin that if ever the Eternal Blue Sky had dealt a blow of fate, Temujin could regard Togril as a father.

At the time of the winter migration, the forty thousand families rode to the southwest and escaped the Arctic winter of driving winds and snows. They set up camp in the forests near Lake Baikal.

The sky was deep blue streaked with strings of white clouds. Snow melt flowed down from the high peaks to the immense blue lake which the Mongols called The Ocean.

The shaman Tab Tengri said that no man knew how deep the lake was, but that he had made a trance journey to the bottom, a mile into the earth. On his journey he had seen blind albino fish which were not good to eat. The waters of the blue-black lake contained enough fish to feed all the nomads in the world as long as the world would last.

It was the task of the younger boys to provide the family with fish and small game. On one of the small tributaries of the river which fed the lake, Temujin set a line with an iron hook. Such items were traded from the forest people who knew the metal arts. He went to lie under a tree. This was a good place to fish. The water flowed clean and clear from the mountains and there were rocks where the fish liked to hide. He always caught more than enough for his tent.

Resting on the bank and watching cattails waving in the gentle breezes, he looked across the river and saw the boys from the commoner's camp tending the sheep and goat herds.

The river branched off into a shallow creek where the animals could drink. The animal herds filled up the prairie that lay between them and the mountains in the far distance. Closer, where the river was wider, Temujin watched the sons of the nobility tending the horse herds. He loved the horses best of all the animals. Mongol horses were indispensable for steppe warfare. Muscled and tough, the little Mongolian ponies had more endurance for war and for the migrations than the Arabians his father traded with the Muslims in the oasis towns. In a few years, Temujin and Khasar would tend horses.

The two boys had set out early that morning with poles and baskets and had been at this spot, near a stand of willows and larch since daybreak. It was mid-morning; the sun was getting high in the sky and the likelihood of Begder catching anything was small. Begder disappeared into the woods for most of the morning, then came back to the riverbank and set a small net in a bad place.

All morning long, Temujin had gone about his business seriously while his half-brother Begder, Sochigil's eldest son, had thrashed about in the woods flushing game. Temujin was six months younger than Yesugei's son by Sochigil but Temujin was the son of the senior wife, so Temujin was recognized as the eldest son, He was the heir, destined to be chief of the clans. Begder felt cheated. The resentment never went away.

Temujin's line bobbed and he took a fish off the line and put it into his fish basket. He kept the basket turned away so that Begder could not see his catch.

Begder had a booming voice and an aggressive manner. He had made a racket but hadn't shot anything. He came to the riverbank. "I didn't get any game. Our tent can't go hungry. Give me one of your fish."

Sochigil was not as well-born as Oyelun and had not taught her son the ways of the nobility, otherwise Begder would have known his place. Begder enjoyed making trouble. It gave him pleasure to pick a fight.

"If you stop making so much noise, you'll shoot a bird. You're a good shot. You'll have plenty of food. Keep your voice down. Don't scare the fish. I have to catch enough fish for everyone in our tent."

Begder told Temujin to mind his own business.

Temujin ignored the provocation. He got up and baited another iron hook and set a second pole in the water. Begder started to criticize, his voice rising.

Begder went to get a pole and cast it into the water then lay back under a tree alongside Temujin. His mood seemed to have brightened, but he kept trying to make conversation.

"What do you like best, horse racing or wrestling?" he asked. Begder's voice floated out over the water.

"Hunting," Temujin whispered. He held his finger to his lips. "Be quiet. You'll scare the fish away," Temujin whispered. Yesugei had told him many times that he wanted Temujin to set an example, but with Begder it wasn't easy.

Temujin's pole dipped. He jumped up and pulled three times before he succeeded in getting the fish out of the water onto the bank. It was a small trout, shiny, gasping for air. He picked up the lid of his fish basket and flipped the fish inside to lay with the others he had caught.

"Give me that one to take home with me."

"You wasted the whole morning in the woods. It's getting late and the fish will be biting, Catch your own,"

Temujin turned his head, distracted by a movement in the water. He ran over to the bank and sucked in his breath. Then he saw the fish. "Don't move. It's Fat Blue."

Fat Blue was the name Temujin had given to a trout he had been trying to catch last winter, the grandaddy, judging from the size of him. He grabbed his net and kneeled; his body arched over the water. Fat Blue was visible in the water, his scales shining in the sunlight. He was backing up and preparing to swim into his favorite hiding place, a fish hole in a canyon of river rock. Every time he hid in his favorite fish hole, Temujin lost him.

The trout positioned himself, swished his tail against the current and nosed into canyon. At precisely the moment the wily trout got his momentum and rammed his body forward, Temujin scooped his net into the water and slipped it over his body. The net came up dripping. Fat Blue's big body glistened with rainbows in the bright sunlight.

"Hooowee!" Temujin exulted, holding the net high, look at his trophy. The fish flipped his tail and gasped for aur, his gills flailing, his eyes wide. Temujin couldn't believe his luck, even with Begder doing his best to scare the fish away. He turned and saw Begder resenting his moment of exaltation.

Temujin opened the lid of his fish basket and slipped the trout into the basket. Fat Blue was lying on the pile of trout, his gills heaving. "He is going to taste delicious. One fish will feed the whole tent."

Begder said, "Why do you think you are better than everyone?"

"Go check your pole. Look. It's bobbing."

Begder pulled up the line, but it was empty. He grabbed his net. He lay across a boulder and swiped his net down into the water. He missed, and when he held up the net, it was empty, dripping water.

Begder got up and walked to the tree where Temujin's fish basket lay. Temujin followed him with his eyes and warned him. "Stay away from my basket."

"Don't be so greedy. You have more than enough. You're acting just like father.: He mimicked, "*The khan shoots first, the khan eats first. In all things, the khan comes first.* I'm the oldest. I should be khan after father dies, not you."

Temujin refused to react to the taunt. "We both do what we're told. Stop acting like an idiot."

Temujin gathered up his poles and came up the hill for the basket. "It is time to go home."

Temujin's back was turned. Begder reached in and took the big trout. Temujin turned in time to see Begder close Temujin's fish basket and shove Fat Blue in his own fish basket. Then Begder took off up the hill, racing back to camp.

"Put him back," Temujin called after him.

It was two miles back to camp. The sun dipped lower in the sky and the light turned golden. Temujin reached his mother's tent and went in. Oyelun knew something was wrong right away. Temujin's face was flushed.

"Come with me," he said.

"Where?" she replied.

"I finally caught the fish I was looking for last year. Begder wasted the morning and then he had nothing, so he stole my fish. He's giving it to Sochigil."

"Let him have it," she said.

"It's not fair. It's mine."

"Do you want them to have supper? Look at all you've brought for us." She went about making a broth for the meal, adding the wild onions and herbs to the cooking pot suspended by a hook over the fire.

"Never mind. We have enough," said Oyelun.

Sochigil came to their tent-door to give thanks. She was small, with long glossy black hair and the eyes of a doe, glistening.

Temujin grabbed his fish basket and handed it to her. "Take these and give me back my fish. I'm going to come to your tent and get the fish myself."

Oyelun said, "No, you're not."

Sochigil looked confused. She did not know her son had stolen the fish. "I've already cut it up and put it in the pot." Begder was nowhere to be seen.

"Where is he?" Temujin demanded. "Hiding in his mother's tent? Avoiding the trouble he caused? I'm going to teach him a lesson."

"No, you're not." Oyelun rushed up to Sochigil and took back the disputed basket of trout. "The boys were quarreling again. Begder took Temujin's fish."

"I'll bring it back," Sochigil said.

"Keep it. We have plenty," Oyelun said. She had a position to protect. She commanded respect in the women's camp. She could not be seen to be quibbling over a fish.

When Sochigil left, Oyelun said to her son, "I am senior wife. I have a duty to protect the second wife. Sochigil is the weaker woman. Your father wants peace between his wives and peace among the clans that camp with us. He is famous for it. You have to stop this fighting."

"He started it."

"This rivalry between two sons will come to no good end."

"You should have let me teach him a lesson. You shouldn't let him get away with it. The whole camp will know. He will brag that he got the better of me."

"When your father is away making war, I am khan," his mother said.

4 The Boys' Hunt

1177

The Yellow Steppe was a favorite place for small game: hare, weasel, fox, marten.

A foot of snow had fallen during the night and transformed the woods into a hushed whiteness. The cold air was fragrant with the smell of Baikal pine. The only sound was the shrieking of a red hawk circling overhead.

Thirty ponies, gray, white, black and brown, their breath hanging like smoke in the air, were drawn up in a straight line, hooves pawing the snow.

Mounted on the shaggy horses were thirty ten-year old boys, all of them good riders. Dressed in fur coats and caps, their light bows laid across their saddle horns and quivers on their backs, the boys held their mounts still and sat up straight at attention waiting for inspection.

At the edge of the birch and pine forest, the only sound was the crunching of snow under Temujin's pony's hooves. Holding his gray pony's head high, reining him in tightly, Temujin trotted down the line like a young general. He wore a fur cap with earflaps. His red hair fell in twin plaits down his back. Under a coat of skins, he wore belted tunic and riding trousers tucked into leather boots, the same uniform as the rest of them.

Temujin would report to his father about the boys' performance. Not even Etchigin, the most boisterous of the boys, tried to play one of the pranks for which he was famous. Begder, who liked to make trouble, had a place in the line, but he did not stand at attention.

Temujin, as the Khan's son, was commander of the hunt and he took his job seriously. Temujin fixed his gaze on each boy in turn, examining his equipment, his bow and arrows, his uniform.

First in the line of boys was Khasar, Temujin's younger brother, the best archer among them. Sitting astride a silver-white gelding, he was short and stocky and worshipped his older brother. Temujin saluted him, fist over his heart, and leaned forward to whisper something. Khasar threw his leg over the horse's back and dropped out of the saddle to tighten his stirrups. He saluted and climbed back into the saddle.

Temujin nodded and continued down the line. He told Otchigin, his next younger brother, that he did not have a full quiver of arrows. Otchigin got down and ran to the leather pouch under the big pine where the boys stored their spare quivers.

Temujin next inspected Belgutei, the younger son of Sochigil, his father's second wife. "Tighten your reins. You have a spirited pony. Keep him under control when we close the hunting circle. If he bolts, he'll frighten the game. If he breaks the circle and the game will escape."

Next was Begder. "Your stirrups are slack. Tighten them. You could fall off your horse." Begder did not move. Temujin dismounted and tightened the stirrups himself.

Begder smiled, pleased because Temujin had had to dismount. Temujin ignored him and said, "You've got that quiver overstuffed. When you pull an arrow out, they'll all fall out."

Belgutei leaned over and spoke to his brother in a fierce whisper. "Do what he says. Stop causing trouble."

"I should be in command," Begder whispered. "I'm the oldest son."

Temujin walked around the pony and shortened the stirrup on the other side. Belgutei leaned over and told Begder to stop. "How could you command the hunt if you act like this in front of all of the boys?"

Temujin lowered his voice so that only Begder could hear him. "Pay attention. Do what you're supposed to do. The hunt will give your tent food. You and your brother have a duty."

Begder threw his leg over the pony's back. He removed the extra arrows and placed them in a piece of ox-hide at the foot of the big pine. Temujin saluted Begder, but Begder did not return the salute. Temujin rode down the line.

Temujin reached the end of the line then rode back and faced the boys. "We make a libation to the Eternal Blue Sky."

He dismounted and took off his cap. The boys followed. He had brought a pouch of *koumiz*, fermented mare's milk. He turned it upside down and sprinkled the thick white liquid on the ground. He said a prayer, his voice ringing out in the snowy silence.

When he completed the ceremony, he announced the riding order, two wings and a center, the same as that of an army going to war, his breath making clouds in the cold air.

"I will ride in the center of the line with Khasar at my right," he said. "He has earned the position because he is the best archer." Khasar gave his pony spurs and trotted up and took his position.

Temujin gestured cutting out ten boys to the left and ten to the right. "You ten are the left wing, and you ten, the right. The rest ride in the center wing with me.

"String out along the forest edge in a line. Everyone keep pace with the line. No straggling. Stay in line until we get to the clearing. When I raise my arm, close the circle. When the left and right sides meet, in the center will be foxes, birds, mice, marten, marmot, hare. No one shoots until I give the command.

"As the khan's son, I shoot first. Khasar is also the Khan's son. When I raise my hand, he will shoot second. Then I will give the command for you to shoot. After the hunt is over, I will take game first for my tent. The rest of you will divide the game fairly and evenly between you. Each soldier will take some back to his tent for his family," ordered Temujin.

The boys lifted up their bows and shouted an old hunting cheer that they had heard their fathers chant at the Grand Hunts.

"Forward," Temujin commanded.

The line of ponies advanced over the snow stretching out for a quarter mile. Boys and ponies passed from the winter sunlight into the dappled shade of the forest. High overhead, they heard a jay rasping out its warning to the forest birds. As the ponies fanned out across the forest floor, Temujin could hear the footfalls as the animals ran away from the hunters—they were prey, smelling, hearing and sensing danger.

In the forest, Temujin lifted his hand and the riders began to close the circle. The first animal, a small fox, scurried across the forest floor, then a hare. Ten or twenty hare followed. Riding in precision, the boys kept to the line, driving the game ahead of them in terrified flight. The riders at the end cantered closer together, forming a circle. Small animals were coursing every which way, running ahead of them now, a pair of martens and a white wolf cub.

When the circle closed one hundred yards across the forest floor, Temujin held up his hand. Everything was still except for the sounds of the animals scurrying, keening, howling their distress.

He raised his bow and shot, killing a plump snow hare with a brown spot shaped like a cloud on its back, He shot again, bringing down a fox with a bushy tail, a pointy-nosed marten and a young wolf with ice-blue eyes. He told Khasar that he was finished. Khasar got off a spectacular shot, bringing down a young deer.

Temujin made a diagonal cut in the air with his hand, the signal for the rest of the boys to begin taking their game. A pony whinnied and reared, breaking the circle. Some of the game escaped, while the rest of the boys held the circle and kept shooting. The boy riding the spirited pony struggled to get his mount back under control. The circle closed again. Forty minutes later, they dismounted and began to truss the game and place it in bags to carry it back to camp.

Temujin saw Begder take the snow hare which Temujin knew was his first shot of the day. He recognized it because of a brown cloud-shaped spot on the animal's back. Begder pretended the kill was his and put it in a sack. Khasar loaded his game and the rest of Temujin's kill. It was plenty for their tent.

Temujin's temper boiled inside him. He did nothing, but he was keeping score, and he added this to his list of Begder's offenses against him.

Yesugei and a few of his men had come to the hunting ground to supervise the division of the game. He taught his son. Each tent in the camping circle got a fair share. Afterward, Yesugei took Temujin out and taught him how to make a libation of thanks.

Evening fell and in the family tent, Yesugei asked Temujin to place knucklebones on the earthen floor and explain why he positioned each of his riders and which boys were skilled riders and shots. Yesugei moved a few of the bones. The hunt was the basis of cavalry warfare and Yesugei wanted Temujin to think. Yesugei wanted to open his mind to possibilities.

Khasar lay on the floor beside Temujin. Imitating his father, he moved three knucklebones. "He's leaving some of the story out. I was here. I shot this way and got the fox. I got the deer later, but I almost missed it because the circle broke, and the animals were getting away. Egsen fell off his horse. Belgutei helped get Egsen up on his horse and

42

back into line. I filled up the vacant spot until he got there." Khasar interrupted the conversation. "You didn't tell father I was the best shot."

"He knows you're the best shot in the whole Mongol camp. The best I ever saw. Everyone knows that."

Yesugei laughed at his younger son's eagerness. "Good job, Khasar. Good thinking. Well done."

Temujin stared at the lay of the battle, lost in his vision of the hunt. "You were very good, little brother. Very good," said Temujin.

Yesugei said, "I'm proud of both of you. The bonds you forge now will make you good companions in war. You must trust one another completely, for one day you will put your lives in each other's hands."

Khasar told his father that Temujin had killed a hare with a cloud on its back and Begder had stolen it.

Yesugei frowned. "Theft is against the rule of my camp. My own son cannot be a thief. I will talk to him about that, son. That's not the way a soldier acts."

Yesugei surprised Temujin when he said, "You're growing up, son. Your mother has said it is time that we found you a wife. We will go to the campground of the Khongirad."

The Khongirad were his mother's people, the marrying clan of the Mongols, renowned for the beauty of their women. They were considered as more civilized than the Mongols, from their proximity to China. They were lettered and could keep accounts, from trading at the emporia on the border with the Jin Empire. This was a momentous event.

Temujin looked into his father's face. He was ten. He would be betrothed and would not return to his family's tent until he was fifteen when he and his bride would marry, set up their own ger tent and produce children.

It was the custom for the newly betrothed groom to stay for some years in the tent of his new family while the bride's family became acquainted with their new son-in-law. When the betrothed reached the age of marriage, the ceremony was held and he returned to his people. If he married the daughter of a chief, she would bring servants and herds with her.

Oyelun was proud, but her eyes told him that she did not want him to leave yet. Khasar began to cry when he realized that he would be separated from his brother.

"I almost forgot, Khasar," said Yesugei gently. "You will have lessons from the Archery Master of my Army. I have a bow made of two layers of the finest horn for you. It shoots further and has a stronger pull than your brother's new bow. While Temujin is gone, you will lead the hunt."

Khasar smiled. "I will have an archery master? I will lead the hunt?" He looked at his brother, and a smile crossed his lips. He was considering that Temujin's absence might have advantages. "What will the master teach me?"

"Marksmanship and weapons. Arrows for different types of game, for war, for killing. Target shooting. The making of composite bows."

Khasar nodded as though he were a grown man accepting an important post.

"As for you, Temujin," Yesugei said, "Wear your finest skins and tunic tomorrow and bring the new bow and arrow. We'll take a trip to the Khongirad lands. It will be good for the family to have our eldest son betrothed."

Later when the family had gone to bed and the brothers were in their feather beds at the back of the tent, Khasar whispered to Temujin, "I hope you find a beautiful girl."

"So do I," said Temujin.

In the morning, Oyelun held Temujin close, then kissed his face and let him go. Her tears dampened his tunic. His father summoned the grooms and told them to bring saddled horses from the corrals. The pack animals had been provisioned with dried meat and vegetables, and *koumiz* for the journey.

Temujin hugged Khasar and whispered to him not to let Begder bully him. Yesugei held Oyelun close. She clung to him and whispered "Safe journey" in his ear and sent her greetings to her people.

Temujin took his gray pony--Yesugei had given permission. They set off as the sun rose over the Donkey Back Steppe. As they rode away, Temujin looked back toward camp. His mother was waving goodbye. Khasar watched until the riders were out of sight.

44

On the sixth day of their journey, father and son were riding along the bank of a stream when they saw a camp. A nobleman in fine clothes stood in the middle of the camp with two servants who were roasting a lamb on a spit.

The tents were painted with images of waterfowl. The camp belonged to a man of means, for this was a custom among the Khongirad tribe. In the steppe country, nomad travelers were always coming and going. It was an old steppe custom to invite passers-by to join a feast. The nobleman dispatched a servant to invite them to join him and rest from their journey.

Yesugei thought it was time for a rest. The smell of the roasted meat wafted over. They had brought dried provisions for making broth. Yesugei saw an opportunity of gossiping with another member of the steppe nobility. He was eager to hear news of this part of the world. A khan had to be informed.

Father and son rode into the camp. A groom took the reins of their horses and took the animals to feed and water them. Yesugei took specially cured jerky out of the saddlebag of his pack mule and offered it to his host as a hospitality gift.

Yesugei introduced himself and his son. The host Dai said that he had heard of the reputation of Yesugei Khan and was gratified to have a distinguished guest. He invited them to join. Yesugei sat down. A servant poured a flagon of *koumiz* filled to the brim. The host, a rich man judging from his fine clothes and beautiful tents, introduced himself as Dai Sechen, which means Dai the Wise.

The cook carved thick slices of lamb and piled them on a platter and a manservant offered food. Yesugei took a slice with his knife, then urged Temujin to eat.

Dai asked where they were going. Yesugei told Dai about the great occasion, a betrothal journey. Dai fixed his attention on Temujin. Dai was a man of the world and could see that the young man had an aura about him and the light of intelligence in his eyes.

Dai drank his cup of *koumiz* and explained himself as a man of the world. "I had a prophetic dream last night. In my dream, I saw a white falcon holding the sun and the moon in its claws. It flew down from the sky and landed on my head. Whenever I've had the sun and the moon in my dreams, it was always from a distance, but this white falcon brought them and put them in my hand."

Yesugei's eyes widened. "The falcon is a symbol of the Borjigin clans." He meant his own people, the clans of the Blue Mongols.

"Your son has a fire inside him, a sign of great spirit."

Yesugei saw no need for false modesty. His son was outstanding, a born leader, even at his young age. "I have known my aon was exceptional from the moment of his birth. You are a stranger and quick to observe. I thank you for noticing." Temujin was moved by his father's pride in him.

Dai got right to the point. "Let me propose something to you. Interrupt your journey and come to my camp. Let me receive you in my tent. I have a daughter of marriageable age. I'd like you to meet her before you ride off to his mother's people. We're in your marrying clan. Come to my pastures and see if my daughter might make a suitable match for Temujin."

Yesugei shook his head. "I promised the boy's mother that we would go to her people. You understand how it is."

Dai would not be put off. "Listen to me, Yesugei Khan. I have a feeling about this. From ancient times we Khongirad have been protected by the beauty of our daughters and the loveliness of our granddaughters, so we've stayed out of battles and wars. When the Mongols elect a new khan, we take our loveliest daughters and place them on carts. We harness a black camel to the cart and we strike his haunches and make him trot off to the khan's tent. We offer our daughters to sit beside a khan and be a *khatun*. We don't challenge empires and we don't make war on our neighbors. We just put our daughters in the front of the carts and send them off. That way, we have a new *khatun* as our shield against war. A tried but true method for us."

(*Khatun* was the name of the wife of a Khan, a title of respect.)

Yesugei laughed. "All right. We'll meet your daughter. If we don't feel there's a match, we will only have a day's ride to Olkunug pastures. We'll come with you."

46

The felt tents of Dai's camp were decorated with paintings of herons and cranes with their wings in flight. Yesugei was impressed by the size of Dai's encampment, a settlement of thousands of white felt tents. The horse herds were almost as big as Yesugei's. The herds were so numerous that they filled the space between the two mountains, Chegcher and Chikurku, visible on the distant horizon.

All the men in Dai Sechen's camp had clothes made of fine cloth and their weapons were ornamented with carving and metal tracery. Yesugei commented to Temujin in a voice too quiet to be heard by Dai or his servants, that the weapons of these people were too ornate to be of use in war.

Dai welcomed his guests to a large tent and invited them in. By the glow of the hearth-fire, Yesugei could see saw that the tent was furnished with beautiful and expensive objects, luxury goods traded by the merchants from the Muslim lands--horses, furs and hides traded for pottery from Persia, carpets from Afghanistan, metalwork from China.

Dai introduced his wife, Nambi. She wore the high-waisted, yoked dress of the Khongirad women and leather riding boots. She wore her hair in long brown plaits, and her brown eyes shone. Her cheeks were bright red, from her life outdoors, and her expression was pleasant. She wore strands of beads of silver, turquoise and coral.

Nambi welcomed their guest when her husband said Yesugei was a respected and powerful khan. This was an important man with a son of marriageable age. The boy had a striking presence, an aura, a confident manner, aware of the behavior of a young khan. The light of understanding came into her eyes. Yesugei assessed the woman favorably. She was quick and trusting her husband, did not need winded explanations.

At the back of the tent, a small girl was arranging the family bedding. This was the daughter. Dai summoned the girl and she came close to the fire. Temujin sucked in his breath when he saw her. The girl's face shone with light. She was full of bright energy and healthy. Her eyes were filled with the fire of intelligence.

About the same age as Temujin, she had dark brown eyes that glistened and shiny black hair hanging loose to her shoulders. She wore

47

a cherry-colored high-waisted dress in the Khongirad style and had cherry-colored boots to match.

Dai said that she was ten, but she was small for her age. Her name was Bortai. She looked from her father's face to the boy's face and regarded the young khan with a level stare. She could see that he was not intimidated by her father.

Temujin felt as though he had been standing out on the steppe in a lightning storm and heard a thunderclap. The girl seemed calm and unperturbed. Temujin averted her gaze, pretending that the beautiful objects in the tent occupied his attention.

Yesugei understood why Dai had wanted the two children to meet. As a father, he could see that they were suited to one another. Yesugei saw what Dai saw. They would make a good match.

Bortai walked to her father's side. He had loved and protected her from the day she was born and she trusted him more than anyone else in the world. If this boy was to be her future husband, she liked him. He was self-possessed, even among strangers. He knew his place in the world. She saw his attention drift to the tent-door. She saw that he wanted to be out of the atmosphere of the tent full of adults.

"You two children go outside." Nambi told her servant to bring tea and yak butter for the men.

Bortai ran to the back of the tent and rummaged among her things, putting a small package in her pocket. She led Temujin out into the fresh air.

Yesugei was a self-contained man who was not overly eager as he discussed the betrothal. He said, "I'll be honest with you, Dai. I could pass over her in order to take the boy to his mother's people as I promised I would, but I see that your daughter and my son like one another and get along. Let me sleep on it, my friend, let me talk to the boy. We will discuss the matter in the morning."

Outside, the girl pointed to the horse corrals and asked Temujin if he would like to see the black pony that her father had given her on her birthday. A groom brought the horse, saddled and ready to ride. She mounted standing on a bucket. In her red dress, sitting straight in the saddle, she looked pretty and Temujin said so.

She invited him to go for a ride. The groom brought Temujin's pony. Together they rode into the countryside. There was a stream nearby where the horses could nibble water lilies.

She took him to a pine forest and showed him the cave in the side of a cliff where she played with her friends. She presented him with a gift, a small silver bell that she said had come from China. He held it up and they listened to its clear tone. He reached in the pocket of his tunic and gave her a little bronze mirror from China, which his mother had given him to offer his betrothed.

She shined the mirror with the hem of her skirt and looked at herself in it. They picked flowers and looked at their reflection in the stream.

They galloped across the grasslands and she saw that he let her ride ahead of him and only once showed off his prowess in riding, so she would see how fine he was.

Their knowledge of connection happened quickly. She didn't need him to dismount but she let him help her. He was giving her his allegiance even though she was still a girl. This was the real gift of betrothal.

Bortai and Temujin came back from their ride flushed and excited and told the adults what a good time they had.

Dai knew that father and son needed time to talk privately. Nambi told her servant to prepare a tent for their guests.

Dai said, "Rest a while. Then join me for a cup of *koumiz*. We'll have a good dinner. Make yourselves comfortable."

When father and son were alone, Temujin said that he would like to have Bortai for his wife. Bortai was a beauty, his son's for the asking, of a good family of the old nobility.

He told his son that they could hold out and pass her up and take Temujin to his mother's people, but in fact, marrying into this bone of the Khongirads would offer a better alliance than marrying into the Olkunugs.

The Khongirads had excellent trade relationships with the Chinese and the Muslim merchants from the West. This might be more valuable to Yesugei than treasure. The Chinese most certainly had spies among the Khongirad. It was only a matter of time before diplomats from the

Jin court or Jin spies in the lands beyond the Great Wall would report to the Son of Heaven who was the Jin Emperor how strong the Tatars had grown in the steppe.

The Jin Emperor would switch allegiance, because the only invasion they had to fear was from the mounted archers of the steppes. If the tribes were fighting each other, they would not plan an invasion of the Jin Empire.

As Khan of the Mongols, Yesugei might well be the nomad leader chosen to be the next Great Khan. He would then become a vassal of the Jin Emperor, as other Mongol khans had in the past. He, not the Tatar, would receive titles and gifts from the Golden Emperor. (Jin, the name of the Manchu dynasty, means "Golden.") The Mongols would rise again to prominence in the steppes, a prominence that they had not had for four generations, while the Golden Emperor played the tribes off against one another, "using barbarians to check barbarians."

At dinner, a girl from the commoner's camp came to play the pipes. This hospitality put Yesugei Khan at ease. He had a few cups of *koumiz*. He congratulated Dai on the beauty of his daughter. He said that Bortai would doubtless have many suitors and would produce heirs that any nobleman would be proud to call grandsons.

Yesugei praised the hospitality of his host and agreed to betroth his son to Bortai.

Dai's voice boomed with good cheer. "I could hold back and make you request her again and again and then let you have her, but who would think it was praiseworthy to stall like that? I could make you ask me twice, and no one would curse me for giving in too quickly. No, this girl's fate is not to grow old by the door of the tent she was born in. I'll be happy to give you my daughter, but now you should go and leave your son with me, so we can get to know him."

He congratulated himself and took credit for making the match. Had he not had the portentous dream? He was not named Dai the Wise for nothing. He had realized the outcome all along.

Dai proposed a generous dowry, a sable cloak decorated with many of the finest thickest sable tails that he had bartered from the people of Sibir. It was a magnificent dowry present. Yesugei said so.

The two men grasped each other in a bear embrace to seal the betrothal. The marriage business concluded, Yesugei decided that he would return. Dai asked him to stay longer. Yesugei wanted to return.

Bidding farewell to his host, Yesugei said, "I'm glad we've forged a tie of kinship. I leave him in your hands. He is a good boy and destined to lead my clans. Take good care of him. Oh, and before I leave, you should know that my son is afraid of dogs."

"Don't worry, my friend. I give you my solemn word that I shall treat your son as my own." Dai had his men give Yesugei fresh horses for the journey. "It's good to see the kind of relationship you have with your son. My daughter is marrying into a family with strong ties. This is the way she has been raised. Come as often as you like, as my guest. And if he is as talented as you say, he shall lead the young men of my clans in the hunt. Farewell and a good journey home."

"Farewell. Come to my tent and I will return the hospitality."

Yesugei embraced Temujin and admonished him to be a credit to the Borjigins. His voice cracked when he said farewell. A groom brought fresh horses. Yesugei mounted up for the return ride.

Temujin watched, fighting back tears, as his father set off in the direction of home.

A year passed. Temujin and Bortai became as close as brother and sister. The young khan became a member of Bortai's family. He rode better than the Khongirad boys and soon the senior nobility invited him to take command of the young men's hunt. From the first hunt, he provisioned the family with plenty of meat to dry for winter stores.

It was traditional that the young couple would marry at fourteen. He could begin riding with his father in battle when he was thirteen. The time was not far off. He would begin riding with his father when he returned.

Bortai learned the duties of organizing a household from Nambi. Her mother taught her to organize the women's camp, supervising the serving women and slaves. She learned the management of the tanning of hides and the manufacture of felt: the shearing of sheep, the carding of shearings, beating of the felt into sheets. She learned the collecting of wild herbs and onions and the drying of meat into jerky. In preparation for her marriage, she was given a dowry of tents, herds, commoners who would follow her to her new home and live in her camp. She had a talent for trading with the merchants and kept her profits in copper coins and silver in a locked box.

Bortai wanted to buy a Chinese carpet as for Temujin's twelfth birthday. She said the carpet would decorate his tent when he established his own camp. The Chinese merchants lived in towns and villages on the borderlands with the steppe country. The Khongirad had learned numbers and accounting from long trading with the Chinese.

This was a mixed town and village. Outside the town were farmhouses, fixed dwellings whose inhabitants owned plots of land where they grew millet, sorghum and rice.

Temujin had never been to a village, for out on the steppes, there was nothing but grassland as far as the eye could see. There were horse trading sites on the caravan trails where the Muslim caravan merchants came to visit and present their wares. But the sedentary world, the world of towns and villages, was a different world.

Bortai took Temujin to a shop in the center of a village. It was his first experience of a village. The street was alive with hawkers, peddlers, and street vendors. He saw shops and an inn for travelers, stores where artisans displayed items made of carved wood and cinnabar, and a textile factory where women dyed silk. A wine shop displayed a wooden sign with a carved bottle. He asked what the peasants did in the winter. Bortai replied that they waited to plant in the spring. Temujin said that the people who lived on farms were slaves to the seasons. The nomads migrated before the winter, and rode back to their lands in the spring.

The two of them walked down the street of shops--Temujin remarked that the Chinese merchants shot glances at him, dressed in tunic and riding trousers. He was different from them. He was tall and towered over the Chinese, even the big peasant boys. Old women whispered, pointing at his red hair that he wore in plaits.

They passed a couple of young toughs standing outside the wine shop and one of them called out something to him, something that sounded ugly. "Do you understand his language. What is he saying?" Temujin asked Bortai.

"They call us barbarians," she nodded, hurrying along. "Don't look at them. Not the merchants we deal with. They are polite."

He slowed down, looking at them, his fists clenching and unclenching. He was big for his age and fearless. He looked like a man of eighteen. He walked toward where the toughs were standing. The youths, sensing he was not intimidated, turned and walked away.

"Barbarians? " He spat on the ground. "I haven't seen a decent horse in this place. The Chinese buy our horses from the Muslim caravan merchants. I could bring herds here and do business. I'm not afraid of them. "I could take three of them."

She took his arm and pulled at his sleeve. "This is the border country. It's the frontier. We do business with them. Some of them are rude. Not all."

They entered a shop where she knew the owner. Chinese goods of all kinds lined the walls: medicines, tea, porcelain, rice, items of manufacture: silks and brocades; fabric embroidered in gold; metal shields painted with lacquer; carved ivory; cast bronze; stoneware pottery; leather quivers of exquisite workmanship.

Behind the counter, the Chinese proprietor fingered an abacus, a counting machine. His name was Mr. Ho and he wore a coat of padded cotton and straight-legged trousers with soft shoes.

Mr. Ho spoke the Khongirad tongue to Bortai, then called out in Chinese to his wife who was minding their two children in the rooms behind the store. "Our guest is here. Bring tea."

A petite woman in a silk coat and long skirt, her hair pulled back in a bun, came and poured fragrant smoked tea in tiny porcelain cups. The tea was offered in the Chinese style, green without yak butter and salt.

Temujin drank the tea and put the cup down. Mr. Ho had honored them as guests. When the woman came back, she had a baby in her arms and a little dog running along behind her. When the dog saw the big Mongol with the red hair, it began yapping and tried to nip his boot. Suddenly the little dog bit Temujin on the ankle. His boots were made of deerskin, soft leather, and the little dog's teeth sank in. The dog shook his head.

He winced and shook his foot and flung the dog away. The picked up the dog and apologized. "So sorry," she said.

"Never mind," said Temujin. "We have big dogs, mastiffs, for the hunt."

She put the dog in the back room and shook her head. A big strong boy like that afraid of a little dog!

Bortai introduced Temujin to the proprietor and said that they had come to look at carpets. She spoke halting Chinese. In the back room, she knew, were the most valuable rugs and fine porcelains, the luxury items he showed to his best customers, who had copper cash to spend.

Mr. Ho motioned for them to come into the back, the dark wood interior of the store. He motioned to two wooden chairs. They sat down and the shopkeeper brought out three carpets. "My best," he said.

Temujin passed over the first two and admired the third. It was made of wool and was deep blue with two birds with long feathers in the center and a rainbow pattern on the border. The wool was soft to the touch.

Bortai said it was a betrothal gift and Mr. Ho smiled and offered his congratulations and his wishes for a happy family. When is the wedding?" Bortai said in a year.

"It's an auspicious year by the Chinese calendar. In honor of the occasion, I will give you a discount, a good price, it will bring us all prosperity. Besides, I have never seen a Mongol with golden eyes like your future husband."

Bortai thought the price was too high. She bargained with the Chinese man as she bargained with the Muslims. The Muslims regarded commerce as a long drawn out game, but the Chinese style of bargaining had begun. He couldn't afford to let the rug go for her price. It was priceless. A fine work of art.

Bortai listened politely and translated for Temujin. He was no stranger to the bargaining that went on in the khan's tent.

"Come," he said to her. "I don't need the rug. I've got a Persian rug. Let's leave." This was the time-honored maneuver when bargaining.

The Chinese defended the superiority of Chinese goods over Persian.

Temujin laughed. "Your price is too high, Mr. Ho. You're robbing me."

Bortai reached the wooden doorframe and as she was stepping over the raised threshold, the proprietor called out "Come back, come back, you can have it for the price, but you're taking food out of the mouths of my children.

Mr. Ho's demeanor changed. She came from a good family and this boy comforted himself well. Family was everything.

"Oh, I am honored that my carpet will fill your tent. I know this young woman well. She is of good family. I hae done business with her mother as well. I thought this young man was your brother because unmarried Chinese girls don't go out with young men alone."

Bortai used silver ingots to pay. She laughed. "I ride and I own horses. Chinese girls don't do that either."

"No, no, they don't."

Mr. Ho had rolled up the carpet and carried it to the cart.

Outside in the sunlight, the three Chinese toughs jumped him when he came outside. He swung and knocked one in the jaw. He stepped in and struck again, the same spot, and hit with such force that the jawbone broke and the youth spat out a tooth. Blood trickled down his lip.

Two of them attempted to get hold of his arms, so a third could hit him. The Chinese were strong from working the fields, but he was a distance rider and was stronger. Without a look, he shrugged off the two as though they were bothersome children and attacked the one in front of him.

He picked the Chinese up off the ground and slammed him against the side of the wooden building. The Chinese slid down, doubled over then fell on his rump.

They got in the cart and rode back to her father's camp. His time in the Khongirad lands taught him an important lesson. He had a taste of the Chinese attitude about the barbarians.

Yesugei Khan traveled to the Khongirad lands once a year to see how Temujin was doing. Father and son took pleasure in each other's company and discussed family affairs and news of the camp.

They discussed the marriage, the biggest event so far in Temujin's life. When Temujin returned to the Valley of Two Rivers, they would hold a wedding and have a great feast. Temujin would take up his duties assisting his father and learning to govern. He would become the Khan of 40,000 tents when his father died and his father wanted him to be prepared.

Temujin was gaining experience and wanted to know of his father's thinking about relations with the Jin Emperor, the ruler of North China.

Yesugei explained how it stood. The Tatar were the vassals of the Jin, the most powerful tribe in the steppes. Once this position had belonged to the Mongols, but the Mongol kings had grown too powerful and represented a threat, for the Emperor of China feared the horsemen of the steppes. The Jin switched sides and formed an alliance with the Tatar.

Yesugei explained that the Jin Emperor's armies could not conquer nomad armies because the nomads were better horseman and superior archers.

Temujin observed that the farming life made the Chinese soft and the nomad life made the Mongols hardy. The Chinese had to leave family and village and town behind to fight. The nomad armies brought family with them.

Yesugei was pleased. His son was intelligent. He wanted Temujin to understand the situation in North China. North China had been divided among three different kingdoms ever since the fall of the Tang Dynasty, a magnificent period in which China was the richest and most cosmopolitan kingdom on earth.

Tang was China's golden age, but it could not maintain its defenses at the frontier. Other nomad armies came down and conquered. A Jin Emperor ruled in the North and a Han Chinese ruled in the South. The Jin had the northeast. They were a nomad tribe who were excellent fighters and took the northeast.

Yesugei had a map. The Xi Xia lived in Northwest China astride the caravan trails that led over the high mountain passes at the Roof of the World. They were tough fighters, the last remnant of the Tibetan empire.

The Jin were the problem. They meddled in the affairs of the steppes to keep their kingdom safe. They wanted the steppe tribes to be weak. Their strategy was to divide and conquer.

Yesugei said, "They call it "Use barbarians to check barbarians." That means Mongols against Tatars and Tatars against Mongols. We fight each other and do not ride south against them. The Jin Emperor will come back to us when the Tatar get too powerful," Yesugei said. "For now, they come against us."

Trade with the Mongols was important to the Jin Emperor because he needed horses for his army and for this, he needed the Mongols. In return, the Mongols traded the Chinese for tea.

Yesugei entertained the Muslim caravan merchants who traded in the Chinese capital. It was the way of khans to show hospitality i their tents. In passing an evening, Yesugei gathered intelligence from the merchants. They assured him that hundreds of thousands of soldiers guarded the cities of China.

The soldiers had war chariots. Their infantry supported the imperial cavalry, armed with long spears and shields. Waves of them repelled cavalry attacks.

"Remember our advantage and do not be afraid of their numbers," Yesugei said. "Our cavalry are superior to their chariots. The chariots are a clumsy way of making war. They cannot maneuver as we do."

The visit between father and son ended. Temujin had almost grown up in the year he had been away. Yesugei told Temujin, "Remain here for one more year. Then you will return to our valley. We will have the marriage feast. Then we will all be together again."

The first day of his journey homeward, Yesugei rode at the edge of the cliff formation that fronted the mountain range. On the fifth day, he came upon a group of men feasting on the Yellow Steppe. One of the men called out to him to join them for food and drink.

Yesugei thought, why not? Hours of daylight remained. He would be glad to rest a little from his journey. The food smelled good. A flask of *koumiz* would refresh him. His heart was sore leaving his son. He decided to eat with them and ride on, to make his own camp.

As he drew near, Yesugei got a look at the men who were roasting a deer on a spit. They were lean, with their skins greased against the cold nights. They had a look in the eyes like hungry wolves. Yesugei did not recognize the men as Tatar, but one of them, the one he named Weasel Face in his mind, recognized Yesugei the Brave as the man who had defeated them in battle many times, the man who had killed his brother and killed other kinsmen in battle.

Yesugei thanked them for the invitation. He walked to the stream and filled his flask. He sat down and drank *koumiz*. Then he sat down and drank a flask of koumiz, resting and watching them tend the grill with the meat.

The second one, the one he named Narrow Eyes, removed the deer ribs from the fire and waited for the meat to cool before he cut it up. Out of Yesugei's hearing, the two Tatar conferred and agreed that something should be done, some revenge extracted.

Weasel Face, the tall one with the rangy cheekbones, said, "I say let's do away with the bastard. He killed ours. He deserves it."

Narrow Eyes agreed. Weasel Face went over to his horse and reached into the saddlebag. He felt around inside, searching for the pouch of poison he got from the Siberian shaman. The poison was made from berries and worked very slowly. This Mongol khan would be days away by the time he realized he was dying.

After he rested his bones from the days' ride, Yesugei got up and joined them at the fire, Narrow Eyes made a great show of sharpening his knife and carving the deer meat. He smiled and offered Yesugei a good slice of the deer rib.

Weasel Face poured him a cup of the poisoned *koumiz*. They exchanged the gossip of travelers. Narrow Eyes congratulated Yesugei on the good fortune of arranging a match for his son. Yesugei ate his fill and drank down the cup, The two Tatar exchanged glances. They pretended nothing was wrong and ate and drank and continued their friendly conversation.

Several hours of daylight remained. Yesugei thanked the strangers for the meal. He made his farewells and left them eating the ribs, the firelight shining in their eyes.

The sun was not yet low in the sky. Yesugei rode on. Dusk arrived and his organs felt like they were on fire. He slumped forward and rode hunched over the saddle horn.

Darkness fell and he pulled a blanket out of a saddlebag. With effort, he managed to make a fire. He lay down, pulled the blanket over him. He felt a stabbing pain in his liver.

In the morning the pain had not left him. He mounted up and rode on. Only six more hours and he would be in the Borjigin camp, if he could stay on his horse.

His legs felt numb and a little while later, his arms felt heavy. He saw Burkhan Khaldun, the sacred mountain of the Valley of Two Rivers.

By the time he reached the Blue Mongol camp, he could barely feel his limbs. The poison began working on his vital organs. He could hardly speak and his vision was blurred. His tongue felt thick and swollen in his mouth. Servants lifted him from his horse and carried him to his tent. Oyelun came, and he told her that he was dying.

Yesugei told Oyelun that she would rule the clans as *khatun* until Temujin came of age. Yesugei's personal servants came to his bedside, kneeled and kissed their khan's hand in farewell and promised to obey Oyelun until Temujin could assume leadership.

Oyelun summoned the chief nobles of the Taijyud clans, the second branch of the Blue Mongols after the Borjigin. Their names were Targutai and Todogen. Yesugei lay in his bed staring with empty eyes. He knew them all but didn't recognize any of them. Oyelun did not think that Yesugei would last until the chiefs arrived. The shaman said prayers and sprinkled the tent with *koumiz* to drive away the evil spirits.

Yesugei whispered in the ear of Munglig, his most trusted manservant. "My sons are still young. Take care of them like they were your own brothers. Take care of my wife like she was your elder sister.

His last wish was to give orders regarding Temujin. "Go quickly, Munglig, Bring Temujin back to this valley. Don't tell Dai what happened. He might keep my son for a slave if he finds out that I am dead. Tell Dai that I miss my son and want him in my tent. I fervently hope that you return before I leave the earth."

The funeral of Yesugei Khan was held in the Valley of Two Rivers. Soldiers drove wooden posts into the earth in the form of a circle a mile in circumference to mark Yesugei's burial ground. Streamered banners whipped in the stiff wind. The shaman Tab Tengri performed the horse sacrifice, breaking the backs of a stallion and a mare, to give the animals an instant death. He hung the skins and ribs from a tall pole, This was the custom with the death of a khan.

After intoning the prayers and making the libations, the shaman sacrificed Yesugei's horse and favorite concubine and put them in the grave with him. The soldiers removed the posts and grass grew over the grave, leaving it unmarked.

Temujin began sleeping in his father's tent, a boy trying to become a man.

Two old women stood on the crest of the sacred mountain looking down into the valley. Their sides were heaving, as they were catching their breath. Yesugei the Brave was dead. It was time to destroy his widow. By leaving her out of the ceremony which connected the clans with the spirits of The Ancestors, they had branded her an outcast. Oyelun was unprotected while they had grown sons who could take over the clans.

Orbei and Sokhati were the widows of Ambaghai, the last powerful Khan of the Mongols. Their hands were wrinkled, but their faces held the memory of a beauty that was remarkable enough to secure marriage to a khan. Their vengeance had been a long time coming.

Orbei and Sokhati had been rivals when their husband was alive, rivals for his kisses, his gifts, the bearing of his children and the honor of sitting beside him at banquets and feasts. They jealously counted the numbers of nights he spent in the tent of these two wives. They competed in giving him healthy sons, a woman's competition.

Once they were widowed, these two ceased their rivalry. They became as close as sisters because they had a common enemy in Oyelun.

Yesugei had named Oyelun regent until Temujin could take his father's place.

Several generations back, the Chinese had tricked Ambaghai into attending a banquet in his honor and then, in treachery, they had poisoned him.

Under Ambaghai, the Mongols had amassed so much power that they were the dominant tribe in the eastern steppes. The Chinese Emperor was informed of this and the officials of his court advised him to switch vassals and offer their alliance to the Tatar, the rival tribe, the mortal enemies of the Blue Mongols. This was Chinese statecraft: use barbarians to check barbarians. By barbarians, they meant the unlettered. Outside the civilization defined in the Chinese classics. Ignorance of government not defined by the philosopher Confucius.

The Jin Emperor made an offer to the Tatar and they became his vassals and reigned supreme as lords of the steppes while the Mongols declined in prestige and power. Through a twist of fate, Ambaghai's successor named Yesugei the Khan instead of his own son. The new khan should be one of their sons, not the son of Yesugei. It was a matter of succession. What was right was right.

The proof was that Yesugei Khan had the reputation of bringing peace and good governance to the Mongols, but he had not defeated the Tatar and restored the Mongols as the most powerful tribe. Yesugei blamed it on the Chinese meddling in the affairs of the steppes. Why did the Chinese do this? To keep the mounted archers from invading China. It was a matter of power.

Yesugei made war on the Tatar many times but did not have the strength or the numbers to defeat them. Now that Yesugei had died, a new khan would have to take command. Yesugei had designated his son Temujin as the next khan. The two old women had devised a plan. The two old women did not want Oyelun lording it over them until her son came of age.

Orbei and Sokhati had come to the sacred mountain to perform the The Ancestor ceremonies. Oyelun should have been with them, but they excluded her. Why should her son become khan? Why not their sons? Why shouldn't they have the power of mother of the khan.

Oyelun's husband was dead and her son was too young and inexperienced to protect her. So the two old khatuns asked themselves, why should she rule over them? Why should their sons not take command?

They celebrated together, for they had been forced to swallow a bitter anger for many years.

They would leave her unblessed, outside the circle of The Ancestors, an exile. They would eat the burnt offering themselves. By leaving her out of the ceremony which connected the clans with the spirits of The Ancestors, they branded her an outcast.

The two old women had performed the Ancestor ceremony for many years as senior women of the Taijyuds.

They removed their shawls. They got down with difficulty and touched their foreheads to the earth nine times. They lay a clean cloth on the ground, spread the utensils--bowls, platter, brazier, coals, skewers--and prayed over them. Sokhati's gnarled fingers took a long time to unwrap the strips of raw meat which were to be roasted as an offering. Orbei removed from her pocket a flask of *koumiz* for the ceremony.

Sokhati built an offering fire out of cypress and wormwood chips and arranged the meats for burning. The meats sizzled and burnt on the brazier and a delicious smell rose up, an offering to The Ancestors, those who had migrated with their herds on these steppes from time immemorial.

The two old khatuns prayed for the clans. Sokhati removed the meats from the fire, placed them on a tray and raised them up for the spirits of The Ancestors to eat. The smoke from the fire drifted skyward.

Orbei poured a stream of *koumiz* on the ground in each of the four directions then poured a ceremonial circle. A golden eagle flew overhead, drifting on the high winds.

They recited the prayers. *Grant us good grazing, healthy herds, many fine grandchildren, good health, long life. Grant us safety from lightning and thunder. May the winter not be too severe.* The prayers lifted to the sky.

They touched their foreheads to the earth nine times. The ceremony had been performed. Their duty was done.

Sokhati divided the offering food between them, making sure each of them got the juicy succulent bits of roasted lamb, goat, horse and yak. They ate all of the meat, licking the fat from their fingers.

Oyelun walked the mountain path enjoying the view as she ascended higher and higher above the valley floor. Below her were pine trees whose fresh scent filled the air and lifted her spirits. Above was the Blue Sky, covered in fish scale clouds. Below her were the rapids of the river, the clear water rushing with the sound of low rumbling thunder as it coursed down the side of the mountain to the valley floor.

The walk on the sacred mountain before the ceremony always made her feel closer to The Ancestors.

Coming here, performing this duty as Yesugei's wife, made her feel closer to him. He had not been dead a month yet. Her mourning was not yet over. She had grieved alone in her tent. in silence.

During the shaman's prayers at Yesugei's funeral, she did not make a public display of grief. She held everything inside. Sochigil, the junior wife, wailed and tore at her hair. Oyelun felt as numb as a piece of wood. Reaching deep inside, she discovered an iron will. She and she alone would rule as regent until Temujin was old enough to be elected khan by the nobility. Yesugei had chosen her. It was his dying wish.

She reached the cliff-top and saw the two old khatuns finishing the offering meat. One look at their faces told her all that she needed to know. These two old witches had gotten a chance to get even with her. She would not give them satisfaction. She took off her shawl and faced them, waiting for an explanation. The two old khatuns got up and gathered the utensils and put them in a sack.

She said, "You excluded me and I belong. I have the right delegated by the khan. I condemn your actions before *Koko Tengri*, the Eternal Blue Sky.".

Neither of the old women responded. She was left out, an outcast, and Oyelun knew it.

Oyelun's voice was cold. "You must be saying to yourselves that Yesugei the Brave is dead now and his sons are still boys. You are making a big mistake if you think that gives you the right to leave me out of the ceremony, I am khan. Do you really think you can leave me out? Leave nothing for me? Do you think I'm such a fool that I'll just sit by and let you insult me? Remember my words, old crones. The Ancestor prayers are without form and substance when they come with a false heart. *Koko Tengri* will not hear them. Without me, there is no ceremony."

Sokhati said, "From now on you should wait for us to invite you before you join in a feast. Tell us, didn't you say to yourself all those years, Ambaghai Khan is dead, I am khatun, I can insult his widows? "

Orbei said. "If you are a powerful *khatun*, what are you doing arguing over a scrap of offering meat?"

Oyelun's voice thundered. "I did not know that so much hatred has been festering in your hearts. I swear I never intended to put you down. I always gave you respect. Never mind. I have a flask of *koumiz*. I shall perform my own ceremony. *Koko Tengri* knows a sincere heart."

Oyelun walked away from them and bowed down, closed her eyes and said the prayers. Then she poured the flask of *koumiz* on the ground. She kneeled and touched her forehead to the ground nine times. Without another word, Oyelun turned and walked back down the mountainside.

Deep inside her chest, she felt her will turn to steel. She did not care how long it took. She would settle the score.

The two old khatuns walked back to the Taijyud camp. Night in the steppe falls swiftly. The sky turned indigo, flaming red, orange and at the horizon, the sun sank behind the mountains, a red disk.

Orbei said, "We must convince our sons to take their place as Ambaghai Khan's rightful heirs."

By the time they reached the Taijyud camp and found their sons' tents, the blue of the azure vault spread across the grasslands.

Targutai and Todogen took counsel with their mothers. Orbei and Sokhati would have preferred to talk to their sons without their wives. The wives would have preferred it if their husbands didn't go running to their mothers every time their mothers snapped their fingers.

The old khatuns had no trouble inflaming their sons' sense of dispossession and their foolish wives' ambitions.

Orbei related what had happened on the sacred mountain. "The time has come. We must split camp. We don't need the Borjigins anymore. The boy cannot govern us. If they want to come with us, let them. If they want to stay behind, let them. I say we leave in the morning and find our own pastures. What do you say?"

Targutai was the older and stronger of the two brothers. He had been close to Temujin when he was growing up and had taught him how to ride. "Who are we to challenge the Khan's decision?"

Orbei said, "You were too young to rule when your father died. Yesugei took over. Now the situation is reversed. Temujin is too young, so one of you must take over."

Targutai mused aloud. "You're right, mother. Temujin is only twelve. He won't be able to lead the clans for years."

The two daughters-in-law understood immediately. If their husbands became khans, they would be *khatuns* and have first place in the ceremonies, even above these domineering old harpies.

Todogen's wife Margut had a moon-shaped face and ruddy cheeks. She was used to her husband taking time to deliberate, and often urged him to action.

She put her hand over his. "This is our chance to gain the khan's tithe for ourselves. We will be rich." The khan's tithe was paid every year, ten per cent of the herds of nobles and commoners. The khan's herds grew larger and the trade in animals grew more profitable.

Targutai's wife Zeni was a beauty. Zeni resented Oyelun's beauty, her way of carrying her head high and the necklaces of coral and silver that she wore on special occasions. She coveted the earrings of precious lapis. "Oyelun has insulted us many times over the years. Why do we camp with them? We have our own people to take care of. Let us leave them behind. We have to think of ourselves."

Zeni would be the wife of the khan and take precedence at assemblies and feasts.

Todogen was slow in making decisions. He remained silent, turning his thoughts over in his mind. Todogen said, "We could do this, but. . ."

"But what?" Margut said, exasperated. "This is the time. Make a decision."

Todogen said, "We have a problem. How would two brothers share the position of khan?"

Margut drew in a breath and explained. "This is a time of mourning, but we must think of the future. Will the clans survive with Oyelun as the khan? The people will be persuaded. Two brothers will take leadership to make sure of the survival of our clans.

Targutai apprehended the situation. "I owed Yesugei allegiance. He was a man of experience and I gave him my respect. I cannot give a boy of twelve my allegiance. We take our clans."

Todogen said, "Then in the future, we make decisions together. We divide the tasks of khan. You lead in battle and the hunt. I manage the camps and the migration."

Targutai embraced his brother. They made plans to circulate the word among the tents. Targutai and Todogen had decided to separate the clans.

At dawn, Todogen gave orders to the Taijyuds to break camp. They were going to migrate fifteen miles down the Onon River: The men loaded the tents into wagons and hitched the wagons hitched axle-to-axle. Then they hitched oxen to the wagons.

Temujin had insisted on sleeping in his father's tent. His mother told him that he would become khan when he turned sixteen. Until then, he would have the duty of inspecting weapons and tackle.

A servant awakened Temujin with the news that the Taijyuds were breaking camp. He dressed quickly and went outside and found Targutai and Todogen breaking camp and heading down the river as they did at the season of migration.

"Kinsmen, what are you doing?" Temujin asked.

"We're making our own camp," Targutai said.

"Why? Are we not all one people?"

"Everything has changed. The deep waters of the river are dry. You are a boy and a shallow stream."

Temujin rode down the line calling out to the clans. "Even if you found good grazing ground, would we all not be better off keeping both bones together, than if you Taijyuds go off on your own? The Tatar outnumber us. We need to stay together to fight them."

Many Taijyud wagons agreed with Temujin and broke out of the line of departing wagons and rode back to camp.

In his youth, Targutai had a reputation as a champion wrestler at the annual festival. He had muscular shoulders and thighs. He looked massive, mounted on his war pony. Temujin ordered a servant to bring Oyelun.

Targutai laughed. "You are yet a boy, calling for your mother. We can't wait for you to grow up to be khan. We will lead ourselves."

"I call my mother because the clans respect her more than anyone of us, including you."

Todogen rode down the line of wagons and gave the command. They were ready to pull out, but at the sight of Yesugei's son riding down the line and calling them back, more of the Taijyud unhitched their wagons. They shouted to him that they had decided to stay.

Targutai rode to the head of the line and ordered the caravan of wagons forward. The women drove the carts and the men drove the herds behind the wagons--horses, sheep, goats, camels.

The women urged the oxen with reins and the wagons began rolling away. The migration noisy with the shouting of humans and the whinnies and bleatings of animals.

Old Man Charaka was a faithful steward in the khan's tent. Todogen was within reach. He stepped forward and grasped the reins of Todogen's horse. Todogen kicked the old man away, but the old man had strength and held on.

Todogen leaned down and pushed the old man backwards. "Keep your mouth shut. The khan is dead. The pledge was to the khan, not to the son."

Charaka lost his footing and stumbled, falling to the ground. He scrambled to his feet. His leg was injured. He limped, walking down the line of wagons shouting at the people who were leaving.

"You don't know if the Taijyud brothers can lead you. How can you abandon the widow of Yesugei the Brave? This is wrong."

The Taijyud soldiers guarding the train commanded the wagons to keep moving. Charaka kept walking, limping down the line, beseeching the women who were driving. Some of the women had tears in their eyes. Two more wagons left the line.

Todogen rode after Charaka and shouted at him,

Spitting at Todogen, Old Man Charaka continued walking down the line of black wagons, beseeching the clans to remain. Three more wagons turned their ox teams and left the line.

Todogen, blinded by fury, reached across his saddle and pulled a spear out of its case. With one swift killing lunge, he drove the spear deep into the old man's back.

Old Man Charaka fell forward and landed on his face. As though in a dream, he felt the spear wave back and forth and fall out of his flesh. The wound made a loud sucking noise as his lifeblood seeped into his tunic. Determined to deny Todogen the pleasure of watching him die,

Charaka half-crawled, half-dragged himself to his tent. Behind him he heard the wagons rolling. He dropped himself into the bed. .

Temujin heard what happened. He rushed to Charaka's bedside and found the old man lying in a blood-soaked bed. He rolled the old man over and looked at the wound. No one could do anything for him.

Temujin cradled the dying old man in his arms, his second act as Khan. The first had been to command the clans back to camp.

Charaka made the effort to speak. "I stood with you. The Taijyuds were taking away the people your father assembled, I stepped out and protested. That was my only crime. For that, look what Todogen has done to me."

"Do not worry for me. I will make this right if it takes my life to settle the score. Yours is the loyalty I will demand in my days as khan. Loyalty to the death."

Moments later, Charaka died. Temujin got to his feet and left the tent and saw the line of wagons moving out of camp.

He went outside and saw Oyelun riding down the line of wagons. She raised Yesugei's banner, that contained the spirits of The Ancestors.

"Stand with me," she said to them. She wanted them to look her in the eyes before they abandoned her.

She called out to touch the hearts of those men who had been bullied into leaving, to those who had been in battle with Yesugei, to those who had received booty from their victories. Her voice was lost in the din. She did not know if they could hear her over the noise of the cart wheels and horses.

Some wagons dropped out of the line. Some ignored her and kept moving.

The sight of her demanding the right to rule in Yesugei's stead, using all her strength to lift the standard into the wind, caused half the wagons to drop out of the caravan and return.

She saw a cloud rising up in the distance and riders coming toward her. The Taijyud brothers reined in their horses and ordered those who had left the line to return, telling them they would perish if they stayed.

Those who were defiant lost the courage that Oyelun had inspired and joined the caravan again. Some of them looked back at her. Some of them did not. They were leaving her to her death and they knew it.

An expression of grief froze on her dirt-stained face. Her throat was raw. Her voice was ragged. The dust choked her, filling her nostrils and throat. Not one of the traitors looked at her. No one turned back at the sight of her.

Fatigued and heartbroken, she gave up. Her legs felt so heavy she could hardly walk. She let the banner fall in the dust. Temujin ran after her and picked it up but the caravan had moved off. There was no calling it back.

Devastated, she went back to the campground. She looked at the empty valley, where only a short time ago had been forty thousand tents and felt her gut tightening in fear. Her face was drained of color. She held out her arms and gathered her children around her.

She had to find strength, otherwise she and her children would die. She looked up and saw Sochigil standing there with her two young boys. Tears were running down the younger woman's face.

"There are forty tents left," Sochigil said.

Forty left out of forty thousand. Those who stayed assembled outside her tent and stood before her, waiting for her to command them.

She found the strength in organizing the camp of forty tents. When winter came, life would be hard. The first task was to lay in enough food to get through the winter. They dried meat and vegetables, to make broth to last the season of violent winds and snows.

Oyelun gathered her skirts up. She took the women and servants and went up and down the banks of the Onon gathering garlic, onions and wild pear. The boys found needles which they bent into fishhooks to catch a few misshapen fish.

Oyelun dug roots while the boys hunted mice and marmots. They made nets to fish in the river and they caught tiny fish and dried them.

Temujin worked harder than the other boys because he felt that as eldest, he had been unable to prevent disaster. He could no longer look forward to managing horse herds which numbered in the thousands. He could not look out over forty thousand tents that he would rule. He could not stand night watch duty with Khasar over clans that he knew would be his.

Gone were the hunts with the boys his age. Gone was the father who protected him. On many occasions, he went up to the sacred mountain alone and prayed to the Eternal Blue Sky. His brother Khasar was closest to him, he told Khasar what was in his heart.

Oyelun held her head high, an example for her sons. Daily she reminded her sons that they were khans of the steppes. Daily she repeated to Temujin that he must restore the family to its former glory. He must never forget that he was the son of a great khan and that by ancient law, the clans belonged to him. The Taijyud had violated law and custom and must be punished. This was Temujin's task.

Winter began and it was fierce. Soon even those in the forty tents could not afford to stay. Even these begged her forgiveness and packed up their wagons and left to join the Taijyuds.

The servant Munglig who had come for Temujin in the camp of Dai the Wise, had sworn to Yesugei on his deathbed that he would protect Yesugei's wives and sons, but he suspected the winter would kill them and he left.

Oyelun and Sochigil were alone with their children and a few servants. The valley beneath Mount Burkhan was empty.

Winter was coming and the family could not migrate to Lake Bailkal. They would have to endure the winter in their native pastures.

They decided to move into the caves on the side of the sacred mountain. They laid in stores of food to last the six months of the cold season. They put an extra layer of felt on their tents. They made felt blankets for their nine horses, all that remained of their huge herds, or the animals would freeze to death. They made sheepskin jackets for themselves.

The family had come down in the world. Their wealth consisted of two round white felt tents, a herd of sheep, nine silver-gray geldings and a yellow mare, and a few servants. The horses grazed in a clearing in the forest, where the couch grass was lush after the season of rains. A year from now, Temujin would become khan, but khan of nothing.

Temujin's younger brother Khasar was the best archer in the old days of the camp of 40,000 tents. He put his skill to work and hunted every day and brought home enough game to keep the women busy drying the meat. He made every arrow count and wasted nothing. The women foraged for roots and vegetables in the hills and dried them.

Something happened in the time of abandonment. Temujin's fifteenth birthday came and went. He felt the humiliation of his family's lowered estate. He had lost his future. It was not a joyous occasion but they had a small celebration.

At night, in their tent, Khasar said, "You've changed. You've toughened, brother."

Temujin replied. "When forty thousand tents filled the valley, Mongols quarreled and fought. Family killed family--fathers, sons, brothers, cousins. This was nothing new. The old stories were right. If we stand together, we are strong. Divided, we are weak. Our enemies know this. When I am khan, I will put an end to tribal warfare."

Khasar believed in his brother's vision. This was a future that he would share. He swore to be Temujin's right hand.

Begder continued to steal. He moved from fish to game. He robbed Khasar's game bag of a fat hare. Temujin saw him do it. He could not tolerate a thief.

Temujin found his mother carding the wool from the sheared sheep. She and the women would pound it into felt.

The shock of Yesugei's death and the splitting of camp had taken its toll on her. The color had gone out of her face. Her hair was pulled back and streaked with gray. She worked harder than she had ever worked in her life. She looked at his face and knew something was wrong. "What's the matter?" she said.

He could hear the exhaustion in her voice. "Begder is at it again. He's lazy. He does nothing. Then he steals from us."

Khasar backed up Temujin. "It's true. Yesterday, he stole the game birds I shot in the woods. Today he took a hare. I wanted that hare for all of us for tonight. I could taste it."

Temujin said, "Do something with him. Get his mother to do something with him."

She threw the wool in a basket and sat up straight, rubbing her back. "I told her about the fish. She spoke to him. She can do nothing. He is feeding his tent. We have enough for the winter. We'll get through. Let it pass."

Temujin insisted. "He has no loyalty. That is a danger to us."

"Try to see it my way," Oyelun said. "Sochigil is the junior wife. She is weaker than I am. I am senior wife. It is my duty to protect her. That is your father's rule in his camp. The women get along."

"We have worked hard," Khasar said.

"I'm grateful," his mother replied, her voice drained of emotion. "We have nothing. The only horsewhips we have are hairs from the horsetails. We have no one to fight beside us in war but our own shadows. How will we ever get revenge on the Taijyuds with you two fighting your own flesh and blood?" She got up and grabbed up a bucket. "Let me pass. I have to milk the mare. We have to stick together or we will not survive. Enough."

Temujin's blocked her way. "No, mother, not enough. Do something about him or I will. I am almost grown. You will not rule me in this."

Oyelun got past him and turned at the tent-door. "You were born clutching a clot of blood in your fist. Your father said that you were destined to rule all peoples. Now you want to destroy a life."

She left the tent.

"Let her go," Khasar said, grabbing him by the arm.

Temujin pulled away from Khasar's grip. "We all have to live by the same rules. Father taught me his way of the khan. Begder refuses."

"I am with you," Khasar said.

The first snow fell in October. The forest of pines, spruces and cypress was covered in whiteness. The riverbanks had a powdery white blanket. The horses grazed in the forest clearing, pawing the ground to search for grass, a special talent of the Mongol war pony.

The four sons of Yesugei went hunting in the woods--Temujin, Khasar, Begder and Belgutei. They split up near the clearing. Khasar put his game in a sack under a pine, then went off into the woods. He and Temujin spent the morning hunting. They returned to the clearing at mid-day and approached from opposite sides of the clearing. They saw Begder taking a hare. Begder heard them approach and stood still, holding the hare.

By moonlight, the valley was transformed into a glistening white landscape The stars seemed closer, clearer, sharper. By November, the Orkhon River was frozen into a thick sheet of ice.

The servants lined the large caves with carpets for warmth. The family piled their down beds with blankets. They made hearth-fires. They had stored dung fuel for cooking and logs for heat. These were stored in a cave to keep them dry. The hard work of gathering and hunting that summer had given them enough food.

To fish, they cut holes in the ice. They used an old leather shield for sledding. They glided across the ice on makeshift skates, competing to outdistance each other. One day when they were catching their breath from their version of a hockey match, they saw an new encampment on the other side of the river.

They heard the jangling of harness bells echoing through the woods as the carts of the Jajirat clans pulled up and made camp on the opposite bank of the Orkhon. Overhead the sky was white with blue patches and the pine forest was covered in snow.

Thousands of wagons rolled into the valley with their livestock. A youth of the same age as Temujin and Khasar was skating on the ice alone, He held a willow branch between his hands for balance, sliding across the ice on snowshoes like the reindeer people of Siberia wore. The new boy was not as tall as Temujin. He had a slender face framed by dark hair, which he wore in two plaits. He was lively and athletic and had shining black eyes.

On the steppes, the nobility introduced themselves by way of announcing their lineage. The princely yurts may have had little in the way of material splendor, but they took great pride in their forebears. The boy called out to them. "I am Jamuga, of the Jajirat Mongols. I am a descendant of Bodonchar the Fool."

Temujin said, "Then we are kinsmen. I am Temujin, son of Yesugei the Brave, khan of the Blue Mongols. This is my younger brother, Khasar. We are also descended from Bodonchar the Fool."

The two young men had much in common. Twelve generations back they shared a common ancestor. In the tents of the steppe nobility, this was important. So began their friendship.

Jamuga captivated Temujin and Khasar with the tales of the migrations of his people. The young men told him of their recent misfortune. They spent the first days of their meeting playing games on the ice.

The powdery snowfall hardened. Their footfalls crunched as they walked. When they found bare willow branches of the right size, they cut them with knives they kept in their saddlebags. Holding the branches, they skated a serpentine, twining around each other. They skated for hours at a time, sliding across the ice in circles. Khasar, being younger, tired sooner. His brother and Jamuga had more stamina and continued together. Khasar would return to camp, jealous of his brother's new friend.

At night, in the cave, Temujin reassured his brother. No one would ever come between them. The Eternal Blue Sky had given him a sign. He was forgiven. He had killed his brother and *Koko Tengri* had sent him a new brother, better than the brother who showed no love.

Khasar understood. If Temujin were to restore the Borjigins to power, he would need allies among the sons of the nobility. The relationship with Jamuga was the *anda* bond, the bond of sworn brothers. The sons knew about this because their father had told them of his own sworn brother. These meant victory or defeat in the war.

Temujin and Jamuga became great friends, putting on snowshoes and hunting snow hare. They played games of knucklebone dice in Jamuga's tent on the frozen banks of the Orkhon. They rode together.

One day in the forest, under the tall snow-covered spruce, Temujin told Jamuga about Togril, Lord of the Kereyid, his father's *anda,* sworn brother. Why has he not come to help you, Jamuga wanted to know.

"Maybe he wants to see if I am able to survive on my own," Temujin replied. "One day I will go to Togril and claim the rights of a son. My father instructed me to do this if anything happened to him. I have to wait. I do not want to go as a beggar."

Jamuga said that in the meantime, Temujin should have a sworn brother. They had a ceremony in the forest, a ceremony as old as the tribes, cutting the wrist and mingling blood and they became *anda*. They swore that for life each would come to the aid of the other no matter what. Temujin gave his friend the knucklebone of a roebuck and Jamuga gave Temujin a knucklebone of brass.

That spring, when they were hunting, they declared themselves *anda* for the second time. Jamuga took two pieces of calf-horn, bored holes in them and made a whistling arrowhead which he presented to Temujin. In return, Temujin gave Jamuga a beautiful arrow made of cypress-wood.

Temujin said, "The elders say that if two men become *anda* their lives become one. I swear to you, If our camps separate, we will meet and cherish one another again. I will never desert you and will always defend you. This is the way we'll act from now on. I give you my solemn pledge."

Jamuga agreed, "Our lives are now one. If our camps separate, we will meet again and be loyal as before. I will never desert you and I will always defend you. I give you my solemn pledge."

Temujin had found a good companion. He did not dream that one day they would become rival princes who wished to rule the steppes and that he would have to hunt Jamuga down and kill him.

Rumors spread like brushfire from horde to horde on the steppes. Around the hearth fires of the tribes, the nomads said that the eldest son of Yesugei the Brave had not died of exposure but had lived, was grown to manhood and sought revenge against his kinsmen for the great wrong done to him.

Upriver in the Taijyud camp, Targutai, wrapped in a thick robe of bearskin, was intoxicated from drinking *koumiz*. He thought that he had made an error by not killing Oyelun and her family when he had the chance.

"That evil brood must be able to fly like the wind on horseback by now." He was slurring his words, talking to no one for he was alone in his *gēr* tent. "Then they were children, still dribbling in their mother's arms. What fools we were not to finish the job."

Several years had passed. Targutai had grown used to being a rich and powerful lord and didn't like the thought that he had an enemy who would like to take everything from him.

He shuddered at the thought of how treacherous the young man might have become, because he was old enough to remember life as it had been when his father was alive. He was dangerous, a prince forced to be a common laborer, who had had years to nurse a festering ill will and to suffer indignities.

Targutai had heard the tales of what an excellent archer Khasar was and had no doubt that Khasar had vowed to put an arrow in the hearts of the two Taijyud brothers. It was logical. That's what he and his brother would have vowed had Temujin and Khasar stolen everything from them.

After all, Targutai told himself, nodding, his chin on his chest, he had done nothing wrong. No alliance among the clans was permanent. When a chieftain died, ties of loyalty ended.

Lesser nobles had the right to break camp. As the leader of one bone of the Blue Mongols clans, Targutai had exercised an ancient right. It was the way of the steppe. Now he had a predicament on his hands. It would only be a matter of time until Temujin would want to claim the peoples that had given their loyalty to his father.

Yesugei's heir would know the ancient ways. He would want to exercise his right. In Temujin's place, Targutai would have done the same. The yearly tithe paid to the khan meant wealth. Targutai's herds had grown immense, and with the wealth, came greater power. Targutai had no intention of giving the clans back.

"Why didn't I kill him?" he lamented to himself and in his drunken state, he answered himself. Because I am a sentimental imbecile. When the boy was young, I trained him the way one trains a two-year old horse and I had a fondness for him. He sent a servant to bring the old khatuns, both of whom were still alive.

"Bring my brother, too," he shouted after the servant left by the tent door.

The brother Todogen had grown arrogant, swollen with importance and power. He saw at once what state Targutai was in, inebriated again, his mind haunted by the dark feelings that he imagined dwelling in Temujin's heart.

Todogen had spent many evenings listening to his brother's laments and he was tired of it. Todogen believed in the rule of might. They took what should have been theirs. That was the end of it.

The old Taijyud khatuns, wizened with the passage of time, as spiteful as ever, came into the *gēr* hunched over. They walked with curved backs and sat at the hearth-fire and listened to Targutai rant.

In the firelight, Orbei and Sokhati looked like crones who had been present at the formation of the earth. They compensated for the ravages of age by wearing more jewels than they had worn in their youths when they were the senior wives of a powerful khan. On their arms, necks and fingers, were silver, coral and turquoise, bracelets, necklaces and rings.

In the thick atmosphere of the smoke-filled tent, Orbei rasped, "How could that woman have survived the winters? What bargain has she made with a shaman of the dark arts that the snows have not buried her? That she and her brood have not starved?"

Targutai looked into the fire. He tried to speak but his tongue was thick. He gathered his bearskin wrap about him. A malevolent light came into his eyes, the courage he gained from drunkenness.

"There is still time to prevent the boy from taking revenge. We will ride to the pastures where we left them and put an end to Yesugei's line. You're right mother. Either the woman has paid a shaman or the whelp is possessed of a demon will. We will do what we should have done long ago, find him and kill him.""

Orbei's voice cracked as she gazed into the firelight, "Yes, my son. This is right. You are the khan of the clans now."

Todogen was enthusiastic. "At dawn we will ride downriver to the pastures where we left them. We will cut down the forest if we must and find him."

Oyelun heard the earth rumbling. She saw the horde of riders approaching across the open country. Terror rose in her heart and cut off her wind. The Taijyuds had come back. This time they would kill them.

She ordered all of them into the thickest part of the forest. Oyelun hid the younger children, Otchigin, Temuge and their little sister, Temulun, in a cave formed by the crevasse in a cliff. Oyelun brushed away her daughter's tears and told her, "Don't come out no matter what. Wait until one of us comes for you." The three little girls huddled together, their eyes wide with fear.

In a clearing, Belgutei chopped down young trees while Temujin and Khasar erected a barricade. Khasar was the best archer and he took his place behind the barricade. Temujin stood beside him. Oyelun took cover.

Targutai reached the edge of the woods, reined in his horse and shouted, "We're not here to fight the family. We've come to get Temujin. Spare yourselves. Send him out."

Khasar began rapid fire volleys of arrows, aimed at raining down on the approaching riders. Temujin and Belgutei joined the volley.

Oyelun ran out from behind the barricade and untethered the gray-white gelding. She led the tough little horse to the barricade and held out the reins to Temujin.

"Run," she ordered. "They're here to kill you. Don't worry about us. Hide. Don't let them find you."

Je hesitated. He did not want to run.

"You can only help us if you live. Don't come back until they've gone. I swore on Yesugei's grave that I would see his eldest son grow to manhood. And I will. Run."

Khasar said, "She's right. They'll kill you on sight. You're no good to us dead."

Oyelun shoved the reins in his hand. "Go. We will hold them off as long as possible."

At the foot of Mount Burkhan, a vast forest of cedar, larch and pine covered the upper reaches of the Onon River. Temujin took the reins, mounted his horse and galloped into the deepest part of the forest. He was hidden under the thick canopy of leaves. A Taijyud soldier spotted a lone horseman leaving the camp and shouted to the rest to follow.

Temujin disappeared. The Taijyuds reined in at the edge of the forest. These woods were too thick for them to ride in after him. He knew the terrain. He had a quiver full of arrows. He could wound or kill riders if they came in one by one. He couldn't remain hidden for long with only berries to eat. They could starve him out.

Targutai called to his soldiers, "Surround the woods. Don't let him escape."

Temujin waited and watched. For three days and three nights, no warriors came into the forest on foot to track him down. By the third day he needed food. He thought to himself, "They must have called it off. It's safe to leave."

As he led his horse to the edge of the cedar forest, the saddle fell off the animal. He backtracked to the spot on the trail where the saddle had slipped off. The breast strap was still buckled and the belly cinch was tight. He was puzzled and thought, "The saddle could have slipped back with only a fastened belly cinch, but it could never have worked itself off with the breast strap still buckled."

He looked around him. He knew the woods well. He had hunted here with Khasar for years. High above him were the tops of the pines and spruce. Beyond that was the deep blue sky. All he heard was birdsong. It must have been a warning sent from the Blue Heaven, he thought. It is the will of *Koko Tengri* that I stay in the forest longer. He turned around and went back into the woods to wait another three days and three nights. Outside the forest the Taijyud were waiting.

He was so hungry his stomach was growling. Again he decided it was time to leave. He rode along the trail when a massive white boulder slid down the mountain and rolled down to block the path in front of him. Once more he rode the horse back into the thick cover of trees and waited three days and three nights. By this time he had been without food except for wild berries for nine days. He had slept fitfully out of fear and he was exhausted. He was going to starve if he didn't try to escape.

"I don't want to die in this forest, hiding from my enemies, forgotten and nameless," he said to himself. "I'd rather take my chances getting out than stay here and die like a trapped animal."

Using the knife, he cut a path through the dense brush around the big white boulder. As he led his horse out, the Taijyud fell on him from all sides, took him prisoner and took him back to their camp.

It was a custom of the Mongols to detain criminals before execution by passing them from yurt to yurt in each of their camping circles. Targutai intended to kill Temujin after the Feast of the Full Moon. Not wishing to take any chances with his prisoner, he ordered his soldiers to put Temujin in a cangue, a wooden stock that rested on his shoulders and encircled his neck and wrists. He told the soldiers to tell everyone in his camping circle, "Let our prisoner spend one night in each tent. Keep an eye on him."

His wrists chained, his neck chafed from the rough wood, Temujin moved from tent to tent for more than a week. He was grateful to be alive, angry with himself for being captured, incensed that the Taijyud would order his execution.

After days of staying with people who mistreated him, the boy was sent to the tent of the *koumiz*-maker, Sorkhen Shira. The family knew of his reputation and was drawn to him. They removed the cangue so he could sleep. They spoke among themselves when Temujin was supposedly asleep and said that he seemed a proud young chief. Sorkhen's son remarked how noble and beautiful the light emanating from his eyes was. The daughter thought he had eyes like a hawk. And red hair!

Sorkhen Shira's sons were the same age as Temujin and said they would have liked to follow their prisoner rather than the greedy brothers.

The Taijyuds were always cheating at the khan's tithe. They were greedy and they were drunkards. Temujin was their idea of what a khan should be.

On the sixteenth day of the first summer moon, the Taijyuds held a great hunt. Afterward they gave a Full Moon feast on the banks of the Onon. The smells of roasting meat and the sounds of feasting, music and dancing enticed the Taijyud from their tents just after the sun went down.

They were in a \mood to celebrate. When the moon rose, everyone went to the feast ground and only one spindly youth was assigned to guard Temujin.

Later some of the men returned to camp, but they were drunk and went to their tents to sleep off the alcohol, dazed from their bouts of gluttony.

Temujin, alone in a tent guarded by a dimwit, heard the far-off sounds of the feast. This was an opportunity. If he did not try to escape now, he would be killed. But how would he do it?

The cangue was locked. The weight of the wood pressed down on his neck and chafed at his wrists. Temujin called the guard over to him and said that he needed help to relieve himself.

When the boy bent over, Temujin threw the weight of his body forward and yanked the chain with his free hand. He swung the cangue with all his might, slamming the cangue into the guard's head and knocking him unconscious. Temujin waited, poised like a cornered tiger. His heart was pounding in his ears, louder than a shaman's drumbeat. Moments passed. Nothing happened. No one came. The noise of the feast drifted into the tent. He didn't hesitate.

The massive wooden cangue slowed him down, so he decided against running into the woods. It was the obvious hiding place. The moon was full. The Taijyud knew these forests and would look for him there. Blindly stumbling, Temujin ran down to the riverbank. In water, the heavy cangue would float. He would be able to move.

Digging his heels into the soft wet earth, struggling to keep his balance, he slid down the brambled bank and splashed into the icy water. It was summer but the river had its source up in the mountains and fed on melted snow. He found a place near the rocks and thornbushes where

84

the current couldn't force him downstream. Using the cangue as a float, he lay in the water with only his face visible. How long would he be able to stay here without dying of exposure, he wondered.

The guard came around and stumbled toward the feast, rubbing his sore head and croaking, "He's escaped. Temujin's escaped."

The Taijyud searched the woods on horseback. Everyone, commoners and nobles alike, were ordered to join the search. Riders fanned out into the woods. Commoners searched the riverbank. The women went from tent to tent.

They thought he would hide in the forest. No one thought to look in the river. Sorkhen Shira looked and saw Temujin leaning back in the water, floating with the cangue still around his neck with only his face visible. He had braced himself among the rocks by the thorn bushes to keep himself from floating downstream.

A wave of pity went through Sorkhen. What could this youth have done to deserve such a death? Sorkhen Shira knew that he was risking his life and that of his entire family, but he had been loyal to Yesugei Khan and Targutai and Todogen had stolen Yesugei's people. Sorkhen figured he owed Targutai and Todogen nothing. Anyway, life had been better under Yesugei Khan.

"Don't be afraid," he whispered to Temujin. "Stay right there. I won't tell them I've seen you. I've got to go back or they'll miss me and suspect me."

Sorkhen rejoined the search party. An hour later, Targutai called off the search. The riders left the forest; the commoners, on foot, went back to the feast ground.

Todogen was not in the mood to celebrate. He threw down his ribs of lamb and said, "How can we feast with an escaped prisoner out there? Let's search again. If he gets too far, we'll never catch him."

Targutai said, "You're right, brother. Everyone, go back to the place he just searched and search again."

When Sorkhen reached the riverbank, he held a torch up and saw Temujin hiding between the rocks. Temujin had been in the water for almost two hours and his teeth were chattering.

He said through his clenched jaw, "I have to get out of the water soon or I'll die."

Sorkhen whispered, "Your lips have turned blue. But you have to hold on. They've come to look again. Wait just a little longer."

Once again, nothing came of the search and Targutai had to call it off. It was late. The moon cast pale light over the deep pits where lamb and deer and boar were roasting. The prisoner's escape had ruined the festivities.

Sorkhen praised the clear *koumiz* which his family had churned and tried to get everyone to drink. He said, "Brothers, we lost the man in broad daylight. We'll never find him tonight, even with a full moon. Let's have one more look. If no one spots him, we can search first thing in the morning when we're sober. He can't get far with a cangue on his neck."

Todogen drunkenly agreed. Riders combed the forest again. Sorkhen sneaked to the riverbank. "*Koko Tengri* must be protecting you tonight. They're going to look one more time and then give up for the night. Lie there quietly until they leave. Then you can get out of the water. I'll help you, but if you're captured, promise me you won't tell them I helped you."

Temujin, floating in the shadows, nodded, his teeth chattering. He watched the torches of the search party of commoners who had gone out on foot. He heard the sound of the hooves coming closer, the shouting of men in the woods, and at long last, the sound of riders returning to camp. Finally all was quiet. Temujin made his way up the steep riverbank, stumbling under the weight of the cangue. On level ground, he sat back on his haunches dripping wet and let the water run off him.

After a while, his teeth stopped chattering. His shoulders had been rubbed raw and his neck and back muscles ached. He would never get very far with a slab of wood on his neck. He had to get the cangue off, but how?

It was madness, but he went back into the Taijyud camp. His only hope was to find Sorkhen Shira's tent and ask the *koumiz*-maker to remove the cangue. He knew how to find the tent. He could smell the *koumiz*. They stored the mare's milk in leather jars all day and churned it all night until it turned clear and potent. They would be up tonight working even after the feast. He would listen for the sound of the churning.

When the river water ran out of his clothes, he made his way back. In the dark, near the tents of the commoners, he listened for the rhythmic sounds of churning. He found the tent and slipped inside the door. The family was startled out of their wits when he came through the tent-door. Sorkhen's face went pale. "What are you doing here?" he whispered. He rushed over and dragged Temujin inside and closed the tent door. "I told you to go find your mother and brothers."

Chimbai, the eldest son, put down a leather sack and said, "Wait a minute, father. You saved him a little. But obviously it wasn't enough. We have to help him the rest of the way. He'll be killed if we don't."

Chiluku, the second son, paused in his churning, "Now that he's here we cannot abandon him now. Help me take off the cangue."

Sorkhen Shira's wife scolded all of them for involving the family but his daughter, Khadagan, went to help her brothers. Chimbai and Chiliku sat Temujin down on a churning stool and used their tools to remove the wooden collar. They got the lock open just as they had when he stayed in their tent. He slumped forward when they slid the heavy wooden beam off. They hid the cangue under a pile of shearings which lay at the back of the tent.

Khadagan looked for a salve. She rubbed the medicine on and whispered that she prayed for his protection. He took Khadagan's hands in his and told her that when his clans were restored, she would be rewarded. She gave him tea with yak butter and some food which he ate hungrily and by then it was daylight.

When he saw the sun rising, Chimbai said, "You can't stay here. They'll find you for sure and kill all of us. The women are making felt. Hide him in our wool wagon. If anyone comes looking for you, no one will think anything is amiss if our sister acts as though she's spinning and sits near the wagon. It will be warm in the wool, but they won't find you. When they leave, we'll figure out how to help you."

Temujin hid in the cart. The brothers covered him well. The Taijyuds conducted a daylight search. Once again, they combed the woods and the surrounding area and found nothing. They searched every day for two days and when they could find no sign of their prisoner, decided that someone in the camp must be hiding him. Targutai ordered a search of all the tents.

Soldiers entered Sorkhen's tent and looked in the bedding. One of them saw the wool cart and decided to pull the wool out of it. They were tossing heaps of the shearing on the tent floor when Sorkhen Shira pretended to be offended by the mess they were making and said, "By the Eternal Blue Sky, you are destroying my poor family's coverings for next winter. My daughter has worked hard sorting that wool. She makes the best felt in this camp. No one would be able to stand the heat of that wool on a day like this."

The Taijyud soldiers looked at the wool they held in their hands. "He's right." The soldiers threw the shearings in the wagon and left the tent.

When they had gone, Chimbai and Chiliku helped Temujin out of the wagon.

"You've got to get out of here," Sorkhen said. "You will get us all killed. Go and find your mother and brothers."

For the journey, they gave him a fat mare which was barren. Sorkhen stewed a fat lamb which had been fed by two ewes and gave him two leather buckets of *koumiz*. The *koumiz*-maker said he could not spare a saddle or a flint to light fires, but he gave Temujin a bow with two arrows so he wouldn't stop to hunt on the way home. Now he had done his duty to his dead khan.

The next night, the family returned to their churning and Temujin mounted up and roude out of the Taijyud camp. He went downriver and went to the place where his family had built the fortress in the forest, but no one was there. He got off the mare and read the tracks they left in the grass.

He followed the banks of the Onon until he reached the spot where the Kimurga River enters the Onon from the west. He found the new camp near Korchukui Hill. He rode into camp on the mare.

Oyelun ran to him and embraced him and said they had been praying that he hadn't been killed. He said they wouldn't be safe there, so they moved their camp to Blue Lake in the Sengur River Valley. This was in the Gurelgu Mountains where they would be within sight of the sacred mountain.

Safe among his own people once again, Temujin looked up through the smokehole of his yurt. He vowed that he was going to destroy the

Taijyuds and restore the Borjigins to their rightful place. He swore the solemn oath with Khasar as his witness and Khasar pledged his loyalty.

Temujin went up the mountain alone to give thanks to the Eternal Blue Sky.

Temujin was hunting and Khasar was cutting striplings to make arrow shafts. They had to work to survive.

High up on a rotted tree trunk in the forest, a crested woodpecker hammered. The woodpecker stuck its beak in a hole, digging for worms.

Temujin bent down and removed a small fox from a trap. He wrung its neck and disentangled its broken leg from the leather mesh and put it in his game bag.

Above him, the tapping of the bird stopped. The woods were silent. Temujin heard horses galloping. He started running toward the pasture.

He ran to the clearing where the family's nine silver-white geldings were grazing.

A Taijyud raider mounted the lead gelding and gave the animal his spurs. Another Taijyud mounted a second horse. The lead horse ran out of the camp and the rest of the horses followed. It was over in an instant.

Temujin slammed a tree with the flat of his hand. "Where is Belgutei? Where's the mare?" They had an old straw-colored mare that they kept for milking.

Khasar said, "Belgutei took the mare to go hunting that morning."

"When he returns, I'll go after them and get the horses back/"

Khasar said, "*I'll* go." Temujin said, "You heard what I said. You stay here and protect the others."

At sunset Belgutei came sauntering back to camp leading the mare, a full burlap sack swinging back and forth from the saddle horn. He was stocky, with powerful arms, a gap-tooth smile and thick black plaits. Belgutei wanted to prove himself to Temujin and Khasar. He did his share of labor, organizing the family's stores of weapons, tools, and riding tackle. He shouted, "Everyone in camp tonight will eat fresh game."

Temujin grabbed the reins and unwound the sack of game. "Where the hell have you been? Taijyud thieves broke into the camp and stole the silver-whites. We've been waiting for you for hours."

Temujin mounted the horse. "Khasar, tell Oyelun where I've gone. Dress the game and make sure everyone eats. I'll be back." Temujin and Khasar were checking traps they had set in the forest, when Temujin grabbed Khasar by the sarm and said, "Listen!" They heard the sound of horses galloping in the distance.

Temujin ran to the pasture. Their nine silver geldings were gone. The horses were all that stood between them and destitution, the only thing which proclaimed their status as aristocrats.

They ran to the pasture and saw a band of Taijyud thieves chasing their horses. One of the thieves mounted the lead gelding, grabbed the mane and gave him spurs. A second Taijyud mounted another horse and whipped him. The other horses followed the lead. The thieves took off across open country. It was over in an instant.

Temujin spat on the ground and cursed. "Those pieces of manure. Without those horses, we are nothing. We have descended to the ranks of commoners.

Khasar was the best archer in the steppes. If his father had lived, he would have been ready for military service and would have a command of ten soldiers. He was spoiling for a fight. "Not if we get them back."

"How? How will we get them back?" Temujin demanded. "We have no horses to ride after them."

"We have the mare," said Khasar.

"Belgutei took the mare and went hunting. He won't be back for hours. Meanwhile, we stand around like fools."

The old mare. their one remaining horse, was used for milking.

"There's nothing to do but wait," Khasar said. He sat down on his haunches. "I know you're angry. You're not the only one who lost a future. I did, too. We're in this together. That life is gone. So we look to the future."

"Good idea. When Belgutei gets back, I'll take the mare," Temujin said.

Khasar was silent, but in their dispossession, the brothers found strength in each other.

At sunset Belgutei walked into camp on foot, leading the straw yellow mare with the hairless tail. A full sack of game hung from the mare's saddle, swinging back and forth. He called out. "I've got fresh meat for all us."

Temujin ran over and grabbed the mare's reins. "What took you so long? We've been waiting all day."

91

"What's wrong?" said Belgutei.

Khasar said, "Thieves broke into the camp and took all of our horses." Khasar grabbed the reins. "I'll go after them."

"No. What a disaster." Belgutei moved faster, untying the game bag from the saddle.

Temujin took the reins. "Khasar, you stay here. Belgutei, dress the game and take it to Oyelun. She'll be pleased. I'll ride after them." He grabbed his bow and mounted the horse. "I'll put arrows through their black hearts. Khasar, go back to the tent and tell mother I've gone."

Temujin rode after the Taijyud, tracking the geldings. For three nights, he slept under the stars. On the fourth morning, he came upon here a young man sitting on a leather stool in the tall grass milking a mare.

Temujin saw In the distant pastures a herd of thousands of horses. He had arrived at a prosperous camp. The youth was wearing clothes made of fine cloth and had boots of the finest leather. Temujin called out a greeting. The young man waved.

Temujin rode up and dismounted. "Have riders come by here with nine white horses? They're my horses. They were stolen from my camp."

Bogorji nodded, getting up and greeting the stranger. "They came by hours ago. I'll show you the tracks." He walked over to a clearing and bent down. "They've got a lead."

He followed Temujin's gaze. "Those herds belong to my father. His name is Nagu the Rich, chief of the Arulat.: You can see why he's called rich." Bogorji laughed. "My name is Bogorji. I'm his only son."

"I'm Temujin, the son of the Yesugei the Brave, Khan of the Blue Mongols."

Bogorji said, "I know who you are. The whole of the steppe nobility is talking about you. Here, have a drink." Bogorji reached up and offered Temujin the leather bucket of mare's milk.

Temujin drank and wiped his mouth with the back of his hand. He handed the bucket back.

Temujin ran his fingers over the tracks. "Those are my horses, all right. Taijyuds raided our camp and stole them from me. I am really furious."

Bogorji said, "You're chasing them. I don't blame you. I would too. I can't stand a thief."

"Neither can I. It pisses me off."

Bogorji said, "Your horse is tired. You'll never catch the Taijyud on that old nag." He went to the pasture with a rope and lassoed a white horse and saddled it up for Temujin.

Temujin accepted the reins and thanked him. "I'll be going. I don't want them to get too much of a lead. I'll return the horse."

"Listen," Bogorji said. "You're tired, riding by yourself. The Taijyud camp is three days from here. Let me come with you. I know you're in trouble, but it's the kind of thing that could happen to anyone. I'm an only son. The herding life is not for me. I'm bored out of my mind. You'd be doing me a favor."

Temujin mounted up. "All right. Come with me, but hurry. They've got a head start." Bogorji hid his leather bucket in the tall grass and saddled up. The two young men rode off in the direction of Taijyud country.

The sun was bathing the foothills in golden light when they came to the Taijyud camping circle. They saw Temujin's horses grazing with the Taijyud herd.

Temujin said, "You stay here. I'll ride into the camp and drive them back this way. Keep them here until I come back."

Bogorji argued, "Don't insult me by making me wait here like a girl in a tent. I came with you to be your companion, not to let you ride into an enemy camp by yourself."

"All right. If you want to risk your hide to help me, you're on." Temujin gave his horse spurs and Bogorji followed.

The sun had set but there was still enough light to circle through the forest around the back of the camp. At the horse pasture, Temujin clicked his tongue and Playfoot, the lead horse, pricked up his ears. Temujin slipped a bridle over the animal's head and took the reins. He jumped on his back, nudged him in the ribs and galloped off. Bogorji leaped on the back of a second horse and they rode west with the other horses following behind them.

The Taijyud ran out of their tents shouting. They mounted up and took off in pursuit. Their leader rode a stallion and held a lasso pole with a noose on the end out in front of his horse. This was what the nomads used to capture horses.

With the sound of hooves pounding in his ears and sweat running down his face, Temujin looked back. The Taijyuds were gaining on them.

Bogorji shouted that he would stay back and hold them off with a bow. Temujin shouted no. He pulled an arrow out of his quiver, turned in the saddle, aimed over his galloping horse's flank, and shot the leader. The Taijyud fell off his horse. Temujin fired again. Bogorji began firing. With his first shot, Bogorji picked off another Taijyud, the arrow biting into his shoulder.

The Taijyud dragged at the reins of their ponies and turned back. Temujin and Bogorji shouted congratulations to each other and rode through the quick-falling darkness. They had gotten away without being injured, but they still wanted to put a good distance between them and their pursuers. They rode all night and, in the morning, they stopped beside a stream and let their horses rest and drink.

Bogorji said, "When you're a khan, you'll make a good commander."

Temujin praised his new companion as a soldier. The well-born youth was fearless, almost reckless, and loyal. He was a skilled rider and shot, avid for war.

Temujin said, "Camp with me. Bring tents and herds. I invite you to be part of my enterprise when I take my place among the young warlords of the steppes."

Bogorji considered the offer. "I have to say that was the best adventure that I've had in years. I'm not cut out to be lord amassing herds and sitting in a tent. I'm a man of action. I accept. I'll make camp with you."

On the banks of the stream, watching the horses drink, they swore themselves *nukur,* companions-in-arms. This oath was the second most sacred of the nomads, the oath of men sworn to fight to the death for one another.

A day later, they reached Nagu's pastures. They took the horses to the pasture where the straw-colored mare was chomping on grass. She whinnied a greeting when the silver-whites came to drink at the river.

Temujin clapped Bogorji on the back. "My new friend let's divide the horses between us. You deserve half."

Bogorji laughed. "I don't want your horses. I'll ask my father for a herd of my own and come to your valley with my own horde. I know horse breeding. We can re-establish your herds."

Bogorji spun around in the direction of the camp. "My father! I didn't tell him I was leaving. He must be out of his mind with worry. Come and meet him. Help me explain."

In his youth, Nagu had been a powerful man, of a domineering personality but in age he had become sentimental. They found him sitting in his tent, weeping because a servant had found the leather bucket in the grass. Nagu thought his son was dead.

Bogorji said, "It was thoughtless of me to leave without a word but I have found myself a companion-in-arms." He introduced Temujin. Together the two young men related the tale of their adventure.

Nagu got over his worry and was amused at their excitement. "I should reprimand you for making my heart sore, but I won't. It's a rare thing to find a true companion-in-arms. You should appreciate your good fortune. And you, Temujin, your misfortune brought you luck.Now that you've found each other, never abandon each other."

Nagu ordered food and drink and before long, servants brought roasted goat and lamb. Temujin had not eaten as well since the death of his father.

The next day Temujin began his journey back to the Mongol camp leading the silver-whites. When he arrived, Khasar congratulated him for getting the horses back. Temujin embraced his brother and went to see his mother.

Haggard and care-worn, she hugged him and wept. "Thank God you're alive. I haven't slept at all since you left." She told him to sit and served him a broth with dried meat and vegetables."

"I have my first vassal, mother. Our fortunes have changed. The lean years are over. I can collect the khan's tithe from the clans that did not camp with the Taijyud but are scattered over the steppes. I can rebuild our herds and camp."

Temujin accepted a cup of tea with yak butter from his younger sister Temulun. He turned to Khasar. With the family as witnesses, he made a solemn pledge. "Khasar, with the family as my witness, I tell you this, I will gather many men around me, but no one will ever come between us. You will always be at my right hand. Let us drink to a new beginning."

The clans began returning to make their camp with Temujin. He had enough young warriors to protect the camp and he set about organizing it as it had been in his father's day. Bogorji had come and joined the camp. They organized a hunt and Temujin observed the strengths and weaknesses of his followers.

At night in a fine felt tent in the men's camp, Khasar offered advice. "Brother, something is missing. If we are to resume the life of noblemen, you should claim the girl promised to you long ago. She will bring a dowry of tents, servants and herds."

Temujin agreed. "I'll need a wife. Not a day has gone by when I haven't thought of her. Much time has passed. She would have no lack of suitors. She may have married another. She is the one that father chose for me. I lived in her father's tent for four years. We had only one year more to wait for our marriage."

Khasar said, "If she feels about you as you do about her, she will be waiting."

"Then come with me. We will ride to Khongirad country in the morning and we'll see. Besides, Khasar. You need a wife too. You should have been betrothed when you turned ten, but the family had nothing to offer. After I marry, we'll arrange a marriage for you."

In the morning Temujin found Belgutei currying the white horses. He was painstakingly inspecting their coats and legs for wounds, sores and cuts, and their feet for split hooves.

"Belgutei, I'm organizing camp. You'll be master of horses in the new camp," said Temujin.

"And weapons?"

"And weapons. Come to Khongirad country with me. See how the civilized tribes live. You'll be amazed at their painted tents. They have writing and know how to keep records. I'll find a wife for you so you won't wind up a graybeard bachelor."

"Are the Khongirad women really so beautiful that I should ride all that way?"

Temujin nodded.

"Then I'll go."

Temujin said, "You can see the Great Wall of China from Khongirad country.

Chancellor Yeh-lu heard many times from Genghis Khan that Bortai brought him status and wealth when he most needed it.

The Chancellor was taking down the history of the Supreme Khan for future generations. He could read and write Chinese and was often seen in his tent with grinding ink from an inkstick to write with his beautiful brushes on rice paper.

Yeh-lu had been an official at the highest level of the Jin government before Genghis Khan recruited him to be his personal secretary, a post that was called *bicigeci*. Yeh-lu understood the art of governing a civilization. He was a master of the Chinese classics and a poet.

So Yeh-lu became the great statesman of the Mongol Empire. He wrote down the history of the new dynasty so that future generations could learn from the past. In his history, Yeh-lu called Genghis Khan by the title of *Taizu*, which means in Chinese, *Grand Progenitor* or *The Founder of a Dynasty*.

Recording the history of the previous dynasty was standard practice among the Chinese scholar-officials who rant the vast bureaucracy of the Chinese government. The idea was to learn from the past.

The Chinese were the greatest historians in the world. The Mongols had no history for they did not have a written language until Genghis Khan gave them one at the Great Assembly of 1206.

Yeh-lu was an eyewitness to history and he knew the principal actors in the imperial drama. He also had the skills and the talent to do it. His fellow scholar-officials had fled to the South to serve under the Southern Song Emperor, who was a Han Chinese. They felt superior to the Mongols and considered them barbarians. Yeh-lu painted a different portrait, and he had stood beside the Khan on the battlefield and he had served him at court.

Yeh-lu believed that one man could change the course of history. He wanted to preserve Chinese civilization from the worst of Mongol ways, and he did. He told the Khan that there was more profit to be made from taxing the population rather than killing it off. He also told the Khan that the empire may have been conquered on horseback, but it could not be government from horseback.

He was a man of letters in a military government, but he played his part. He served Ogodei after the Supreme Khan's death, and was hounded from office by Ogodei's shrewish wife, but he saw the succession of power from the Supreme Khan to his named successor. He served for thirteen years and Ogodei benefited from his advice.

One of his great achievements, which went unrecognized, was that he advised Princess Sorghagtani to move to North China and take up residence in an estate confiscated by the Mongol generals from a former governor of the province. He advised her to ask Emperor Ogodei for an estate for her second son, Khubilai. The way to glory in Mongol aristocratic society was in the military and Khubilai was born too late to participate in the great campaigns. Yeh-lu told Princess Sorghagtani that there was no future for Khubilai in the capital. He was a minor prince in a minor branch of the imperial family. He spent his days hunting and carousing with the young aristocracy in the capital.

North China was in a state of chaos from having endured twenty-five years of warfare. Yeh-lu advised Khubilai to assemble a coterie of Confucian advisors and govern North China using Chinese methods. The people would understand the regular taxes and they would stop the mass exodus on the roads to the South. He advised Khubilai to become the imperial family's expert on China. The Princess was extremely wise and listened to Yeh-lu's advice. Ogodei granted her and her son lands and titles and the result was that Khubilai Khan eventually became Supreme Khan. It is so sad that Yeh-lu was hounded out of office and accused of amassing a fortune from his position. The bad-tempered empress found no evidence for her accusation. But this is a story for another time.

Temujin was thirteen years old when his father arranged the marriage to Bortai. He was smitten with puppy love for Bortai from the first moment he laid eyes on her. But there was more. Hardship had matured him. Relying on his mother's wisdom after the abandonment of the relatives, he realized that a wife was a valued support. Bortai financed his early career. Without her, he would have been a minor figure in the politics of the steppes.

Bortai told their story from her point of view. Yeh-lu asked her if she had any idea of the man he would become. She laughed at her youthful romanticism. "He was always imbued with an aura of light. He was young, but he had a sense of destiny. I loved him from the time I was a young girl. I was the first principal wife. Of course, others came afterward, but I was the first and our bond was unique. We grew up together."

"That is a bond that stands the test of time," said Yeh-lu. He asked her to go on with her story.

"News travels fast on the steppes. My family heard that Temujin had been betrayed and abandoned by greedy relatives. My father knew that my future husband had lost everything. Yesugei Khan had been a wealthy and important khan when the marriage was arranged. My father did hot want to marry me to a pauper.

"My father wanted to arrange another marriage for me, but I refused. My father said I was wasting my life, with no husband and no children, but I was adamant. My sisters thought I was mad to wait for him. They said he would never return, but I knew that he would come back for me. I was right."

Bortai spoke with satisfaction. "I remember the day Temujin came for me. What a sight he was, not the magnificent conqueror that he later became. He wore old riding clothes. He was wearing his fur-trimmed war helmet. He loved that helmet. He wore a sheepskin jacket and he carried a war bow.

"Strung over the cruppers of his wooden saddle were his provisions for the trip, a bag of koumiz and dried jerky from his camp, a gift for my father. It was a humble gift, but he did not come empty-handed. He had a way of making a humble gift seem important. It was his manner.

"Yesugei's death changed him. He had grown tougher. He had no fear. He had no illusions about human nature. He had a strong presence. He was nobody's fool. I knew he saw deeply. He was the essence of nobility and he justified the faith I had in him. He always said that he had a destiny. He was my destiny."

The retainers from Dai's tent rode out to meet approaching strangers. They recognized Temujin immediately. They rushed him to my father's tent and announced his return. They spoke of him as though he were a visiting dignitary."

Temujin arrived in his own whirlwind and entered and greeted the family. He observed the ritual politeness of the khans of the steppes, but he wasted no time.

"Is your daughter still betrothed to me or has she married another?"

Dai was growing old. His hair had gone white and he walked with difficulty. He knew that his daughter was a desirable match. He was providing her with a generous dowry. 'First let me say I am sorry. I heard tales of your misfortune but considered it my duty to protect my daughter's interests."

Temujin said, "I understand. You're her father. You were doing your duty. I do not bear a grudge. The past is behind us."

He said, "She is not married. She has refused other offers of marriage."

"I have dared to hope. My father is no longer with us. The last time I was in your tent, he was alive, so the moment is tinged with sadness. May we hold the marriage ceremony right away."

"I was the one who proposed the betrothal when we met. You still have the aura of light about you. You survived. This is admirable. I could hold back and make you ask for her again, but I want to see my daughter married. I want grandchildren. Let's have the marriage ceremony."

What did Bortai do while she waited for her future husband to free himself of his difficulties? Bortai was busy. The women of Bortai's camp were working, and as they worked, they shared the gossip of the women's camp.

The commoners in her camp churned *koumiz* that brought a fancy price at market. Her women made good quality felt that commanded the top price with the caravan merchants. She bought the secret of a fine tanning solution from Arab caravan traders. Her commoners made the softest tanned skins for gloves and boots. The caravan traders bought them for the Chinese market, for they traded in the Jin capital, Zhongdu.

She had her own private treasury, lock-boxes full of Chinese cash and silver ingots. She had a sister Alikha who worked with her, but who constantly told her that she was a fool for keeping herself for a loser. Alikha was younger, but had married and had her first child, while Bortai was alone.

Bortai's industry relieved her loneliness, but at feasts when shepherds sang love ballads and young couples went off to put up the urga, the lasso that signaled a young couple wanted privacy, she longed for Temujin.

She heard a rider approaching and she saw him. She got up and ran to meet him. Temujin jumped off his pony while it was still galloping and ran toward her. He swept her into his embrace. She was trembling.

"I have missed you so much that my heart ached," he said. "I've never stopped thinking of you . . . Did you doubt me?" He held her hands and looked at her. "You're still the most beautiful girl I ever saw." He embraced her again.

"I knew you would come," she said. "I begged my father to help you, but he said you had to prove yourself worthy."

"I know. He told me. I can't blame him. He thought he was doing the right thing for his daughter. It's in the past. Let's look to the future. We're going to be married right away."

She turned to her sister Alikha. "We're having a wedding!" The sister took a dim view of the engagement and pursed her lips.

"I can't believe it," Bortai said.

"Yes. We'll have a life together."

Bortai appeared in her father's tent in a long red dress, a silver headdress on her heavy plaits. Around her neck she wore a necklace of lapis lazuli. She smiled and the gathered family and friends saw that she was filled with joy. When she looked at him, her gaze was as steady and penetrating as he remembered it.

Temujin bought wedding clothes. He wore new tunic and pleated riding trousers and boots, waiting when his bride stepped into the light of the hearth-fire. His bitterness at the years of hardship and his grief for his father evaporated at the sight of her.

At seventeen, she was a proud and accomplished young woman. She was also rich.

Khasar stood beside his brother "You're lucky that you've won such a prize."

The shaman said prayers and sprinkled koumiz on the ground. They chanted for an abundance of children and good fortune.

102

When celebrating, the Mongols abandon themselves to the feast. The bride and groom led the dances and sat on a dais at the banquet table accepting the good wishes and the presents of those who had come to the wedding feast.

The beauty of the Khongirad women is justly renowned all over Mongolia. They danced in their high-waisted dresses, the coins of their headdresses jingling, the ropes of coral and turquoise around their necks, their bracelets of silver and long silver earrings, keeping time to the music, their eyes flashing in the firelight.

As the moon set, Temujin took his bride to the wedding tent. Bortai sipped from a silver cup and offered it to him. He drank and passed the cup back to her. Passion overcame him and he fumbled with her, grabbing at her. He was too hasty, trying to make sure she wouldn't get away from him. She pulled away from him, speaking to him sweetly. Her voice calmed him down.

The wedding night passed and after that night, he knew that she was his.

Two days later, Dai gave orders to the servants to put the belongings of his daughter into the marriage cart. Nambi presented Temujin with the dowry present promised to Yesugei so many years ago: the magnificent cloak of sables.

Bortai rode in the lead wagon of a wagon train containing her dowry, the oxen and herds, the families of servants and slaves, the property given to her father. The lead wagon contained her tent and her furniture and possessions.

Her clans brought their tents and their families, and her slaves tended her herds: horses, cows and sheep. She was the wife of a khan, and it would be her duty to care for the women's camp, her animals, and her clans, and when he was away making war, she would rule in his place. She would trade on his behalf, and she would hear disputes for judgment when he was away.

As she did in her father's camp, she would supervise the making of felt, the milking of mares, the production of koumiz, the tanning of hides, and the splitting of sinews for the sewing of sheepskin jackets.

It was the custom for the bride's family to escort the new couple on their journey to their new home. Dai the Wise rode as far as Uragh Chol and turned back.

Nambi accompanied her daughter to her new home on the Senggur River and stayed with Bortai until she was satisfied that her daughter's horde had been settled in a manner befitting the daughter of a powerful chieftain.

Oyelun instructed her people to create a women's camp, like the one that she had in Yesugei's time. Bortai's tent was in the center, with her servants' tents surrounding her.

Seeing Bortai settled, Nambi returned to the Khongirad lands, escorted by nobleman sent by Dai Sechen.

The entire Borjigin clan rode to the Senggur River to bid Nambi farewell.

At night, lying under a fur blanket, staring at the hearth fire, Temujin drew Bortai close to him. "I will take the place my father had and be the most powerful khan in the steppes. I swear to you that you will be mistress of all that I rule. Your sons will inherit all that I have."

The couple began their new life. Their happiness was contagious. The camp prospered.

Temujin was once again a man of means and he had followers which gave him the ability to defend his camp. He was no longer afraid to occupy his ulus, his father's native pastures. He gave the order for the Mongols to move from the Senggur River back to the Valley of Two Rivers.

Temujin began his rise in the world. He established himself among the lesser nobility of the steppes. He had acquired vassals, men came and made camp with him, who trusted his leadership.

Bogorji asked Temujin to arrange a marriage for him. This was the duty of a khan. Temujin arranged a marriage to Bortai's cousin.

Temujin had a collection of companions, men who had joined him as vassals and who became his commanders in war. Each was appointed by merit, no matter how humble their beginnings. Jebe, who was a blacksmith's son, was exceptionally talented and given a command. This was the beginning of the Council of Generals, his greatest strength.

He took his place at the head of Yesugei's table and spoke to his commanders. "Among us, it is considered wise to accept the counsel of women, for the shamans say that women hold up the earth and men hold up the sky, and both must be in balance. My mother was the wife of a khan. She never ceases to remind me that it is my duty to do restore my family's honor. Our camp is still small. I need the protection of a powerful lord. My father has given me a legacy.

"I will take Togril Khan, the dowry gift brought to me by my wife and ask him to accept me as his vassal.

Bogorji had a swashbuckling glamor about him. He was handsome, an aristocrat, a brilliant horseman and always in high spirits and devoted to Temujin. He swore when he heard of Togril's obligation. "Togril is the most powerful man in Mongolia. The bond is the legacy your father left. Why haven't you invoke this obligation sooner?"

Temujin said, "No one respects a beggar. I wanted to go to him when I could hold my head up."

Bogorji said, "You're right. You made the right choice. You want respect. Much time has passed. Will he honor the bond?"

Khasar was tending to the bows that he had made for him, the special composite bows that were good for distant targets. "My father told us many times that we were to invoke the bond. Togril swore an oath to treat us as his sons, down to the seed of our seed."

Temujin said, "I had to wait until I could perform the duties of a vassal. I'm ready."

In the morning, the three set off for Kereyid country.

The Mongols call the Bogdo-ula Mountains the dwelling place of the gods. They resemble a row of dragon's teeth jutting into the sky. The range separate the Kerulen basin of Temujin's native pastures from the basin of the Tola River, the river that runs through Ong Khan's country.

On the Ong Khan's side of the range, rolling foothills covered with Baikal pine slope down to the Black Forest, a vast woods full of game offered splendid hunting. On the banks of the Tola, in a clearing of the Black Forest, Togril Khan made his royal encampment.

Temujin and his party rode through the border region where the marshlands meet the Gobi, then traveled the stretch of the Silk Road that ran to the Great Wall. They reached Kereyid territory.

This was Genghis Khan's first visit to Khara Khorum, the Kereyid capital. The name meant Black Rock. The Mongol quarter was a city of felt tents. The foreign quarter had fixed dwellings, including a bazaar with shops and neighborhood factories. Arab and Persian traders who plied the caravan routes of the southern Gobi made Khara Khorum their home.

Thus, Khara Khorum was international. It had mosques *and* Buddhist temples. The Kereyid King converted to the Eastern rite of Christianity a century ago. This Nestorian Christians were people of the book and many of them could read and write, which accounted for the belief that Christians were more civilized than shamanists.

Guards met Temujin's party at the entrance to Togril's camp, and escorted them to a palace-tent, a pavilion tent made of cream-colored silk with tent-posts of cedar trimmed in hammered gold. The tent was so enormous that it could hold hundreds of people.

Silk is a fine material for a tent, for it keeps out rain, is warm in winter and cool in summer. The sides of the tent shimmered and shone in sunlight and when the gentle river breezes blew, it seemed to breathe, gently billowing in and out. Beyond Togril's tent, was a felt tent that served as a church and atop it, a crucifix of solid gold.

The Tola River had good water with excellent pasture on both banks of the river. Togril Khan was a rich man and owned huge herds of horses: Mongol ponies, Arabians and Akhal-Tekes, the Horse of Heaven, prized by Chinese emperors. The Akhal-Tekes were a prized mount with glistening coats of gold or black and were imported from the Muslim lands in Central Asia.

On the far bank of the river were the herds belonging to Togril——the Five Snouts and a herd of camels that Togril acquired as tribute from the camel drivers who brought goods from the West: Russia, Turkey, Iran and the Central Asian capital of Bukhara.

Beyond Togril khan's camp was the smaller camp of his brother, Jakha Ghambo. Jakha was a talented administrator, a practical man who had a great mind for figures. Jakha set up a tent for the Treasury and there he conducted Togril's dealings with the ortagh, the trading guild of the men from the Muslim countries in the West.

The ortagh had a fixed building in the foreign quarter where they kept count of the goods brought in by the caravan traders and the amount of business done in Kereyid territory. Jakha kept records of the duties and taxes owed to Togril. The tent also served as a treasury and exchange bank where the merchants and their customers exchanged metal money for goods.

Temujin told Khasar, "We have nothing like this. We have a lot to learn from our father's sworn brother." Khasar agreed. This alliance would bring a new understanding of the world. Togril's camp was a trading hub for the whole of the Southern Gobi.

Guards ushered Temujin and Khasar into Togril's presence. The Khan of the Kereyid rose to greet them. His fingers were covered with jewels, rings of lapis and malachite. He wore a silk brocade Chinese robe trimmed with fur. Togril liked showing off his wealth and took pleasure in impressing his guests with his lavish surroundings.

His tent was filled with pieces bought from the caravan merchants. The floor was covered with red Persian carpets woven in intricate designs. Around the hearth-fire were kang beds, sofas of rosewood for his guests to sit. The high Chinese sofa beds had wicker matting underneath. Coal-burning braziers placed underneath for warmth in winter. The beds were made of rosewood piled high with cushions of Chinese silk brocade. Around the perimeter of the huge tent were rosewood armoires from China, cupboards and chests of carved red cinnabar lacquer from southern China and tables made of fragrant woods from Burma and Annam.

Temujin was impressed. Togril invited his guests to come in and sit and have refreshments. Serving women poured grape wine from the Uighur country and offered a toast to their health. He welcomed Temujin and Khasar and introduced his son Nilkha, who went by his title, the Senggum.

Jakha Gambo had been a friend of Yesugei's. He came to the tent to meet Yesugei Khan's sons. He drank the toast with enthusiasm, but Nilkha lounged among the pillows of a kang bed, making no effort to drink the toast.

To Temujin, Nilkha seemed petulant and ill-mannered. He disliked the arrival of strangers to whom his father owed loyalty. The son had already calculated that these strangers represented a threat to him.

Togril Khan was a few years older than Temujin's father would have been had he lived. Temujin's voice caught in his throat when he realized that in his memory, his father was always young.

Temujin spoke in a manner befitting the son of a khan. "Because in the old days you and my father Yesugei the Brave were sworn brothers, you are as a father to me. I've come to tell you that I have married a Khongirad woman and I've brought you the wedding gift."

Khasar laid the cloak of matched skins on the cushion beside Togril.

The cloak was a deep black, made of the finest fur, wide pelts, soft to the touch, light in weight and warm against freezing weather. Togril picked it up, felt its softness, the lightness of the skins, and was delighted. He wrapped it around his shoulders.

"You do me great honor. This is a gift fit for a king. I thank you."

Temujin held his breath, waiting on Togril's pronouncement.

"I regret that I did nothing to help you. Your father helped me. He rescued my throne. Without him, I would not be here. I owed you a debt, but I waited to see what kind of man you were before I took armies to war in your defense.

"Hear my decree. The clans your father gathered belong to you. For the respect you've shown me, I'll round up the people who gave the oath of loyalty to your father and return them to you. This is only just. I should have done it long ago. The tithe belongs to you." Togril struck his breast. "Let my promise live here."

The Senggum objected. "Their father performed a service long ago. Why should you repay it so many years later? Why should we make war on the Taijyud for nothing when we could make war on the Naiman and take over the trade routes of the Western Gobi?

Nilkha's rudeness embarrassed Togril. "Excuse my son. He has no manners."

Temujin ignored the Senggum. Togril had made the offer. Temujin intended to seal the bond. "Restore my father's peoples to me and I swear that I will support you in all you undertake."

Nilkha shrugged. "He has no army. How much support can he give us?"

Togril addressed Temujin. "If you're half the man your father was, you will be an excellent commander. Come. Take the oath of loyalty."

Temujin went down on his knees, took off his cap, closed his fist over his heart and took the old hunting oath of the steppes.

"I pledge you my loyalty and the loyalty of those that follow me. I shall turn over a part of all booty to you and all the women we capture and give you first choice of game in the hunt. I will pay a tithe for your protection. You are my khan and you command me in war and in the hunt."

Togril put his hand on Temujin's shoulder. "I accept you as my vassal. In exchange for your service to me in war, I will extend my protection to you. I will turn over to you a portion of booty that I take. I swear on your father's grave that I will restore your clans and all that is rightfully yours to you in fulfillment of the bond.

"It's done. I've pledged to be your lord. Let's toast the memory of your father. A better man there never was."

Temujin raised his cup and drank.

The sacred mountain turned pink in the first light of dawn. Rosy light cascaded to the foothills but darkness covered the camp. A raiding party galloped into the valley.

Bortai was sleeping in her tent in the women's camp. One of her serving women slept nearby. Her bed began shaking. She woke up and rushed to the tent-door. Riders galloped across the river. The leader had deer antlers on his helmet; another had a horse-tail flying in the wind. Crude-faced Mergid. It was a raid.

She had not been among the Mongols long and she panicked. Where was Temujin? The serving woman said the family were running to the cave at the foot of the mountain.

Bortai froze with fear, but willed herself to run. Her body felt heavy. In the camp, panic and confusion were everywhere: women running, children crying, servants grabbing children. In the distance, she Oyelun with her youngest child under her arm. She called out, but with the whinnying of horses and the grinding of cartwheels, Oyelun didn't hear her.

She started to run after Oyelun, but a team of oxen almost ran her over. She leapt out of the way and twisted her ankle and fell. The fall knocked the wind out of her. At the corral She saw Temujin saddling a pony, calling her name. He had a mount for her. Come, he was calling. Her ankle felt like it was broken.

She saw Khasar and Belgutei, getting a horse ready for Sochigil. Khasar called to her, "Take the deer path to the hiding place."

Temujin was shouting commands. The noise and commotion frightened her. She got to the corral, but the horse they saddled up for her got loose, running from the confusion. The horses ran past her, running away from the raid. Her pony was gone.

She saw Old Lady Khachigan, who sheared sheep with Oyelun, hitching a wagon to a speckled ox. The old woman jerked her head. "Get into the cart. Hurry! We'll catch up to them."

Bortai stepped on the wagon wheel and felt a pain in her ankle. She tumbled over into a pile of sheep shearing.

Khachigan snapped the reins on the animal's back and the cart lurched forward. She looked back. "They're Mergid. Forest people from the north." The old lady was short of breath, but the cart rode away.

Bortai turned and watched as the raiders rode through the camp, flattening tents. They were making certain no one was waiting to ambush them.

A Mergid rider spotted the wagon and rode up alongside the wagon. "Who are you?" he demanded.

He smelled like yak butter, and Bortai remembered Temujin telling her that the Mergid rubbed fat on their bodies to keep warm. Khachigan flicked the reins. "Stay hidden or they'll take you."

Bortai felt sick to her stomach. She was the perfect target. The scout rode off to report to his chief.

Three chiefs had banded together for a raid. Togtoa, Dayir-Usun and Darmala. This was a vendetta, payback for the theft of a wife from a Mergid. They had come to steal a woman as payback for the crime that Yesugei had committed in taking Oyelun on her wedding day so many years ago. Bride theft was the only crime more serious than horse theft.

Khachigan cracked the whip over the ox and tried to speed the animal along the bank of the stream. Bortai heard a loud crack and the back of the cart slumped down. Khachigan got out to look. The axle of the cart had snapped in two. They were in serious trouble.

Togtoa was a fierce little man who wore a leather helmet with reindeer antlers on the crown. His long black plaits were bound with feathers and he had bear grease smeared on his face.

A soldier took the reins from Khachigan and pushed the shearing aside. He dragged Bortai out of the cart by her arm.

Togtoa smirked. "A woman who wears the jewelry of a princess. You must be Temujin's new wife," he said.

Bortai was shaking, unable to speak.

"Can't answer?"

Bortai summoned her courage. "I have done nothing to your people."

"Where's your husband?"

Bortai said, "I don't know where he went. I brought a rich dowry to this camp. Take what you want and leave."

Dayir and Darmala, rode up to see what Togtoa had discovered. Dayir was a bearish stocky man in a fur coat. He was more interested in wealth than in revenge. He wanted booty. "Let's go. If you want her, take her."

Darmala was leading a fawn-colored pony with Sochigil slung across the horn of its saddle. She was hanging limply like a rag doll, unconscious.

Togtoa wanted to impress the other chiefs. "A highborn woman too good for a Mergid, eh? You're coming with us."

Darmala said, "She'll do!"

"Leave her alone," Khachigan pleaded. "She only just came to live among us."

"Silence," Togtoa threatened. Bortai glanced up the mountain.

Togtoa followed her gaze. "He went to the mountain. Good riddance."

Darmala wiped sweat from his forehead. "Forget him. Why hunt him anyway? The debt is paid."

Dayir said, "Let's go."

Togtoa grabbed Bortai by the arm. With one pull, he dragged her onto his horse.

The three chiefs lifted their clenched fists skyward in victory. Togtoa ordered his soldiers to ride north.

Beyond the Donkeyback Steppe, the wooded steppe meets the Siberian taiga. The Mergid raiders crossed the Ili River. The steppe zone gave way to the forest zone, an immense woods of spruce and poplar that stretched to Sibir, the Land of Snows. Once they were back in their own lands, the three chiefs separated, returning to their own camps. Togtoa ordered his man to put Bortai in a cart. He put Khachigan at her side.

The cart rumbled into the encampment of birch houses. It was a poor camp, with children running about in rags and women with sad faces washing clothes at the riverbank. Bortai knew then that her future was going to be far less pleasant than her past. She drew in her breath and closed her eyes. She knew that Temujin would come for her. She had to believe that.

112

Chilger the Athlete was Togtoa's youngest brother. He had a wrestler's physique. Among his people he was admired for his skill in hand-to-hand combat. He was the most famous athlete among his people.

The raid on the Mongols enhanced Togtoa's position among his clans. This bride taken in revenge went to a member of the family. He allowed the old crone to stay with her mistress.

I must survive this, she told herself.

Temujin realized that Bortai was gone when the family gathered in the caves in the hills.

He said, "They were Mergid. Togtoa and his cronies. I recognized them. I know where they camp. This was vendetta against me, for my father kidnapped my mother on the day of her wedding to a Mergid and he married her."

Oyelun nodded. "It's true. Yesugei saw me and kidnapped me."

Bogorji shook his head. "Revenge for the kidnapping of a Mergid long ago. What a waste."

Temujin said, "The tribes are a cauldron of endless warfare, generation after generation, because there is no strong man to put an end to it."

Belgutei returned from searching the camp. "They took my mother too."

Oyelun said, "Where's Khachigan? She's not here. She had a wagon. Maybe Bortai is with her. Maybe they're hiding."

Belgutei said, "I searched the camp. Bortai is gone."

Temujin said, "This is my fault. I did not set up sentries at the edge of the camp. They would have warned us of a raid. That was the way my father organized his camp. I've been a fool. I'll need an army to get her back."

Temujin took two companions and rode to Kereyid country for an audience with The Ong Khan. He strode through the camp with such purpose that the guards fell into step behind him. Togril Khan stopped in mid-sentence when Temujin entered the tent. Nilkha, the Senggum, pushed his plate back. Nilkha looked like trouble had just entered his world.

Temujin did not stand on ceremony but came right to the point. "O my father, a great misfortune has befallen me. Three Mergid chiefs raided my camp and took my wife. I need your help to get her back."

"Why am I not surprised that he wants something from you?" said the Senggum. "Once a beggar, always a beggar."

Togril snapped. "Shut up, Nilkha. This is a tragedy. Of course I will help you get her back." What was power if it was never exercised? It was nothing.

"Temujin, your father rode to war for me and restored me to my throne. I need to get my blood moving. If we are going to war, let us act quickly. How many men can you contribute to a campaign?"

"Five thousand. My vassal Bogorji will ride with us. Khasar will command troops. My brother Belgutei will command troops. We will need more men. I have an ally, a sworn brother, Jamuga. I have not seen for many years. He has become Khan of the Jajirat Mongols."

Togril said, "Good. I know him well. He is my vassal. I know where he makes his camp. He is a promising young khan who has won many campaigns," said Togril. "Some years ago, he lived in my tent with me and waited in attendance on me, bringing me my cup and hunting with me. He has many followers. Tens of thousands of the Jajirat bone of the Mongol clans camped with him in the Khorkhanagh Valley."

Temujin received the news with astonishment. "Amazing! I did not know that my old friend had risen so high in the world. He will honor the old bond. I'm sure of it."

Khasar mumbled, "Don't be so sure of him."

Togril replied, "Of course Jamuga will honor the oath. The bond is for life. This is what you must do. Send a message to Jamuga. Send someone who will not be intimidated by Jamuga, someone smart enough and observant enough to inform you of the composition and training of Jamuga's troops.

Temujin did not hesitate. "Bogorji, this is the perfect assignment for you." Bogorji nodded and saluted.

Togril ordered a banquet. "I have not waged many wars in recent year and you are inexperienced in command. I suggest making Jamuga commander of our troops."

Temujin agreed.

Togril laid a map of the steppe country on a table. "Bogorji, tell Jamuga that I have taken Temujin as a vassal and I have joined this campaign. I am committing 20,000 men, two *tumens*. Ask him to join and contribute twenty thousand troops. Tell him that I will be the Right Wing of the army. He will be the Left Wing.

"Let him decide when and where we should join forces. In the meantime, Temujin and Khasar, return to your pastures and gather your forces. When you hear from Jamuga, send a messenger, and tell me the time and the place we will join our armies. Then we will meet."

In the morning, Temujin returned to the Valley of Two Rivers. He organized his army. Belgutei was Master of Horses. Khasar was Master of Weaponry. Dodai Cherbi was Master of Provisions. He had word from Jamuga. They would join forces in three weeks. He called for a hunt and began training his 5,000 cavalry.

Bogorji arrived with Jamuga's message. "'Tell my sworn brother that it has been years since we swore allegiance, but when I hear Temujin say, 'They've emptied my bed', I grieve for his loss. I will help him crush the Mergid.'

"Tell my Elder Brother Togril and Temujin that I will make the sacred offerings as custom dictates. Say this: I will raise my black horse-tail standard at the head of my army. I will beat the black bull-hide drum until it sounds like thunder. Without delay, I will mount my black warhorse and put on my armor made of leather and tanned as hard as iron. Then I will raise my steel lance. For my *anda*, I will place on my bowstring a deadly arrow laced with peach-bark poison and mark my enemy along its shaft. For the *anda* of my childhood, I will unsheathe my sword. Let's all die together fighting the Mergid or destroy them until there's nothing left of them but smoke.'"

Bogorji had an energetic way about him, a physical vitality, and people rarely took him as a threat. The agreeable manner disguised a keen eye. He made a detailed report on the situation in Jamuga's camp. " Do not fear these enemies. In the time it took me to get back to you, the Mergid will have split up. A confederation of forest people lasts only until the plunder from the raid is divided.

"Togtoa will go back to his camp on the Steppe of Male Camels. Togtoa becomes frightened when he hears someone strike a horse blanket--he thinks it sounds like a war drum.

"Dayir Usun camps at Talkun Island where the Orkhon and Selenga Rivers meet. He is also a coward who retreats as soon as you shake a quiver at him.

"As for Darmala, Jamuga says he camps on the Steppe of Karaji. He runs as soon as he sees an uprooted weed blow across the steppe."

This was the kind of moral support that Temujin needed. Khasar was annoyed that he and Temujin had to accept second in command. "Get to the point, Bogorji. Where does he want the armies to join forces?"

Bogorji had a good nature and was not offended. "At the head of the Onon River in three weeks. He's got ten thousand soldiers and he'll raise ten thousand more."

"Khasar lets Jamuga irritate him. It's not worth it."

Bogorji continued, "Jamuga thinks we should make for the Kilgho River where the river-reeds grow. He suggests that we cut reeds and lash them together to make rafts to transport our army across the river. From there we go into the forest and take them by surprise. That's his battle plan.

"Our army will descend on them as though we leapt down through the smoke-holes of their huts. We'll fight until Togtoa's wives and sons are dead. We'll break down the door-frame where Togtoa's guardian spirit lives. We'll stop fighting when nothing is left of the Mergid but thin air."

He was the least powerful of the three khans, but still wished to make a good showing. This was his first major campaign, if you could call a campaign against a forest tribe a war. It was a tribal skirmish. Temujin discovered in himself a passion for war.

The Mergid were the least of the tribes; it was best to test his strength against them, to make his mistakes where they could cost him the least. The forest tribes eked out a living by selling timber to Chinese and Muslim traders. They were decent hunters but mediocre horsemen. They hunted in the woods and did not organize the Grand Hunts of the Mongols. They lived too far to the north to be one of the serious contenders for power in the steppes.

He told Khasar that the Mergid had given him a test and they would regret it. He would make them pay. Strategy, the only mental activity that drove Bortai from his thoughts, consumed him. He was in command of the smallest number of troops in the alliance but organized his men and his equipment with great care.

A messenger arrived from Togril's camp to inform Temujin that the Kereyid Army had departed and was riding toward Mergid territory. Temujin was ready. He had organized the departure of his small army. On the day of departure, he flew his father's standard the battle shield with nine white streamers. He gave the command and the war drums rolled.

Temujin, dressed in the same uniform as his soldiers and wearing his war helmet with the sable brim, stood on a platform and made a speech to his soldiers. "The Mergid do not want me to come after them because they think they are abiding by an old custom, paying me back for a crime that was committed before I was born. I say this is not right. I say this type of tribal warfare must end. We must have leaders who can put an end to the cycle of retribution. We will ride to war to right the wrong done to me. My wife has been taken from me. I ask every one of you to fight bravely. I will fight alongside you. I will ride at the head of our forces. I swear my loyalty to you. Swear yours to me!"

A chant went up from the men. "Temujin! Temujin! Temujin!" They banged on their shields with their swords. A streamered flag snapped as it unfurled in the breeze and the sound of kettledrums filled the valley.

He held up his hands for silence, looking out over the men. He felt a surge of love for the enterprise, for those who would follow him. "We are joining forces with the mighty Kereyid Army of Togril Khan. We

117

will camp below Burgi Cliff in front of Mount Burkhan. May the Eternal Blue Sky protect us all!" From the throats of the Mongols, another cheer rose up.

"Jamuga Khan is my sworn brother and he will be our commander. Give him your loyalty as you have given it to me. You will ride with me in the Army of the Center and I will command you personally. When we have my wife back, we will celebrate long and hard. Let us ride north!"

The commanders of *tumen*, units of ten, and commanders of one hundred and one thousand, were nobility; commoners were the rank-and-file cavalry. Following the army, was a wagon train that provided food, with commoners at the reins of the teams of oxen. Commoners tended the herds necessary to feed the army. That was the war train, the nomad way.

The movement of Mongol troops to the Tana Stream took five days. Togril arrived with his army of ten thousand and Jakha Gambo brought an army of ten thousand. The setting up of camp at Burgi Cliff and the uniting of armies and organization of supplies took several more days. By the time the combined Kereyid and Mongol forces arrived at the headwaters of the Onon, Jamuga had been waiting for three days and he was furious. He was the commander of this operation and his orders had not been followed.

He greeted Togril, Jakha Gambo and Temujin with a violent display of temper. "Didn't we agree that even if there was a blizzard or a rainstorm, no one would arrive late? The word of a Mongol khan is supposed to be sacred. In days of old, any lord who didn't live up to his word was run out of camp."

Togril Khan apologized. "We are in the wrong, Jamuga. The departure was sudden. For the sake of unity, let's overlook the mistake. Let's keep sight of our goal."

Jamuga was not appeased. Temujin was surprised that Jamuga did not get control of himself. This was not the way aristocrats behaved. He kept his counsel, but he didn't like the way Jamuga's leadership.

Togril put an end to Jamuga's display of temper. "We have breached discipline. If you want to make an issue of it, decide who is to blame and what his punishment should be."

Jamuga backed down and the moment passed. Jamuga had decided on a surprise attack. The khans and their commanders moved the army across the Kumur Mountains down the Menja Valley, to the shore of the Kilgho River, in the heart of Mergid territory. Under cover of night, they built rafts, crossed the river and reached Togtoa's camp.

A sable trapper and a fisherman from the river crept into Togtoa's camp and warned him that an army was coming. Togtoa and Dayir Usun sneaked out of camp with a few followers taking nothing but the clothes on their backs. They fled down the Selenga River to the eastern shores of Lake Baikal and made camp.

Togtoa's camp was built at the edge of a forest backed up to the river, with a clearing in front of it. There was room for Temujin's army to maneuver.

Jamuga ordered Temujin to ride directly into the camp. He would encircle the camp from the right, Togril from the left. Temujin liked it. "A classic pincer movement. Copied from the hunt?" Temujin asked.

Jamuga smiled. "Of course."

Temujin's cavalry swept across the settlement and at first encountered no resistance. They crashed into Togtoa's encampment and set fire to Mergid huts, burning them to the ground. Men, women and children emerged from their huts screaming and running for their lives.

The Mergid preferred to ride close and use swords, knives and lances. Mongol archers, keeping, brought the Mergid down in droves as the Mergid rode in for close fighting. Temujin had been riding at the head of an attacking Mongol unit, more commanding than fighting. A Mergid rider came in at him from the side, slashing at him with a knife.

Temujin was bigger and stronger than most of the forest men. He reached out and grabbed the man by the neck and threw him off his horse. He saw a rider attacking Khasar and took Yesugei's bow from his saddle horn. He was seeing everything in battle reality, slow time.

A messenger rode up and shouted that Togril and Jamuga had circled the camp and were decimating the Mergid.

Temujin saw Togril's men driving the Mergid toward him. It was as though they were bringing down game, killing the Mergid riding toward them with Togril and Jamuga at their rear.

Togril sent a messenger to say that they had taken the camp.

Temujin raised his bow in victory. Watching the troops fan out, following his orders, he felt satisfaction.

He found Togtoa's hut, a large cabin with deer antlers adorning the door.

"Strike down the doorframe," he ordered a soldier. According to Mongol belief, this was where the suldé, the guardian spirit, lived. The shamans said that to destroy the household spirit brought bad luck. Temujin gave the order to his men to set fire to the house, He waited as the flames licked upward, and watched it burn. He ordered. "Take women and children captive. Put the men to death." He had seen enough. He rode off.

Temujin grabbed one of the women taken captive and asked where their chief had gone. Mute with terror, the woman pointed to the river. Temujin rode like a madman, exorcising his fury.

Khasar shouted that Togtoa had escaped.

"We'll find him later," Temujin shouted to Khasar. "Help me find Bortai."

It was a hellish scene. A wall of beasts and humanity was fleeing from the raid on foot. The camp was smoking. Bodies of horses and people lay everywhere. Temujin felt no pity. The punishment visited on these people was just. Abandoned by their chief, people were fleeing in terror.

Temujin rode through the camp shouting his wife's name.

Bortai was running with the Mergids who were fleeing down the river, leaving behind huts, tools, wagons, possessions, and herds. In the dark, Bortai was thinking only of escape, but turned when she heard a voice calling her name. She looked around, then decided she must be imagining it. Bortai stopped in the middle of the chaos and let the foot and wagon traffic flow past her.

Again, she thought she heard a voice calling her name. She looked but saw no one who resembled Temujin. Khachigan drew alongside her, managing the reins of a cart. Bortai waved frantically and the old woman dragged on the reins. The wagon stopped. Bortai clambered aboard to avoid being trampled to death. The din of the battle was a deafening cacophony, clattering of sword on shield, screaming of men in their death throes, cows lowing, horses screaming, the crashing of wagon wheels against rocks, the wailing of women and children, the shouting among soldiers, the crashing of timbers as flaming arrows lit haystacks and burst into flame, the crashing of burning roofs. The whole village was smoking and her eyes were running with tears. She had to watch where she stepped for people had dropped bundles and belongings and dead animals and children, cats and dogs, were everywhere. Death and destruction surrounded her on every side.

She was certain that she heard his voice! She jumped down from the slow-moving ox-cart. "Come on, Khachigan. Get down. Temujin is here. We're saved!" The old woman struggled to get down.

Bortai half-ran, half-dragged Khachigan in the direction of the voice. They dodged the wagons and bumped against people and horses. Bortai looked up and recognized Gray Ears, Temujin's favorite horse.

She grabbed at his stirrup. She shouted up to him. She reached up and seized his riding boot. He looked down, saw her and uttered a cry, He dismounted and embraced her. She was alive. He hugged her to his chest and whispered her name. The din of the battle was deafening, but she heard him.

All around them, bodies of dead men and horses littered the clearing. In the river, bodies floated in the slow current and in places the water ran red with blood.

Temujin grabbed her arm. She placed a boot in his stirrup and swung up onto the saddle. He got up behind her. He shouted to one of the soldiers and ordered the man to bring the old woman and her cart. With one arm around Bortai and one hand holding the reins, Temujin rode out of the Mergid camp.

Jelme saw them and rode up and saluted Temujin. He was a blacksmith's son, a commoner by birth. Temujin told him to take a message to Togril and Jamuga. "I have my wife. She is safe with me. I've got what I came for. Let's end this quickly and make camp for the night."

He ordered the Mongol Army to retreat, to ride to the camp on Talkun Island. There they would be safe from a counter-attack.

Jelme was not good with words, but on this occasion, he was eloquent, proud that he had been assigned the calling off of war. He found Togril and Jamuga and delivered the message.

Belgutei spotted Chilger the Athlete running away in the dark and ran him down. From his horse, he caught Chilger with a lasso around the neck. "You are supposed to be a strong man. Why are you running away in the night?"

Chilger said, "She's gone. She's not with me. I don't know where she ran. My life is worth less than a pile of sheep dung. I was running into the canyons to save my life. I had nothing to do with taking her. That was Togtoa. I am a man of lowly station. . ."

Belgutei tightened the lasso on Chilger's throat. "You lie. You're the chief's brother."

Chilger coughed and pulled at the rope around his neck. "Don't kill me. I'm the chief's brother but I brought disaster on my people. They will want to kill me. To you Mongols, I am forest people. I desired a Khongirad noblewoman. I am like a black crow that desires to mate with a swan. My life is over."

Belgutei lifted his sword and was ready to strike when a soldier rode up to him. "Your mother is captive somewhere in this camp. We don't know where. Come with us. Let's find her. We're getting ready to ride out."

Belgutei put his sword in its sheath. "You're a lucky man, Chilger. Today, you live. Keep your head. For now."

Chilger uttered a blessing and escaped into the night. Belgutei followed the soldier and found his mother's tent. He entered, but she went out by another door. Belgutei ran after her and caught up with her. He grabbed her arm and turned her to him, searching her face. He asked, "Mother, we've brought an army to rescue you. Why are you running from me?"

Sochigil had madness in her eyes. She clawed at her son's arm as tear streamed down her face. "Oyelun always said that my sons would be princes and you are a khan while . . .I can't look you in the face." She wrenched free and she ran away to hide in the deepest part of the forest. Belgutei searched everywhere, but he couldn't find her.

In a rage, he took up a quiver of blunt arrows and shot every person of Mergid blood he could find. He wanted their pain to be as great as possible and the bloodletting as profuse as possible. Yet this did not satisfy his rage. He assembled any Mergid he could find and executed them along with their children. After the battle, they took women as spoils of war, concubines and slaves. From the women, he took one that was beautiful. They loaded the women and the booty onto carts. Children became servants to open and close the tent-doors of the Mongols.

There was nothing left in the camp but the wind. They rejoined the camp.

Khasar came to his brother's tent and asked permission to wed a Mergid woman whom they had taken as spoils of war. It was the oath of the hunting peoples that the khan had first choice of the women taken in war. Temujin gave his permission.

Temujin tried to dissuade Khasar from marrying. He wanted Khasar to wed a Khongirad woman, but his brother had seen a raven-tressed beauty and had been taken with the woman's wild look. Temujin relented.

Temujin said, "Wait. We will have the marriage celebration in our own pastures. Speak no more of this now, brother. See to it that the booty is put into carts."

Dirty and bloody from the battlefield, Jamuga entered Temujin's tent bearing a cup made of carved ox-horn. He was delighted that Khasar was present. His *anda* Temujin never made a move without consulting Khasar, Jamuga wanted Khasar to hear the speech he was about to make.

He raised his cup. "*Anda*, we have fought together. Let us unite the Jajirats and Borjigins. It is time the Mongols rose up."

Khasar saw Jamuga's eyes cutting back and forth, watching where Temujin ordered the carts full of booty to be loaded. The old feeling of distrust returned. This campaign had proved that Togril was past his prime. His brother and this man were the principal contenders for rulership of the steppes. Temujin wrapped his arm around Khasar's shoulder and said in a low voice. "Don't leave me alone in the tent with him."

Temujin said, "This is a good idea, but let's take the time to talk it over. I go to see about my wife."

"Of course. Congratulations on your first victory. Let it be the first of many. I hope she's unharmed."

"So do I." Temujin held open the tent-door. He had not missed the meaning of Jamuga's comment. His *first* victory, stacked against Jamuga's many. "I owe you a debt of gratitude. Without your help, I would not have her back."

Jamuga laughed. "The day will come when I ask a favor of you. The bond works two ways. What shall we do about the booty?"

"We'll divide it tomorrow. Tonight, I think we deserve a rest. Let the army see its reward by the light of day."

"Good enough," said Jamuga.

They forded the stream on horses. Khasar asked, What orders shall I give about making camp? Are we travelling on or staying here?

"Let's make camp with the Jajirats in the Khorkhanagh Valley. Our fortunes are changing. I want the steppe nobility to realize that our strength is growing." Khasar would not question him about his decision until they were alone.

When all the Mongols returned to camp, Temujin distributed booty among his commanders. The commanders took care of the junior officers, who took care of the men under them. This was the system of distribution of goods taken in war.

Temujin found Bortai in his tent. She was dressed not as a princess, but in coarse-woven clothes. She looked at him the way she had ever since she was a child, seeing into his inmost thoughts. He tried to kiss her.

"Forgive me. It's so good to hear the sound of your voice. I have missed you so much . . . You'll never know . . . " The man she had married was transformed by his first war, a war undertaken for her honor.

"You're different. I'm different. You have no idea how crude these people are."

He said, "If there is blame, it is mine." He went down on his knees in front of her. "I have brought an army to get you back. I have slaughtered an entire tribe because they dared to harm you. There is nothing left of them." He was shaking and weeping. "What else can I do? Tell me and I will do it, or come to me now as my wife."

Her shoulders shook. She was sobbing. "You don't understand," she said, her voice torn by her private agony. "I was pregnant when they took me. The child is yours."

"Are you hungry?" he asked her. It was an inane question but feeding her, giving her animal comfort seemed the easiest thing he could do. She shook her head no.

"Do you have wounds that need attending? The shaman Tab Tengri is with the army." She shook her head no. Munglig's son had learned the shamanic arts from the old shaman. He was out in the camp with his satchel of herbs and plants, tending to the sick and wounded and seeing to the burial of the dead.

"Do you want something to drink?" She nodded yes. He poured a cup of *koumiz* for her She drank it and it seemed to calm her nerves.

She said, "How could you. . .. you left me." The words came on a river of her pain.

His voice cracked. "I'm sorry. I'm so sorry. I thought you were with us."

"You were sworn to protect me. You know that I had never been in a raid before."

"I know." He gathered her in his arms. She tried to drag herself away from him, but he held her and quieted her.

He spoke to her in the circle of his arms, remembering for her the vigor and beauty of their lovemaking the night before she was taken from him. He said that he knew the moment the child was conceived. "The child is mine.".

"Look at me. You're not badly wounded, you have surface scrapes and scratches. Your inner wounds will heal in time. I am overjoyed that my wife will give me my first child. No one will dare say anything about it."

He sent for the shaman to bring her a sleeping potion. The servant brought the tea and she drank it. "Temujin, you know my feelings for you. In my heart I have never betrayed you."

"I know that. I swear I will make it up to you. I make you a solemn promise. I will never put you aside for any other. Your sons and your sons alone will inherit the lands I conquer. For the rest of our days, let this be our understanding and let us never speak of this again,"

She lay down and he lay beside her and held her in his arms until her breathing grew deeper and calmer and she fell asleep. He got up and went out to look at the stars.

The next day, Togril ordered the Kereyid Army to strike camp. Before he left, Temujin asked Togril Khan to muster the troops and stand with him as he made a speech of appreciation.

"Because you joined me when I needed you, O my khan, my strength was as great as Heaven and Earth combined. With the help of the Eternal Blue Sky, we've torn out the hearts of the Mergid warriors, pulled apart their livers, and emptied their beds. We've killed their sons and captured their women and they are no more. The job is done, let's leave this place Let us salute the brave men who fought with us." A cheer went up.

The Kereyid Army left the forest lands and rode to the far side of Mount Burkhan. They provisioned themselves by hunting their way down the Hokortu Valley before returning to their camp on the Tola River.

The Mongol Army left Mergid territory. Bogorji had captured a Mergid scout who guided them to the Khorkhanagh Valley. There he made camp with Jamuga.

A few months later, Bortai gave birth. The new father gave his son the name Jochi and invited all the people living in white felt tents to a feast.

He had won his first campaign. His alliance with Jamuga had given him a large army. He had his first heir. Many clans came to his camp to congratulate him. They brought gifts--furs, vessels of pottery, cups made of carved bone, arrows from the arrow-maker, a bow from the bow-maker, flasks of fermented mare's milk from the *koumiz*-churner, hides from the tanner, meat from the hunters.

The fame of the two young khans spread all over the steppes. Thousands of people came to camp with them.

Word of the victory spread. Around the campfires, the people began to sing of a hero who would restore the Mongols to their former glory.

After the rescue campaign, the two main branches of the Mongols made camp together in Jamuga's pastures in the Khorkhanagh Valley. This was a place of power, of mythic significance. In this valley, the last Mongol king had been crowned. It had a Great Branching Tree, an oak thirty feet high with a huge expanse of branches,

The two young khans inspired many clans to follow them for they seemed blessed by the Eternal Blue Sky. No one could resist them. Some clans who had left Temujin to camp with the Taijyud came back, A member of the Mongol royal family--Altan Khan—joined them, giving them the legitimacy of the old Mongol royal line.

The two young khans organized a Grand Hunt that lasted for a month. Several thousand riders took part, the line of riders extending for two miles, including several hundred mastiffs and beaters. Temujin shot well and took several deer, a wolf, a small bear, a panther. The men killed a huge quantity of game, Temujin, as commander of the hunt, enjoyed himself more than he had in years. He wished that his father were alive to see the great spectacle.

The young khans gave a feast for their followers, an epic bout of eating and drinking, music and dance. Cooks set up outdoor kitchens as assistants dressed thousands of animals. They roasted meat over open fires--deer, hare, boar, goat, sheep--and boiled meat and bones of yak, fox, wolf and marten in huge caldrons of water with roots and vegetables, wild chives and garlic to make Mongol stew. The light of the full moon bathed the camp in silver, huge bonfires flared up against the night sky, stars hung in the heavens, music filled the valley. Nobles and commoners celebrated. The clans ate voraciously and consumed vast quantities of *koumiz*. The feast reached its crescendo as dancers held hands and made a circle around the Great Branching Tree.

An event like this possesses a rhythm. In the early morning everyone in camp rested from the revelries of the previous evening. By afternoon, the excitement built for another night of festivity. As the moon set, the mood of the feast changed. Musicians played soft sad ballads and young men and girls courted.

The feasting went on day and night. On the eighth night, seated at the banquet table, Temujin and Jamuga reminisced about their childhood adventures. They recalled seeing their breath in the air as they skated on the ice of the frozen Onon River and they remembered the arrowheads they exchanged in the forest.

Temujin, always moderate in his consumption of alcohol, abandoned himself to the victory festivities and was happily inebriated. He stood up and toasted Jamuga. On this occasion, he felt sentimental. His eyes glistening, his heart overflowing with gratitude, he turned to Jamuga. "Let's declare ourselves sworn brothers again. What the elders say is true. Bonds forged in childhood should last until death."

A hard drinker, Jamuga rose to speak, unsteady on his feet, almost pitching over. He turned to those gathered below the dais and spoke loudly enough for all to hear. "Let us declare ourselves brothers until the end of our days," he said. He was slurring his words.

Temujin leaned over and whispered something into the ear of one of his grooms. The man went off into the night. When he returned, Temujin stood up holding above his head the gold belt he had taken from Togtoa. A second manservant led Togtoa's horse right into area in front of the dais, a beautiful yellow gelding with a black mane and tail.

Jamuga hung the belt over his shoulder and stroked the horse affectionately. With a grand show of noble generosity, he dispatched his own groom. The man returned and Jamuga presented Temujin with the gold belt that had belonged to Dayir. He handed Temujin the reins of Dayir's horse, a gelding as white as a newborn lamb and pledged his loyalty. The Mongol chiefs cheered as Temujin and Jamuga saluted each other in the old nomad way and embraced.

Musicians struck up a dance tune, and men and women danced again under the spreading leaves of the Great Branching Tree, circling the tree so many times that their feet pounded a ditch into the earth a foot deep.

Mukhali, a commoner loyal to Temujin, stood looking up at the tree and said what all of them were thinking: that a new Mongol khan would be elected by them and proclaimed under this tree. He stepped into the circle of firelight and lifted his cup. "In days of old, we Blue Mongols elected a khan in this place. Let us do so again."

That night, Temujin pitched his tent next to Jamuga's and the two of them began sleeping under the tree.

With the khan's tithe, Temujin was prosperous in his own right, no longer dependent on his wife's dowry. The tents under his command numbered in the thousands, formed five camping circles, His herds grew and he grew wealthy, receiving one-tenth of the horse herds from the nobility, one each of the five snouts from the commoners.

He had ideas about the organization of a camp and set about structuring his camp and his army. No other nomad khan in history, no Hun or Turk, ever mastered men and resources well enough to rule a civilized society. Genghis Khan was the first and his genius for organization e was obvious from the beginning of his career. The future Genghis Khan chose equipment for his army: light armor made of leather fortified with metal plate. (He was familiar with metal armor but thought it too heavy to wear on horseback).

He decided that his soldiers would bring five remounts, their own saddles, and dried food and blankets for their horses. In addition to his other equipment, each soldier had a silk shirt that he wore underneath his leather armor. Twisting the fabric of the shirt was an ingenious way to remove an arrow from a wound.

Genghis Khan began training exercises, The simple circle formation of the Grand Hunt was the basic pattern for the riding order of the Mongol Army. Then he invented formations, the lake array, the chisel array, the thorny bush array, for different attacks. An entire wing of his army fought as a unit, the only army on the steppes trained to such precision. He rode at the head of his army into every battle and he was victorious in all of them. He lived in a tent like his men, wore the same uniform they wore, and ate the same food that they ate. He knew his commanders intimately and made assignments according to their strengths and weaknesses.

He saw the necessity of creating a command structure. No one had a better eye for talent than Genghis Khan. His commanders were without equal and his command structure was the finest in the world. At the beginning of his career, he appointed a Council of Generals: Khasar,

Belgutei, Bogorji and Jelme, a commoner, became his first generals. He raised Mukhali, who had fought brilliantly in the Mergid campaign, to the status of nobleman and gave him the rank of general. He promoted his men on merit, not by birth.

Temujin divided his army in the traditional manner, in units of 10, 100 and 1,000. He appointed junior commanders from men he had come to know in the Mergid campaign and the hunt. The camp was spread out over many miles and Temujin liked to be informed. He set up a system of Near Arrows and Far Arrows, spies and informants, so that he would know everything that was going on in his camp. His mother and wife reported the gossip of the women's camp.

Even in the midst of the good years, he and Khasar shared a confidence. He and Jamuga were both princes, and both were ambitious. Only one of them could rule the steppes. When would friendship turn to rivalry, Khasar wondered. He did not know then that it would only a few more years.

A year passed, and then another. Khasar was so caught up with his new responsibilities, integrating the tents of the many clans that had come to join them into the structure of camping circles in the valley that he was spending very little time with Jamuga. Each camping circle was ruled by a commander. The men had to be assigned a circle under the command of each of the newly appointed generals.

Temujin summoned Khasar to his tent. "I asked you to go falconing with me and Jamuga. You refused. You don't come to my tent at night. I wonder why. Are you avoiding me?"

"It's not you. It's him."

"Why? What has he done to you? Hasn't he brought us good fortune?"

"Oh, please. You think the sun rises and sets on him. He looked like a fool at the Grand Hunt, showing off in front of all the men what a great archer he is. He can't shoot worth a damn."

Temujin grew defensive. "Everyone know what a great shot you are, Khasar."

"Believe me, I'm not jealous of him. I challenge him to an archery contest any day of the week, including one on horseback "

"Then what is it?"

"I don't like the way he tries to outshine you. He interrupts you when you speak. He thinks his ideas are better than yours and says so publicly. I don't like the way he treats his horses. Neither does Belgutei. You are too blind to see it. I think he's using you."

"Using me? It is I who am using him. As for his being jealous of me, he has five times more than I do. Why should he be jealous of me?"

"Outside, maybe he's richer. But deep down, he knows you're the better man. He resents you for it. He's trouble. It will come to no good, but I know you will never listen to me. So I say nothing and I stay away. Don't badger me to spend time with him. I don't like him and I don't like who you become when you're with him."

"Your jealousy is the only flaw in your character, Khasar."

"I'll falcon with Belgutei. I prefer his company." Khasar picked up his bow and left the tent.

After every Grand Hunt, Temujin and Jamuga threw a feast for the whole camp. Two evenings before they had had a drunken revelry which lasted all night long. The commoners were dismantling the feast-ground. Khasar spotted Bortai standing under the Great Branching Tree not far from Jamuga's tent. She was wearing a purple dress and silver bracelets and earrings. Motherhood agreed with her.

Her silver earrings tinkled when she moved her head.

"I liked the old days when he depended on no one but us. I should be happy that he has found something of the pride and dignity he lost, but I'm not."

Khasar said, "I'm annoyed with him. He's got a big army now. He should be thinking of taking revenge on the Tatar, not of hunting and feasting with Jamuga."

"Come on, little brother," she cajoled. "You and I know him better than anyone alive except your mother. The desire for revenge against the Taijyud is still the driving force of his life."

"You're right. I don't trust Jamuga, 'What do we really know about Jamuga that we should trust him so much? None of us saw him for years. He never came to us in our time of troubles."

She lowered her eyes. "My father always felt ashamed that he never offered any help,"

"I understand your father's reasoning, but what was Jamuga's excuse?"

"Khasar, Khasar, you men are all alike. There will never be war enough to satisfy you. Sometimes I long for the peace of my father's camp. What if Temujin dies making war? What will I do?"

"I know his mind like I know my own. He will never make a move against the Taijyud before he is ready. He knows his limits. He will never attempt what he cannot achieve."

"Why can't you just forget the past and live in peace like my people?"

Khasar was curt. "You have never known hardship, Bortai. Your father never lost his wealth. When Temujin became Togril's vassal, that that was the first step. Joining forces with Jamuga is the second step. Temujin is at the beginning of his enterprise. My brother believes he has a destiny."

"If you must know, I agree with you about Jamuga. My husband is too sentimental about the *anda* bond."

"You speak more like a general than a wife."

"Not really. Did I tell you I'm pregnant again?"

The future Genghis Khan within the space of six months made a momentous decision. Mukhali told him that Jamuga had organized a hunt and had not invited him, nor had Jamuga given his brother khan a share of the meat.

Among the nomads, the khan acts as judge in the settlement of disputes. A Borjigin aristocrat came to Temujin complaining of high-handed treatment he had received from Jamuga, who had been acting as judge in a pasture dispute with a Jajirat.

Jamuga had not delivered justice and the Borjigin man complained about it to Temujin. It was not a complicated case. Temujin listened to the details and rendered a decision in favor of the Borjigin. The Jajirat man protested and went to seek redress from Jamuga.

Jamuga reversed Temujin's decision, not by principle, but by clan prejudice. Jamuga told the man that his word was final, that Temujin was merely a second-in-command. The gossip went around the women's camp and the Borjigin man repeated the conversation to Khasar.

Temujin's mother Oyelun spoke to him of the matter, and he told her that he was biding his time. He was generous to Taijyuds who came to him from Targutai and Todogen's camp, even going so far as to give one of his best horses as a gift of good will to a Taijyud traveling through his pastures.

Before long, the tribes who had belonged to his father came to Temujin's camp. He was building an army to wage war on the Tatar. He told Khasar that Khasar might have thought he had forgotten about revenge on his greedy kinsmen, but he had not.

The time of the spring migration came. Temujin and Jamuga had an argument about where they would camp. Temujin wanted to camp by the riverbanks so the horses would have water to drink. Jamuga wanted to camp on the hillsides where the sheep and goats would have good pasture.

Temujin decided to break camp with Jamuga and take his clans with him. When the Jajirats stopped to make camp on the first night of the migration, the Borjigin wagons kept moving all through the night. In the morning, they stopped to rest. 13,000 tents had come with him, more than he had anticipated. The Jajirat clans had split up. Some remained with Jamuga; some joined him. When the lesser chiefs had seen that the royals and the aristocrats and all the senior nobility had chosen to camp with Temujin, they had gone with the Borjigins. Temujin was powerful on his own and Jamuga was his rival. The division was out in the open.

A month later, they arrived at Lake Baikal. Bortai went to the birthing tent. Her labor was long and difficult, but he had a new son. He went inside and stood by while the shaman, Tab Tengri, gave his son a blessing.

The child was bright red and bald when he was born and was a colicky difficult baby. He decided to name his son Jagadai. He had not had any recent victories, but Jagadai was born in a time of consolidation of camp, of organization and building of power, this was what attended his birth. Tab Tengri said that the baby was colicky because Bortai had been so distraught about Jamuga during her pregnancy.

When they arrived at Lake Baikal, he organized a hunt and gave a feast in Bortai's honor and in honor of his second son.

The whole camp brought gifts and congratulations as the couple sat on the dais. The people drank *koumiz* and danced. The throat-singers warbled their ballads and sad old herder's tunes.

When the winter season of migration was over, Temujin moved his camp to the shores of the Blue Lake in the Gurelgu Mountains. As they moved through Taijyud country, tribes that had formerly camped with his father joined him. More of the Mongol royals also joined him.

When they had set up camp at the Blue Lake, Altan Khan, the most senior member of the Mongol royal line, summoned Temujin to his tent. Two other senior Mongol royals were present: Daritai, the grandson of Khabul Khan, and Khuchar, a member of the senior branch of the Borjigin royalty.

Altan spoke for all of them. "We want to elect you khan." They had decided that two khans could not rule them. They disliked Jamuga's manner. They stood, fists over hearts, and pledged their loyalty to Temujin.

Altan Khan called a Grand Assembly and stood on a dais before all the people and made the announcement that the Mongol royals had elected Temujin and given him the title Genghis Khan, which means, in the Mongol tongue, Oceanic Khan. Then they publicly enthroned him as their khan. His commanders brought a throne of horse-skins and Altan placed a square of white felt on it, symbolizing that Genghis Khan was the ruler of all who lived in felt tents.

He sat down on the throne and his commanders lifted him up over their heads and paraded him through the crowds. The royals clenched their fists in the ancient salute. With one voice, the nobility solemnly invoked one of the old hunting oaths.

"We will ride with you against the enemy. We will deliver to you from the spoils of war, the most beautiful women, and the most beautiful virgins for your palace-tent. Also, we will turn over the prize geldings and mares, all the long-legged horses will be brought to you trotting. At the hunt, we will drive the game of the steppe to you so that their bellies touch and the game of the mountains so that they stand leg to leg, for you to have the best of all we have. If any one of us should disobey you in battle, take that man's possessions, his children, his wife and cut off his head and leave him to die in the dust. If we disobey your orders in peacetime, abandon us to our fates at the time of migration. Leave us without protection. This we swear to you."

Afterward, in the open space in front of the tent, the people gathered and thousands of voices rose up chanting, "Genghis Khan! Genghis Khan! Genghis Khan!" The new Khan of the Mongols accepted the accolade of his people.

In his tent, he received his followers and distributed booty. A man of the Uriyang tribe came to camp to join them. He strode forward and spoke in a loud clear voice and said his name was Subudei the Brave. He was lean and tall, with not an ounce of fat on his frame and carried himself erect, with a military bearing. He made a speech and asked Genghis Khan if he could join his camp. He was something of a poet for his speech was full, composed of beautiful words unlike the primitive utterances of the faithful commoners. In return for the khan's protection, Subudei made his oath. "I'll be like a rat and gather up others to follow you. I'll be like a black crow and gather great flocks of people to surround you. Like the felt blankets that cover our horses, I'll gather soldiers to cover you. Like the beaten white felt that guards a tent from the wind, I'll assemble great armies to shelter your tent."

Genghis Khan said, "Join us. If you excel in the field, I will give you a command." Subudei saluted and took his place among the nobility.

While he was receiving the congratulations of the nobility, a messenger came bringing word that his kinsmen the Taijyud brothers had joined Jamuga. The Taijyud felt afraid and thought they needed protection. They surmised that it was only a matter of time until Temujin, the wolf cub, came to take over the pack.

Munglig, the boy who had fetched him long ago from Dai Sechen's camp, came forward. Genghis Khan uttered a cry of surprise. "Where have you been?"

Munglig was ashamed and asked forgiveness for abandoning the family when the Taijyuds deserted so long ago. Now he wished to join the Mongols.

Oyelun stood beside the throne of horse-skins. She whispered in Temujin's ear. She had seen Munglig privately and had forgiven his desertion of the family. Munglig had once had a wife, but she had died and he had seven grown sons. He asked Oyelun to marry him and she had given her assent with the one provision. Normally Mongol widows did not remarry so that they could be joined with their husbands in the Land of the Ancestors. Oyelun asked that right would belong to Yesugei. Munglig agreed and they were married. Genghis was happy that his mother would no longer be alone in her tent.

They celebrated with a feast. By the end of the evening, Bortai was wrapping her foot around his under the table, toasting him and kissing his cheek. She whispered that she wanted to leave the feast ground and go to his tent. He rose, took her hand and bid good night to the company.

The next morning, after Bortai departed for her own tent, he summoned Khasar who had left the feast ground early.

"Brother, we have to inform Togril about my election. If he does not hear from us, he will think that we have declared war on him. His forces could easily destroy ours."

Khasar agreed. "I will bring word. I will be your ambassador."

The Kereyid Camp

Khasar arrived in Ong Khan's camp and announced the news of Genghis Khan's election to Togril Khan.

Togril received Khasar in his luxurious tent and offered hospitality and a rest from the journey. "That's good news. I'm proud of Temujin. He's up to the job. Send word of congratulations to my adopted son,"

"I will," said Khasar.

Togril said, "Temujin sent this message because he does not want war with me."

Khasar said, "That's correct. Temujin did not want any misunderstanding. He has no intention of riding against you."

Togril said, "I'm in favor of this. The Mongols should have a khan. Otherwise, there will be a vacuum of power in the central steppes. And the Naiman or the Tatar will try to conquer the Mongols. Then we will have war in the north and I do not want trade to be interrupted. I get richer in peacetime."

Khasar said, "That's what Temujin thinks. I'll tell him you see it the same way."

Togril invited Khasar to the hospitality of his camp, but Khasar said that his new duties occupied all his time. He invited them to visit the camp.

Khasar took his leave.

The Senggum spat on the earth. "Old man! Why do you not step down in favor of me?" He pushed away the servant who had come to fill his cup, "We should go to war. We control the roads through southeastern Gobi. If we conquered the Naiman lands, we would be the richest men who ever ruled the steppes."

Togril shook his head in disgust. "You don't understand anything. I knew the way Altan Khan's mind works. Altan is lazy. He wants Temujin as a puppet to do the work of hunting and fighting, while Altan lives the life of a royal. I wonder if Altan Khan really understands the man he has put on the throne?"

The Senggum said, "Maybe, father, you are the one who doesn't know Temujin. What will Temujin want once he had taken his revenge on the Tatar? He will want all of it. We have the greatest army in the steppe and do nothing but sit around like old women."

Togril snapped. "I don't want war. I want to enjoy my old age. You're my flesh and blood, but I don't like your ways. Besides, if I stepped down, what kind of a khan would you make? If you spent less time gambling at the horse races, I might delegate kingship to you, but you have no taste for duty. I am going to the office where the men run my counting house."

" Jamuga and I could forge an alliance. We could rule the steppes. We could take on the Naiman and we would have the revenues from the Western Gobi."

"You're too greedy, Nilkha. Be careful that your ambitions don't outstrip your talents. Do what you want when I'm gone, but I would advise against thinking you and Jamuga will rule together. He is inconstant and, Heaven help me, so are you. Leave me alone. I go to my counting house where I trust you will leave me in peace."

Togril sent a messenger to Temujin, addressing him by his new title of Genghis Khan. He included a gentle reprimand to remind Temujin that a vassal owed it to his lord to seek permission for changes in his status. Temujin had not asked his permission, but no matter.

Genghis Khan! How excellent that you have been elected, my son. I congratulate you on your good fortune. I don't know how the Mongols have survived all this time without a leader. If you had consulted me beforehand, I would have approved.

Jamuga was furious when he heard the news of Temujin's election. He thought he would have made a far better Khan of the Mongols. He sat with his companions and wondered aloud why the royals had gone behind his back and offered the position to Temujin. What were they up to? Why were they eliminating him from consideration?

Jamuga sent messengers to the Mongol camp accusing Temujin of insulting him, of leaving their camp in the middle of the night without a word of his departure and taking with him many Jajirat clans. He said that he knew that the two of them were rivals in the competition for leadership of the steppes.

He admitted to his companions that he knew that Genghis Khan had bested him.

His message was a taunt.

Why didn't Altan and Khuchar elect Temujin to be the Mongol khan when we all camped together? Why did they not select between the two of us in the presence of all the people in white felt tents? Why wait until we split camp and each of us was half as strong?

*I entreat Altan and Khuchar. Uphold the solemn oath of loyalty you have sworn to my **anda** Temujin. Serve him with a loyalty which never falters as long as he sits upon the throne of horse skins.*

Genghis Khan gave an open-air feast on a clear night under a canopy of stars. He sat on his throne of horse-skins at the center of the head table. Bortai sat next to him, dressed in a silk jacket with a silver and turquoise headdress and long silver earrings inlaid with turquoise.

Oyelun's hair had turned gray. She was, getting on in years, but retained her elegance in her yoked Khongirad dress decorated with fine rainbow pattern needlepoint.

Commanders filled the seats at his table: Khasar, Bogorji, Jelme, Subudei. Bodyguards, the only men wearing weapons, surrounded the area.

A nomad orchestra played a lively dance tune. Men and women went to the dance floor, the men linking their arms across each other's shoulders dancing in front of the khan, women winding their arms through each other's arms, dancing in front of Bortai.

Genghis traded jokes and stories with his generals. The whole table was in a festive mood enjoying the drinking and dancing.

Hundreds of servants went from table to table pouring *koumiz* and serving platters of food, while at the open pit, Genghis Khan's chief cook, Shikiur, a man with a thick torso, a cheery face and arms of steel, supervised a staff of fifty in his open kitchens, saw to the roasting and serving of game killed in the hunt.

A Guardsman approached the dais, saluted the Khan and delivered a message. "Urughud, Manghud and Jurkin warriors have arrived from Jamuga's camp. Hundreds of them. They say that they want to leave his camp and make their camp with us. We removed their weapons and had them walk between the fires."

The Jurkins were members of the senior branch of the Mongol royal house. The shaman Tab Tengri put cauldrons of boiling oil at the entrance to the camp, for the removal of demons, according to the belief of the shamans.

"Bring them before me," the khan ordered.

A cordon of Guardsmen led the way. The music trailed off and dancers parted to allow a band of big men with huge arms and shoulders, make their way to the dais. A murmur went through the crowd. They carried themselves as great warriors.

Khasar spoke in his brother's ear. "We will use them in the army if they swear loyalty to you. His loss; our gain."

Genghis looked at Khasar. "I will trust them until they prove themselves. Jamuga could be laying a trap, sending spies into my camp. I will allow them to make camp with us, at the extreme edge of the camp. Surround them with our most trusted sentries. I'll give them a chance to prove their sincerity."

Khasar nodded. The newcomers saluted Genghis Khan and introduced themselves. Jurchedei, the head of the Urughud clans, went down on one knee and announced his lineage. Khuyildar, the head of the Manghud, did the same.

Genghis welcomed them as great warriors from tribes of renowned fighters.

Jurchedei said, "We live by a code of honor, khan. Every nobleman deserves a prince's death," Jamuga violated the code. He spilled blood on the ground."

Shamanists believed that spirit resides in the blood and that if blood is spilled upon the ground, a warrior could not join The Ancestors. The method of execution was to wrap the offender a carpet and trample him to death with horses.

Khuyildar said, "Jamuga ordered that a Mongol nobleman be taken prisoner and boiled alive in seventy iron kettles." This was a punishment the nomads learned from the Chinese.

"I heard the piteous howling that rose up to the vault of the Blue Sky. Jamuga took pleasure in the suffering. The cries echoed through the camp, I went to him and asked that prisoners be allowed the traditional death, Jamuga refused. Jamuga also rode his black horse to the place where the head of the Chinos clan, Chaghaghan, was being held prisoner. He got down from the horse, drew his sword and cut off the man's head. Then he tied the bloody head to the tail of his horse and rode through the camp dragging it behind him. This was when I decided to leave. The others felt the same way that I do. We ask your permission to join your camp."

Genghis grunted in disgust. "Tell me what led to your split from Jamuga."

Khuyildar said, "I'll be honest with you, sir, in Jamuga's camp, I have seen things I would rather not see in a khan".

Jurchedei was blunt. "We want to make camp with a man we can respect. We're paying a tithe and we're fighting. We've heard that you would take the garment off your back and give it to a man if he needed it, that you would get down off your best horse and offer it to a man if he had none. Is this true?"

Khasar answered. "My brother has done this many times, even for the Taijyud who wronged him."

"Then you're the leader we're looking for.

"Join us. You're my kinsmen and you have legitimate grievances."

Jurchedei said, "Khan, I compliment you on the prosperous look of your camp. We hear that there is no fighting and murder in your camp. If this is true, sir, then you are a khan fit to lead the whole steppe. We will join you and fight alongside you. You know our reputation. You and your generals have seen us in the field. We will help you destroy your enemies"

Genghis said, "Welcome." He lifted a cup of *koumiz* and drank with them. He introduced them as new members of camp to the clans gathered for the feast. They applauded the newcomers who left the feasting to make camp.

The Jin Emperor sent a splendid envoy dressed in the tailored uniform of the diplomatic corps, deep blue with black trim, and a jade badge of office, polished boots and a sword at his side. The man saluted smartly and introduced himself. He unrolled out a scroll and read a decree that announced that the Emperor had bestowed a formal title on Genghis Khan, *Pacifier of the North.* He lifted a jade amulet. Genghis Khan bowed his head, and the envoy placed the amulet around his neck.

In those days, a title from the Emperor of China impressed him.

Genghis Khan replied, enunciating the Chinese words with care, "Pacifier of the North. The Jin Emperor gave Togril the title of *Wong Khan, King of the Khans.* He pronounced it Ong Khan in the Mongol tongue.

The envoy asked him to perform the *ketou,* the knocking of the head.

He got down on his knees, inhaled the fragrance of mother earth, and prostrated himself before the envoy of the Son of Heaven. The envoy was pleased and congratulated the barbarian khan, then read a list of tribute that he would pay annually for the privilege of being a vassal.

Horses, skins, and hides. Ten thousand of each. Temujin had Uighurs to work in his treasury because they could read and write and they knew administration. His personal secretary Tatatonga counted up the tribute and put it in a cart.

Later Genghis Khan discussed the matter with Khasar. The Emperor of China did not fool Genghis Khan for an instant. He wanted to wage war against the Southern Song because the emperor who sat on the Southern Song throne could rule all of China and dump the Jin from the throne. If the Song came to the North, they were a threat. Unfortunately, first emperor of Song had forsaken warfare. They made several feeble attempts, but they could not take back the North/ So the Jin Emperor had to pacify the North, namely the new Mongol Khan, so he could ride to war in the south. He needed supplies from the barbarians to make war on the Song. He needed horses for war. He got them from Genghis Khan. Such were the politics of North and South.

Genghis Khan told Khasar, "I gave the best of our goods as tribute."

The brothers watched the soldiers loading up the carts with the finest pelts--sable, ermine, marten, fox, and wolf. As a personal gift, Genghis Khan sent the Emperor the hide of a bear, a magnificent gift.

Once they had the raw materials, Chinese artisans could manufacture whatever military equipment the Jin Army required.

Khasar made a joke. The Chinese are making equipment from our goods and taking our horses so they can one day fight us with our own supplies.

Genghis said, "I have to keep the peace with him. That's the way of the world. I also sent a herd of 1,000 Akhal-Tekes, from the West."

Khasar said, "The Horse of Heaven. That's a very expensive present."

Genghis Khan "They are the finest horses in the world. "

The cavalry masters of the herds rounded up the high-stepping desert horses who would follow the army back to China. I don't want him to think that I am an ignorant barbarian."

"And what did you receive in return?"

"The Emperor always makes a show of his return gifts. He doesn't want anyone to think he needs the tribute. So I received a lavish present. In return the Son of Heaven gave me 10,000 bolts of dyed silk and 1,000 ingots of silver. I also got 10,000 boxes of tea. Horses and tea. That's the way it has always been between us and the Chinese. I care nothing for clothes of silk. I wear a Mongol uniform. This exchange of presents was not the point. I had a motive.

"What was that, brother?" Khasar asked.

"I requested permission from the Son of Heaven to campaign against the Tatar."

"That took a lot of nerve."

"It was a test. I wanted to know how much freedom I had to wage war in the steppes. I asked if the Emperor would join me in punishing the four tribes of the Tatar. The envoy asked me when I intended to go on campaign and I told him in autumn, when the weather cooled off.

"He said that the Jin Emperor had no interest in such a campaign, but that I had permission to conduct the war.

Khasar said he had to hand it to his brother. "You can destroy the Tatar with no fear that the Chinese will attack. When I am done with the Tatar, I will be the most powerful man in Eastern Mongolia. The imperial envoy realized that I was unifying the tribes and training them for war. I imagine he reported to the emperor."

"Was it necessary to supply the Jin Imperial Cavalry with horses?" Khasar asked.

Genghis Khan nodded, "I am conducting myself according to established order. This has been the custom for centuries. We give them horses. They give us silk and tea. I don't want them setting up trade with Xi Xia. I don't want the two states in North China ganging up against me. So I am their supplier for horses. The distance is shorter and it is more convenient to collect tribute horses than to pay for them. I sent 10,000 war ponies. Besides, I have a score to settle with the Tatar."

Seventy Felt Cloaks, Tatar Country, 1202

Autumn came and the weather cooled. Cool weather meant the fighting season had begun.

Genghis Khan made a tour of inspection of his Army and its horses, weapons and equipment. He planned extensively for every campaign. He went into every detail and left very little to chance. He ordered his army into the field.

The Mongol Army rode east until they reached a place called Seventy Felt Cloaks. Genghis addressed his commanders and fifty thousand soldiers from the back of his warhorse.

"I wish to lay down rules for the conduct of war. If the Tatar forced us to retreat, every man is ordered to return to the place where the formation began and stand ready for my command to counter-attack. Do not leave the field.

"These Tatar are skilled at our style of nomad warfare. They may feign a retreat, lure us into a chase and wheel about on us. Any man who disobeys my orders will be killed. If our army wins the engagement, no one is to gather spoils. That is an order. I will divide the Tatar possessions equally among us."

The men banged their swords on their shields and cheered him.

The war drums rumbled across the grasslands, booming.

The Tatar were waiting at the place called Seventy Felt Cloaks. He saw the four Tatar clans, arrayed for battle. The horses were well cared for. He knew from the spies he had sent to the Tatar camp that the men were good riders but they were undisciplined and relied on war paint to frighten his troops. Their horses were not used to riding in close ranks. He decided to use the battle formations he had developed to force the Tatar to ride close together and frighten the horses.

The Tatar charged. He laid his bow across his saddle horn and raised his hand to the signal corps who rode behind him. He had devised a system of signal flags to tell the men which of the formations--Chisel, Thorny Bush, Hammer, Lake Array--he wished the army to assume. He had no need to send messengers to his commanders with his orders. Messengers could be captured and give up his battle plans. The flags

146

allowed him to coordinate large numbers of troops across large distances.

He chose Chisel Array for the Army of the Center, going down the middle of the Tatar troops and splitting them in half. Thorny Bush for the wings. Lake Array for the retreat--wide and thin, when they would not be a target for the Tatar by that time would be scattered. White for advance, black for retreat, and combinations of colors for the various formation.

The flags went up and Mongol war ponies trotted out in a line a mile long. Genghis heard thunder and looked up. The weather would hold. The storm was far away, beyond the hills, and there was no wind.

The Tatar spurred their horses and galloped toward the enemy. The Mongol light cavalry fired, raining down volleys of arrows.

Genghis Khan rode at the head of the Army of the Center and Khasar rode beside him. He was destined to govern all people. He would be victorious.

Genghis gave the signal for the change of formation. The flags went up and the ten thousand troops divided.

Ahead, Genghis saw the Tatar chief riding a massive black horse, wearing a headdress of feathers. The chief had bear grease on his face and carried a huge war bow. "There he is," Genghis shouted.

Khasar was using his lighter bow. He changed and brought out his heavy bow, and the cypress arrows that were light in flight and shot great distances. "I've got him," he shouted into the din of the advancing cavalry.

Genghis held out his hand to halt his brother's fire. Khasar looked across at him. Genghis put his fist to his heart. He's mine, the gesture said.

Khasar held his fire. Genghis took aim. The first shot missed. He took aim again, picking off the man to the chief's right and to his left. One man fell backward and was trampled by a horse. Genghis lowered the great horn bow and notched an arrow. It flew straight and true.

The horse rolled over, but the Tatar was fast, rolling away to prevent himself from being crushed.

Genghis pulled on his reins. His horse slowed and he jumped down off his horse. Arrows whistled by his head. Next to him an arrow killed a man. In front of him an arrow killed a horse and a man staggered around the field.

In the midst of the chaos of the battle, Genghis strode forward pulling his knife out of its sheath. The chief had gotten to his feet but he was stunned from hitting the ground so hard. Genghis reached out and the world slowed down motions. He grabbed the Tatar and spun him around.

A savage with a face painted black, swollen red lips and huge teeth faced him. The man reached down for a knife in his boot. Genghis raised his arm high and watched the Tatar come up at him with the knife in his hand.

Genghis gauged the man's reflexes. The man crouched, waiting for an opening and lunged, coming at him, mean-looking. Genghis saw his opening. He grabbed the man by the neck. He pulled to the side, to snap the windpipe but the man had a neck like a bull and his neck did not break.

Genghis reached down and placed his iron grip on the chief's wrist. He pulled and twisted and heard the bones crack as he broke it. The man shouted in pain.

Genghis stepped back, to get the weight of his body behind his swing. He drew the knife through the air and with one swipe, slit the Tatar's throat, spit in his face, and flung the bleeding body to the ground.

Khasar slid out of his saddle and dragged Genghis away by the arm. He had slipped into the Slow Time of battle. Everything was silent in the world and then the sounds of the battle filled his ears and he came to himself and saw the battle going on all around him.

The world resumed its motion and he heard the clank of sword against shield, the shouting, scuffling, yelling and the death cries. He smelled blood and dust in the air.

An arrow came out of the air and struck the ground beside him. Another hit him, but it plunged into his leather armor. He yanked it free and pitched on the ground beside him. Bogorji rode up to see if the Khan was safe.

Genghis mounted his horse. He placed his boot in the stirrup and swung into the saddle. Khasar mounted up, and looked to see that his brother was safe. Genghis touched the brim of his war helmet. Then he rode into the fray. Khasar followed.

The signal corpsman found the Khan. He made a hand gesture. The black and white flags went up and Genghis and Khasar moved back from the forward advance, so Genghis could observe the the wings of his army to closing in the death grip.

The heavy cavalry rode through the ranks of the light cavalry; the light troops dropped back through the gaps in the line.

He heard the whinnying of horses, the pounding of Mongol swords on Tatar shields, the shouting of men, and the clashing of horses.

He saw Subudei take aim and bring down a man. Mukhali was in command of the advancing wing. Bogorji and Belgutei were riding with him.

The Tatar exhibited battle fatigue. One fell down off a horse. He was not mortally wounded but had an arrow sticking out of his side. He took his knife and slashed the saddle belt of Khasar's horse. Khasar fell but charged with his sword, slashing at the attacker's sword arm.

An officer came up with a mount for Khasar. The Tatar's horse reared up and tried to trample Khasar. Khasar managed his bow and shot the rearing horse.

Mukhali and Subudei outflanked the Tatar and surrounded them. The Tatar ranks were closed in the Mongol array, like game in the hunt. They were fighting so hard that they did not realize they were herded into a trap. Genghis and Khasar led the charge through the center. The circle closed, the Tatar chief shouted to his men to ride out of the closing circle. Some escaped. Others were defeated. The enemy who escaped ran for the hills.

The Tatar Army paused, gathered themselves together and counter-attacked.

Genghis raised his hand and the red and black signal flags went up. The Mongol cavalry advanced in the thorny bush formation, all troops firing from a bush array.

The Tatar had been masters of the steppe for so long that they faltered against the cavalry maneuvers born in the mind of Genghis Khan.

Each time the Mongols gained ground, the Tatar retreated. Each time the Tatar retreated, the Mongol cavalry wheeled and counter-attacked, pushing the Tatar back. The Mongol advance was relentless.

149

Finally, the Tatar could stand no more and broke ranks and fled. The Tatar lay in heaps on the battlefield, and so did many of their horses. At the edge of the field, the Mongol women who followed in wagons were already salvaging weapons and gold jewelry from the dead Tatar. The Mongol Army pursued them to the edge of the battlefield and began taking captives.

Once the battlefield was under Mongol control, Genghis ordered his generals to take control of the Tatar campground, tents, possessions, peoples, and herds.

Black with grime, the sweat pouring down his face, Genghis Khan raised the victory flags. Across the field, Khasar saw the flags and raised his flags and shouted to his men, his cry bouncing off the hills in the waning light of day.

Genghis dismounted and ordered a servant to bring him a cup of *koumiz*. He found a place where no blood had been spilled on the earth and removed his leather war helmet.

He poured the *koumiz* on the ground. He threw his helmet down. He saluted The Ancestors and thanked them for victory. He asked that the spirit of his father witness that he had been a dutiful son.

Khasar came and stood beside him, watching for enemy who might have been hiding in the hills, and who had sneaked up, wanting to kill them. Overhead the clouds rushed across the deepening violet of the sky.

The Khan called the Council of Generals to meet in his tent. He sent his men to Megujin's tent to claim the plunder, all the gold given to him by the Qin Emperor and all his possessions. The remaining Tatar could not live. He would wipe them from the face of the earth. He would show them no mercy.

Genghis inquired after the condition of officers and men and listened to Subudei and Mukhali's report on the cost of the victory, the numbers of killed and wounded.

Khasar had minor wounds. Subudei had a deep wound on his thigh and Mukhali had taken an arrow in shoulder. His armor had protected him. Jebe's fingers were bleeding because he had shot the huge double-faced horn bow so many times.

Genghis Khan's younger brother Otchigin wore armor with nails in it. He had killed twenty Tatar but had taken a lance in the side. Genghis knew that battle wounds could poison the blood. He did not want to lose his brother. He ordered the shaman to bring his herbs and poultices and tend to him.

He sent a messenger back to his ulus, to his camp in the Valley of Two Rivers, delivering news of the victory to Bortai.

He drank a cup of *koumiz* and wiped his hand across his mouth. "Kill every male higher than the hub of a wagon wheel. Keep the women, children and small boys. We need slaves. Let's divide them amongst ourselves. Let them be of some use to us." Then he went out to see to the horses. One of his commanders brought a small boy, the son of the chief. His name was Shiki Kutuku. "Keep him. He will live in the tent of my mother. She is alone. She will adopt him."

Genghis ordered Jebe to bring the cart-loads of plunder to his encampment where he personally saw to the division of spoils among the generals. His generals cast in their lot with him in the hopes of prospering and he gave them their share of the plunder.

Genghis rewarded his most trusted commanders and divided the booty among them. He gave them the task of dividing their shares among the junior commanders.

Jebe came to report that Daritai, Genghis Khan's uncle, and Khuchar, his cousin, had gone to the Tatar camp and were taking many things of value that by right belonged to Genghis Khan.

"They told me that they were your family and said you had exempted them from the rules," Jebe said.

Genghis whipped the words out. "Go back and tell them that I laid down rules for the division of spoils and my family is no exception to any rule of mine. If they violate my code, I will punish them as I punish anyone else. A thief is a thief. Take possession of the goods they have taken. Bring them before me at once."

Genghis ordered Mukhali to bring the chief Yeke Cherbi's daughter to his tent so that she could become his wife. "Have her arrayed in her finest clothes. The rest of you may divide the women among you." This was the ultimate act of revenge, to hold the daughter of his enemy in his arms.

Jebe dragged Daritai and Khuchar into Genghis Khan's presence. The Khan chastised them. "You breached my orders. You forfeit your share of the booty. You countermanded my orders to my men. Don't ever do it again!"

An uncle and a senior royal, Daritai protested. "You have no right to punish me in this manner." Two Keshig Guardsmen unsheathed their knives.

"Silence. I have given my orders," Genghis Khan commanded. Daritai stuttered and fell silent.

Then Genghis Khan retired to his tent. He enjoyed taking what belonged to the enemy, his possessions and his women.

Genghis Khan looked at the battlefield, littered with dead. He found a place where no blood had been spilled on the earth and removed his leather war helmet. He poured a cup of koumiz on the ground. He got down on his knees and asked that the The Ancestors witness that he had been a dutiful son. He bowed his head to the earth and gave thanks for victory. Khasar came and stood silently, watching for enemy who might be waiting to kill him.

Overhead the clouds rushed across the deepening violet of the sky. He had a messenger system of Far and Near Arrows. He sent one of the Far Arrows to inform Bortai of the victory.

Genghis called the Council of Generals to meet in his field tent. There were no luxuries. This was the way the soldiers lived in the field.

"Send Dodun Cherbi to the Tatar chief's tent to claim his plunder, the gold given to him by the Jin Emperor. Take all the valuables." Dodun Cherbi was the Master of Provisions.

"What is to be done with the survivors?" Subudei asked.

The generals discussed the matter. Bogorji asked, "Should he let the remaining Tatar live, take them as slaves, bring them back to camp?"

Khasar said. "They cannot be trusted. They are devious and knew no loyalty or gratitude."

Subudei agreed. "Show the Tatar prisoners no mercy. They killed our fathers and grandfathers." He drank another cup of *koumiz* and wiped his hand across his mouth. He spat.

Bogorji said, "Wipe them from the face of the earth. Make a lesson of them."

Genghis Khan spoke. "Kill every male higher than the hub of a wagon wheel. Keep the women, children and small boys. We need slaves. We'll divide them amongst ourselves. Let them be of some use to us. That one boy, the son of a nobleman, Shiki Kutuku, bring him. He will live in my mother's tent. Her tent is empty and he will be her adopted son."

"Where is the wife of the chief? Yeke Cherbi."

"She's a prisoner."

"Send her to my tent."

He asked after the condition of officers and listened to Subudei and Mukhali's report of the number of killed and wounded. Khasar was hit, an arrow in the back, but his armor protected him. Bogorji had minor wounds. Subudei had a deep wound on his thigh. Mukhali had taken an arrow in the arm. Jebe's fingers were bleeding from shooting the horn war-bow so many times. Genghis ordered a Night Guard to get the shaman to tend to Subudei. Untended, he might get blood poisoning. The shaman had herbs. He came and applied a poultice.

Genghis ordered Jebe to bring the cart-loads of plunder to his encampment where he saw to the division of spoils. He divided the plunder among the generals. His generals cast in their lot with him in the hopes of prospering. They divided their share among the junior commanders. They divided their share with the men.

If the younger officers and the commoners grew wealthy, Genghis Khan would have the undivided loyalty of the army. First Genghis rewarded his most trusted commanders.

While Genghis was dividing the Tatar possessions, Jebe came to report that Daritai, Genghis Khan's uncle and Khuchar, his cousin, had gone to the Tatar camp and had taken many things of value. By right, all of the plunder belonged to Genghis Khan.

"They said they were your family and were exempt from the law," Jebe said.

Genghis said. "I do not want my commanders to think that my family gets preferential treatment when it came to war. No one is exempt from my code. My relatives need to be taught a lesson as well. They will be punished like anyone else. Take everything from them and bring them before me at once." Jebe left the tent.

Genghis commanded Mukhali to bring Yeke Cherbi's daughter to his tent so that she could become his wife. "Have her arrayed in her finest clothes and bring her to my tent. The rest of you may divide the women among you."

He told Khasar, "There is no pleasure like holding the wives of your enemies in your arms, to hold the daughter of his enemy in your arms.

His relatives entered and were too unwise to show humility. "Daritai and Khuchar, you two breached my orders about taking spoils. Neither of you will receive a share of Tatar booty."

Daritai protested. He was an uncle and a senior royal and the young khan had no right to punish him in this manner.

"Silence," thundered Genghis Khan. "I have ordered."

Two Keshig Guardsmen unsheathed their knives. Daritai sat down.

Her name was Yesugan and she was tall and willowy. The daughter of the Tatar chief, she wore a long dress of orange silk brocade and a headdress of silver coins. She had put rouge on her cheeks. She wore embroidered slippers. He sent the servants away and told her that she did not have to be afraid, that he did not wish to harm her.

He said that her chiefs had done his people a great wrong and that he had avenged his ancestors. He would see to it that she had her own household and herds. All the while he spoke to her, she had tears running down her face for this was the man who had just murdered her father and had destroyed her people.

He told her to take off her clothes. She did as he asked. He told her to lie down on his bed of rough blankets and pillows. He took off his tunic and trousers and she saw his fine masculine physique. His men called him a Man of Iron. He had black and blue bruises all over his body.

She read his expression. He needed a woman. He took his time and then he pulled away from her.

He slept for a while then he took her again.

In the morning he had food brought. He told her that her tent would be in the woman's camp. That she would be provided for. That his principal wife was Bortai, and she was the manager of the women's camp. He said she had nothing to worry about.

She exhaled a breath. She had won his affection. She would live. He could have turned her over to a commoner or a general. He could cut off her head or give her to a slave.

"Did I please you?" she asked, forcing a smile.

"Yes," he said.

"Then I have something to ask of you. I have an older sister, Yesui. She is more beautiful than I am and would make a good wife."

"Why do you ask such a thing?"

"You have taken my father and brothers and uncles and cousins. She has no one. I do not want to leave her alone. She was married a short time ago and when the battle ended, her husband grabbed her and dragged her off, I don't know where they are, probably in the forest. If your soldiers find her, they will kill them both."

"My soldiers will find her. If I take her, her husband will die."

"I will not be alone in your camp if she comes."

One of his Guards brought Yesui to his tent. He said that the soldiers found a man in the forest fleeing. He said that he was the husband of the chief's daughter, Yesui. He had run away because the soldiers took his wife away. The husband still loved his wife. The wife belonged to the Khan. The husband was no more.

She came to the Khan's tent. Her hair was bedraggled and her clothes were torn and tattered, but she was beautiful. Genghis Khan looked her over. "Your sister has made a request of me. I will take you for a wife," he said.

"You will have her own tent. Make sure there is peace between you. I do not tolerate trouble among the women in my camp."

Then Genghis Khan consummated the union with the Tatar chief's second daughter.

Genghis Khan's Camp, 1201

One evening while Genghis Khan took his ease, spending an evening in Bortai's tent enjoying her company, Bogorji tapped his sword twice against the tent-post.

"Sorry to interrupt you, sir. It's important."

"Enter," said the Khan.

Bogorji said, "Riders came to camp, commoners wearing hats with ear flaps and leather armor. They threw down their weapons and walked between the cauldrons of fire. They asked to see you, Khan. They said that they escaped Jamuga's confederacy in Alkhui Springs. They bring news that Jamuga formed a coalition against him

"You spread the word that you would offer riches and a place in the nobility to anyone who brought information. They took you up on your offer. They're here. They want to see you. They want to deliver the message to you, for your ears>"

Genghis Khan looked at Bortai. She knew that where war was concerned, she completely disappeared from his thoughts. "It's all right," she said. "I understand. Go. Really, don't worry."

"Bring the men to my campaign tent. Summon the generals."

Genghis pulled on his riding trousers and tunic and stepped into his boots. Wrapping a scarf around his mouth, he opened the tent-door. Outside was a sandstorm. He armed himself with dagger and sword, wrapped a scarf around his mouth and nose and went out into the sandstorm. He raised his arm against the driving wind. Grains of sand stung his face. Leaning hard into the wind, he pushed his way toward the tent in the men's camp, cursing the weather.

Subudei and Mukhali were waiting for him in his tent. Bogorji brought the commoners, the two men who had come from Jamuga's camp.

Genghis Khan looked at them. "Is this a trick? A trap of some kind? Has Jamuga sent you here?"

The first one, named Kenzei, said, "No, khan. I swear it. If I'm lying, may lightning strike me dead."

Genghis said, "Then, speak."

"We have risked our lives to come to you. Will you give us a reward?" Subudei put his hand on the hilt of his sword.

"You'll be well compensated," said Genghis.

"I bring a warning. Jamuga has gathered sixty thousand troops, your enemies, and they have made camp with him. They elected him to be their ruler and gave him the title *Gur Khan,* meaning *Supreme Khan.*"

Khasar said, "We had not realized that Jamuga put together an army of that size."

Genghis lifted his hand for silence. "Continue," said the Khan.

"He declared his intention to defeat you and to rule the whole of the steppes by himself."

The second man spoke up. "He's proud of the men who joined him. He has your enemies."

"Who exactly joined him?" Genghis asked.

The Oirad, a forest tribe, had come down from the north.

The Tatar had come from their lands in the east. Now that the Chinese Emperor had abandoned them, they had nowhere else to turn.

Buyuruk Khan was a white shaman and ruler of the mountain-dwelling Naiman, whose lands extended from the Altai Mountains in western Mongolia north to the Irtysh River.

Buyuruk and his brother, the Tai-yang, had divided Naiman lands when the old Naiman king died. Buyuruk had taken the slopes of the Altai Range while the Tai-yang ruled the plains. Naiman grazing grounds, the most extensive in the steppe lands, lay to the southwest of Mongol-Kereyid territory,

The Naiman lands were an important prize. They occupied an important strategic position in the steppes. To the west, Naiman pastures bordered on Uighur lands—these were the oasis cities on the Silk Road. Beyond them was the kingdom of Black Cathay. This meant the Naiman controlled trade and riches flowed into the treasury.

The Taijyuds had joined because they knew that Genghis Khan would eventually ride against them.

A small band of Mergid joined him--these were the chiefs Togtoa, Darmala and Dayir Usun, his old enemies. They came from the northwest of Mongol territory, the woods surrounding Lake Baikal.

The forces were led by four generals--Aguchu of the Taijyud; Buyuruk, of the Naiman; Khudu of the Mergid and Khudukhu of the Oirad.

The forces that Jamuga commanded were as numerous as the combined Mongol and Kereyid armies.

When the weather broke, Jamuga planned to ride from Alkhui Springs and attack Genghis Khan.

"Your information is valuable. I am a man of my word. I invite you to camp with me. I will give you each a tent and horses from the best of my herds. Belgutei, give them uniforms and weapons. There is a reward in silver."

They thanked the khan and struck their chests with their fists. They followed Belgutei.

Genghis spoke with the generals. "I expected that my enemies would come against me. Jamuga wants a showdown. Him or me. Let's not take any chances. If he wins, he'll become the Khan of the steppes. The storm won't last more than a day. Jamuga's forces are too numerous for us to fight alone. Send word to the Ong Khan. Tell him the size of the forces arrayed against me. Tell him to come with an army."

Mukhali rose to take his leave. "If you win this battle, my khan, *you* have only the Tai-Yang to defeat and *you* will be ruler of Mongolia. I, for one, will be glad to see it. I predicted it long ago." He smiled.

"Mukhali, go. The rest of you, prepare the army for war. Subudei, Mukhali, you will lead the Junghar, the Army of the East. Subudei, you will lead the West Wing, the Baraunghar. I will lead the Khol, the Imperial Horde. Khasar will ride with me. Jelme will take the Rear Guard. If the army must wheel about, he will lead the advance forces." They saluted and left and the Supreme Khan was alone in his tent.

Genghis Khan decided to visit Tab Tengri, the white shaman whom he admired as a Speaker to Heaven. The Khan consulted the shaman on many occasions. The young Khan was undertaking great ventures and he needed counsel. Tab Tengri was the only man he had ever thought might possess an intelligence superior to his own. The man was his junior by six years.

Genghis Khan discussed with his wife and his mother when they spent time together that Tab was a shaman of great power, learned in

159

healing, the consulting of oracles and trance journeys. "You saw the way he conducted the horse ceremony when Yesugei died," he said. This was the most sacred rite of the tribes performed for the funeral of a khan. The shaman had cut a mare and a stallion in two, roasted the meat and hung the horse skins from tall poles around the burial ground.

Khasar was skeptical of the man's influence and let his brother know it. Khasar said the shaman was trying to take Khasar's place as the closest advisor to the Khan. "Why?" Genghis Khan asked.

"I'm in his way," said Khasar. "The man who is an obstacle feels the manipulation of the usurper. He is no good."

But Genghis Khan scoffed at his brother. Genghis Khan wanted to know the will of Heaven.

The Khan rode with two guards through the. The shaman pitched his tent in the birch woods of the foothills. The sandstorm had blown itself out. The wind had died. Genghis left his guards outside and went in.

The tent-walls were painted with images of rainbows, snakes and ladders, symbols of the journey of climbing to heaven. Piles of objects lay on the floor, animal bone, dried plants, bark, skeletons and skins of animals.

Tab Tengri sat in front of the fire, shaking a rattle and chanting in a voice which sounded as though it emanated from the bowels of the earth. He wore a headdress of deer antler and a tunic made of deerskin with branches and bark and beads sewn on it. He had paint on his face, stripes of blue. He threw a yellow powder into the flames. Brightly colored sparks flew into the air.

Tab looked up, his drug-glazed eyes seeming to penetrate Genghis' soul. "I was waiting for you, Genghis Khan I've taken the sacred drug. The mushroom, the *amanita.*, I made the Voyage to Heaven to consult the spirits of The Ancestors,". said Tab Tengri. "What counsel may I give you?"

"My *anda*, Jamuga, rides this way with an army. I have sent for the Ong Khan. I plan to go to war against Jamuga."

"My vision is filled with rainbows, a good omen for you."

"The problem is the old vows you took as a sworn brother. He had broken the bond."

"My mother and Bortai looked into Jamuga's heart long ago. Khasar never trusted him either. I thought that they were jealous. I did not take their counsel."

"He is an enemy now. Free yourself of the old bond and become a true genius on the battlefield."

He began cleaning the mushrooms of their stems. These are from a forest tribe in Sibir the Land of Snows, where the people herd the sacred reindeer. He muttered an incantation over a small cauldron. He threw herbs into the water, then the mushrooms. He stirred the pot.: He poured the soup into a bowl and offered it to the Khan,

"Soup of *amanita muscaria.*"

Twenty minutes passed. Then a rainbow of colors filled the Genghis' vision, colored the shaman's face and the walls of the tent. Tab Tengri acted as if he were holding the reins of a horse and galloped around the tent. He described his journey down to the center of the earth. He made animal noises to speak with the totem animals, the wolf, the horse, the yak. Then the shaman said he was making the celestial voyage. He was climbing among clouds and rainbows.

Genghis saw himself riding a horse as white as the mountain peaks, into the Eternal Blue Sky. He rode all over the sky and conversed with the Ancestors. He did not know how long the vision lasted. He fell into a deep sleep.

He awoke in the morning with Tab Tengri sitting beside him watching him. The hearth fire had burned out and the coals were cold.

"The Ancestors said my war was just. I will not be punished for fighting my *anda.*"

" Whatever happens is the will of the Eternal Blue Sky. Make the libations before the battle."

"I will. I always do."

"You are Beloved of Heaven. It is your destiny to rule all peoples. Whatever happens is the will of the Eternal Blue Sky.

"From this time forward, you ride white horses. You drink *koumiz* made from the milk of snow-white mares. Go to your tent, take the gifts which he gave you when you declared yourselves brothers and burn them. Throw this powder into the fire. When you win this war, I will receive the post of chief priest. I will be your closest advisor. Closer than your blood. Now leave my tent."

The request unsettled Genghis. What did the shaman want? Prestige and wealth for many would come to consult him and bring him gifts.

Genghis went to find Khasar. When he found him, he looked him in the eye and admitted that Khasar's judgment about Jamuga had been correct. That was enough for Khasar.

"The Tatar who remain know we have the backing of the Jin Emperor. The Naiman joined him because they know that once we conquer the rest of the Tatar, once we dominate the east, we will ride against the West. The Mergid, all that is left of them, and the Oirad, are forest people, are small in number. The Taijyud have no choice. They are alone."

He paused and sighed. "It seems so long ago that we all skated on the frozen ice of the Onon. So long ago."

"When we were poor. And now, thanks to you, we are rich again. Don't worry about him, brother. We will put an end to the troubles he has caused us. I will ride beside you."

Genghis Khan's voice caught. "I told you that no *anda* would ever come between us. You always have been and always will be my right hand."

Khasar said, "If you win, you will be Lord of all Mongolia."

"Togril is Lord of the Steppes and I am his vassal. I owe him a debt of gratitude. I am second-in-command. When Togril dies, everything will change. I will deal with the Senggum. We will have to fight Jamuga sooner or later. Now is the time, when we can command the Ong Khan's army. We will create a Mongol-Kereyid empire beyond the wall of the Chinese."

Khasar nodded. "I will give the commanders your orders."

Several days later, the Ong Khan arrived with his army and pitched camp.

Genghis Khan left his bodyguards outside and entered the tent of the Ong Khan. By the light of the hearth-fire, the man who was like a second father to him was examining his bows and arrows. Even on campaign, he liked luxury. His bedclothes were of the finest silk, his bedding of down and woven cotton. The Ong Khan's hair was white and his movements were slow.

He welcomed Togril and they agreed on the route, down the Kerulen River. The Golden Emperor would not realize what was happening until it was too late. The two khans bid each other goodnight.

Koyitan

Genghis Khan went to war with his sworn brother, the companion of his youth/ Genghis bid farewell to his youth. His sworn brother had become his rival.

The combined Mongol-Kereyid army faced Jamuga's confederation by afternoon. Their standards were flying and their war drums pounded. Genghis Khan estimated Jamuga's forces at six *tumens*, sixty thousand men. General Subudei, his chief strategist, agreed with the count. Subudei was a blacksmith's son, a commoner, who had risen up through the ranks to be his top general, a man with a mind for strategy in war that matched his own talent.

Khasar rode with Genghis at the head of the Army of the Center. The Armies of the Left and Right formed a line a mile long. "They outnumber us," Genghis said to Khasar.

Khasar said, "He'll see the Ong Khan's battle standard. We have a disciplined fighting force. He has an unproved coalition. He will know that someone from his own camp betrayed him."

In the morning, Genghis Khan gave the order for the light cavalry of the Mongol Army to rain down arrows on Jamuga's forward troops. Jamuga had put infantry in front and the arrows killed masses of troops.

"That is his first error," Genghis Khan said to General Mukhali.

The air grew black with whistling arrows. The arrows tipped with peach bark poison and were dead in minutes, turning blue.

Signal flags appeared at the commands of the generals. The light cavalry dropped back, riding in tight ranks as the horses of the heavy cavalry rode through.

The banging of the war drums never ceased and filled the plain and the cliffs, echoing up to heaven. Genghis' commanders were visible in the field--Belgutei, Subudei, Mukhali, Jelme, Bogorji. The two of them remained close to one another on the field, both of them drawing their horn bows. The armies charged one another like waves, forming, breaking, reforming, breaking again.

Genghis looked up to the hill where he had posted Mongol sentries. They raised signal flags to inform him. No reinforcements were on the way to aid Jamuga's confederation.

A black and white flag announced that Jamuga was not moving the wings of his army into position. At the Khan's signal, red flags were lifted, a signal to his commanders for them to mount a flanking movement, encircling the enemy troops.

Jamuga saw the encirclement. It meant the end for they would be surrounded. "Send for the shamans," Jamuga said.

Buyuruk Khan and Khudukha, went to a place at the rear of the fighting and made a sacred circle. They used river rock and river water and rubbed the stones. They conjured a storm. On a cliff, a tornado appeared, a black funnel sliding down to the battlefield.

Genghis Khan was in the thick of battle when he saw the storm bearing down on his army. Thunder rumbled and lightning bolts shot out of the sky. He wheeled around on his white horse and rode to a place behind the fray and snatched his helmet off his head. He bowed down and held his fist over his heart and prayed to the Eternal Blue Sky. He asked to be given victory this day as a sign. He looked skyward.

The winds changed course and the funnel changed direction and crashed through Jamuga's forces. It wreaked havoc in his army. It picked up horses and riders and flung them through the air. The flanks of the army broke, turned and galloped from the field in terror. Men were swept into ravines shouting, "The Blue Sky has turned against us!"

The army dispersed. Buyuruk Khan took his troops and rode away, to the West, to his lands to the Altai Mountains. Khudukha abandoned Jamuga in the field and took his clans and rode north to the Selengge. Aguchu led his Taijyuds back to the Onon River. In a blind rage, Jamuga rode back from the battle to the camp where his confederacy had proclaimed him Gur-khan and pillaged and robbed everything they had left behind. Then he took his men and rode down the Ergune River where he and the Jajirats had made their camp.

The tornado followed the retreat. It blew for hours, ravaging the countryside. Jamuga's confederation split forces. At last, the storm whirled up into the mountains where it spent itself.

The Ong Khan saw the storm dissipate. He pursued Jamuga down the Ergune River. Meanwhile Genghis Khan set out after the Taijyud.

He delivered the justice the Taijyuds so richly deserved.

When Aguchu, the leader of Taijyud, reached their camp and ordered his troops to make a last stand against the Mongols.

The Mongols felt the protection of the Eternal Blue Sky and they fought long and hard. Night fell and both armies, exhausted, made camp on the battlefield so that they could fight again at dawn. Enemies were camped so close together they slept almost side by side.

After the battle, Khasar could not find Genghis Khan anywhere in the camp. Khasar rode across the field looking for his brother but night was falling. He could hardly see. He got off his horse and led it as he walked over the battlefield.

Some of the women who followed the army searched the bodies of fallen enemy looking for items of value. Others searched for their own troops gathering up weapons and arrows.

Genghis Khan was lying on the ground. He had been hit in the neck by an arrow. His life blood was running out of him. He had begun to see the white lights and he was hallucinating which meant that he was dying. He heard someone calling his name.

Jelme was walking through the battlefield looking for his khan in the dying light. He found the Khan lying in a pool of blood, a piece of arrow protruding from his neck. His eyes were clouded over.

Jelme took hold of the arrow and gently removed it. The arrow came out in one piece. Jelme sucked the wound and spit out the blood.

Genghis Khan saw his father beckoning to him, floating above the sacred mountain. Yesugei urged his son to return to his body. It was not his time to join The Ancestors.

Jelme's mouth and chin were red from blood and he felt sick.

Suddenly, Genghis Khan opened his eyes and spoke. "I'm thirsty. Give me something to drink."

Jelme laid his khan's head on the ground and covered him with a saddle blanket. He went to the enemy camp wearing nothing but his loincloth. He stepped over the bodies of sleeping soldiers, searching for a flask of water or mare's milk. They had freed the mares from their carts and had whipped them until they ran away. This was so that if their

166

enemies took the camp, they would not find food. In an abandoned wagon, he found a bucket of churned curds. He made his way back to where Genghis Khan lay, weak but alive.

He put the bucket of curds down and went to find a stream so that he could mix the curds with water. He found a rivulet and made a liquid that the wounded khan could swallow them. He returned to Genghis Khan's side, picked up his head and held the cup to his lips. The Khan drained the cup and asked for another. Jelme gave him another and then another. Genghis had lost so much blood that he was weak.

"My strength is returning," Genghis said. He took hold of Jelme's arm and sat up. "The mists have cleared from my eyes."

It was dawn. The sun was rising. Mongol-Kereyid soldiers were mounting up and moving into the Taijyud camp.

Genghis Khan looked around him and saw blood on the ground and asked what it was. Jelme told him that he had spit it from the wound. The sight of his own blood stunned him.

"Why didn't you spit further away?" he demanded.

"I was afraid to leave you because your life was hanging by a thread. I couldn't swallow any more blood."

"I remember you taking off your clothes and running away to the enemy camp. Why did you leave me? If they had captured you, would you have given me up to them to save yourself?"

" I took off my clothes because I had to get you something to drink, I was gone only for a short time. If you thought I abandoned you, forgive me."

"No. No. You saved me. I will not forget the service you performed for me."

"Then grant that I will always ride at your side, Khan."

He heard a woman's voice calling "Genghis Khan! Genghis Khan!" and saw her running across the battlefield.

"A woman calling my name? Who is it?"

A woman broke out of her hiding place and threw herself on her knees. "I am Sorkhen Shira's daughter, Khadagan. Do you remember me?" She lifted up her face.

The Khan recognized the woman who was kind to him when his neck was in the cangue and took it off in secret. "I remember you. You lied to the soldiers for me when Targutai took me prisoner. You gave me warm milk to drink and massaged my sore wrists."

"Yes. Yes. That's me. Your soldiers have captured my husband. They're going to kill him. Please, spare him. I ask for your mercy."

Jelme helped him mount a horse and he rode to the Taijyud camp. He arrived too late. His soldiers had already killed her husband. The woman was torn apart by grief.

"Don't worry," he said. "Nothing can make up for this, but you have my protection."

Genghis Khan ordered his soldiers to take spoils from the Taijyud brothers, all that they had of value: silver, carpets, pottery, weapons, and silks. Genghis claimed their possessions. He gave Khasar permission to execute the brothers, sons and grandsons for the crime of disloyalty. He ordered his soldiers to pitch camp and commanded the army cooks to prepare a victory feast.

He sat with the daughter Khadagan, fed her choice bits from his knife and offered her a place in his camp. His guards brought her father, Sorkhen Shira, the *koumiz*-maker who had saved him from execution. With tears streaming down her face, Khadagan ran to embrace her father.

"Welcome, Sorkhen," said Genghis Khan. "I will reward you and your sons for taking the wooden cangue off my neck and helping me to escape. You must have heard of my victories. You know I reward loyalty. Why has it taken such a long time to leave the brothers and join me?"

Sorkhen spoke in respectful tones. "Forgive me, Khan. I was afraid. I am a poor man and would not have been able to take my family with me. I was afraid the Taijyud would put out the light of my hearth and that my name would cease to be. Many times, I had to hold back from doing what my heart wanted to do. So I waited until the time was right. When I heard you had defeated them, I came. I hope you remember the services I rendered to you."

"I respect a man who protects his family. You are welcome here. I will find your daughter a Mongol nobleman for a husband that she may give you more grandchildren for your tent."

Sorkhen Shira ate like a starving man, for he had been hiding a day and a night and had not had food.

"Another man came forward. "I shot the arrow that wounded you. I took aim from the mountainside. I want to join you." He seemed ready to meet his fate. "If you take my life, I will fertilize a plot of land the size of man. Let me live and I'll serve you."

He waited for an answer.

Genghis Khan studied the man "You have nerve. You come to my camp, admit that you killed me and have the courage to face me. I *will* spare your life for I would have an army made of men like you. What is your name?"

The man told him. He had camped with the Taijyud.

"From now on, your name is Jebe. It means 'the Arrow' in commemoration of your deed. From this day forward, aim your arrows against my enemies. Join the feast, Jebe One of your arrows pierced the spine of my warhorse. You killed a valuable animal. I will miss that horse. He was a noble animal."

"I will find you a herd of horses to replace him." And he did. A few years later, Jebe was ordered to clean up the territory where an old enemy of Genghis Khan was closing down the bazaars and persecuting Muslims. Religious toleration was a hallmark of the Khan's empire, so Jebe hunted him down and executed him. Then he rounded up a herd of the Horse of Heaven, the Akhal-Teke, prized by the Chinese emperors, with shining golden coats.

The elder Taijyud brother Targutai escaped to the forest, but he was found by one of his servants, Old Man Shirgu and his two sons. The old man contemplated bringing Targutai to the khan in the hope of gaining a reward, being made a nobleman and having a herd of his own.

The old man decided against that course of action because Targutai weighed three hundred pounds and could not mount a horse even with help. They loaded him into a black ox-cart. They set out for the Mongol camp, but Targutai's sons saw their father in the cart and came to rescue him.

The Old Man held his knife at Targutai's through and sat on his chest. "Call them off or I will slit your throat."

169

"Don't come for me. Don't worry. If he takes me to Genghis Khan. The khan will not execute me. When he was a boy, I taught him to ride. I taught him to train a colt. I hear he has acquired wisdom with his years. He won't kill me."

The sons turned away. Mongol soldiers took the survivors as prisoners and slaves.

Driving the ox-drawn cart to the Mongol camp, the old man began to have second thoughts. He said to his sons, "We've laid hands on our khan. When we get to the Mongol camp, Genghis Khan might punish us for this is a breach of tradition."

They released Targutai close to the Mongol camp where scouts would find him, then went on foot.

They went to the tent of the Khan. "Why have you come?" he asked them. "How do I know that you are not assassins sent by Targutai?".

They told him that they had captured Targutai but let him go.

Genghis called for silence. "If you had come into my camp with your khan as your captive, I would have killed you and all your children. Since you did your duty, I will accept you and let you camp among my people. Let it be known among those who follow me that I have shown mercy to those who are loyal."

The old man went down on his knees and knocked his head to the floor. The Khan ordered Dodai Cherbi to give him lodging.

Genghis Khan looked around him at the smoking ruin of the Taijyud camp. The next morning, the Mongols struck camp and rode back to their valley.

This was the summary of events that followed in Chancellor Yeh-lu's history.

During the next few months, many of the Kereyid clans came to join Genghis Khan because the Ong Khan had fallen on hard times. He lost his position as the most powerful man in the steppes through his own deeds. He opened the way for Genghis Khan.

There was a family dispute. Togril did not even have time to request an alliance from Genghis Khan. He was forced to flee west, past Naiman country. He spent time in the oasis cities of the Tarim Basin where the Uighurs, Christians like his own people. lived and prospered. He travelled further west and at last sought refuge in the Muslim lands west of the Chui River with the Khan of Khara Khitai.

Togril was arrogant and difficult to get along with, and soon he quarreled with the leaders. He left and returned east, travelling through the Uighur lands and the Tangut kingdom until finally, in greatly reduced circumstances, with nothing of his former wealth remaining, he entered the region of Lake Gusegur. He was so poor that he was living off the milk of five goats and the blood he could prick out of a stringy camel. The once mighty Khan of the Kereyid now had only a blind yellow horse to ride.

When Genghis Khan heard of the fate of his former protector, he remembered the bitterness of his own years of privation and took pity on him. Genghis ordered two of his riders to find Togril and bring him back to the Mongol camp. Genghis announced to the people of his camp that Togril would come to live among them.

*"He will come to us weary and hungry and we will provide for him," the khan said. He was in his early thirties at this time, a man and he believed in repaying his obligations even when Togril had not done the same. "I will honor my father's **anda** bond as Togril did when I was so sorely in need."*

That year, Genghis used his tithe to provide for Togril in a princely manner. Genghis also took an army into the field and waged a war to gather the Kereyid people together for Togril.

After that, Mongol and Kereyid noblemen hunted together in a Grand Hunt and Genghis gave Togril the first shot and the best meat. When winter came, Mongols and Kereyid migrated together.

Togril returned to his camp near the Tola River. He was once again master of his own lands but his status on the steppe would never be the same again. Togril had proved himself a weak and vacillating ruler. Genghis knew he could never place his future in the hands of one so unreliable. The Senggum was no better.

Khasar advised his brother that it was time to make a move. Khasar said, "It is not easy to decide to put Togril aside. Ask yourself this. Who would be the better Supreme Khan? Togril or yourself?"

Genghis replied, "The choice is clear."

Khasar said, "I would say that after he lost his kingdom, and you restored it, you are no longer a vassal. In all ways, you are his equal. You cannot afford to put the fate of our people in his hands. His judgment is flawed. He is weak, and his son is no leader for us."

"You're right," said Genghis Khan. "We must wait on the timing. For us to take over, the clans must follow. They will follow if they see just cause."

The Ong Khan's Camp, 1203

The Ong Khan gave a feast in Genghis Khan's honor. Genghis Khan brought Khasar and some generals to the feast, a small contingent.

Togril made toasts acknowledging Genghis Khan's prosperity and the size of his following. He acknowledged Genghis Khan's position as a vassal of the Jin Emperor. Gurin, a Kereyid commander, sat at Ong Khan's left. Genghis Khan sat at his right.

Genghis Khan was the most powerful man in Mongolia, but the Ong Khan liked to play the role of the grand old royal of the steppes.

Togril may have suffered adversity, his wealth may have diminished, but he had always loved loved luxury and he still loved it. He sat on a throne of solid silver chased with scenes of the hunt.

Commanders from both armies sat at the table. Togril toasted Genghis Khan and praised their connection through the generations and through many campaigns.

The Kereyid commanders had served in battle with him. They were impressed by the organization and equipment of Genghis Khan's troops, the performance of his cavalry and the innovations of his battle tactics. To a man, they liked serving under his command.

The Ong Khan raised his glass and declared he and Genghis Khan were father and son.

The Senggum sat several places away from his father, with the Kereyid commanders. He had been wounded in battle and had a bandage on the side of his face. When the wound healed, the shaman said, the Senggum would have a scar. His senior wife and children and they had been taken captive. The Senggum was in a bad mood, his temper spoiled even further than was usual the case. His rival's status had increased. His own had decreased. He was spoiling for a fight. The way he saw it, he had to protect what was his. Who would follow his father was the question.

"Let's make a solemn pledge," Togril declared: "When we do battle with an enemy, our armies will ride together. When we hunt wild game, we will have joint hunts. If anyone is jealous of this bond, like a snake with sharp teeth provoking us to fight one another, we will not be swayed by slander. We will never allow anyone to come between us. We will only believe what comes from the other man's mouth."

Togril emptied his cup. The Senggum, stony-faced, did not drink the toast. People were staring at him. His senile old father had just pledged the Kereyid kingdom to this man of a lesser tribe. By the time Togril died, Genghis Khan would have consolidated power over Mongolia and would be too powerful to defeat.

"Let's seal the bond," Genghis said. "Let us unite our houses. This is the way of khans. My eldest son, Jochi, is ready to marry." Jochi stood. "He is my first-born, a fine young man. Give him your daughter, Chagur Beki, in marriage. In exchange, I'll give my eldest daughter in marriage to Nilkha's son."

The Senggum spit out a mouthful of wine. His face reddened. "We marry into your house? Are you mad? My sister won't be treated as a Kereyid princess living in a Christian tent. If she marries one of your offspring, she'll be a slave for a Mongol brute who worships the Eternal Blue Sky. She'll have to sit at the back of the tent and wait for her lord to finish eating before she is offered a bite. We don't treat our women the way you do. I will die before I see my sister married to your son."

A hush fell over the table. Genghis Khan waited for Togril to reprimand the Senggum, but Togril said nothing.

He left the tent. Khasar and Bogorji followed. "My relationship with Togril is done, turned to ashes. We leave these lands. We strike camp."

The time had come to go against the man who had been his lord. He rode back to his own pastures.

174

Time passed and Genghis Khan received a message from the Ong Khan saying that he had changed his mind and had decided it would be good to arrange a marriage between the two houses. Genghis Khan still wanted to make an alliance and began making preparations to go to Kereyid country for the betrothal."

His father left Togril as a legacy and Temujin wanted a connection to his father. His mother persuaded him not to go. She didn't trust Togril. She said that when he arrived for the feast, Togril could take him prisoner, execute him and take over his army."

"Don't forget, son, I knew Togril in the old days when your father was still alive. He has a weak nature." Khasar agreed with his mother.

Genghis Khan sent word to Ong Khan that his horses were too thin to make the journey. He said that he would wait until the end of summer when his horses had fattened. The betrothal feast should be held in the autumn.

When Ong Khan took counsel with Jamuga, the younger man said that his sworn brother had seen through the trap.

Then two commoners arrived at Genghis Khan's camp after riding all day and all night for three days. They refused to divulge their message to anyone but Genghis Khan. When ushered into his tent, the one named Badai expelled his breath, touched his forehead to the earth and rocked back on his heels, wiping a forearm over his grimy face. Badai's words came tumbling out. "Sir, I overheard the lords making a plot against you. When dawn breaks, the Kereyid Army has orders to ride against you. It will take them a week or more to get here. Make haste to defend yourself or they will catch you unaware."

"How do you know this," the Khan asked.

Badai replied, "I am a servant in the tent of Altan Khan's younger brother." These were the royals who had left Genghis Khan's camp.

"I was working in the tent and Yeke was telling his wife about the plan. She is a mean-tempered woman and hissed at him to be quiet in case someone overheard them and went to warn you.

"When his son came into the tent, Yeke told him the plan. I heard Yeke tell Narin to prepare for war. The Kereyid will ride at dawn, Khan.

175

They mean to take you by surprise and take you prisoner. We rode all night to warn you. You still have time to escape."

Badai repeated the news that had circulated in the Kereyid camp. "Jamuga met with the Senggum and the royals in the Desert of Weariness and convinced them that they had to attack you. The Senggum asked for the Ong Khan's permission. Some of the senior Kereyid officers spoke for you and against Jamuga and the Senggum, but Togril Khan listened to his son and gave the orders."

Genghis told the two commoners. "If what you tell me is true, I will reward you. If you're lying to me, you will both die."

He called his generals and repeated the story. "I know the mind of my enemies. They fear my power, so they think they must strike before I am too powerful. Jamuga resented my victory over the Tatar. He resented the royals electing me Khan. He chastised them for not considering him. He has wooed them to his cause at last.

"Nilkha wants war in the west and he is afraid that I will inherit his father's kingdom. Jamuga thinks he can rule Nilkha and Nilkha thinks he can rule Jamuga. Both are using their alliance as the last chance either one of them will have to rule the steppes.

A Guardsman stood at the door. Genghis issued his command. "I'm ordering a retreat. We will break camp immediately. We will travel east to Tatar country. Give orders for the clans to take nothing that will slow us down." The Guard left and within minutes the din of the breaking of camp and the rounding up of enough herds for food broke apart the quiet of the night.

Within hours the forced ride began, a train of thousands of riders followed by household wagons. Genghis Khan chose his battleground. It was a place where he had fought a battle and knew the terrain.

The Mongol Army rode all night. Morning came and at nightfall of the following day, he ordered his commanders to see that the people let the horses drink water. He ordered the people to take several hours, get down from their wagons, stretch their legs and eat. Four hours later, he gave orders to resume the retreat.

By noon of the third day, they had gained enough ground to stop and rest again. By the end of the week, they had used the dried provisions.

The commanders came to him and asked permission to hunt. Genghis refused.

The men opened veins in the necks of their ponies and drank the blood. Ir was their only source of nourishment. A week later they arrived at the extreme boundary of the lands Genghis Khan had taken from the Tatar. This was the basin of the swift-running Khalka River at the foot of the Khingan Mountains.

Genghis reached the place where the Khingan Range began. Thick forests covered the foothills leading into the high mountains. The Supreme Khan took his people through the pass and when he reached the valley, gave orders to halt the retreat and set up camp. He sent for Jelme and gave him orders to hold the pass to the valley with a Rear Guard of 1,000 crack archers.

In this country, where the Gobi Desert meets the marshlands, the grass is sparse and the grazing, difficult. The only water was muddy and had a foul odor.

Servants of the Mongol chief Aljigidai were out on the steppes tending herds when they saw a great cloud of dust rising. They went and looked and saw the mighty Kereyid Army riding in battle formation with their battle standards flying. They were riding toward a place called Red Willows. They went to see what was causing the dust clouds and looked over the ridge. Below them was the Kereyid Army, riding in battle formation with their battle standards flying.

Aljigidai grabbed a horse and rode to Genghis Khan's camp. Khasar, He was taking council with his generals, discussing the condition of the army. Aljigidai told Genghis Khan, "The Kereyid Army has reached Red Willows and is riding in battle formation.

The man left and Genghis Khan told his Council of Generals, "We have come to the end of the retreat. Here is my battle plan. It is a time-honored tactic of nomad warfare. The army will wheel around and counterattack. Raise the standards, the signal corps will take its place beside me. To victory,"

The commanders left. Messengers carrying Jamuga's standard arrived. Guards took their weapons and escorted them to Genghis Khan's tent. They delivered Jamuga's message.

The Ong Khan is old and his heart is not in the fight. The Senggum envies you and is a poor soldier.

The Supreme Khan glared out from under his war helmet. "Is that all? I have no secrets from General Mukhali. Speak."

"Jamuga Khan instructed me to tell you the Kereyid order of battle." This duplicity surprised Genghis Khan. "Then tell me."

The man recited the battle order, as though he had repeated it to himself a hundred times. "Jirjins in the front lines lead by Khadagh. Tubegen behind them, fierce fighters, ten thousand. Donghkayid clans behind them, ten thousand fierce fighters. Imperial Bodyguards behind them, one thousand troops led by Khori Shimesun. Behind them, the Army of the Center."

Mukhali helped the Khan into his armor and buckled it. Genghis picked up his wrist guards. He thanked the man and ordered two Guards to take him into custody. "I'll deal with you later."

One Guardsman remained behind awaiting orders. Genghis said, "Tell the generals and Jurchedei and Khuyildar to come to my tent. And Officer? I know this is your first battle under me. If you serve me well, when you are ready, I will give you a command."

"Thank you, sir," said the man and left.

Mukhali said, "Jamuga has the loyalty of a flag fluttering in the wind. He is not sure of Ong Khan's victory. He thinks you might win. He thinks you owe him for the information. He'll want to share power with you."

Genghis Khan handed him a quiver. "It's too late for that."

Jurchedei, the commander of the Urughuds, arrived with Khuyildar behind him.

The generals entered. Genghis Khan gave his battle order. "Your Urughud and the Manghud will form the forward ranks. They're my fiercest fighters. They'll soften up the Kereyid front line."

"What do you say, Uncle Jurchedei?" Genghis Khan said. "Will you lead the first charge for me? Kereyid forces outnumber us, so you'll have your work cut out for you."

Jurchedei struck his breast. "I will lead, Khan."

Khuyildar stepped forward: "Sir, I will lead the first charge for you."

Jurchedei laughed and said, "There's enough glory to go around. We'll both lead the charge."

"Done. Tell the army to mount up," said the Khan.

Khuyildar stopped at the tent-door and turned to the Khan. "Promise me one thing."

Genghis was strapping his sword. He looked up. "What is it?"

"If I go to The Ancestors, provide for my children."

"Without fail. Now, let's do battle with the Kereyid Army."

Genghis raised his battle standard and rode to the plain. Khasar mounted up and joined him at the front of the Army of the Center. Together they beheld the spectacle of the Kereyid Army in full battle array facing their Army.

The Ong Khan rode down the line of commanders with Nilkha beside him. Then Ong Khan took his position. The fierce Jirjins charged across the plain. At the command of their leader, the Urughud of the Mongol line charged to meet them.

The pounding of their war-horses made the earth rumble and the mountains shake.

The Urughud rode in line, the shoulders of their horses close together, the Chisel Formation, the rhythm of thousands of warhorses, gaining ground on the enemy, their legs pumping, their hooves drumming.

The Urughud unleashed their arrows and the volley blackened the air. The Jirjin line looked steady until men the front ranks started falling. A second volley took another row of men down.

A Mongol commander took an arrow in the abdomen, fell from his horse and was trampled by the troops coming up behind him. A younger soldier took an arrow in the shoulder but he wheeled and one of his fellows rode up and pulled him from his horse.

He ripped off his armor and pulled the man's silk shirt off. The arrow came out of the wound and the man scrambled back to his mount.

Genghis commanded the officer of the signal corps to his left. The white and black flags went up and the Manghud charged. They spurred their ponies into a gallop and fired arrows. The Jirjin began falling right and left as the fierce archers and their heavy bows rained down arrows. Horses turned aside as the charging Mongols crashed through the Jirjin line collapsing their attack formation.

The force of the attack drove the Kereyid soldiers back on themselves, as horses coming up from the rear crashed into those already engaged. Animals fell, trapping men under them. Many fallen soldiers were trampled to death by the oncoming troops.

Kereyid archers receded before the tidal wave of the Mongols attack units in an eddying whirl of men. Horses fell knocking men from the saddle as the front ranks broke. Mongol arrows struck targets in the chaos at the front ranks, reducing the enemy. Mongol horsemen avoided the tangle of legs, arms, bodies and drove on deeper into the ranks.

In close fighting, Khuyildar shouted his command. The cavalry switched weapons and deployed swords and lances. Khuyildar ran a man through with a sword.

Genghis held his troops back. He wanted the Kereyid to spend their energy early in the contest. The Ong Khan would be more reckless if he believed that he was winning.

Khasar rode into the fray with a corps of crack archers and was decimating the forward ranks of the Kereyid. An arrow glanced off Genghis Khan's leather armor. One stuck in one of the leather plates. He looked down, pulled it out and threw it on the ground.

On the Kereyid side, Achigin the commander of the Tubegen led his troops in a countercharge against the Mongols. They fell on the Manghud troops. Achigin let an arrow fly. Khuyildar was struck and fell from his horse. His bodyguards, a cordon of ten, closed ranks and took him from the field.

Genghis surveyed his reserve troops standing in ranks on the plain. He raised his arm and gave the signal. The flags rose. The heavy cavalry rode to the battleground with ferocity.

Genghis saw a small hill where a group of officers was observing the battle. Among them was the Ong Khan. The Dongkhayid rode into the fray. The Urughud fell back, re-grouped and counter charged. The Dongkhayid broke ranks and fell back in disarray.

The Senggum led a charge against Jurchidei. An arrow hit him in the chest and knocked him off his horse. When he fell to earth, the Kereyid Army drew ranks around him, protecting him from being trampled to death.

Amid the Kereyid arrows filling the air around them, Genghis and Khasar charged into the midst of the battle and fired their war bows. Genghis and Khasar paid their Guards no heed. They charged forward firing and all around them, Kereyid fell like the leaves of autumn.

Genghis looked over at Khasar. His brother wore archer's gloves made of unborn calf and hit his targets with stunning accuracy. Genghis Khan thought that riding into war was a beautiful sight.

Khasar looked over and shouted, "To your right." A Kereyid with a lance had gotten inside the circle of guards and was charging him. Genghis pulled his reins off to the right, got out of the way of the horse's charge, The man rode past him, straight into the lances of his guards.

Bogorji rode up, his face grimy, his sword raised. He pointed his sword in the direction of the front of the line. "The Senggum is down."

Genghis rode up to the front where the forward troops were driving the Kereyid back. He looked for Jamuga but did not see him.

Genghis began firing again. He looked up and saw the arrows leaving the bows of his troops like rain, whistling, arcing, flying through the air and killing Kereyid and he exulted. He looked around. Khasar was gone.

The battle had been waged for hours by this time. Fighting was so fierce that dead men and horses littered the plain, with arrows jutting up from bodies, severed limbs, bloody trunks, swords embedded in them, the detritus of war, the stench of death was everywhere, sickly sweet and macabre. The losses were heavy, but the Mongols were moving forward across the plain; the Kereyid were losing the battle.

The light turned gold as the sun set in the foothills. The fighting had begun at dawn and had continued all day. The Mongol Army had destroyed the Kereyid battle formation. They tried to regroup, to form a line on the field. Togril's thousand imperial guards rode through the broken ranks of the Dongkhayid and attacked the Mongols.

Jurchedei and the Urughud fought with the energy of madmen and forced the Kereyid into retreat. Its spirit broken, its prince wounded, the Kereyid forces gave up. The exhausted soldiers turned their horses and ran from the battlefield. A cheer went up from the Mongol side.

Genghis lost sight of Khasar during the battle. He located Subudei and Mukhali and rode back to camp with them. He asked the generals to check with the juniot commanders and report to him, He wanted to know the performance of the units and the numbers of their losses. He was worried about Khasar. Subudei said that Bogorji and Boroghul were missing.

Khasar was nowhere to be found. The women went to the battleground and gathered weapons and valuables in their skirts. No one saw him among the dead on the battlefield. The Manghud returned bearing Khuyildar on a litter and carried him to his tent.

Genghis summoned Tab Tengri, the shaman, to see to the wounded and the dead. Tab applied a poultice to Khiyuldar's wound. Genghis knew that the man would not recover when the shaman Tab Tengri shook his rattle and began the dance to assist the spirit in leaving the body and joining The Ancestors.

Genghis Khan summoned his Inner Council for a report. Mukhali looked stricken. "Bogorji and Boroghul have not returned. Subudei is with us. We have sustained heavy losses."

"I have no choice," the Supreme Khan said. "Give orders to deepen the retreat immediately."

The Mongol Army rode out under cover of darkness and continued the eastward journey rode for a day and a night without stopping. Genghis gave the order to make camp. He made a tour of inspection with Subudei and Mukhali and listened to their reports.

Mukhali said, "I'm sorry to bring you this news, Khan. Ogodei is missing. Bogorji and Boroghul have still not returned. Ogodei was riding with them."

The news struck the Khan like a hammer blow. "What of Khasar?"

Subudei said, "Sir, we have not found Khasar."

Genghis closed his eyes. "I saw a horse shot out from under a man Maybe it was Ogodei. Find him. Dead or alive."

Subudei gripped his Khan by the shoulder. "If Bogorji and Boroghul are alive, they're with Ogodei."

Mukhali said, "One of my men saw Khasar taken prisoner."

Genghis Khan said, "The Ong Khan will not kill Khasar."

Subudei said that was good news. "Ong Khan will try to use him as a hostage."

Genghis turned back to his tent. "Station double shifts of scouts at the perimeter of the camp. Put the horses to graze. The Kereyid may come after us. We won't travel until we have news of Khasar and Ogodei. Tell the commanders to ready their troops to resume the retreat."

The sun rose blood red over the mountains. A scout rode at breakneck speed and reported to Genghis Khan's tent. He had seen a lone rider, silhouetted against the sky, riding toward the camp. Mukhali rode out to meet him.

It was Bogorji. He had ridden all night. He was short of breath, thirsty, exhausted and famished. His uniform was torn and dirty, but he was not wounded.

A groom took his horse while a servant helped him to Genghis Khan's tent. The Khan rose and poured him a cup of water. The sight of his old friend mad Genghis Khan hopeful. Bogorji drank, but he swallowed too fast and spat up the water.

Genghis attempted a battlefield joke. "I knew I picked a good man when I let you join me. Not even the Kereyid can kill you."

Bogorji managed a weak grin. "I'm too damned beautiful to die and I have too many women to satisfy."

"Good. I need you. You have to satisfy me."

"I'm sorry, Genghis. Ogodei was with me. I tried my best to find him. An arrow hit the Senggum and he fell. A cordon of Kereyid came out on the field to protect him. They surrounded him and carried him off the field.

"I charged at the troops and my horse was shot out from under me. I ran off the field on foot. When the Kereyid Army stopped to guard Senggum, they left a packhorse with its pack sliding off. I stole the horse and tracked you. I'm lucky I found you."

"That's enough for tonight, Bogorji. You need rest." Genghis called his Guardsmen, "Put the general in his wagon. He can't ride in his condition. Feed him. Don't give him heavy food."

Bogorji threw off the Guards and tried to stand by himself. "Don't treat me like an old woman." He staggered and his knees buckled under him. Genghis caught him and held him up.

"Take him to the wagon," said the Khan. "This is no time for pride. I need you."

Bogorji relented and allowed the Guards to support him. At the tent-door, he said, "The Army would have found Ogodei's body by now if he were dead."

The sky was streaked with mauve and apricot clouds in the dying golden light.

A uniformed soldier ran up and reported, "A Mongol officer is riding into camp carrying a wounded man over the horn of his saddle. His legs are hanging down over the side of the horse."

"Let's go," Genghis said to his men. He strode to the entrance of camp, feeling his spirits rise as he beheld the vast sweep of the steppes around him.

Boroghul had ridden after the Army slumped in the saddle, his body covering Ogodei's limp body. Boroghul had blood all over his tunic and his lips were cracked.

His voice croaked. "I've got Ogodei. The Kereyid have turned back. They're retreating. Help me, Genghis, I found him on the battlefield. He's badly wounded. He's bleeding to death. Do something."

Tears came to Genghis Khan's eyes. His men took Ogodei's limp body from the saddle, as gently as if he were a newborn.

Genghis said, "Tell Tab Tengri. Slay an ox, remove the entrails. Put Ogodei inside. It's the only thing that will stop his loss of blood.'"

Ogodei was unconscious. Boroghul had wrapped a makeshift bandage around the wound in his side, but the bandage was soaked with blood. Genghis gently unwrapped it. Ogodei had a puncture wound on the side of his neck, a great gaping hole which had festered.

Genghis Khan cradled Ogodei's head, waiting for the light to come back into his eyes. Ogodei, his sweet-tempered son. He closed his eyes and communed with the Eternal Blue Sky.

The shaman Tab Tengri slit the ox from its neck to its groin and removed its entrails. The Supreme Khan's men lifted Ogodei and put him inside the cavity. The animal was still warm and the blood pouring into the cavity equalized Ogodei's blood pressure. Ogodei stopped bleeding.

Genghis stayed and watched over him. Several hours later, Ogodei opened his eyes. He spoke and moved. All night long, Genghis remained

184

beside his son. At dawn, the shaman ordered Ogodei removed from the cavity. His son was going to live. By mid-morning, Ogodei sat up and drank water and with great effort swallowed clear broth. He spoke to his father and told him that he felt stronger.

Genghis Khan touched Ogodei's head and said a prayer. He believed that The Ancestors had sent him a sign. They were telling him that the Blue Sky would grant his destiny. He reached deep inside himself and the will to victory broke out of his soul and flooded his body, his whole being.

He strode out of the tent, summoned his commanders and gave the order to break camp at sunset. "We will deepen the retreat. I will lead my army to the east and I will lure Ong Khan to his destruction."

Genghis Khan's Camp, Tatar Country

These were Genghis Khan's darkest hours. The retreat took him into unfamiliar territory, the edge of Tatar territory in the east. The pastures were sparse and the rivers, few.

He split his forces and ordered a hunt along both banks of the stream. He had ten thousand six hundred men left. He had to feed them. An army of empty stomachs was no army at all.

Genghis Khan had no message from Ong Khan.

The Khongirad surrendered without a fight. They were Bortai's people and they knew him. This gave him room to maneuver. He had the freedom to move at will in their territory without fear of being attacked.

He sent a message to Ong Khan and asked why he was making war on his loyal vassal. Did he think that Genghis Khan deserved a punishment for some transgression? A vassal had the right to know why a lord waged war on him.

He reminded Ong Khan that the two of them had pledged that neither would allow anyone to come between them. That they would speak directly to each other.

Genghis Khan sent word to his former companions-in-arms, those who had formed a coalition against him. He insisted that he had not committed wrongs against any of them. He asked for their reply. He wanted to know what was going on in their minds.

Genghis Khan knew the answer. Jamuga and the Senggum had badmouthed him and convinced the Kereyid camp of Genghis Khan's treachery. They thought it was a matter of survival to make war on Genghis Khan.

Genghis Khan addressed a message to the Mongol royals. He wanted to know why had they abandoned the Mongol camp. He told them that they had elected him to rule them. If they wanted to camp with the Ong Khan, they owed it to him to tell them. Their abandonment of him was underhanded. He hoped that they showed more loyalty to Ong Khan than they had to him.

He sent a message to the Senggum. He told the Senggum that he was fomenting trouble. He was jealous because Genghis Khan had found favor in Senggum's father's eyes because the Senggum was a son who failed his father. He did not carry out his duties, but constantly advocated for war. Genghis Khan leveled the charge that the Senggum and Jamuga were to blame for the split.

Genghis Khan was satisfied that he had put fear in the mind of the Senggum.

"Subudei," he said, "I am fond of my *Yasa*, my Code of Laws, I believe in justice. But with those who cannot be persuaded of the law, I am fond of vengeance. You ride with me. You know me. You know that I always settle the score. Those who have gone against me will get what is coming to them."

"And more," said Subudei. "I don't doubt you, Khan. I'm with you."

The Mongol Army reached the shores of Lake Baljuna. Genghis Khan called a halt to the retreat. He made camp in the marshy lands surrounding the lake. It was a sad place hung over with gloom. A tribe camping in that place surrendered and asked to join the Mongols.

The first night they made camp, he stood before his people and saw weariness in their faces.

"Because those whom I counted as friends betrayed me, I have a bitter fate. Those of you who have remained with me at Lake Baljuna, hear me.

"The Eternal Blue Sky has promised me that it is my destiny to rule all peoples. I *will* prevail against the Kereyid. For your fidelity to me, I give you my word that you will always have first place in my camp. This is the covenant I make with you, because of your loyalty. Let none of you doubt me."

He ordered them to rest and see to their families and equipment. They would need their strength in the days to come.

They were working at surviving the turn of fate when a stroke of good fortune came. A Muslim trader named Hussein had been trading with the Chinese in the border country of the Great Wall. Hussein and his camel caravan rode up to Lake Baljuna with a thousand head of sheep and a white camel. Genghis Khan bartered with the trader for the sheep. Then he fed his people.

One of his corps of men dedicated to keeping him informed of events throughout the steppes arrived and delivered a message. "I bring good news, Khan. Khasar is alive. He's filthy and thin, and his legs are sore from riding. His tongue is thick: his lips, crusted and dry. He has not eaten in days, but he'll recover. I should prepare you, Khan. He looks terrible."

Genghis said. "Where is he?"

Two guards entered the Supreme Khan's tent supporting Khasar's weight, his arms around their shoulders. He was unsteady on his feet. They eased him into a chair. Genghis poured a cup of the black water of the lake, but Khasar was too weak to lift the cup to his lips. Genghis held it for him.

Khasar turned up his nose at the foul smell of the water. He tasted and spit it out. He looked up at his brother. "I can't drink it!"

Genghis smiled. "If you have strength to complain, you will be well again. It's all we have. I'm sorry."

Khasar drank, wincing at the bitter taste. "I'm hungry. I haven't eaten." Genghis ordered a serving woman to bring food.

Khasar ate. The color returned to his face and his strength returned.

"Bogorji said your wife and children were captured with you. Tell me what happened."

"They're alive. Ong Khan kept them as hostages. Don't worry. "Togril swore that he won't harm my children. He thinks I have come over to his side. They'll be all right.

"I met Kereyid people, soldiers who are loyal to you. They sneaked me out in of the camp in the middle of the night. I rode east to Khongirad lands. The Khongirad did not believe that I was your brother because my clothes are in tatters. I convinced them. I proved I was your brother by telling them that I knew Dai Sechen and described his tent. I described Bortai and her children. They believed me and told me where you'd gone. They said they had submitted to you peacefully."

"They did," Genghis said.

Khasar managed a weak smile. "I know the way your mind works. You didn't want the Kereyid to assert rule over the Khongirad because the Khongirad could provision their army."

Genghis nodded. "You know me. You're right. Besides, they prefer to be ruled by me. Let them provision my army."

"How *did* you find me? The country is vast."

"Some herdsmen told me about a bitter place with a muddy lake and said that new peoples had just arrived and made camp there. It had to be you." Khasar looked around.

Genghis said, "What about Ong Khan?"

"He realized that he made a mistake in breaking with you. Jamuga made an alliance with Nilkha. Nilkha wants to take over. "The Senggum thinks that he will be the next Khan of Mongolia. Jamuga intends to be Khan of Mongolia. Ong Khan blames Jamuga for the situation."

Genghis said, "They have no unity. They outnumber us. If we wait until they attack, they'll wipe us out. We must take the offensive. Otherwise, it's the end of us."

Khasar's eyelids drooped shut and his chin dropped to his chest.

"Take him and put him to bed," Genghis said.

By noon the next day, Khasar appeared in Genghis Khan's tent, well enough to walk without help.

Genghis had thought deep into the night. "I want you to ride back to the Ong Khan's camp. Leave right away. The way will be shorter. They'll have some distance toward us. Find a good hiding place. Send Togril a message."

"Saying what?" Khasar asked.

"Say, 'No matter how I searched for him, I could not find anyone who had news of him. My wife and children are with you, Ong Khan, and I would like to make my bed in your camp. Guarantee me that no harm will come to me, and I will return to you.'"

"And I go back to the Kereyid camp?"

Genghis nodded.

"And do what? What are you going to do?"

"You arrive in camp, you tell him you had to return because you would have died of starvation otherwise, you behave as though you are bewildered and sad, because you have lost me."

Khasar left the Mongol camp, Genghis ordered the Mongol Army to mount up and pull out. The Army followed Khasar some hours behind. Genghis hid the army behind in the hills. Tens of thousands of troops surrounded the Kereyid camp.

Thousands of Kereyid campfires lit up the night sky. The sound of music filled the air and the sounds of laughter and merriment. The Ong Khan was holding a feast. From the sight of the roasting pits, and the amount of game cooking over open fires, Togril must have called a Grand Hunt to provision his army and had called for a celebration before his army rode east.

Khasar sent messengers to Togril. "Tell the messengers to say that I'm waiting for Ong Khan to send a man I recognize with a guarantee of safe conduct and I will come to his camp."

The messengers returned with Iturgen, a Kereyid whom Khasar knew well. The Kereyid party rode up to the knoll where Khasar was waiting. Iturgen looked down. Too late, he saw campfires and realized that Genghis Khan had laid a trap. The Mongol Army was lying in wait.

He broke from the Kereyid party and tried to escape to warn Togril, but Khasar fired an arrow and knocked Iturgen's horse out from under him. Khasar and one of his men captured Iturgen and dragged Iturgen out of the saddle. They brought him to the tent of Genghis Khan.

"Khasar, decide what his fate should be," Genghis Khan said.

"If I let him live and he gets back to the Ong Khan, my wife and children will be killed." He dragged the man outside by the scruff of his neck and unsheathed his sword and killed him.

Khasar went back to camp and found the Council of Generals assembled in his brother's tent.

Genghis told his commanders, "Our friends betrayed us. Our allies broke faith with us and attacked us with no cause. They caused us to retreat across far terrain, but our escape, our retreat, was not in vain. We have discovered the bonds of loyalty among ourselves.

"Generals, take pleasure in this campaign, for when we defeat the Kereyid, we will be masters of Eastern Mongolia. Order your soldiers to mount up and surround the Kereyid camp.

"To victory!" said Subudei.

"Hear! Hear!" said Mukhali.

"To Genghis Khan!" said Bogorji.

"To Khasar," said Genghis Khan.

The sound of the feast grew louder as the Mongol Army approached the Kereyid camping circles. The tents were deserted because all of the people were attending the feast.

Genghis gave the order. The army attacked, descending on the Kereyid soldiers while they were drunk and full and carousing. The Mongol troops rode through the camp using swords to cut off heads, arms, run men through the trunk.

Khasar's archers cut down Ong Khan's Guard with volley after volley of arrows. Genghis rode up to the dais looking for Togril and the Senggum, but the two of them had the protection of a small cordon of guards, and rolled down from the dais, and got away. Genghis shot three of the Guards in rapid succession. The musicians of the nomad orchestra dropped their instruments and ran from the center of the feast-ground, but a cordon of Mongol archers shot them down where they had only moments before been playing a dance tune.

Subudei worked the outer perimeter of the camp. By this time, many of the Kereyid men had gotten to the corrals and mounted up, and Subudei's heavy cavalry were engaged in close fighting with them, with sword, knives, lance.

The butchery in the main part of the camp went on. Thousands of men were too drunk to fight and by the time they were shocked into consciousness, saw only the helmets of Mongol riders, the breath of Mongol war ponies, swooping into camp swinging an axe to take off their limbs. They were like ducks swimming on a lake, helpless because they could not get to their mounts.

The feast-ground turned to mud as the Mongol horsemen rode around as though it were a race track, killing ten men on a circuit, one at a time, at a pass through the camp, until their arms were sore from swinging sword or axe and their lower quarters were covered in blood for their targets were on foot, or sitting down, or running away and few of them were mounted.

The screams and howling were piteous, rising up to the vault of the sky. Women dragged children away, but many of them were trampled under horses' hooves. None of the Kereyid could get to their horses and

191

many were slaughtered. Some did manage to get to their horses, but by now the Mongol ranks were swelled with the men who wanted to be ruled by Genghis Khan.

By first light of day, the Kereyid Army surrendered to Genghis Khan. The commanders came forward on foot holding aloft their battle standards. Behind them, the junior command, those who had survived.

Corpses of men, women and children littered the camp, thousands of them. Genghis Khan's commanders took the surrender of the officers and ordered Mongol soldiers to make a search of the tents. They had orders to gather the women and children who were hiding and tell them to load up their carts and follow the Mongol Army.

Mongol soldiers put male prisoners men in a corral, their hands on their heads, then surrounded the corral under heavy Guard. Mongol commanders ordered their troops to collect Kereyid weapons. Genghis gave the army permission to loot and plunder. Khasar went to the women's camp to find Enju and his children.

Genghis Khan walked as in a dream surveying the remains of the battle, dead campfires, horses and men. He finally arrived to the Ong Khan's magnificent tent. Genghis sat down at Ong Khan's table of rosewood and had a glass of grape wine from a cup made of gold.

Togril's wealth, his lands and herds, his city of Khara Khorum, the Silk Road which ran through his lands, the taxes, the trade, everything in Southern Mongolia, belonged to him. He was rich beyond his wildest dreams.

He picked up a piece of porcelain then set it down. He ran his boot along the Persian carpet. From the Ong Khan's carved ivory chair, he asked for the commanders of the army to be brought to him.

His Guard came back and said that Togril and the Senggum had escaped. Jamuga was gone. Gurin Noyan, the Kereyid general, came and surrendered formally. Genghis accepted his surrender. Eastern Mongolia, all of it was his.

The chief of the Jirjin, who had left the Mongol camp after Genghis Khan's reprimand, survived the battle and now came to Ong Khan's tent and went down on his knees.

"I let the Ong Khan escape. I pledged him my loyalty. I fought for him because he was my khan and it was my duty to protect him. Now that you are master of the Kereyid, will you accept me into your service? I will give you my skill as I gave it to him. Otherwise, kill me here and now."

Genghis Khan toyed with the golden cup. "You ask to be my vassal and we have old ties. Everyone on the steppes knows that I value loyalty, but you left me once before. You have no loyalty and are no one to trust. This is what I will do for you. My great warrior Khuyildar died of the wounds he received fighting for me. Because of his great service to me, I will provide for his orphans down to the seed of his seed.

"I will let you live and allow your hundred best Jirjin to serve Khuyildar's wife and sons. If any of these Jirgin have daughters, they will not be married, but will serve my brave warrior's wife and sons."

Subudei and Mukhali came to the tent to request Genghis Khan's instructions as to the fate of the prisoners.

"This is my command. The Kereyid will cease to exist as a people. All of them, nobility, soldiers, slaves, and hostages, will become members of Mongol clans.

"I will divide Kereyid military units among our commanders. They have fought together; they will live together as one people and one army united under my command. All will camp with me.

"The ten thousand Tubegen who gave their loyalty to Ong Khan are to be split up and divided among Mongol commanders; the same is true for the Dongkhayid and the Jirgin. There are no Kereyid people anymore, only a Mongol people, with allegiance to my commanders, not to their own clans."

Genghis sent for Jakha Gambo, Ong Khan's younger brother.

"Jakha," he said, "Do you have any objection to an alliance between our houses? I'd like to marry your eldest daughter and I'd like to give the youngest to my son Tolui, my aide-de-camp, who will become Khan of Mongolia when I die."

"I would consider it an honor to unite our houses," Jakha said.

"You're a wise man. Send for your daughters. Tell them to dress in their finest. Get Tolui in here. We'll have the marriage now. On the Kereyid charnel ground. As a reminder of the punishment of those who think themselves better than I am. We'll have a Christian priest if you have one among you, because I know that Sorghagtani is devout. And a shaman for Tolui."

Genghis Khan took the elder daughter, Ibakha Beki, Lady Ibakha, for himself. He secretly was fond of the younger, Sorghagtani Beki, who was his idea of what a woman of the steppe nobility should be but did not think it right to make her a fourth wife.

"Better she became a principal wife for his son. She was a steppe aristocrat of the stock that produced both he and Bortai. She would produce fine heirs for Tolui.

The dark elegant beauty and the regal bearing of the Lady Sorghagtani, as she entered his tent and bowed with great dignity, moved him as a man. She was holding a string of Christian beads in her hand which had a cross dangling from it and did not seem afraid of him although she did not know what her fate would be. When he announced to her that he wished her to marry his son, she went down on her knees and uttered words of greeting to him as her new father-in-law.

Her gaze was direct and steady, her thick black hair fell in lustrous sheets around her shoulders. He was seized with the desire to possess her. It lasted one blinding moment then passed. She spoke strong words to him that expressed her joy and her desire to bring honor to his house. She said that she hoped his son would find her pleasing and that she would bear heirs worthy of being his grandsons.

"The union of you with my son Tolui," he said, "will be blessed. The issue will be good."

She asked how he knew.

"I have a good eye for a match. Tolui will have a Kereyid princess for a wife. Give me good grandchildren. I have much to leave behind."

She laughed and at that moment his heart leaped. He stumbled over his words for the princess was level-eyed. She had managed to make him feel like a boy rattling on about the white horses that the Retainer of the Studs bred for him. No woman had ever done that to him in his life and this one could not have been more than sixteen.

Genghis decided that the Ong Khan had done him a favor by opposing a match between Chagur Beki and Jochi. This woman was a greater prize. Tolui, who would one day be Khan of Mongolia, would have her.

194

Genghis Khan gave Jakha Gambo permission to live among the Mongols again, since he was now a member of Genghis Khan's immediate family. Genghis liked him and allowed him keep his tents, herds and peoples.

Genghis Khan gave a great feast in the middle of the raucous celebration and the gargantuan bouts of gluttony and drinking, sent for the two commoners who had brought him word that the Senggum was coming against him.

"Badai and Kishlig, you brought victory over the Kereyid. Your actions saved my life and my throne. Because of this, I give you the golden tent of the Ong Khan just as it sits here with everything in it, golden goblets, basins and bowls, and all his servants to carry them for you. The Ongkho clan of the Kereyid will become your personal bodyguard from this day forward.

"You are free men, down to the seed of your seed, entitled to wear a quiver and arms, drink *koumiz* and partake of the offerings at the ancestor ceremonies. When we take spoils, you will have a share; when we hunt wild game, you will have a share. Whoever rules after me, remember the deeds these men have done and honor them."

The two went down on their knees and touched their foreheads to the ground. Genghis Khan retired to his tent to savor his victory.

1204

Genghis Khan returned to his pastures in Two River Valley. The feasting in the Valley of Two Rivers went on for weeks while the ox-carts laden with booty and treasure rumbled up to the white velvet tent. The moment of disbursement was at hand and the excitement among the people grew. Being a provider of riches was an excellent trait in a leader, a Supreme Khan

The Guards helped Genghis Khan distributed the plunder among the high command, the men of the nobility: bolts of silk fabric' objects of gold and silver; coats, blankets, rugs of fur, all manner of things made from hides.

Genghis Khan called for a Great Assembly. He was master of the eastern steppes. It was a new era and he intended to lay down new rules. He made a speech.

*"Today we become **Yesse Mongol Ulus**, the Great Mongol nation!"* Cheers rose up from the crowd.

"From now on, there will be no tribes: no Mongols, Kereyid, Tatar, or Mergid. I am breaking the tribes up and giving them a place with each of my top commanders. Your loyalty is to your commander and to me and to the Great Mongol Nation.

"My law, the Great Code, the Yasa, is the law of the land. All of the commanders will have copies of the Code. All of you will obey it. The Great Code applies equally to all."

He divided up the empire and gave fiefdoms to his family and to the senior nobility. They would collect tribute from the clans and forward it to him. From the revenues, he would pay them annual stipends. The fiefdoms would civilian officials appointed by Genghis Khan to oversee the collection and forwarding of tribute. Each fiefdom would have a military official to maintain the Khan's order and enforce his code.

He controlled the family by controlling the purse. Goods flowed through the system. Goods moved through the system. Genghis Khan could apportion new materials and new inventions to locations where he deemed they were needed. This was the way of The Horde, everything in motion.

Every member of Genghis Khan's family had an official government administrator attached to his *appanage*; a man loyal to the central government appointed by the Supreme Khan.

Part of the tribute was the conscription of troops for military service. The Khan's official would take a census every year and conscript military service. When the Khan had the need, the troops would fight his war.

In fulfillment of his promise to Bortai, he issued *yarlighs*, decrees, creating fiefdoms for their four sons.

Jochi received the lands of the "forest nations" in the extreme northwest "as far away as the hooves of Mongol horses had trod." Among the Mongols, it was customary for the eldest son to receive lands furthest from the father's pastures. Jochi received nine thousand households.

Batu, Jochi's eldest son, was of an age to join the army and Genghis had promised him a place in his tent as a member of his Keshig Guards. Batu became an aide-de-camp. The boy admired his grandfather and could not wait to join the Imperial Guards.

Jagadai, his second son, was a stern disciplinarian. His interest was in the law. He had a legalist approach and had mastered the Yasa, the Code of Genghis Khan. Jagadai received the lands south of the Ili River and eight thousand households.

Ogodei was a great favorite with all types of people, from officials to common soldiers and spent his time in the company of Shiki Kutuku, the master of the treasury and Tata-tonga, the Uighur scribe. He also took a strong interest in administrative affairs. He received the Southern Altai Range, and lands near the Imil River as well as five thousand households.

Tolui inherited Genghis Khan's pasturelands in Mongolia and was given five thousand households for income. Tolui had shown such great talent for military life. Genghis Khan appointed him his Chief of Staff.

Tolui's wife, the Princess Sorghagtani, gave birth to her first child, a healthy son whom she named Mongke who would one day be a successor to Genghis Khan. Of all the women his sons had married, Genghis thought she had the makings of an empress.

Khasar received four thousand of the newly conquered households in the old Tatar lands in Manchuria. Belgutei received one thousand five hundred.

Genghis Khan had more innovations. He announced a new organization for his army. Kereyid were integrated into the main body of the Mongol Army. All Kereyid officers would serve under Mongol generals where they would train in Mongol tactics.

He divided up the army and appointed commanders. He created posts: Master of Provisions, Master of Weapons, Master of Horses. He created positions for formal assemblies, so the Great Assemblies were more like a court with officers.

His adopted brother Shiki, orphaned during the Tatar campaign and raised in his mother's tent, was the Secretary of the Treasury. Revenues from the trade routes in the Southern Gobi and elsewhere in the empire belonged to Genghis Khan. Shiki was to keep the records and supervise the merchants' activities in the capital.

The old system was gone. Genghis Khan created a government composed of scribes and administrators from Uighur country, because the Uighurs knew record-keeping. He named the officials who would held responsibility for horses and weapons. He appointed a Master of Provisions.

He rewarded people who had performed special services for him and to whom he had promised reward. Sorkhen Shira, the *koumiz*-maker who had helped him escape from the Taijyud camp long ago, became a nobleman. He was also given dispensation to break the law nine times without punishment.

He ordered the creation of a system of post-roads, good roads with shelter every twenty-five miles. He created a system of Near and Far Arrows to bring him information and news from the far quarters of the empire. Anyone bearing an imperial seal could obtain a clean bed and food, and a fresh mount. The empire was connected.

Finally, Genghis Khan created the *Keshig*, his corps of bodyguards. They were the young commanders who served him in his tent, six in the day, six at night. Many had a reason to want him dead. He rode with the Guards, trained and hunted with them. He knew each man's skills in war. He observed the character and talent of each man at close range. From their ranks he assigned their commands.

Khasar paid Genghis Khan the compliment of creating an efficient system. Money and troops flowed to the Khan. Income flowed to the nobility. Nobody fought, stole, raped or killed, or they would be subject to punishment under the law.

In winter, his spies informed Genghis Khan of a dangerous development. The Tai-yang had given protection to a coalition of Genghis Khan's enemies--Jamuga and Togtoa, the Mergid chief who had been an enemy since Genghis Khan's youth. The Mergid was living on the western shores of Lake Baikal. Another tribe, the Oirad, joined the coalition. Genghis and Khasar and the Council of Generals thought this was an ominous sign and that they had better prepare for war. Sooner rather than later, said Genghis Khan. Preparedness was his cardinal rule of war. He liked to be first in the field.

Genghis Khan gathered intelligence from the West, information about Naiman troops, culture, army, fighting tactics, and supply routes. He sent spies to the oasis cities. This was where the Tai-yang supplied his army. The merchants of the bazaars passed information to his men.

The spies informed him that Tai-yang had large numbers of troops and these were reputed to be the best army in the steppes. The Naiman Campaign would be a great military challenge, perhaps that Genghis Khan had faced so far in his career.

Genghis Khan called for a Great Assembly. Genghis Khan told the nobility that he had decided to bring all of the steppes under his command. The Tai-yang was the last of his enemies. He was the ruler of the Naiman in the West. The Naiman were a Turkish people. They were Christians and considered themselves more civilized than all the other tribes of the steppes. They had writing and were wealthy from trade in the oasis cities of the Silk Road--Khotan, Yarkand, and Kashgar.

and announced that he intended to ride west with as large an army as possible. He wanted family and senior nobility to donate troops. Then he took counsel with Subudei and planned the campaign.

He sent out scouts to find the route across the Gobi Desert. A season passed and his scouts returned with maps of the routes the Mongol Army would take. He would traverse the distance during spring and make camp for the summer. The fighting would begin when the cool weather came.

Genghis Khan climbed steadily up the rocky path of Burkhan Khaldun. At the top, he poured a libation of mare's milk and surrendered his will to the will of Koko Tengri, the Eternal Blue Sky. He removed his belt and placed them on the ground. He took off his cap and placed it on the ground.

In May of the year 1204, Genghis Khan set out with 45,000 men and rode west. He defeated the Naiman Army in an epic battle at a place called Chakrimat.

The Supreme Khan was fortunate in his enemies. Tai-yang was inexperienced in command and reluctant to go to war. The Tai-yang did not have the loyalty of his senior command. They called him "late-born" and weak, because he had been born when his father was late in life and his seed was weak. But Tai-yang had a son Guchlug who argued in favor of war and he convinced his father. Tai-yang's mother, Gorbesu, had the loyalty of the troops and she asked them to fight for Tai-yang.

The Tai-yang went to the battlefield of Chakrimat, but his character was not that of a great leader. He was weak, perhaps because he was late-born. He watched the battle from a pavilion on the hillside. Genghis Khan rode at the head of his troops.

The Mongols attacked, Togril and Jamuga abandoned Genghis Khan in the field and Jamuga went to the Tai-yang's camp. The Mongol Army retreated in the middle of the night and regrouped, waiting for the right moment to renew the attack. Kogsegu pursued what he thought was the retreating Genghis Khan and fell upon the Kereyid Army and destroyed them.

The Mongol Army attacked in waves, backing up the Naiman army to the cliffs. They came, wave after wave, relentlessly. The Naiman Army had nowhere to run. It was a tactic of choosing the battlefield and using it to advantage.

The Ong Khan lost his life and the Senggum escaped with only the clothes on his back. When the tide of battle turned against the Naiman, Jamuga switched loyalties and made his way to Genghis Khan's tent claiming that he had struck terror in the heart of the Supreme Khan's enemy. He pretended to Genghis Khan that he had helped assure a Mongol victory.

Genghis Khan granted him asylum. During the final stages of the battle at Chakrimat, a cordon of Mongol guards escorted him to Genghis Khan's tent. True to his old self, Jamuga greeted his old friend wearing arrogance like a cloak.

Genghis greeted Jamuga. He was formal, not the friend he had once been. Jamuga understood that his fate was in Genghis Khan's hands. He made a show of grace under pressure.

"Such formality with an old friend?" Jamuga said. "Really, is this standoffishness necessary? I don't have a weapon and if I couldn't kill you on the battlefield, I certainly wouldn't try here. Aren't you going to offer me something to drink?"

"Untie him," Genghis commanded his Guards. Genghis Khan knew Jamuga's bravado was for show.

The Guardsman cut off the ropes. Jamuga rubbed his wrists. "My dear brother, let me make this easy for you. As long as I draw breath, I will be a threat to you. You have no choice but to execute me. I would kill you without a moment's hesitation if our situations were reversed. I have only one request. If I'm going to die, I want some dignity. Give me the death of a prince. "

"Let's be clever about this. Guard, give him something to drink. Forget your pride."

"What do I have left but pride?" Jamuga asked. "I have lost the contest of wits with you. I give up."

"I hate disloyalty in any man, and you have it in great measure. I will spare your life. Here are the terms. I will make you a commander in my Army, a junior commander under one of my generals."

Jamuga said, "Genghis, you still have a soft spot for me." He shook his head. "After all I've done to you, don't let sentimentality get the better of you. Let me die with honor. Today you achieved a great work.

You united the peoples of the steppes under your banner. The world is yours.

"What use would you have for me? I would be a thorn in your side, a louse in your jacket-collar. Be rid of me and do it swiftly but let me die without my blood flowing into the ground. Bury me with ceremony on a mountainside, I will look over you and your children and grandchildren and protect them forever. I come of a noble line and have been defeated by one of a noble line. Do it quickly and do it now."

Genghis Khan replied, "You are a warrior of great skill. I could use you, but you are weary of life. You are weary of yourself. About that, I can do nothing."

Genghis Khan ordered one of his Guards, "Put him to death without spilling his blood and bury him with honor."

Genghis Khan's commander took Jamuga out. They rolled Jamuga in an ox-hide they soaked in the river. They placed it out in the sun. The heat dried the skin and suffocated Jamuga. Genghis Khan gave the men orders to bury him on the mountain overlooking the plain.

Genghis returned to the battlefield. The plain was littered with men and horses. The shamans gathered the wounded and administered medicines. The families were walking among the dead, searching for their relatives. The Mongol Army was lining up the prisoners.

The next day Genghis rode into the camp of the Naiman Khan and took possession of his tent and his treasure, and his concubines, servants, and slaves. He looked across the battlefield. His rivals were dead. The steppe wars between the tribes were at an end. He was master of the Western steppes. He was the supreme power in Asia.

The Kharadal Forest, Autumn, 1204

After he defeated the Naiman, Genghis Khan ordered the return to his native pastures. On the way, he decided to eliminate the last of his enemies, the Mergid. They had been a thorn in his side since he was a young man. He made peace with them during the Naiman campaign. He even allowed them to guard his booty. While he was fighting, they stole the booty and returned to their forest.

He assigned the job of putting an end to them to his commanders. He retired to plan the return to the Valley of Two Rivers.

A captain brought a captured Mergid chief and his daughter to Genghis Khan's tent. Her name was Gulan and she was destined to be the love of his life.

In the Kharadal Forest, where her people camped, soldiers from both sides, Mongols and rebels, roamed everywhere. Dayir found a Mongol officer named Naghaya, gave his weapons to the officer and said that he trusted Genghis Khan's reputation for forgiving those who submitted to him. Naghaya said that he would escort them to the Supreme Khan's tent in three days' time. In the meantime, he gave them shelter in his tent.

Dayir commanded his daughter to dress in her finest clothes--he was a defeated Mergid chieftain and he was bartering for his life by offering his daughter in marriage.

Although she was the daughter of a chief, she had not married because she despised the men in her father's camp. The crude Mergid chiefs were at the bottom of the social hierarchy. Because of the precarious situation of her people, she had so far been successful in refusing to marry.

She was seventeen. Her gleaming black hair fell to her waist. She had a sweet expression, a bow-shaped mouth, a graceful bearing. She wore a high-waisted dress the color of red wine.

Genghis Khan was in his early forties--she was young enough to be his daughter. Dayir had prepared a speech. He stammered as he explained that her dowry was a tent made of leopard-skins and a leopard-skin bed cover.

Gulan was young, but she was no fool. She knew the fateful moment of her life had come. The man who stood before her was a man who could give her the world. Gulan had been hearing of the man who stood before her for years. The Mergid called Genghis Khan the Man of Iron. His chest and shoulders were massive, and his eyes were the eyes of a bird of prey. He carried himself as a man of power.

She bowed to him, smiled, and spoke a polite greeting. From the moment he saw her, Genghis Khan was thunderstruck.

The Khan questioned Naghaya. "What is your name, officer?"

"Naghaya, sir," the man replied. He stood at attention, his fist tapping his heart.

"Dayir says that he and his daughter spent three days in your tent. Why did you keep a woman promised to me in your tent?"

"I was cleaning up the last of the hostile troops. I wanted to leave my camp in good order, sir. I was doing my duty, sir. I left guards to watch her. She was safe. I was not in the tent."

"I will have you executed if you took her for your own. She is spoils of war and she belongs to me."

Naghaya swore on the lives of his children that he had never laid a hand on the woman. "I told myself, 'She is the possessions of the Khan.' If I have broken my pledge of loyalty, kill me here and now." He offered his sword and Genghis Khan took it in his hand.

Dayir interrupted. "As a father, I would not have permitted her to . . . I would lay down my life on it. She has preserved herself."

Genghis Khan bellowed for silence. "I know you, Dayir, and I know the treachery you've committed in your life. Your words mean nothing to me. If you did not have this daughter, you would be joining The Ancestors. I would have killed you myself."

Gulan had a little dagger up her sleeve. She slid it out and held it to her throat and looked into the Khan's eyes. Her voice broke the spell of the Khan's anger.

"Great Khan," she said, "I swear that this officer was only concerned with his duty to you. My father and I intended to set out for your camp but we had no military escort and the officer warned us that the countryside was not pacified and that soldiers in that country might give us trouble. Without him, we would never have reached your camp unharmed. I mean no disrespect, sir, but instead of asking *him* what transpired in his tent, you should ask *me.*"

She felt light-headed, as though she were sailing down the river in a boat.

"I am to be your wife. Why don't you examine me and see if I am as I was on the day I was born."

The Khan's anger abated. "You have good sense. I do not allow weapons in my tent." He held out his hand. "Give me your knife." She placed the knife in his palm.

"How did you get this past my guards?"

"No one searched me, sir." She lowered her head, suppressing a smile.

"I shall see that my men are not so careless in the future." He turned to Naghaya. "If you are telling the truth, I will promote you for rendering a service to me.

"She remains with me. Leave us."

He picked up the leopard skin and tossed it across his bed. "Your dowry gift is pleasing to me. I accept you as my wife. The ceremonies will be held later. Come to me. Here, on your leopard skin."

Soon he realized that she was telling the truth. She did not take her eyes off him as they consummated the marriage.

Genghis sent the Army of the Left under the command of Chimbai, Sorkhen Shira's son, in search of the rest of the Mergid. He gave them the order to exterminate them for the trouble they had caused him for his entire life.

The Mongol Army spent that winter at the base of the Altai Range. As the tempests of snow came to an end, Mongol commanders came frequently to report that scouts had chosen the route of return. As soon as he could get through the passes, Genghis Khan sent Mukhali to inform Bortai that he had taken a wife.

Bortai was the manager of the women's camp. Gulan would have a tent and clans in Bortai's camping circle. He did not want to surprise Bortai with his marriage. The two Tatar wives lived in Bortai's camp.

He informed Gulan that she would be his fourth principal wife. He told her that Bortai was Empress and that her sons would inherit the empire. He also told her that it was a cardinal rule of his camp that the

205

women got along. By this time, he had a harem of several hundred concubines, gathered up as spoils of war. Many of these bore him children. This was the private life of Genghis Khan.

He knew that Bortai would see the grand passion he had conceived for Gulan. He also knew that Bortai was secure in her position and would accept matters as they stood. This was life. Things happened. Who could account for fate? Still, he sent Mukhali to prepare his first wife and the companion of his youth so that she was not taken by surprise.

There was a difference. He had married Bortai when he was young, weak and penniless. He was a man of burgeoning power when he married Gulan.

Prince Yuan-qi of the Jin Imperial Army arrived at the entrance of the Valley of Two Rivers after the Great Assembly that bestowed the title of Genghis Khan, meaning Oceanic Khan, on the man known by his birth name of Temujin.

His party had passed miles of pastureland where herds branded with the owners' name and tribe grazed. He saw the outer camping circles of the Mongol people and thousands of wagons rolling into the Valley and setting up camp.

Yuan-qi sent his military escort to find out the reason was for this massing of people. The commander returned with news that the Pacifier, as Temujin was known, had summoned the Mongol nobility to this place to attend his coronation as the new ruler of Mongolia. His name was now Genghis Khan. He was making a government and laying down laws. He had just given his people a written language.

When he arrived at the boiling cauldrons of oil at the entrance to the camp, Yuan-ji showed his jade pendant, the insignia of his rank, and told the Keshig Guardsman that he was an envoy of the Jin Emperor. Yuan-qi spoke with the authority of his rank. He said, "Genghis Khan is a vassal of the Jin Emperor and the Emperor wished to know why his vassal had not paid tribute owed to the Dragon Throne for two years. I am here to collect the debt."

The Guards detained him at the entrance to the camp and asked him to pass between the cauldrons of boiling oil to rid himself of demons. He submitted to the barbarous custom.

Yuan-qi waited for the Guard to announce him to the Khan. He told his attendants that he was surprised. A vassal of the Jin Emperor failed to notify his Lord, who was the Son of Heaven, of an event of such importance.

Temujin or Genghis Khan, as he was known, was remiss in his duties. The Emperor of China, who was Yuan-qi's aging uncle Madaku, would not be pleased.

Genghis Khan received the Chinese prince in the Ong Khan's splendid pavilion tent. He welcomed the prince and asked to know his business.

The theory behind Chinese conduct of foreign relations was, that all came and submitted in order that they could benefit from the proximity to the brilliance of Chinese civilization. The occupant of the Dragon Throne counted it as a mark of prestige: the higher the number of foreigners who came to the Celestial Court annually to make obeisance to the Son of Heaven and pay tribute, the greater the prestige.

Genghis Khan had not paid tribute and this was an insult to the Son of Heaven.

Yuan-qi reminded Genghis that for some years past sent the usual nomad goods--tanned hides, furs, sable, tiger furs, bear skins and horsetails. The Son of Heaven had given him presents worth four times the amount of his tribute, in bolts of silk, ingots of silver and chests of tea. Genghis Khan said that he was well aware of the amounts of goods he had sent to China and had been sent documentation on the amounts of good which the Emperor Madaku had sent to Mongolia.

Yuan-qi said, "The Son of Heaven considers your failure to pay tribute a mark of insolence on the part of a vassal. The Son of Heaven has sent me, his nephew, as a rebuke. I come to remind you of your obligations. I come to collect and remit the two years of tribute that you owe to the Dragon Throne."

Genghis Khan regarded the man who stood before him in his imperial Jin robes.

Yuan-qi asked why the Khan had not sent a representative to the Jin court in the capital of Zhongdu.

"Because," said Genghis Khan, "I was too busy making war. I was bringing all of Mongolia under my banner.".

The Chinese aristocrat was accustomed to deference and knew that he was being slighted. "Then on behalf of the emperor, I congratulate you."

The Imperial Prince was dismissed by Genghis Khan and returned with no tribute.

Yuan-qi informed the Emperor that Jin should begin making military preparation against the barbarians at once. The Emperor was old and reluctant to fight at the frontier. He wished to live out his old age on his throne and felt safe because the Gobi and the Onggud separated him from attack by the nomads.

He ordered an entry to be made in the Chinese annals. This was the first mention of Genghis Khan in Chinese history, but certainly not the last: *On the banks of the river Onon, the Mongol Temujin has declared himself Genghis Khan.*

1207

In the spring of 1207, Genghis Khan moved his headquarters to the Ong Khan's old capital of Khara Khorum on the trade routes of the southern Gobi Desert. Khara Khorum or Black Rock was situated in the Ordos Loop of the Yellow River. The country was steppelands, like the grasslands of Mongolia, good for horses, but closer to China.

The reason for the move was simple. From Khara Khorum, it would be easier to supply the Mongol Army, now numbering 150,000, while it was on campaign.

The Supreme Khan kept his beloved Valley of Two Rivers as a place to visit for long periods of rest and recuperation. In keeping with tradition, he invested his youngest son Tolui as Khan of Mongolia.

Khara Khorum was a city of tents divided into four quarters, Mongol, Chinese, Muslim and Christian. The Muslim and Chinese quarters had populations of artisans and craftsmen who were able to make armor, weapons, carts, and other equipment for the army. The merchant guilds, the *ortagh*, kept the prices fair and represented the interests of the Muslim and Chinese capitalists to the Khan, and coincidentally gave him a never-ending supply of spies. The forest and river provided more resources for the civilian and military populations.

The Mongol quarter housed his family and his government. Genghis watched his fortune grow. Shiki Kutuku took possession of the storehouse that held the Ong Khan's treasury and began keeping records.

Early in the morning, Genghis heard the call of the muezzin from the Muslim quarter, at noon he heard the bells of the churches from the Christian quarter and on the Buddhist holidays, he heard the tolling of the huge brass gongs.

Soon after the move to Khara Khorum, four Chinese officers from the Jin Army, together with their families, defected from Jin and came to Mongolia. Guards escorted them into Genghis Khan's presence and the Chinese asked his permission to live in Khara Khorum.

The Supreme Khan welcomed them and gave them good treatment. They supplied him with recent intelligence about affairs in the Jin Empire. He learned from the defectors that the Jin Army was still fierce, a force to be taken seriously.

In the spring of 1207, Genghis Khan put his eldest son Jochi in command of a contingent of troops with a local guide named Bukha. This was Jochi's first command. He was to subdue the Forest Peoples of the Irtysh region. The forest zone of the north, Sibir, was called the Land of Darkness because the sun shone only a few hours a day there. A place of superstition and malign spirits, the forests of this region were so vast that no one knew where they ended.

While an imperial prince was in nominal command of the army, General Subudei was in actual command. Genghis equipped the expedition with iron carts made in Khara Khorum. The new equipment, better for crossing the grasslands than the old wooden carts.

Jochi and Subudei rode into the forest country and took the surrender of the forest tribes. The Kirghiz chiefs surrendered and presented Jochi with gifts of white falcons, geldings, and sables. Jochi brought the chiefs back to Mongolia and allowed them to present their tribute to the Supreme Khan in person.

Genghis was pleased by this mark of respect and commended Jochi's performance.

With the completion of these operations in the North, Genghis Khan had safeguarded the rear of his Army from attack.

He told Jochi, "You went from my tent at my command. You conquered without causing suffering and bloodshed in the lands you took. In recognition, these lands belong to you. Your lands are the furthest west that Mongol ponies have ridden."

Another event occurred which was to be of immense significance. An embassy from the Khitan people who occupied northeast China arrived. They announced that the Khitan people had risen in rebellion against the Jin Emperor.

The Jin had deposed the Khitan and the Khitan wanted Genghis Khan to restore China to their rule. He decided that the time was not right. He sent Mongol ambassadors back to the Khitan ruler saying that he would not invade China until he could throw the whole might of his army into the struggle.

Also of significance, Jochi and Subudei encountered the Shah of Khwarezm in the field. The Shah ruled a vast empire to the west of Khara Khitai across the mountains at the Roof of the World

One of Genghis Khan's enemies was making trouble in the region. Guchlug was the son of the Tai-yang and he escaped after the defeat, He moved to Khara Khitai he married the king's daughter and then deposed the king and took his throne. Guchlug was persecuting Muslims all over the kingdom.

The Shah of Khwarezm had a newly founded empire and he was a vassal of Guchlug. He and his son Jalaladdin were chasing a band of Kipchak nomads who had rebelled, He had an army of 60,000 men in the field. When he arrived at the Irghiz River, he found that the ice on the river was too weak to bear the weight of his cavalry, so he made camp and waited for the season to change and the ice to melt. Finally, he crossed the river and did battle with the Kipchaks on the day that Jebe defeated the remainder of the Mergid.

The Shah spotted the Mongol forces and rode out in pursuit of them, The Shah's troops overtook the Mongols at dawn the next day.

Jochi, as commander of the Right Wing, did not wish to fight the Shah and sent a messenger to the Shah that said he had no orders to engage with Khwarezm. Subudei was the actual commander, as it was Genghis Khan's practice to put a prince in command, with a general to back him up. Subudei was second in strategy to Genghis Khan and the best general in the Mongol Army, The Mongol Army was under Genghis Khan's orders to make war on the Mergids. The Shah sent a reply. He regarded all unbelievers as Infidels and therefore enemies. He would engage.

Jochi had 20,000 men; the Shah had sixty thousand. The Right Wing of each army engaged the Left Wing of the opposing force. Jochi overpowered Jalaladdin, the Shah's son, who commanded the Right Wing of the Khwarezmian force. The Mongols held their own against three times their number for an entire day. Jalaladdin saved the Shah's army from a complete victory.

The fighting stopped when night fell. Usually, the two sides would resume battle the following day. The Mongols set bonfires to make it look like they had made camp, but they slipped away under cover of night. At daybreak, the Shah saw an empty battlefield and realized that the Mongols had abandoned the fight.

Jalaladdin, the Shah Mohammed's son, was a great warrior. He praised the Mongols and said they were superior fighters. The son was not allowed in the Shah's palace by the Shah's second wife, because Jalaladdin was the son of the first wife. It was a tragedy for the Shah, as events would soon reveal.

Shah Mohammed told his son, "I have never seen men as daring nor as steadfast in battle, nor as skilled giving blows with point and edge of sword. I fear them."

Subudei reported back. Genghis Khan thought this a regrettable incident since he was now the neighbor of the Shah and wished to have diplomatic and trade relations with him.

To keep himself informed of conditions inside the Shah's kingdom, Genghis Khan dispatched spies to the cities of Khwarezm.

The great cities of Samarkand and Bukhara were centers of Islamic learning and major stops on the caravan routes of the Silk Road. The bazaars and caravanserais were used to the presence of foreigners. Many languages were spoken and no one took notice of the Mongol spies. They returned with the report that the whole of Ferghana was a seething hotbed of religious war.

Since Guchlug was persecuting the Muslims of Khara Khitai, they might ask for help from the Shah. Genghis Khan did not wish to give the Shah an excuse to annex Khara Khitai. He was glad when the Uighur king Buzar came to his camp and submitted, asking to become his vassal.

Genghis Khan and his brother Khasar were aware of their new situation as political masters north of the Gobi. Events in neighboring states became important.

"My wars have changed the balance of power in the Muslim world. I don't want the Shah summoned into my territory to protect Muslims." He proclaimed a policy of religious toleration throughout the west. The

212

trade would follow. Revenue would follow. The Khan had time to reflect.

At the time the Supreme Khan rose to power, China was divided into three kingdoms: Xi Xia, Jin and Song.

A strategist looks at the present and sees the future. This was a talent that Khasar sometimes referred to as The Eagle Eye. Genghis Khan realized that neither the Xi Xia King to the southwest nor the Jin Emperor to the south felt secure with him, a formidable military power, on their northern borders. General Subudei, who was the greatest strategist in Genghis Khan's world, agreed with him. The two of them often consulted maps that Subudei acquired in the markets owned by Arab traders, for the Arabs were the best mapmakers in their world. They plied the trade routes and mapped them from experience. Chinese maps were fanciful, based on myth, for the Chinese were content being the Central Country. All countries came to China. All roads led to Zhongdu.

The tribal wars in Mongolia disrupted trade along the caravan routes of the Gobi. News of the victory spread across Asia. The refugees and displaced political leaders fled to the oasis towns of the Silk Road.

Each victory created fresh tremors of apprehension in the rulers of the region. Every time Genghis Khan amassed more power, he represented a threat to a new ruler.

Once a khan or king, emperor or shah perceived him as a threat, war was inevitable.

The mightiest of his neighbors, the Jin Dynasty ruled northeast China and lay to the southeast of Mongolia. The Manchu tribe had conquered China one hundred years earlier and had founded the Jin Dynasty. Despite their long sojourn in China, they were still fierce fighters. Genghis Khan was a vassal of Jin and had had diplomatic relations with them for years.

To the south of Jin, below the Yangzi River, the Song Emperor ruled over a brilliant culture made rich by sea-going trade. South of the Yangzi River, the Song Dynasty had created a new culture, mercantile and seagoing in nature, very different from China's old traditional military, feudal culture in the north. New cities, centers of banking and

213

manufacturing, grew up and great wealth was created. This was in part because the founder of the Song was a general who renounced the militarism of the Tang and forced his generals to give up their military titles for civilian posts. Song thus represented a new era in Chinese history. The great cities of Hangzhou, Suzhou, Yangzhou and Nanzhing were unrivalled by the old agricultural and military centers in the north, the traditional heartland of China.

Genghis knew merchants who told him the situation of the Southern Song Emperor. In the tenth century, the Khitan had invaded and founded the Liao state in northwest China. The Song Emperor, a Han Chinese, had fled to the south and founded the Southern Song dynasty. Although he was a Han Chinese and the Manchu invaders were barbarian, the Song Emperor been forced to pay tribute to the man who had deposed him.

In the eleventh century, new barbarians came down from Manchuria, ousted the Khitan and founded the Jin Dynasty. The Southern Song Emperor continued the payment of tribute to the new conquerors. The Song court was divided between the Irredentist Party who wanted to fight to reclaim North China and the Accommodationists Party who wished to maintain the status quo in the South. Many of the Irredentists believed that if they could mount an attack the Chinese in the north would rise up in rebellion and help them regain the Dragon Throne.

The only problem with the dream of reconquest was that the Song had neither the will nor the military skill to mount their war. How would Genghis Khan rule China? One possible solution would be to recover north China and allow the Song to govern in his name. He also thought that the Khitan were potential surrogate rulers. The Song were too far away to be a serious military objective.

The Supreme Khan wanted to avoid giving either Jin or Xi Xia a pretext for invading Mongolia. He did not want to give them a reason for forming an alliance against him. If Jin and Xi Xia became allies, they would be strong enough to destroy his newly founded state. He wanted time to consolidate his power.

Merchants, spies and defectors kept the Supreme Khan informed of the situation at the Song Court. The Song was militarily weak. The Song courtiers of the Irredentist Party finally mounted an offensive against

214

Jin. They crossed the Yangzi River and attacked Jin garrison troops in the frontier province of Honan, a wild uninhabited region full of wild boar and other such animals.

He kept informed of the skirmishes on the long Jin-Song border on the Yangzi. The Jin had a problem at the rear of their army. Forced to protect his long southern border, the Jin Emperor had to send reinforcements to Honan.

The Song were a dangerous adversary for Jin because they were Han Chinese, their dynasty had originated in the North and they could claim the Dragon Throne. The Jin Emperor was too occupied with events in Song to be a problem when Genghis Khan went on the first of his foreign wars and mounted his campaign against Xi Xia.

The Xi Xia kingdom southwest of Mongolia was the last remnant of the old Tibetan empire. Xi Xia was the weakest of the three states. They were a warlike people of Tibetan stock whose army was weaker than the Jin Army, smaller, less well-trained, and less well-organized.

Xi Xia was smaller than Jin, not as well-fortified, nor as well-administered. The kingdom occupied the strategically important corridors to Inner Asia through which the caravan traffic passed on its way to and from the Muslim lands. Genghis Khan decided to take arms against them as his first conquest of a civilized state.

China was always the main objective of Mongol arms.

The Supreme Khan's motive was not the acquisition of territory--he had no intention of occupying China. He intended to rule it from the steppes. He desired prestige--he saw himself becoming the most important political and military power in Asia.

Chancellor Yeh-lu at that time served at the court of the Jin Emperor. As Minister in the highest bureaucracy in the government, the Central Secretariat. He was privy to the best intelligence that the Jin Emperor received. He was in daily attendance at the pinnacle of power in the Jin State. In his possession was the Seal of State of the Jin Dynasty. He knew that the Jin Emperor realized too late that a serious power had arisen in the North.

Why were the Chinese so slow to realize what a threat Genghis Khan had become? This was the answer of the Chancellor to Genghis Khan. Before 1203, the Jin Emperor believed that one or another of the coalitions that had risen up against Genghis Khan would destroy him, but he was wrong. Every confederacy of Genghis Khan's enemies was defeated. After the defeat of the Tai-yang in 1204, the Son of Heaven finally realized that a true menace had appeared in the North.

Unfortunately, In 1205 Jin hostilities with Song began. By the spring of 1206, it was too late for the Jin to take action against the Mongols.

Until this time there were still Naiman and Mergid forces belonging to Togtoa and Guchlug at large in the North who would have been happy to make an alliance with Jin against Genghis Khan. Genghis Khan denied the Chinese this possibility by sending Jochi to eliminate his old enemies.

After the Xi Xia Campaign, Genghis Khan ruled the lands on Jin's northern and western borders. He made an alliance with the Khitan who had a kingdom in Manchuria, to the northeast of Jin.

Jin-Song hostilities stopped in 1207 but there was no peace treaty until 1208 when the amount of tribute Song had to pay was increased. By then it was too late.

In 1209, Genghis Khan received word that the last emperor who could remind him of his duties as a vassal of Jin had died. His old envoy Prince Yuan-qi ascended the Dragon Throne as Emperor Wei. Genghis Khan was not impressed. This was one of the reasons he did not concern himself with hereditary rule. The Mongol nobility elected their leaders. Genghis Khan had defeated too many men who had inherited their thrones to be impressed with hereditary rule.

The paradox of Genghis Khan's rule lies in the contrast between the wise philosophical visionary who was a stern disciplinarian in his own life and who gave his people laws based on common sense and a strong affinity for justice with the ruthless military leader who knew no means but terror for subjugating his enemies.

Meticulous planning was the hallmark of his warfare. Long before his armies rode out of his pastures, everything had been gone into with great care, sometimes for more than a year. Before he went to war, he summoned the nobility and asked them to commit troops. The Supreme Khan established communication lines, supply lines and supply depots. He also sent out spies.

Although the Chinese histories stress the idea of limitless hordes of mounted nomads descending from the high plateaus of Asia, Genghis Khan's troops never exceeded more than 120,000 men and these had traveled across tremendous distances and natural barriers to reach their military objective. The conquest of China had been the dream of nomad khans for a thousand years, but no barbarian power had ever governed a civilized state. Trade or raid was the pattern of the old nomad empires, like the Xiong-nu relations with Tang. It was a matter of the man who was the leader, the man who believed it was his destiny to govern all peoples.

Genghis Khan's Camp, Khara Khorum

The Campaign against the Xi Xia was the first campaign in the civilized world, the first campaign against walled cities and it was a tough fight. The Mongol Army was experienced in steppe warfare, in the open spaces of the grasslands, but they had no experience of siege warfare against walled cities. This was the most difficult campaign of Genghis Khan's career so far, and the Xi Xia became Chinese vassals. Genghis Khan controlled northwest China, its trade routes and the mountain passes where the caravan traffic to and from China flowed on the Northern Routes.

The Mongol Army faltered in the fight and made mistakes. They accidentally caused a flood in their own camp and had to retreat. Eventually they learned the new type of warfare and they beat the enemy. To observers at the Jin court in northeast China, It was obvious that Genghis Khan would most likely be preparing for war with Jin, for Jin was richer and was a bigger prize. Yet the Jin Emperor might not have feared this new enemy, because the performance of the Army was not so spectacular that it would strike fear into an opponent of the size and power of Jin.

Genghis Khan thought that Xi Xia was a rehearsal for Jin.

Keshig Guards escorted a prince of the Onggud tribe into the Supreme Khan's tent. Alakash was dashing, handsome and dressed in fine clothes. He liked being a son of the steppe nobility and showed off his knowledge of protocol when being entertained in a powerful khan's tent. He uttered formal words of greeting.

Genghis Khan rose to greet his guest and welcome him. The two men embraced.

The Khan summoned his generals and sent for Tolui, his fourth son by Bortai, who camp with his father and served as chief of staff. Tolui was part of the Council of Generals and rode beside his father in campaigns. He had a great love of the military and Genghis Khan was proud of him.

When they arrived, Genghis Khan laid on a meal that was the product of a hunt. Alakash ate with great appetite, praised the hospitality and the real Mongol food. They engaged in the gossip that was the pastime of the Mongol nobility.

The Onggud were a branch of the Mongols who had settled outside of the Great Wall. Although they were no longer nomadic, their lands were an extension of the steppe. They were Nestorian Christians and survived by trading with China and had done so for centuries, but they were still, in their souls, people of the steppes. They looked and dressed like Mongols, their country resembled the grasslands of Mongolia and their people spoke a language related to Mongolian. They were Christians of the Eastern rite who had converted a century ago, at the same time as the Kereyids.

Alakash was stricken with love for the atmosphere. He said that this was what it must have been like in the tents of his ancestors. He laughed and joked with the generals and washed the dust of the journey out of his throat with Genghis Khan's *kara koumiz*, the special white koumiz made from Genghis Khan's white mares. It had the effect of a bolt of lightning. The Supreme Khan felt affection for Alakash and waited to hear the intelligence the Prince brought.

After the food and drink, the conversation turned to serious matters. Genghis Khan dismissed his servants and ordered his Guards to secure the area around his tent. "I've received information from servants and underlings many times. So in my own tent, I distrust their presence. You were right to come to me. I commend you. Tell me."

Alakash said, "The Jin have moved troops onto our soil. A Chinese officer, Field Marshall Tu, passed through the Great Wall and entered Onggud territory. He is cutting down the great timbers of our forests. He is building a fortress, a Jin Imperial Army garrison. When it is completed, it will contain a large number of troops who will be permanently stationed in our territory. This bodes ill for me and my people. I am invoking the old bond between our people. I am asking for your protection."

This was preparation for war. The Jin and Xi Xia had been at peace for more than forty years, but when the Mongol Army left Xi Xia territory, the Xi Xia were so furious with Jin for not sending troops to support them that they attacked Jin's western border. The Jin had to defend itself against Xi Xia. They had to go to war, and they knew that the Mongols were the cause. So they were arming themselves against the Mongol. It was only logical to assume that they would be a target if the Mongols had already attacked the northwest.

Genghis asked his commanders what they thought of Jin's move.

Subudei said, "In their situation, I would come against you."

"So would I," said Mukhali. "Sooner rather than later."

Genghis had a legal turn of mind. "You are a vassal of Jin, are you not?

Alakash said, "Yes, but my relationship with Jin is a marriage of convenience. My relationship with the Mongols is a marriage of blood. May I remind you, Khan, that I am a faithful vassal. I fulfilled my duty to you and contributed to your victory when I sent messengers to warm you of the Naiman attack."

Genghis Khan approved. "That you did." He wanted to know the Prince's mind because he disliked disloyalty.

"The Jin have put troops in my land. I came to you to invoke the right of a vassal to be protected from aggression."

Genghis Khan had a legalist turn of mind—to him the way of a Khan meant that he was just in his actions against foreign states.

"Here's the way I see things, Alakash. "For many years you have provided me with timber for construction of carts, corrals, tent-posts, lean-tos for tackle and so on. Your forests are a valuable asset to me. If the Jin deprive me of lumber, I consider it an act of war.

"Further, the Onggud are one people with the Mongols. We speak the same language. Your country is part of the steppes although you have become civilized. From your long association of trade with China, you have numbers and some fixed dwellings, but your people have been Mongol vassals for generations. Your relationship with the Jin is one of trade rather than one of blood. So I deduce that my relationship to you supersedes your relationship to Jin.

Genghis made his pronouncement. "Jin deployment of troops outside the Wall, their entry into Onggud territory means they are taking the offensive. I have rights as far as the Jin are concerned. I am the vassal of Jin. They should have notified me of their movement of troops against an ally who is vital to my interest. I acknowledge your right of protection."

Alakash said, "You should know. I have discussed the matter with my nobility. Not all are with me. Some want the alliance with Jin. We have heard that in Manchuria, the Khitan are rebelling against Jin." The Khitan were a former ruling house of North China.

"They are rebelling. That is true. A defector came to me asking for support in a war. I told them the time was not right. He was a member of the royal house. I considered it, but they do not have the strength to take on Jin."

Alakash said, "I don't come empty-handed Khan. I have a key to the gate in the Great Wall. When the time comes, I can open the gate and let an army enter without a fight. The Jin gave us the keys as a mark of trust. We guard the gates for him."

Genghis shot a meaningful glance at Subudei. Together Genghis Khan and Subudei would create a strategy. They could use the gate to move troops into Jin territory without fighting a battle, without giving advance notice. They could launch a surprise attack against Jin.

Subudei wanted clarification. "We could ride through the gates of the Great Wall without a battle?"

"Yes. I offer unobstructed entrance into Shanxi province."

Genghis said, "There's your answer. That explains why the Jin have built a garrison in your lands."

Khasar said, "Recently, four Jin defectors came to our camp. They were former officials in the Jin government political refugees who had run afoul of the Emperor. One man was a treasury official and he provided me with information about the size of the population. If I go against Jin, this is invaluable information. I gave them a reward. I have information about the composition of Jin troops and Jin defenses."

"What did the man say," Alakash asked.

"He told me that the population of the Jin Empire in 1195 was 48.5 million. That was the size of the tax rolls. He knew, because he collected the taxes. The Jin Army numbered half a million troops. 120,000 cavalry. The cavalry is mixed, Khitan, Onggud and Jin troops."

Alakash confirmed the intelligence. "120,000 cavalry, but they are short of horses." He smiled.

221

Genghis Khan said, "I know. I took away their main supply when I defeated the Xi Xia. My cavalry is the same size. They use the Han Chinese as infantry. The cavalry sometimes fights with body armor, but not always."

Alakash was impressed by Genghis Khan's knowledge of the Jin. He had sources from the Khongirad, his wife's people and the Muslim caravan merchants who crossed the Gobi to trade in Zhongdu, the Chinese capital."

Genghis Khan said, "This is my pronouncement. The Jin committed a hostile act against me. This is not their first hostile act. Prince Alakash, swear an oath of loyalty to me."

Alakash went down on one knee and put his fist to his heart.

"It's about time," said Subudei. He stood up and raised a glass. Mukhali joined him.

Genghis Khan said, "It is the way of Khans to seal an alliance with a marriage between two houses. I have a granddaughter who is of marriageable age."

Alakash said that he had a son."

"Then we will arrange the marriage," said the Khan.

Alakash stepped up and embraced the Khan.

Genghis said, "Bogorji, take Keshig Guardsmen and ride to the Xi Xia capital. Tell the King to send troops for my campaign. Place a garrison in command of the invasion routes that run through Xi Xia territory."

Genghis sent for Shiki Kutuku. "Shiki, go to the Khitan king. Tell him that I accept him as a vassal, have him swear the oath, and that it is his duty to cease contributing Khitan troops and horses to the Jin cavalry. Take Bortai's brother Noyan with you. He will like it that the Khongirad are with me."

Tolui said, "So, father, you have surrounded your enemy with your allies, like animals in a hunt."

"Exactly," said Genghis. "Mukhali, take troops and ride to Onggud territory and attack the Jin forces there. Destroy the fort and remove all Jin troops from Onggud territory.

"Guard, send a messenger to the camp of my son Jochi informing him of my plan for war. Summon my sons Jagadai and Ogodei from their fiefdoms. Together with Jochi they will command the Army of the Right. Give each of them orders to contribute 20,000 troops. Tell them to join me soon as possible.

A Guard announced that a Mongol envoy had just returned from a diplomatic mission to the Song court. "Send him in at once," the Khan said.

The envoy delivered his message. "The Song Emperor refused a Song-Mongol alliance. They inform you that the Song Emperor concluded a peace treaty with the Jin Emperor and paid Jin tribute, tens of thousands of bolts of silk and a similar number of ingots of silver."

"The Song are very foolish," Genghis Khan replied. "Had they made an alliance with me, I could have restored them to the Dragon Throne."

The crossing of the Gobi Desert would take a month and would take place in cool weather--The Armies of the Left, Right and Center, 120,000 men, needed water and food.

The Muslim caravan merchants provided Genghis Khan with information on the caravan routes across the Gobi. The master stroke was that they gave him information about the oases fed by glacier melt. They supplied connections where the Master of Provisions could acquire supplies while the army traveled to North China.

Once the crossing was accomplished, the army lived off the local population. The Master of Provisions confiscated supplies. Once they reached the other side of the Gobi, they would make camp. Men and horses would rest in the steppe lands.

The best time for a crossing was spring when the weather was cooler. The Supreme Khan's army was divided into three wings, each taking a different route, to avoid overwhelming the oases.

With The Horde, everything was mobile. Dodai Cherbi, Master of Provisions, saw to supplies, the herds and wagons that would follow the Army across the Gobi. Belgutei rounded up the horse herds that would go with the army across the desert.

Each soldier brought five horses as remounts so he did not ride his horses to exhaustion. Each man brought the equipment required of a member of the Mongol Army: two flasks of water; rations of jerky; two bows (compound bows made of horn), two quivers of arrows; a silk undergarment; an inflatable raft made of tanned leather sewn together (for fording rivers and also for crossing rivers in night raids when stealth was important and the horses were to be left behind).

Preparation for the crossing took time. The heat of summer passed. The storms of autumn ended. Winter came and went. The Army was ready. Spring was the time to ride. Before the army departed his camp, Genghis Khan offered a libation to the Eternal Blue Sky, submitted his will to the will of the Eternal Blue Sky, and asked for victory.

He was ready. He commanded his generals to muster the army.

The Supreme Khan stood on a platform and listened to the ovation of his army, one hundred twenty thousand troops. They pounded their shields with their swords. Their approval washed over him in waves. He wore the same uniform they wore, he slept in a tent as they did, he ate the same food that they did and he rode at the head of the army. He held up his hands and they fell silent.

"The Jin have meddled in our affairs for generations. In the time of our great-grandfathers, we were supreme among the tribes of the steppes but the Jin killed our great leader Ambaghai. They set the Tatar against us and the Tatar killed my father, Yesugei the Brave. They promoted wars in the steppes without fear of reprisal. They killed our leaders without punishment. For these wrongs against *Yesse Mongol Ulus*, the Great Mongol Nation, I declare a war of national revenge."

The army shouted their approval.

"You men are the greatest, most skilled and most highly trained army the world has ever known, better than the Huns, better than the Turks, better than the Goths. Our Army is more disciplined, better integrated, and better trained, superior in every way to the Army of Jin. The Army of Jin is divided and has dissidence within its ranks. I do not make a difference among the people who join us. The Jin have different nationalities as troops: Han infantry, nomad officers of the Jurchen tribe, and Khitan cavalry. They do not fight as one as our Army does.

"I offer you riches and the glory of defeating the greatest civilization on earth. We will take three paths across the Gobi and we will fight our way to the palace of the Jin Emperor. The Eternal Blue Sky has told me that I am destined to govern all peoples. We will all return to our beloved steppes to celebrate the greatest victory in our history."

The men cheered and he waited.

"You will be rich and you will have glory and I will be with you all the way. We will return to the steppes as masters of Jin."

The men cheered. He announced the battle order. "I will ride at the head of the Army of the Center." A cheer went up from the men. My son Tolui, and Generals Subudei and Mukhali will ride with me.

"My sons Jochi, Jagadai and Ogodei will command the Army of the Right. Bogorji will ride with them. Khasar, Jebe, Jurchedei, Noyan and Tolun Cherbi will command the Army of the Left."

225

The roar of the men was deafening. He dismissed them and went to his tent.

Yu-er-lo, Khongirad Country
June, 1211

Genghis Khan made camp in Khongirad country, the land where he had lived when he was betrothed to Bortai. There the people knew him and he was a welcome guest. It was close to the Chinese border, but he was camped in nomad territory. That was the way he liked it.

This was a border region, close to the mountains that protected the Jin capital.

Genghis Khan took his place at the head his campaign table and addressed the Council of Generals. He welcomed them and brought out a map that had been provided to him by the Muslim merchants who frequented is camp. Then he presented the map with his battle plan for the invasion of Jin China.

The big surprise in the campaign was going to be the Army of the Right, camped in Onggud territory. Bogorji retained the enthusiasm of his youthful exploits with Genghis Khan. He reported on the state of affairs with Prince Alakash. "No Jin forces have been deployed against him. The Jin have no idea that a foreign army is the guest of the Prince."

Khasar said, "Alakash has good security."

Subudei always calculated the risk. He never painted a rosy picture. "The Jin will learn of our presence sooner or later. Our deployment is too large for it to go unnoticed for long."

Genghis Khan pointed to their map. "The Armies of the Center and the Left invade through the mountains in the northeast. Two roads go down the mountains. At the bottom is The Grille, where the Great Wall ends. There are two walls at the bottom. We must not be trapped or the Jin forces will decimate us. Once we pass the Grille, we are on the road to the capital. Twenty-five miles away."

Subudei discussed warfare. "We will be attacking walled forts. This is a different type of warfare for us. That is why we had the campaign against Xi Xia. The Jin have the advantage of superior numbers. We have the advantage of surprise."

Genghis Khan said, "My sons and the Army of the Right are the reserve. I will deploy them as a surprise at the right time. They will form a pincer movement with the other two armies."

He explained the battle plan. "We fight our way down through the mountain passes to The Grille. Our objective is to get to the foot of the mountain, get through the Grille, and take command of the two roads to the capital.

Subudei pointed to the map, "On the way down the mountain road, we have to take three main fortresses, Weining, Xuande and Fuzhou. The walls of the fortresses are made of wood. Thcy protect the border. They were built in lonely desolate places and it is difficult, if not impossible, for Jin commanders to reinforce them. They are susceptible to fire. We have siege engines with us."

Genghis Khan said, "Our forces have better training. We have superior tactics and equipment. *Do not underestimate the enemy.* The Jin Army is experienced in mountain warfare. We have not fought this type of campaign before.

The Khan's youngest son Tolui was a talented officer, a skilled horseman, popular with the men. He asked, "What are the mountain roads made of?"

Subudei said, "The roads are rocky so the horses will have difficult footing. You'll have to take care with the animals. The weather will be extremely cold. Some men and horses may have a hard time breathing. said Genghis.

Subudei said, "We will be outnumbered. Let the men know and prepare them. We don't want them to panic. We cannot afford to lose troops."

A *Keshig* Guards arrived and announced that a defector had come to camp and asked to see Genghis Khan.

"Bring him in," said Genghis. He turned to the generals. "Defectors are of critical importance to us. I guarantee good treatment to defectors. If a Jin general defects, I will offer him a command under one of you. Guide yourselves accordingly. We need their intelligence. Test them. Make sure of their loyalty. Don't fall into any traps. But treat them as fellow officers."

The officer entered the tent with his *Keshig* escort He carried himself with military deportment.

The officer had a military bearing and gave up his intelligence standing at attention. "The Jin command has ordered two armies to ride into the passes to defend the fortresses against you. They approach through the valley of the lower Yang River.

"The smaller Jin force arrived at Wu-sha Bao in August and has already erected defense fortifications. They were under orders to make camp and wait for the arrival of your main army at Yeh-hu Ling. The smaller force waits for you. The main Jin force has not arrived."

Genghis Khan thanked him. "You will have a command under Subudei. We will see to your tent when we return."

He addressed his generals. "All right. Tell the army to mount up. We'll eliminate the smaller army, then we'll engage the main forces. Let's take the offensive. Our first engagement on Jin soil will be against inferior numbers. This will give the men confidence.

"The Emperor thinks if he defeats us in the mountains, we will quit the country. He knows he has the advantage on the mountain terrain.

"Jebe, this is your command, your chance to be the arrow in a great contest. Leave at once. Take the defector. I give him a command with you as his superior officer. He knows the country and will be a valuable guide. Go to Wu-sha Bao and mount a surprise attack. Cut off all possibility of a Jin retreat to Weining."

Jebe asked, "Why do you want the road to Weining cut off?"

Genghis replied, "It is a route of retreat for the Jin Army. I want to take them out of the battle. I want to deny them the chance to regroup and attack when our main army arrives."

Jebe saluted and left. Genghis reached for his war helmet. He went outside and made his offering to The Ancestors. He prepared to take command.

Mongol Winter Headquarters
Lung-hu Tai, 25 miles from the Chinese capital
Winter, 1211- 1212

Dragon Mouth Mountain was a fitting name for the camp of the Mongol khan.

The Supreme Khan's breath hung in the frosty air and his feet crunched in the snow. At the entrance to his tent, icicles hung from the flagpoles that held his standards. It was some weeks before the Lunar New Year and Genghis had given the order for a feast. If his men had to weather a bad winter far from home, he would fill their bellies and give them a celebration.

By the light of the campfire, soldiers played sentimental steppe ballads, haunting melancholy tunes on the instruments of herders: mouth organ, *pi-pa*, butterfly harp, drums and lively dance tunes.

Dodai Cherbi, the Master of Provisions, had a supply of *koumiz* and the men were getting drunk and dancing jigs, unwinding after the hard season of fighting. Army cooks erected spits to roast whole lambs.

Genghis Khan strode through the camp greeting his soldiers. He drank a flagon of *koumiz* with the men and retired to his tent. He took a seat at his campaign table and joined Khasar, Tolui and the rest of his high command. He wished them a Happy New Year. They drank a toast to his health and to the conquest of Jin.

The Supreme Khan went around the table receiving good wishes from his commanders.

A Jin defector sitting at the far end of the Khan's table drinking rice wine, said, "Sir, take advantage of the disorder caused by your victories. Sweep down into the plain of China. You will have more plunder than you ever dreamed of and you will control North China all the way to the sea."

Jebe was fearless, raring to go, a man of exceptionally high spirits. "I'll plunder the plain of North China for you, Genghis. Give me the order."

Genghis Khan gave the order.

When spring came, Jebe took several thousand men and rode across the plain, through towns, small cities, villages, through the open countryside, putting everything to the torch.

He came to the Liao River, frozen with ice. Jebe commanded his cavalry to ride across it. He watched as the men crossed six at a time, their arms on each other's shoulders, the horses close together. From the river he drove straight on Dungjing in the hope of taking it unaware but the garrison was ready and the place was well defended.

He commanded his army to make camp in front of the city. When he was sure that the garrison had seen them, he had troops ride the perimeter of the wall, firing at the garrison. He feigned retreat, leaving the camp and baggage as though the army had given up and departed. The citizens threw open the gates of their town so they could loot Jebe's abandoned camp.

Jebe had ordered a retreat of thirty miles. His army was out of sight. His men changed to their spare mounts and completed the return journey in twenty-four hours. They arrived on the night of the Lunar New Year. It was the most festive night of the year for the Chinese. It was a bright cold February night with crisp clean air and thousands of stars in the sky.

The soldiers had opened the city gates for the New Year celebrations: the New Year ritual was to cast out the evil spirits and welcome in the good spirits. The populace were drinking and dancing, dancing and drinking. The people lit thousands of gaily colored lanterns. A lion dance was in progress. Jebe's troops heard the crashing cymbals and banging drums drifting out into the night.

Jebe's army poured into the city. Distracted by their festivities, the people were caught unaware and offered no resistance. The Mongols took possession of the city with a minimum of killing. The population was terrified into submission.

News traveled to the capital. The Jin Emperor ordered an army to ride out to the great North Plain in pursuit of Jebe, but too late. Jebe had delivered a great Mongol victory. Genghis gave permission to plunder and Jebe let loose the Mongol hordes in China.

He swept through the plain of China all the way to the sea. The barbarians had never seen civilization, a continuously settled region that went for hundreds of miles to the sea. Farms, villages, cities, markets, shops, factories, temples, all this was new to them. The pillaging went on for a month.

The looting began and the dazed of North China watched helplessly, as the riders came on their war ponies. The Mongol Army went on the rampage, looting, burning, killing, pillaging, and raping. The Lunar New Year turned into a nightmare.

Messengers brought the news to the Supreme Khan. Booty and victory. This was the moment Genghis Khan had been waiting for. He had taken his revenge. .

By January 1212, hundreds of towns had been captured, plundered and set to the torch. Jebe packed up the khan's booty on black wooden wagons and returned to Dragon Mouth Mountain in February.

Genghis Khan commended him for his performance and gave him an extra share of his booty. Jebe distributed booty among his commanders and they distributed it among their junior commanders and the men. The Khan provided riches for those who followed him.

Genghis Khan ordered Jebe to take 1,000 of the battle-seasoned troops down the road to the capital for a reconnaissance mission. Genghis Khan wanted to know conditions on the road to the capital. How many troops guarded the road?

Three thousand crack troops of the Jin Imperial Guard met Jebe on the road. They fought bravely and well. Jebe sent back word to the Khan. He was impressed by their courage. He also informed the Khan that the local peasantry were loyal to the Imperial Government.

Jebe questioned a Jin commander about how many Guards held the capital. The commander replied that there were two hundred thousand men.

Jebe told the Khan that he believed this to be an exaggeration, meant to frighten the invaders.

Jebe returned to camp and reported to the Council of Generals. Genghis Khan announced that in the spring they would take the capital.

Jebe said, "The capital is magnificent. Zhongdu is beyond anything any of us has ever seen. We have never had a military objective like this. The walls are forty feet high and eighteen feet thick. The capital covers 18 square miles. It has a million inhabitants. This is civilization, Khan. We have never encountered this."

Genghis Khan said, "It is a building surrounded by a wall. There is a way to take it. My men came for plunder and glory. I cannot leave a battle-seasoned army sitting in camp and give them nothing to do. I know how my men think. They will all be straining at the bit to get their bit of gold. That's why I ordered Jebe to let them loose.

"As to my plan for the spring offensive, I will explain to the men. Listen to me. The battle is in the mind of the enemy. Do not let the Jin defeat you in the battle of the mind.

"I think of it this way. I am fortunate in my enemy, The Jin Emperor has made a tactical error, either from his failure to gather intelligence or the poor ability of his commanders.

"The Jin Imperial Army has failed to place troops between my eastern and western armies. This is to my advantage. They have created a situation that allows me to use my forces as I please. Shanxi is the economic heart of China. The western army will lodge a spear in the heart of the dragon."

In December of 1212, the Jin Emperor sent a message to Genghis Khan. Genghis Khan had been operations in Jin China for a year and a half. This was the first communication from the Son of Heaven.

The Emperor wanted to sue for peace.

The Jin Army had lost so many troops that the Imperial troops were at a disadvantage when meeting the Mongol Army in the field. They had no fresh supply of horses and their cavalry was undermanned. The last remaining source the Jin had for horses were the Muslims traders of the Gansu Corridor in the Far West and the distances were too far to re-supply the army in good time. '

As to conditions in the Jin empire, things were not good. there was a shortage of food, the mountain passes were under the control of an invading army and the rebel king of the Khitan had been installed in the northeast. The Onggud nobility who had been Jin vassals went over to the side of the Mongols.

The Jin had many divisions under arms, most defending major cities and strategic and important towns. As to the rest of the country, the Emperor had informed the commanders of minor towns that they had to defend themselves. The Mongol Army had decimated the best of the Jin forces and was on the offensive.

Genghis Khan saw that it was within his grasp to be the new master of North China.

The Jin Emperor offered booty but he requested that in return, the Mongol Army leave China. Considering the Mongol position, Genghis Khan considered that the terms offered by the Emperor were insufficient.

Genghis Khan asked the imperial messenger to wait in camp and sent for his generals. He told them he had decided to reject the Emperor's offer and continue the war. He had their unanimous support. Genghis Khan sent a letter of refusal to the Jin Emperor.

More defectors came to his camp and asked to join the Mongol Army. These were men of the world. They could read the handwriting on the wall. They knew that this was no mere barbarian raid. They believed that the Jin had lost the Mandate of Heaven. They believed that Genghis

Khan would be the new master of Jin China. They told of a revolution inside the Imperial Palace. A general had killed the old emperor and for a time the Jin had had no ruler. The ministers had to convince the general not to take the Dragon Throne.

Genghis Khan understood now why no one had attempted to halt the operations of his army inside China. The Jin were occupied with a palace revolt. With no one firmly in command, North China could be his.

Genghis Khan made it a point not to overreach. Prudence was another of his cardinal rule of war. A great leader had to recognize his limitations. This requires honest with oneself. Many rulers were dazzled by their own legends and had sycophants who lied to them. This was not the case with Genghis and his Council of Generals.

Lesser men would have tried to capitalize on the situation in the palace. Many would have been driven by greed and glory. Not Genghis Khan.

Another of Genghis Khan's cardinal principles of war was thoroughness, attention to detail. He was a planner, working out every detail in advance, leaving nothing to change, before the first soldier got on the back of a horse.

The winter of 1213 arrived and Genghis Khan told Tolui that did not want to be trapped in the mountains in winter. He gave orders for the Army to withdraw to his winter campground at Dolon Nor.

He announced his intention to return to China in the spring. He left troops to occupy the small border towns on the Khongirad side of the mountains because the towns were supply depots for the forts. He did not want the army to have its supply lines cut.

The Mongols took hundreds of cartloads of booty with them. The Army had been in good condition, well-fed and physically fit, but they had fought for six months and they were ready for their winter rest.

When Genghis Khan left North China, the populace had the winter months to contemplate the fate that would befall them when The Horde returned in the spring.

A mood of uncertainty hung over the capital like a black cloud. The Jin high command debated ideas for the defense of the city. The new Emperor did not have the strength of will to take control of the Army. The Han Chinese at court had divided loyalties. Some supported the foreign rule of the Jin Dynasty. Some wished for the return of a Han Chinese dynasty.

Chancellor Yeh-lu would later become the greatest statesman of the Mongol Empire. At the time of the conquest, Yeh-lu was serving in the Central Secretariat, the highest bureau in the Jin Empire. He was well aware of the disorder in the palace. The government still had to run. Yeh-lu went about his duties as a means of clinging to his sanity.

Genghis Khan passed winter devising his strategy for the rest of the campaign. Spring came and with it came new orders from Genghis Khan.

General Jebe took the most strategic pass in the mountains, a place that was weakly defended. It was said by the peasants that the pass was guarded by a demon that manifested as a yellow wind. Jebe massacred the population and took the pass. He had no problems with the demon or a yellow wind.

A carpet of white bones covered the mountain road for many years to come, a lesson to those who chose to resist the Mongol Army.

To the south of Huailai was a gorge seventeen miles long, a dark-spirited and gloomy place, overhung with gray clouds. This was Liaoyang, the eastern capital, the main garrison of the Jin Army. Crack troops guarded the innermost barricades of the Great Wall, the place where the road to the capital began.

Jebe rode at the head of a large force and attacked the walls of the Jin garrison. The full might of the Mongol Army descended on the best troops of the Jin Army and decimated them. Jebe did not stop.

He turned toward Fei-hu Pass and took it by surprise. He pressed on and fell upon Xijing Pass in a surprise attack. He took every fort and pass on the way to the capital.

Messengers informed the Jin Emperor that the Mongols had destroyed the main forces of the Jin Army. The way to the capital lay open.

The Emperor dispatched General Juhu with troops and orders to prevent the Mongol Army from entering the region of the capital. At the sight of the victorious army, Jin troops broke ranks and fled.

The Supreme Khan took command of the Army of the Center and undertook the final offensive on the capital.

Advancing by forced rides through the narrow road, they surprised the Khitan commander of the northern mouth of the Juyung Pass, He surrendered. His stand against the Mongols had been heroic, but cannibalism had broken out among his troops and he reached the conclusion that resistance was futile.

The Mongols beat the Jin Army back to the southern mouth of the Pass and trapped them. The wings, commanded by Prince Tolui and General Chugu descended from the hillsides while Genghis Khan initiated a frontal attack.

The Jin troops in the field panicked and surrendered but the defenders of Auyung, the local fort, refused to surrender. The commander sealed the gates of the southern mouth of the pass with molten iron. For thirty miles around, the commander had the countryside strewn with caltrops, iron balls with four sharp prongs placed in the ground so that one spike projected upward. This was a last stand.

The Supreme Khan camped before this pass for a month, then gave up. This was the only place that Genghis Khan proved unable to reduce to his control. Behind his army, the road from the north mouth of the pass was littered with corpses.

Genghis Khan led the main army to Jozhou and arrived there on November 10th. His descent from the mountains had been a complete victory. He had taken possession of all the forts and all the roads leading to the capital.

The Supreme Khan left Mukhali to complete the siege of Jozhou and retired to supervise the setting up of his headquarters. The camp was situated twenty-five miles north of Zhongdu with no obstacles in his way.

On November 19, he dispatched a Xi Xia officer in the service of the Mongol Army to offer the Jin Emperor peace. The officer was admitted through the city gates of the capital and escorted to the Imperial Palace where he delivered this message to the Son of Heaven.

These are the words of Genghis Khan, who is Beloved of Heaven. The whole of Shandong and Hobei are now in my possession while you retain only Zhongdu; Heaven has made you so weak that should I further molest you, I do not know what the Eternal Blue Sky would say or do; I am willing to withdraw my army, but what provision will you make to still the demands of my officers?
The Emperor made no reply.

Meanwhile, Jebe took the Army of the Left and fought his way across the plain to the sea. The Mongol hordes charged over the plain and swooped down on villages and towns terrorizing the inhabitants, stealing their possession, torching their villages, raping and kidnapping their women and daughters. They tore through cities, riding their horses down narrow streets scattering children and animals, chickens, dogs, cats. They attacked ninety towns, looted and burned them to the ground.

Jin generals barricaded themselves inside the walled cities of the plain and tried to defend them with armies conscripted from the peasantry. There were no professional soldiers to be had.

The Mongols seized the elderly and women and children who were abandoned in the villages. They drove them as a human shield in front of the army when the Mongols attacked the walled cities with their meager defenses. Mongol siege units launched fire-arrows dipped in pitch and lit with torches; they hurled missiles covered in burning naphtha.

The peasants, nauseated at the sight of members of their families in front of the invading army, disobeyed their officers. Instead of shooting back, the peasants surrendered the cities. The Mongols looted, but they did not burn the cities nor slaughter all the inhabitants.

Genghis Khan was master of North China all the way to the sea. He decided to see for himself what Jebe had conquered.

Riding at the head of the Army of the Center, the Supreme Khan entered the great plain of North China. The sight of civilization, hundreds of miles of continuous settlement, cities, towns, villages, farms, factories, churches, temples, warehouses, wharfs on the river, boats, shocked him. He had never imagined the existence in his wildest dreams of the spectacle that lay before him. He did not comprehend sedentary life and he loathed the peasants, people who lived in fixed buildings, hovels compared to his tent, who stayed rooted to one spot all their lives, slaves to the elements.

Genghis told General Subudei that civilization was not for him. He loved the free open life of the steppes. From one end of the plain to the other, corpses filled rivers and lay in open fields. Disease and pestilence spread through the population and infected the army.

He gave the army permission to plunder the plain. They had been on campaign for two years. He had to reward them or they might mutiny and turn on him. After a year and a half of fighting, Genghis Khan unleashed his army. For six months, the autumn and winter of 1213, the Mongol Army until they had ravished the entire plain.

It was a horrible six months, with the barbarians cut loose from the iron discipline of the army. They attacked ninety towns, looted them and burned them to the ground. The whole plain was scorched, scarred and burned, smoldering, stinking with the smell of burning flesh, burned out cities, blackened forests which had once been verdant and filled with birdsong, emptied of life, charred earth. Rivers were filled with corpses, timbers torn from buildings, dead animals.

On hearing that the Mongol Army was approaching a walled city that they were charged with defending, many Chinese generals barricaded themselves inside and defended them with peasant armies. The Mongols seized the elderly, and women and children who remained in the unprotected villages and drove them, a human shield, in front of the Mongol advance guard. The peasant defenders of the cities, at the sight of members of their own families and countrymen in the enemy vanguard, disobeyed their officers. Instead of shooting fire-arrows which had been dipped in pitch and lit with torches, or hurling missiles covered in burning naphtha, cities surrendered. These were not burned nor were the inhabitants slaughtered.

North China was a smoking ruin. A Chinese chronicler who had joined the Mongol camp wrote: "Everywhere north of the Yellow River could be seen dust and smoke and the sound of drums rose to heaven."

Genghis Khan had achieved his purpose. He had promised his troops booty and glory and he had provided both. The men had slaked their appetites and were ready to follow him anywhere. The Army loaded its booty was loaded into the Mongol carts with the big-spoked wheels and withdrew to the north to the open steppe-like country at Dolon Nor.

At the end of 1213, more defectors came to Genghis Khan's camp informing the Supreme Khan that the Emperor Xuanzang was so hard-pressed for troops that he had pardoned all the criminals in the capital and put them under arms. He gave them good treatment and a place in his army.

Alone with his generals, Genghis Khan told his Council that their adversary was crumbling. He would take pleasure, he said, in destroying him and taking all that he possessed, especially the imperial wives and the imperial steeds.

The fabled and magnificent city of Zhongdu, the greatest and richest prize in Asia, was twenty-five miles away.

Zhongdu, the Jin Capital
May, 1214

Inside the city, an atmosphere of impending disaster hung in the air. The Emperor Xuanzang placed the capital under martial law. Crack Jin Imperial Guards maintained order in the streets.

Chancellor Yeh-lu served in the Central Secretariat of the Jin Dynasty. He was an astrologer and skilled in consulting the oracles. He cast the I Ching and saw the signs and omens that revealed that the Jin Dynasty had lost the Mandate of Heaven. His astrological predictions told him that Genghis Khan was destined to be the new master of China. He was a Buddhist in his private life, and he meditated every day, trying to preserve his equanimity in the midst of disaster.

The Jin Emperor received word that famine had broken out in the province of Shanxi. The war had interrupted the agricultural cycle, and people were starving and were leaving their homes in search of food. Emperor Xuanzang, the former prince who met Genghis Khan in the steppes, sent food from the southern city of Kaifeng

Kaifeng was an old capital, under Jin control. Refugees cluttered the roads in and out of Shanxi so that Jin soldiers had difficulty bringing relief.

Chancellor Yeh-lu was in daily attendance upon Xuanzang, The Emperor expressed many times his regret that he ever given up his military post, his life of action for the Dragon Throne. The occupant of the Dragon Throne confided to his minister that the Emperor of China was little more than Genghis Khan's hostage.

The Emperor was sickened by the terms he had been forced to give the barbarian. Xuanzang had visited the nomad camp. How could a lowlife topple the greatest civilization on earth? It went against everything the Emperor was raised to believe in.

Thinking of his place in Chinese history, he demanded that his chancellor advise him: was an emperor obliged to keep his word to the commander of an invasion force.

Yeh-lu was unfamiliar with military customs regarding the conduct of war. As for political advice, Chancellor Yeh-lu had confidence in his opinion. He reminded the Emperor that he had the duty to be a sage emperor and show benevolence to the people. He still had many divisions of imperial forces. He was still in control of most of the country.

The Emperor ordered the commander of the Imperial Guards to conscript all men capable of bearing arms. These were forbidden to leave the city. The Commander opened the jails and took any man of an age to bear arms and conscripted him into the army.

Unable to bear the tension any longer, the Son of Heaven decided to break his word to Genghis Khan. The original commander of the capital had built four small forts outside the main city connected to the city walls by underground tunnels. The emperor decided to abandon the capital. He was sick of being Genghis Khan's prisoner. He issued instructions that the imperial family was to move into the northern fort; his relatives, to the western fort; the wealthiest citizens of the capital, to the eastern fort; government officials and their families, into the southern fort. He assigned 4,000 soldiers to each. The remaining 20,000 troops of the garrison of the capital remained in Zhongdu.

This done, the Emperor informed the court that he was transferring the capital to Kai-feng, a city in Honan south of the Yellow River. Kai-feng had an abundance of resources and the wide river afforded a natural barrier against the invaders. He was taking his people and fleeing to safety. He was breaking his word to Genghis Khan.

The Commander of the Imperial Guards tried to dissuade the Emperor. "Sir, you gave your word to Genghis Khan that you would remain in the capital. You cannot leave the people to their fate. Forgive me, but I think you should stay behind to give hope to the populace. If the Son of Heaven abandons Zhongdu, barbarian general will take the city and will be the master of North China."

The Emperor replied, "My son the Heir Apparent will remain behind in the capital to give hope to the people. If I stay here, my dynasty will be at an end. From Kai-feng, I have the hope of mounting a resistance and defeating the invaders."

The Son of Heaven took an escort of 2,000 Khitan Imperial Guards and left for Kai-feng. He gave orders to fly the imperial standard as though he were a reigning emperor. Thirty miles from the capital, several hundred of the Khitan officers mutinied and abandoned the emperor. He gave orders for a Jin offensive and offered purses of gold and silver to the officers and men who defeated Mongol troops. A Mongol Army appeared in Shanxi. Another appeared in Honan. Xuanzang sent half-trained infantry out to meet them and the Mongol Army slaughtered them in the field. The dynasty was dying.

At first the Heir Apparent stayed in Zhongdu. Fearing for his son's life, the Emperor ordered the Heir Apparent to join him in Kai-feng. They left the capital under the control of the Commander of the garrison. Chancellor Yeh-lu remained in Zhongdu and was a witness to the fall of the dynasty. He never dreamed it would be my destiny to serve Genghis Khan.

Chancellor Yeh-lu later recorded in his history of the Mongol khan that he served Genghis Khan for thirteen years and never knew him to break his word to his people.

35 Crash, Boom, Fall

Yu-er-lo
Genghis Khan's Summer Headquarters
July 1214

Khitan officers who mutinied rode north to Mongol headquarters and brought Genghis Khan the news that the Jin Emperor had broken his word to Genghis Khan and fled the capital for the old capital. He had taken his family and trusted officers. The officer who came to Genghis Khan's camp had left him.

This was treachery. Genghis Khan had taken the Emperor's word and Genghis Khan was furious. He was disgusted that the Jin Emperor abandoned his capital and his people to fate.

By September of 1214, Genghis rode to Zhongdu to see the capital for himself. It was vast beyond his comprehension. He realized that it was beyond the capability of his Army to take the capital by siege warfare. He would never be able to breach the walls or break down the gate.

He had to force the commander of the city to open the gates to him. He decided upon a blockade. A city of such a vast size needed supplies. Daily hundreds of cartloads of foods came to the city. He blocked the arrival and entry of food. It was more efficient to starve the inhabitants of the capital to death. The Commander of the Jin Imperial Guard would be forced to open the city gates and surrender the city. Otherwise, he would have a city of death on his hands.

He ordered his army to surround the city. On pain of death, no supplies were to enter or leave. The Jin did not have the force to break the Mongol blockade. A few times, Imperial Jin officers managed to sneak a shipment of food in by a secret entrance, but this was the exception.

The blockade continued through the terrible winter of 1214 and for ten months afterward. Autumn ended and winter came and passed. The Mongol Army had been in China for four years. Chancellor Yeh-lu was a resident of the capital during those terrible months and witnessed at first hand the starvation of the population.

244

The Supreme Khan remained in his tent at Lung-hu Tai and spent his time organizing the parts of China already in his hands, dividing the territory under his control into administrative districts and setting up a system for the remission of taxes.

His generals wanted to raze North China and turn it into pasture for Mongol horses. Genghis Khan declined their request.

In March of 1215, Genghis dispatched a Mongol envoy to Kaifeng to offer peace to the Emperor. The envoy delivered Genghis Khan's message: "You used the peace to deceive me. You think you are safer dealing with me from a distance, but you are not. Zhongdu will fall."

Emperor Xuanzang rebuffed the Mongol messenger and sent an army and supplies to the capital in April, 1215.

Genghis Khan heard that three armies were approaching the capital. He dispatched forces to meet them. The relief commander, Li, was drunk and was taken prisoner; the Mongols confiscated his 1,000 cartloads of food. The emperor began making plans for a second attempt at relief.

A defector came out and informed the Mongol generals that conditions inside the city were so desperate that cannibalism had broken out. An astrologer told Genghis Khan that the signs and omens that accompany the fall of a dynasty--chaos, disorder and rebellion--were everywhere.

Zhongdu, after ten months, surrendered to Genghis Khan.

Commanders of the garrison opened the city gates. General Shih-mo led Mongol troops into the city. The Mongol Army plundered and put the city to the torch. Three quarters of the city was on fire. Mongol soldiers sacked all but a part of the capital and slew many thousands of inhabitants. One of the Imperial palaces was set on fire. Zhongdu burned for a month while the soldiers engaged in savagery, looting, murder and rape.

Women jumped from the ramparts to their deaths rather than be taken as slaves by the Mongols. Their bodies rotted in the moat that surrounded the wall, the gauzy fibers of their elegant gowns filthy with river mud and blood.

Shih-mo sent word to Genghis Khan's headquarters that the capital was in the hands of the Mongol Army. Genghis Khan called his senior commanders. Khasar rode at his side for the occupation of the capital. Genghis Khan gave the city a Mongolian name, *Khanbalik,* which means the Khan's city. He thanked The Ancestors for granting him victory.

Word spread through the camp. Mongol soldiers threw their caps in the air. Every Mongol was rich. Genghis Khan was now the supreme political and military ruler in Asia.

Chancellor Yeh-lu stood at the gates of the Imperial Palace contemplating the ruin of the capital.. Rise and fall, yin and yang, this had been the pattern of Chinese history for millennia. Yeh-lu had the seal of state of the Jin Emperor. He detached himself from the horrendous tragedy and with an escort from the Khan, retired to a Buddhist monastery. The great pattern of dynastic change had been set in motion. His world had come to an end.

During the last days of Jin, Chancellor Yeh-lu, a high court official, was powerless to affect the course of events. He worked in the Central Secretariat, the highest agency in the bureaucracy, and he was in constant attendance upon the Jin Emperor. He was a witness to the fall of the dynasty.

By May of 1215, the capital fell. Zhongdu was in Mongol hands. The campaign lasted four years.

When the cold weather of winter began, people in the cities were so destitute that they went into the temples and removed the great statues of Buddha, chopped them up and used them for kindling wood. Even the great bronze temple bells were taken as plunder by the Mongols, so there were no bells to ring out in celebration the day the last of Genghis Khan's army rode north.

What good were worldly treasures and worldly position when Zhongdu was a smoking ruin littered with corpses, the gutters running slick with fat rendered from human bodies?

Chancellor Yeh-lu had observed Shiki Kutuku cataloguing the contents of the Jin Emperor's treasury while the Mongol Army loaded up black carts. The Imperial Treasury contained millions of gold and silver ingots, millions of bolts of the finest silks, satins and brocades, hundreds of thousands of priceless objects of art, carvings, paintings, embroideries, sculptures of precious and semi-precious stone and ivory, porcelains, jewelry, bronzes. The carts rumbled off across the Gobi where they were unloaded in the treasury of Genghis Khan. The gold and ivory Dragon Throne was placed in the tent of the Supreme Khan. A Jin official tried to offer Shiki a portion of the treasure as a bribe, but Shiki refused the bribe and dutifully brought the booty to Genghis Khan's camp at Dolon Nor.

The Supreme Khan ordered General Mukhali to remain behind in command of an army to consolidate the Mongol victory. The capital, the mountain forts, Manchuria, Shanxi, the Liaodong Peninsula, all were in Mongol hands.

Chancellor Yeh-lu told Abbot Hai of the Buddhist monastery where he went to take up residence that it did not matter to him whether he

247

lived or died. He came to envy those who had been quickly decapitated, for it seemed to him that it was easier to die than to survive such horror. At night in dreams, he thought he heard the ghosts of his ancestors calling his name over and over in a howling wind. He did not know whether they summoned him or chastised him.

Spring arrived. Flowers opened in the fields and the snow-laden sky turned from gray to blue. Even the rats were thin. Even as the Mongol carts rumbled out of China, the Mongol generals demanded taxes from the population and confiscated the crops to feed the army.

All was sadness and desolation. Joy left the chancellor and he had no will to live. He had no idea that within a number of years, he would become the most important official in the Mongol Empire.

He embarked upon a quest for enlightenment. He did what was called "shaking off the dust of the world." He studied with Abbot Hai of the Bao-an Temple. This man was a great master. For three years, day and night, Yeh-lu applied himself to his studies. Finally, the Abbot confirmed that he had achieved enlightenment. If he had not sought wisdom, Yeh-lu might have hanged himself with a silken cord for the simple reason that his world had come to an end.

Soon afterward, he received a summons from Genghis Khan to come to his court in Mongolia. Yeh-lu had in his possession the State Seal of the Jin Empire, the seal that was pressed in red wax and affixed to important documents. In the year 1218, the Supreme Khan sent a Chinese general to the monastery. The man wore a seal of authority, a golden tiger **paizi**, a medallion of solid gold embossed with the image of a tiger.

The inscription on the seal in Chinese and Mongolian read: *This is the sacred order of the Oceanic Emperor Genghis who is Beloved of Heaven: All commands are to be executed in accordance with the wishes of his Envoy.*

Yeh-lu left the monastery under armed escort and rode north to Mongolia bearing the seal, a priceless object made of mutton-fat jade.

He made the journey in a palanquin that provided by the khan. The party went through the gates of the Great Wall and entered the barbarian world. Keshig officers, the elite Imperial Guards drawn from the sons of the nomad aristocracy, ordered his party to pass through the fires

248

which the shamans placed at the entrance to the nomad camps to rid visitors of evil spirits.

Guardsmen searched him, for no one was permitted to enter the Supreme Khan's tent bearing arms. They ushered him into the palace-tent. Made of brocade, of immense size, the palace-tent had been taken from the Son of Heaven and was filled with objects from the Jin Imperial Treasury. In the center of the tent was the ivory-and-gold Dragon Throne taken from the Audience Hall. Across it lay the skin of a white horse, the symbol of the Supreme Khan's rule. Genghis Khan sat on the Dragon Throne as though it were a saddle, legs open, torso forward, shoulders squared. He looked as though nothing on earth could unseat him.

Chancellor Yeh-lu was twenty-five years old and had been a courtier all his life. Genghis Khan wore the uniform of the Mongol soldier, a belted tunic with pleated riding trousers and leather riding boots. He had red hair that he wore in plaits and a leather war helmet trimmed in sable. His eyes were amber at the center, ringed in gray. He had wide cheekbones, big shoulders and a broad chest.

Chancellor Yeh-lu was a vain man, over six feet tall and slender in his black silk scholar's gowns. The new Emperor of China fixed his eyes on the man he had summoned. Yeh-lu bowed, asked permission to approach and presented the Khan with the Jin Seal of State.

Under the Khan's unflinching gaze, Yeh-lu knew that he was no mere brute of a military man. The Khan questioned Yeh-lu closely. As a high official in the government of a deposed emperor, Yeh-lu was certain that he was to be put to death. His only thought was to conduct himself with dignity.

"I have avenged you and your ancestors by ridding you of the Jin," Genghis Khan said.

Yeh-lu was offended. No one, not even a great conqueror, was privy to his feelings about his family. He tucked his hands in his sleeves and drew himself up to his full height. "With all due respect, sir, my grandfather, father and I all served the Jin. I would be a liar if I told you that I was happy about their downfall. I would be much happier bringing the seal of state to the Jin Emperor than surrendering it to you, sir."

Yeh-lu waited, wondering from which direction the deathblow would come. None of his soldiers moved.

Then the room erupted with the sound of the Supreme Khan's laughter. He said, "I admire loyalty more than any other virtue, even loyalty to a fallen enemy. If you would be loyal to your vanquished lord even though it could cost you your life, I will trust you to be loyal to me. I offer you a post in my government. I am not an educated man, but I surround myself with educated men. I can make use of your skills."

Genghis Khan was almost fifty, old enough to be Yeh-lu's father. He said that he admired Yeh-lu's accomplishments. Yeh-lu knew writing and record-keeping. He knew history. He was classically educated and could read and write Chinese. He had passed the civil service exams that included the composition of classical Chinese poetry. He was a physician and knew medicines and herbs. He was an astrologer and knew the stars. He was skilled at consulting the I Ching.

The Supreme Khan had to form a government. He offered Yeh-lu the post of **bicigeci**, scribe-secretary in charge of official documents and the position of Court Astrologer. He told Yeh-lu that his generals wanted to turn North China into pasture for Mongol horse herds. Yeh-lu told him that it would be more profitable to tax the population rather than annihilate it. The Mongol generals were taxing at will and bleeding the populace. The populace were packing up and taking the roads that led to Southern China where a Han Chinese emperor sat upon the throne of the Southern Song dynasty. Yeh-lu suggested the taxes that the Chinese populace expected to pay.

"This is what I mean," said Genghis Khan. "You could do a lot of good for your people."

Yeh-lu realized that he was in the position of standing between civilization and barbarism. He was susceptible to flattery although he masked his pleasure well. If the truth be told, Yeh-lu was fascinated by Genghis Khan, who was larger than life, a different order of men from the emperors Yeh-lu had served. Yeh-lu imagined that in antiquity, long before civilization set in, the Chinese once produced men of action such as The Conqueror.

Many of his fellow *literati* had moved to Southern China, refusing their services to the conquest government. Yeh-lu decided that he could save Chinese civilization from the worst of Mongol ways. He had witnessed the horrors of the Mongol conquest firsthand. He accepted

250

employment in the Supreme Khan's court and in the process, gave himself a reason to live.

Little did he know that within a few years, he would become the most important statesman in the Mongol Empire.

A Trade Embassy
1215

Smoke drifted over the walls of Zhongdu. The city was no longer burning, but it was smoldering. Genghis Khan's army was camped in full view of the ruins.

The Campaign in China had lasted four years. The Khan was looking forward to returning to his native pastures. Genghis Khan's brother, Shiki Kutuku, was loading five hundred cartloads of booty, the imperial treasure of China, into black carts for the trip back to the steppes.

It was time to make a final tour of inspection and delegate troops to his Viceroy, Mukhali, who would oversee the garrison of troops after the main army departed. The Mongol Army would cross the Gobi as winter set in.

The Supreme Khan had to decide what to do with the tens of thousands of prisoners who had dug the earthworks for the sieges. He could not transport all of them across the Gobi Desert. Besides, he did not know whether they carried disease. He could not risk bringing them to Mongolia and infecting the population. He decided to execute them because they knew the secrets of his siege warfare. He gave orders to spare artisans and men of learning.

A Guardsman announced the arrival of a trade embassy from the West, from the Muslim lands in Central Asia. Shah Muhammed, the ruler of Khwarezm had sent a merchant named Bahaddin as the leader of the embassy. He carried documents addressed to Genghis Khan from the Shah. There were a number of merchants with their camels and their goods. The camels were in the pen reserved for the animals of visitors.

The Guardsman brought news that Sorghagtani Beki, Tolui's senior wife, had given birth to a second son. She had named the child Khubilai. The child was healthy. Sorghagtani was doing well. Tolui accepted his father's congratulations.

Genghis Khan told the Guardsman to invite Bahaddin to accept the hospitality of his tent.

Genghis Khan was no fool. The conquest of China had been the dream of Muslim rulers for centuries. Genghis Khan guessed that the

252

Shah had heard of the Mongol Khan's conquest of China, and wished to know if it was true that Genghis Khan was the new ruler of China. Travelling merchants made excellent spies.

Shah Mohammed had only recently created his kingdom of Khwarezm, that included the lands to the West in Central Asia, the Kirghiz steppes, Persia, Turkestan and Afghanistan. The Shah Genghis Khan's neighbor. They shared a border in Sibir, in the Land of Snows.

Bahaddin and his fellow traders, congenial but hard-trading men of the bazaars of the Silk Road, entered the tent and Genghis Khan asked them to sit. Six Keshig guards were stationed in the tent. Six more were stationed outside. This was the standard guard for the Khan. He had many enemies and many might wish him dead. Cooks and servants offered roasted meat and tea.

The Supreme Khan made small talk about conquest. Bahaddin told Genghis Khan that as bathing was an important custom in the Muslim lands, and as they had had a long journey, the members of his embassy were anxious to bathe. He did not want to offend the Mongol practice of not bathing in rivers, streams, and lakes. He had heard that the Chinese bathed in tubs heated with coal. He asked if it were possible to find a place to bathe in Zhongdu.

Genghis did not object but agreed to make arrangements. If the man wanted a look at the city, he could have it.

After the meal, the merchants brought their wares. Balchick, who had a prosperous look about him, presented his wares. Textiles were the specialty of the Muslim lands and Balchick traded in the finest and most expensive textiles in Asia. He usually traded his luxury goods to the Chinese court, but as Genghis Khan was now the lord of China, Balchick spread before the Supreme Khan a piece of gold lame.

"Three gold *balish*, Khan, a very good price for gold-embroidered cloth. Two gold *balish* for the silver-embroidered cloth."

Genghis Khan said, "Your price is high. Is it wise to begin commercial relations between our two countries by offering steep prices? Perhaps you don't realize this, but I count many traders among my acquaintance and have been buying goods from the Muslim lands since I was a young man. In fact, I recently bought some cloth just like yours. The fabric is worth no more than 10 to 20 silver *dinars*. I'll show you."

The Khan ordered a guard to go to his tent and bring the goods he had recently acquired from a Persian merchant. The guard returned with a piece of Zandachi cloth, a fine cotton, and also with a piece of Persian cotton. The Chinese kept the manufacture of silk a state secret. They did not have cotton. They did not cultivate the plant. The guard brough Chinese silk.

The merchant apologized for his error, but he had incited the wrath of the Khan.

The Khan told his guards, "Go out to the pens and find out which camels belong to Balchick. Confiscate all his goods as punishment for trying to cheat me."

The other merchants apologized for Balchick's behavior. One of them told the Khan he was embarrassed. "Please don't judge us by his behavior. We have good merchandise and fair prices." He offered an exquisite piece of damask as a gift.

Genghis Khan got over his pique. He liked the damask. Their goods were excellent. He would pay for everything. He was in such a good mood that he forgave Balchick and said that he would pay Balchick 1 gold *balish* for the gold embroidered cloth and 1 silver *balish* for the silver."

Balchick accepted and the evening ended on a peaceful note.

The next day, Mongol soldiers escorted Bahaddin and his retinue into Zhongdu, and they saw what remained of the city that was once the capital of China.

Zhongdu was a charnel ground. The embers of many buildings still glowed and emitted steady streams of smoke. The stone buildings still stood, but many bodies littered the streets and the gutters were greasy with human fat. Mountains of bones lay everywhere.

Outside the south wall were piles of rotting female bodies. Many of the noblewomen had jumped off the wall and committed suicide rather than fall prisoner to the invading army of barbarians. They chose death rather than such a fate. The most beautiful and aristocratic would be married to Mongol noblemen. The rest would become slaves.

Bahaddin and his companions took hot baths in the Imperial Palace, in the former residence of the Emperor's concubines. There in wooden tubs heated with braziers of coal, the Muslims washed for the first time since they crossed the Gobi.

The Muslim party returned to Genghis Khan's camp at Dolon Nor.

That night, one of the Guardsmen came to Genghis Khan's tent to say that several members of the Muslim party had contracted fevers. A Chinese doctor came and examined the patients. He said that there was an epidemic of typhus in the city, because of the rotting bodies. The Muslims had contracted the diseases.

In a few days, all of them except Bahaddin and the camel-pullers died. Bahaddin was allowed to return to the Shah's lands with as many Muslims from camp as he needed to serve as camel-pullers, porters and cooks.

"Why are you releasing them, Khan? asked General Mukhali, who spoke Chinese and heard what the doctor said."

"Because I want him to report to the Shah," said Genghis Khan.

After the departure of the Muslim embassy, the Mongol Army broke camp and returned to Mongolia. It was the last time Genghis Khan would ever see China.

1219

Genghis Khan was eager to establish trade relations with the Shah of Khwarezm, so he sent a trade embassy. It was a luxurious affair. As a sign of respect, Genghis Khan selected a Muslim, a man by the name of Mahmud Ali Khwajah, which translates as Mahmud the Envoy, as his ambassador. Mahmud was a native of Bukhara, a city in the Shah's empire that was a center of Islamic culture and learning, and a lively hub of trade. He chose the man as a mark of respect and a symbol of friendship.

The trade embassy was enormous, 450 people, counting attendants and camel-pullers; all were Muslims. 500 camels carried the merchandise to be sold for the Khan's profit: gold silver, Chinese silk, camel hair, beaver skins and sable pelts. As a special gift, the Khan included a lump of gold the size of a camel's hump.

In the spring of 1219, the trade embassy sent by Genghis Khan arrived in Khwarezm. The embassy only got as far as the city of Utrar, a border town on the frontier. Then the Supreme Khan heard nothing. There was no message of thanks for the golden nugget. There was no expression of admiration for the goods sent for trade. There was no message of appreciation for the selection of Muslims for the embassy. There was nothing.

The Shah lived in a palace in Samarkand. The Persian name for this place was Ferghana; the rivers are called Amu Darya and Syr Darya, *darya* being the Persian word for river. Merchants had used the caravan routes that crisscross the region for a thousand years and the trade had made its citizens prosperous.

The Shah's dream was to become ruler of all the Islamic lands. Long before he encountered Genghis Khan, Shah Mohammed had begun calling himself "The Shadow of Allah on Earth." This did not sit well with the Caliph of Baghdad, the pope and emperor of orthodox Islam. There was a rift between the Shah and the Caliph. The Caliph had sent troops against the Shah and removed the Shah's name from Friday prayers.

The cause of their argument was that the Caliph had refused to renounce all temporal power in favor of the Khwarezmian ruler. Although the Caliph had done this for various other potentates in the region, such as the Seljuk Turks in Egypt, and the Abuyyid Dynasty in Syria, he refused to do it for Shah Muhammed. Things were not going well in the land of Khwarezm.

The Shah thought that China would be better off in his hands than ruled by Genghis Khan. He was insecure. His kingdom had been hastily cobbled together and the army was loyal to his mother who was a Turkish princess. His mother was angry with him because he insulted her for taking a lover in middle age.

His son by his first wife, Jalaladdin, was a great warrior, but the second wife would not allow him in the palace, so the Shah did not have the counsel of his son, which he needed for his own mind had a tendency toward paranoia.

From ancient times, Ferghana had known the greatest of conquerors. Alexander the Great had crossed Central Asia on his way to India and to Afghanistan.

The city walls were surrounded by farms which produced melons and eggplants, grapes and dates; rich with factories where artisans wove cloth of silk, cotton and silver, wove carpets and tooled leather to make exquisite bindings for books, cases of every kind, saddles and cushions; where metal craftsman worked in copper and Chinese from the Oriental quarter made the finest rag paper which was shipped throughout the world of Islam. Every house had a walled garden. Here in this city was the fabulous treasury of Mohammed, a storehouse laden with gold, jewels and pearls.

The Shah was wealthy–his courtiers dressed in gold lamé. He had a vast harem, many prize falcons and many thousands of the finest blooded Arabian horses. Tamed cheetahs roamed his palace.

From Samarkand, in the season, he set out for the desert on his falconing trips where he lived for a month in a resplendent tent surrounded by servants and women.

The Shah of Khwarezm received Ambassador Mahmud and listened politely as Mahmud delivered the Supreme Khan's message:

Genghis Khan thanks the Shah of Khwarezm for his embassy and sends his own in return. Having heard of his power, the Supreme Khan offers to make a treaty of peace with the Shah and place him on a level with the dearest of his sons. The establishment of peace and of safe and profitable trade relations between the kingdom of the Shah of Khwarezm and the Emperor of Mongolia and China would have advantages for both sides."

To Genghis Khan, Shah Mohammed was an inferior, nothing more than a newcomer who owed The Conqueror allegiance. The condescension in the message was not lost upon the Shah.

So he detained Mahmud for a confidential audience and attempted to bribe him. "It is good that we People of the Holy Book remain steadfast to one another. Therefore, you must tell me all that you know about the Khan." The Shah produced a large pigeon's egg ruby as a gift, for he bought from the best traders of the Silk Road who had their shops in Anatolia.

Fearing for his life, Mahmud pretended to agree and accepted the ruby as a "gift."

The Shah asked, "Are his armies superior to mine?"

Mahmud realized that he had to be careful of his reply. Clearly the Shah was attempting to figure out if he had an army that could beat Genghis Khan's. Fearing for his life, Mahmud told an inspired falsehood.

The horses of the Shah's army were Arabians, animals of much greater speed and beauty than the stubby Mongol war ponies. In truth, the Shah had better horses, if one did not count endurance as a virtue. The Shah's army had more beautiful uniforms, though they were probably not as well-equipped. Mahmud knew the Master of Weapons in Genghis Khan's camp because he sold him bridles and stirrups for the Mongol ponies.

Mahmud replied, "The armies of Genghis Khan cannot compare with your own."

"Good. I desire to make a treaty with Genghis Khan."

The next day, the Shah dictated to a scribe and the scribe wrote out the provisions of a commercial treaty

Mahmud departed. Shah Mohammed rode off to Baghdad to attack Caliph Nasir.

A man claiming to be a camel-puller from the trade embassy sent to Khwarezm had arrived in Genghis Khan's camp.

He was very thin and said he had had little food because he had no money and had been lucky to escape from Utrar with his life. The man was in terrible condition, a commoner but intelligent, and refused to divulge his information to the Imperial Guards.

Genghis told the Guardsman to admit the man. The camel-puller dropped down on his knees and touched his forehead to the floor.

"O Khan, I am a humble man and do not know how to address the Great Ones of the earth."

The Khan said, "If it is true that you have escaped from Utrar and bring word of my embassy, you need have no fear of me. I will reward you. Bring him broth."

The man recounted the fate that had befallen the Khan's embassy. "The governor of Utrar stole all the goods. He killed all of your envoys and ambassadors. All are dead, massacred, except for me. 500 camels carrying your merchandise all stolen by that thief, the governor, Inalchik."

This happened two months ago. When Mahmud left the Shah, the Shah sent word to the governor, to detain the Khan's merchants. The Shah said they were spies and that gave him the right to execute every last one of them and to take their goods. The governor carried out Shah Mohammed's orders.

The camel-puller heard that the governor divided the spoils with Shah Mohammed. The goods were sold in the bazaars. By chance, the camel-puller had gone to the bazaar on an errand and had not been detained. That was why his life had been spared.

The camel-puller witnessed the merchants of the bazaar competing to buy the goods that he recognized because he had loaded the goods onto camels and transported them. Those men of the bazaar were excellent at trade and kept so much silver and gold in the bazaar for buying and selling that the camel-puller could hardly believe it. The merchants were gossiping about how the money was shared between the Shah and the governor.

The Supreme Khan rewarded the man and made him a nobleman, with a horde of his own and herds.

Genghis Khan had no desire to engage in a foreign war. He wanted to enjoy his newfound riches, and spend his life in the steppes hunting and passing time with his wives and concubines, for he had many concubines as spoils of war. He was the new political master of Asia. He had to enforce his Code of Laws. If he did not enforce the Yasa, others would come against him. So he gave the Shah one more chance.

The Supreme Khan sent a message to the Shah. This had to be the act of the subordinate. He demanded that the Shah punish the offending official. If he did not want to punish the governor, Genghis Khan demanded that the Shah extradite the governor to him and he would execute him. The Shah sent back a message refusing. To add insult to injury, Shah Mohammed executed the envoy sent to demand punishment. Then he closed the trade routes from Turkestan to China.

These were acts of war. The die was cast. The ruler of Khwarezm had given Genghis Khan no choice.

Genghis Khan sent messengers along the post-roads to the far ends of his empire. He summoned the Mongol nobility to a *khuriltai*, Great Assembly. He informed them that an ambassador of his had been murdered. To Genghis Khan, the person of an ambassador was sacrosanct. He considered the murder of his envoy a gross violation of his Code of Laws. The man had to be punished.

When his wives found out that he was going to the West to make war, they asked him to make a last will and testament, so that if he did not return, they would know his wishes as to the succession. Many members of the nobility asked him the same things. He and Bortai had an understanding. He had promised her that her sons would inherit the empire, but they had four sons. He said that he would leave a will and testament, in writing, when he had come to a decision.

She asked him to leave a copy, in writing, with Tatatonga the scribe. He said that it would be placed in the Treasury with the Code of Genghis Khan, the secret history, and the collection of his maxims that was called *The Biligs*.

He called his sons and generals to his tent. He asked who they thought should rule in the event of my demise. Yeh-lu was in attendance, and he made a copy of the proceedings and wrote it down in Chinese characters.

"Jagadai said, 'Jochi is the eldest, but he cannot be your successor! He is the bastard of the Mergid who captured our mother.'

Genghis Khan thundered for silence. "Be careful of your tongue, Jagadai. I have only so much patience, even with my blood. I have always acknowledged Jochi as my son and have never allowed anyone to say otherwise. Don't ever speak to him that way again.'

Bogorji grabbed Jagadai by the shoulder and shook him. "Your ignorance insults your own mother."

Jagadai apologized, but he was boiling.

"The moment passed. Ogodei made a joke. He said that everyone knew that Jagadai was a bore and uptight, an upright prude making rules for everyone to follow."

"I take this as a matter of the utmost importance. I leave you my life work. I have observed you closely for many years and I have given the matter no small amount of thought.

"Yeh-lu advised me to follow the Chinese practice. The Chinese have hereditary rule, sir. The eldest son inherits and then the other sons, as the father provides. I don't believe in hereditary rule. I have seen its effects in the civilized world and I don't think much of it. I have defeated

261

too many rulers who inherited their kingdoms. The Mongols elect rulers on the basis of their ability and that is a good system. But I will choose my heir."

"Jochi performed well in the Army of the Right under General Bogorji's command. Jagadai also performed well, but the military is not his calling. Jagadai was born to be a judge. He learned my Code of Laws by heart. I had to constantly remind him that when he became a commander, he could not hold his men to the same high standards he set for himself, because some of them were not capable of measuring up. I knew this would be a problem with his leadership and tried to curb him of the habit, but one can only go so far. This is Jagadai's nature.

"My third son Ogodei is a good horseman and loves the hunt. He is a solid but not exceptional commander. Ogodei has the common touch. He I liberal and has a generous heart. I think he is too liberal and too generous with everyone from the grooms and herders to the nobility. From the time he was a small boy, he has been a natural diplomat. He has the nature of a peacemaker. His only flaw is that he is too given to pleasure. He likes to drink and he chases too many women.

"Tolui, my youngest son, is most like me. He is a natural military man. Anyone who loves the military should follow Tolui. Tolui and Ogodei love one another best. I am naming Ogodei my successor because of his liberal nature. Tolui will inherit most of my army. It is his task to back up Ogodei's rule with the army.

"The man who ruled after me is chosen, not on the basis of affection, for I love all my sons, but on the basis of character.

"Jochi and Jagadai do not get along and argue constantly. I have given them lands far apart. This is my wish."

Jagadai received the Central Asian khanate and would see to it that the code of laws was upheld throughout the empire.

Jochi would have the North Country, Sibir and Russia, the furthest west that Mongol ponies rode. It was the custom of the Mongol people to give the eldest son the lands furthest from the father's native pastures. Jochi was to rule the attack wing of the Mongol Empire.

Tolui received the father's pastures, the Valley of Two Rivers and would become the Khan of Mongolia. He was commanded to remind

Ogodei of his duties. He was also to remind Ogodei to uphold the *Yasak*, Chinggis Khan's code of laws. *Yasak*.

"Each of you are to keep a copy of the Great Code in your treasury, and on great occasions, display it and revere it. Jagadai was designated to enforce the Code. Shiki Kutuku, who was named Chief Judge, will adjudicate cases."

Ogodei asked, "What if none of my sons should prove fit for rule? My second son, Guyug, is sickly. My first son died. I have a grandson by him."

"Surely someone of my line will prove fit for rule. Hold a *khuriltai*, a Great Assembly. Let the nobility hold an election," Genghis Khan replied. He was no believer in hereditary rule. The Mongol Army was a meritocracy.

As Chancellor Yeh-lu was later to confide to Princess Sorghagtani, this was Genghis Khan's only mistake. He failed to provide for an orderly succession to the throne, and the heirs would be dealing with it for generations.

My name is Yeh-lu Ch'u-ts'ai. For the past twelve years I have been personal secretary, physician and astrologer to Genghis Khan, conqueror of the world.

In the space of twenty years, with his army, the most disciplined and highly trained fighting force in the world, he has built an empire which extends west from the volcanic mountains of Manchuria on the Pacific Coast to the Muslim lands on the Mediterranean Sea; from the arctic wastes of the Siberian taiga to the jungles of Burma.

The capital of his empire is in the nomad world, in Mongolia, in the city of tents known as Khara Khorum, or Black Rock. He also has capitals in the civilized world, walled cities: in China, he rules from the city of golden tiled rooves, Khan-balik, In Central Asia, he has the elegant old garden city of Samarkand. He also has Bukhara, a great trading city and a center of Muslim learning and culture.

The Mongols have only had writing since Genghis Khan gave them a script in 1206. They have not become accustomed to the writing of history, and have no literary style, nor any ability to keep records. How could they leave a history of themselves?

On the other hand, the Chinese literati *produce brilliant history but how could they abandon their belief in their own superiority in order to tell the story of their conqueror?*

I write this memoir in the year 1227, the year of the Supreme Khan's death in order that I who have stood beside him on the battlefield and at court, I who know something of his personal life, may leave the story of the man called World Conqueror for generations to come.

A Confucian looks for moral order in history. Despite what Chinese literati *say, I have found moral order among the nomads. Genghis Khan was a genius at war. His warfare, far from being ruthless, bloodthirsty and savage, had a morality, an elementary logic, all its own. He never left an enemy population behind the advancing front lines of his army. His Code of Laws has ushered in an era of peace. After the conquest, his empire was as much about trade as it was about war.*

264

Chinese historians will record the bloody deeds of the Mongols, but only I can tell how I helped to eradicate the worst of their ways by serving them.

I am half-Chinese, half-nomad, and speak both Chinese and the languages of the steppes. Yeh-lu, my family name, is the name of the royal house of the Khitai. Originally, we were a cultured tribe who lived to the northeast of the Great Wall, a people who became cultured by trading with China for her fabulous silks and articles of manufacture. From our settlement outside the Great Wall, we envied China, the richest and most brilliant civilization on earth and we saw her weaknesses. The story of my nomadic ancestors was the usual one for the tribes who inhabit the steppe zone outside the Great Wall. We conquered China at a time when Chinese rulers were weak.

The Tang Dynasty, a much-sung Golden Age, the most cosmopolitan period in Chinese history, was a period of military rule presided over by the great Chinese feudal families of the northwest. The central government became corrupt; the Tang could not keep control over the entire country. The dynasty fell when the imperial army lost control of the frontier provinces.

In the chaos which descended on China after the fall of the Tang, China became divided into many small kingdoms. My Khitan ancestors, strong in military ways, came down from the steppe on horseback, sacked the Chinese capital and took over the palace. We conquered Northeast China and ruled for two hundred years as the Liao Dynasty.

We became civilized, seduced utterly by China's culture. Then more vigorous barbarians, the Jurchen who were Manchus, came down from the northeast and defeated us. They formed the Jin Dynasty. The remains of my family fled west and founded a state in a place called Khara Khitai or Black Cathay.

The Han Chinese who fled from the barbarians set up a new capital at Hangzhou south of the Yangzi River. The founder, Tai-tsu or Grand Progenitor, of the Southern Song Dynasty, was a Chinese general of an old family who at a victory banquet asked his commanders to turn in their swords and accept civilian titles. They depended on the river, a natural barrier, to protect them from the northern barbarians and it did.

265

The Song prospered. Their economy was not based on agriculture but on trade and manufacture, not on military families but on merchant families. It was wealthier than Tang and possessed a brilliant culture. Although for hundreds of years ministers exhorted emperors, the Song were powerless to take north China back from the barbarians. How are these events to be explained except that the Chinese dynasty lost the Mandate of Heaven, without which no emperor rules China?

The Jin knew nothing of governing. They depended utterly upon my family, the deposed Khitan royalty who remained in China. My grandfather, father and I all served them as officials. We were mediators between the Chinese literati who formed the vast government of China and the wild Manchus of the steppes whose emperor had untamed tigers roaming his palace and vulgar dancing girls gyrating in a disgusting manner as they held up mirrors to their audience so that the Manchu courtiers might observe the slack look of lust upon their own faces.

The Jin Emperor was all too aware of the danger the nomads in the wild regions of the north represented. After all, that was the quarter from which his own dynasty had issued. He pursued the usual Chinese foreign policy toward tribal peoples outside the Great Wall, _i-i-zi-i_, "using barbarians to keep barbarians in check." The Mongol tribe posed a threat to Jin rule because they had produced strong leaders for generations. To upset the Mongol balance of power, the Jin made allies of the Tatar tribe. In time, the Tatar grew strong enough to menace Chinese frontier forces. Without a shred of conscience, the Jin Emperor abandoned the Tatar and embraced the Mongols, who had so recently been his enemy. The young Genghis Khan, just coming to power in the steppes, became a Chinese vassal. In return for the title of Pacifier and many gifts by the Chinese court, Genghis Khan was given the privilege of paying the emperor tribute. A loyal vassal, Genghis Khan hunted down the Tatar for his lord and wiped them from the face of the earth.

In China, the Central Country, one sees the great patterns of history clearly: rise and fall, ebb and flow, yin and yang, barbarism and civilization. The Jin Emperor was surrounded by weak men, descendants of the old Manchu nobility, drunken sycophants who took over the highest positions of government and shut out the professional bureaucrats, my fellow scholar-officials. The Jin had grown indolent

266

and luxury-loving. The time was ripe for a great leader to rise up in Mongolia. Genghis Khan, with his brilliant generals and his unparalleled army crossed the Gobi and descended from the steppes like a storm.

Genghis Khan's campaign against China was difficult and changed forever his previous ideas about conquest. The method of warfare he used during his rise to power in the steppes was the total slaughter of conquered populations. Under the vast blue sky of Mongolia, the land is empty as far as the eye can see. Populations are small. There, nothing is grown or manufactured. Once he wiped an enemy from the face of the earth, they were annihilated for all time. Civilization in China meant hundreds of miles of continuous settlement: farms, factories, workshops, stores, boatyards, temples. When the Mongols slaughtered the population of a city, within a short time, swarms of people reinhabited the place and before long, it was as though the Mongols had never taken it.

Against walled cities, the Mongol Army faltered. They were men born to the horse. They knew nothing of walls, gates, battlements, fortifications, citadels. Many Jin generals, men of the world, could see that this bold and sweeping campaign was no mere barbarian raid. Genghis Khan was destined to be the new ruler of China. These generals and many Chinese engineers decided to trust to Genghis Khan's guarantee of good treatment and went over to the Mongol side. With the help of these defectors, Genghis Khan mastered the art of siege warfare within a few years. The capital Zhongdu fell in the year 1215.

I fell into a profound depression and retreated to a Buddhist monastery in North China where I meditated under the guidance of an abbot. I remained there for three years. Then I was summoned north, into Genghis Khan's presence, and ordered to bring the seal of state.

I am a classically educated person. Yet I cannot call Genghis Khan a barbarian as many of the Chinese literati do. He was proud of being a nomad who owned vast herds of horses, sheep, goats, yak, oxen; proud of being the unifier of the ceaselessly warring nomad tribes of Mongolia. He loved the free open life of the steppe. He loved being a soldier. He wore the same rags as his men, ate the same food as they,

267

and lived in a tent. He rode at the head of his army into countless battles and was victorious in all of them.

Only at the end of his life, did he allow himself to grow accustomed to the luxuries he had plundered in China. Yet, although he professed to despise the sedentary world, I believe he possessed a great gift for civilization. He was the first nomad khan ever to rule a sedentary culture. He built a system of roads and post-stations connecting all the cities in his empire. His messengers kept him in touch with the farthest stretches of that empire. Most importantly, he gave his world a code of laws called the Yasak. It was more lenient than the Tang Code. It ushered in the era known as The Mongol Peace.

At the time of the invasion of China which began in the year 1211, I was an official in the government of the Jin Dynasty. I must confess to being vain. I am over six feet tall and slender. In my blue silk scholar's robes, I appear very different from the Mongol barrel-chested generals and aristocrats of the steppe.

After the fall of the capital, Genghis Khan refused to live in the palace. Born to the horse, he camped in a yurt on the steps outside the Great Wall. In his tent, he sat upon the Jin Emperor's throne as though it were a saddle, legs open, torso forward, weight balanced, shoulders squared. His eyes were golden amber at the center, rimmed in gray, hawk-wings. He had red hair which he wore in two plaits, under a leather helmet trimmed in sable fur. He was tall, as tall as I am, and straight-legged. The Mongols do not bathe frequently for they are shamanists and superstitious about the spirits in rivers and water. He wore the uniform of the Mongol soldier, a long tunic, soiled from the battlefield, and pleated riding trousers and leather riding boots. His legs spread wide, he looked as though nothing on earth could unseat him.

The Great Khan fixed his eyes on me. Under his unflinching gaze, I knew to the depths of my spirit that this was no ordinary barbarian, no mere brute of a military man.

The Great Khan questioned me closely. Being a high official of a deposed emperor, I was certain that I was to be put to death. My only thought was to conduct myself with dignity. I did not know then how much the Great Khan admired men of learning.

My ability to read and write Chinese, my knowledge of the stars and of medicine, he said through an interpreter, could be of immense value to him.

He asked if I would become his personal secretary. I was stunned. That was his way. He was not an educated man, but he made use of my education. I accepted Genghis Khan's offer and dedicated myself to the task of transforming the nature of his rule.

I have had the chance to observe the Mongols at close hand for almost thirty years now. They are crude by Chinese standards and superstitious. They are gluttons who, at their feast, eat gargantuan amounts and descend into glassy-eyed stumbling drunkenness. They stink from drinking koumiz, fermented mare's milk. In cutting their wide swath across the world, they have left mountains of skulls. I paint a terrible picture of the Mongols, yet I admire their courage, discipline and the skill in warfare which has allowed them to master the world.

Genghis Khan barely comprehended civilized life. He was above all a soldier. To sweep a Chinese city from the face of the earth to create pasture for Mongol horses, seemed reasonable and practical. To stop the carnage, I appealed to his lust for goods, the greed which all Mongols had in abundance. I told him how he might tax the population instead of plundering and annihilating it. I described the silk, grain, precious metals, porcelains and jewels, which he might obtain annually through taxes and tributes.

The Great Khan changed. From the time he conquered China, his court became magnificent. His tent was decorated with gold fabric, rich carpets, precious porcelains, sculptures, objects of carved jade, one in particular I remember as belonging to the Jin emperor, an elephant of mutton-fat jade which had rubies for eyes.

When I went to the battlefield with my medicines, he was grateful that I stopped the epidemics of dysentery and typhus which so often followed the slaughter.

Many of my fellow literati *refused to live under the alien rule of the Mongols. Painters, scholars and officials, men of talent fled to Southern China to the protection of the Song Emperor. He was Han Chinese. He was not strong enough to re-conquer the north, yet the Song Emperor presided over a brilliant culture, perhaps more brilliant than that of Tang.*

I remained with the Mongols and my influence prevailed. Had I not played my part in the Mongol drama, Chinese civilization might have been destroyed.

If I am to find any explanation besides destiny in what inspired Genghis Khan to undertake his life of conquest, I can only suggest this: he was a Mongol prince whose father was the lord of clans numbering forty thousand tents. It was his birthright to one day rule these clans. When the Tatar murdered his father, his future was taken from him. His greedy kinsmen were unwilling to follow a boy, (Temujin, as he was called in his youth) and abandoned him. It was the first of many betrayals. I believe his need to triumph over his helplessness created in him a lust for power which never left him.

As for my own future, after the period of mourning Genghis Khan, the Mongol nobility gathered from the far corners of the empire and held a khuriltai, *a Great Assembly. They deliberated and ratified Genghis Khan's choice of successor, his third son Ogodei. I was delighted when Ogodei requested that I continue as Chancellor. I have told the new Khagan that I will serve him as faithfully as I served his father before him.*

Yeh-Lu Ch'u-Ts'ai
Secretary to Ogodei Khan
Khara Khorum, Mongolia, 1227
His Seal Affixed

270

Principal Characters

Temujin	Genghis Khan's boyhood name
Oyelun	Mother of Genghis Khan
Yesugei	Father of Genghis Khan
Khasar	Brother of Genghis Khan
Sochigil	Yesugei's Second Wife
Begder	Genghis Khan's half-brother
Belgutei	His brother
Bortai	Genghis Khan's principal wife
Gulan	Genghis Khan's fourth wife
Yesui	
Yesugan	Genghis Khan's Tatar wives

Subudei
Bogorji
Mukhali   The Generals
Jelme
Jebe "The Arrow"
Boroghul

Jochi
Jagadai   Genghis Khan's Sons By Bortai,
Ogodei   The Heirs To His Empire
Tolui

Jamuga   Genghis Khan's sworn brother, rival

Togril   The Ong Khan, Lord of the Kereyid
The Senggum   His son, rivals

Glossary

anda	Sworn brother
Blue Mongols	Genghis Khan's Tribe. Borjigins
Caliph of Baghdad	Pope/emperor of orthodox Islam
darugachi	Mongol military governor
ger	Round felt tent, a yurt
Jin Dynasty	Ruler of North China
Keshig	Imperial Guards
Kereyid	Ruler of southwestern Mongolia
Khongirad	Marrying clan of the Mongols
Khuriltai	Great Assembly
Khwarezm	Ruler of Central Asia
Koko Tengri	Eternal Blue Sky
Mergid	Forest tribe in southern Siberia
Naiman	Rulers of Western Mongolia
Tatar	Rulers of Eastern Mongolia
Ortagh	Muslim merchant association
Southern Song	Ruler of Southern China
Ulus	Home pastures
Yarligh	Decree
Yasa	Genghis Khan's legal code
Xi-Xia	State in northwest China

Select Bibliography

Allsen, Thomas T. 1987. *Mongol Imperialism*. Berkeley: University of California Press.

Al-Din, Rashid. John Andrew Boyle, trans. 1971. *The Successors of Genghis Khan*. New York: Columbia University Press.

Atwood, Christopher, 2021. *The Rise of the Mongols: Five Chinese Sources*. Cambridge: Hackett.

_____. 2004. *Encyclopedia of Mongolia and the Mongol Empire*. Bloomington: University of Indiana Press. www.academia.edu/8855875/Encyclopedia_of_Mongolia_and_the_ Mongol_Empire

Biran, Michel Biran. 2013 *Qaidu and the Rise of the Independent Mongol State in Central Asia*. New York: Routledge.

_____ *et al., eds.*, 2020. *Along the Silk Roads in Mongol Eurasia: Generals, Merchans and Intellectuals*. Oakland: University of California Press.

Boyle, John Andrew. 1968. *The Cambridge History of Iran, Volume 5: The Saljuq and Mongol Periods*. Cambridge: Cambridge University Press,

Broadbridge, Anne F. 2018. *Women and the Making of the Mongol Empire*. New York: Cambridge University Press.

Buell, Paul D. 1979. "Sino-Khitan Administration in Mongol Bukhara." *Journal of Asian History* 13: 121-151.

Chen, Paul Heng-chao. 1979. *Chinese Legal Tradition under the Mongols*. Princeton: Princeton University Press.

_____, trans. and ed. 1982. *The Secret History of the Mongols*. Cambridge: Harvard University Press.

Dardess, John W. 1972-1973. "From Mongol Empire to Yüan Dynasty: Changing Forms of Imperial Rule in Mongolia and Central Asia." *Monumenta Serica 30*: 117-165.

Dawson, Christopher, ed. 1980. *Mission to Asia*. Toronto: University of Toronto Press.

Eliade, Mircea. 1974. *Shamanism: Archaic Techniques of Ecstasy*. Princeton: Princeton University Press.

Favereau, Marie.2021. *The Horde: How the Mongols Changed the World.* Cambridge: Harvard University Press, Belknap.

Franke, Herbert. 1966. "Sino-Western Contacts under the Mongol Empire." *Journal of the Royal Asiatic Society, Hong Kong Branch* 6: 1972.

_____ and Twitchett, Denis, eds. 1994. *Cambridge History of China, Vol.6, Alien Regimes and Border States (907-1368.* New York: Cambridge University Press.

Grousset, Rene. Marian McKellar and Denis Sinor, trans. 1972. *Conqueror of the World: The Life of Chingis Khan.* New York: Viking Press.

_____. Naomi Walford, trans. 1970. *The Empire of the Steppes: A History of Central Asia.* New Brunswick, NJ: Rutgers University Press.

Hodong, Kim. 2005. "A Reappraisal of Guyug Khan." In *Mongols, Turks, And Others: Eurasian Nomads and the Sedentary World.* Reuven Amitai and Michal Biran, eds. Brill's Inner Asian Library. vol. 11. https://www.academia.edu/28691612/A_Reappraisal_of_G%C3%BCy%C3%BCg_Khan

Howorth, H. H. 1965. *History of the Mongols: 9th to 19th Centuries.* New York: Burt Franklin Press, 1965. Reissue, 5 volumes.

Jackson, Peter 2005. *The Mongols and the West.* New York: Routledge.

Juvaini, Ala-ad Din Ata-Malik. John Andrew Boyle, trans. 1958. *The History of the World Conqueror. 2 vols.* Manchester: Manchester University Press.

Kahn, Paul. 1981. *Secret History of the Mongols.* Berkeley: University of California Press.

Kwanten, Luc Herman N. 1979, *Imperial Nomads: A History of Central Asia, 500-1500.* Philadelphia: University of Pennsylvania Press.

Lamb, Harold. 1927. *Genghis Khan: Emperor of All Men.* Garden City, New York: Robert M. McBride.

Langlois, John D., ed. 1981. *China under Mongol Rule.* Princeton: Princeton University Press. See "The Muslims in the Early Yuan Dynasty," by Morris Rossabi.

Lo Jung-pang. 1954-1955. "The Emergence of China as a Sea Power during the Late Sung and Early Yüan Periods." *Far Eastern Quarterly* 14: 489-503.

Martin, H. Desmond. 1981. *The Rise of Chinggis Khan and His Conquest Of North China.* New York: Octagon Books.

May, Timothy. 2012. *The Mongol Conquest in World History.* London: Reaktion Books.

Olschki, Leonardo. 1960. *Marco Polo's Asia.* Berkeley: University of California Press.

Perdue, Peter C. 2010. *China Marches West: The Qing Conquest of Central Eurasia,* Cambridge: Harvard University Press.

Polo, Marco. *The Travels.* Ronald Latham, trans. 1982. New York: Penguin Books, 1982.

Prawdin, Michael. Eden and Cedar Paul, trans. 1940. *The Mongol Empire: Its Rise and Legacy.* . London: George Allen and Unwin, Ltd.

Rachewiltz, Igor de. 1971. *Papal Envoys to the Great Khans.* London: Faber & Faber.

_____. March, 1977, "Some Remarks on the Ideological Foundations of Chingis Khan's Empire." *Papers on Far Eastern History* 7: 21-36.

_____. 1962. *"The Hsi-yu Lu* by Yeh-lü Chu-tsai. *Monumenta Serica* 21: 1-28.

_____. 1962. "Yeh-lu Chü-tsai (1189-1243): Buddhist Idealist and Statesman.@ In *Confucian Personalities,* Arthur Wright and Denis Twitchett, eds. Stanford: Stanford University Press, 189-216.

_____, et al, eds. 1993. *In the Service of the Khan: Eminent Personalities of the Early Mongol- Yüan Period (1200-1300).* Wiesbaden:.

Riasanovsky, Valentin A. 1965. *Fundamental Principals of Mongol Law.* Bloomington: Indiana: University Uralic and Altaic Series. Reprint.

Richards, D. S., ed. 1970. *Islam and the Trade of Asia.* Philadelphia: University of Pennsylvania Press.

Rossabi, Morris. 1988. *Khubilai Khan: His Life and Times.* Berkeley: University of   California Press.
_____. 2010. *The Mongols and Global History.* New York: W. W. Norton and Company.
_____. 1970. "The Tea and Horse Trade with Inner Asia during the Ming." *Journal of Asian History* 4:2: 136-168.
_____. 1994. "All The Khan's Horses." *Natural History.*
Saunders, John Joseph. 1971. *The History of the Mongol Conquests.* New York: Barnes and Noble.
Schlepp, Wayne. 1975. "Yeh-lü Chu-tsai in Samarkand." *Canada Mongolia Review* 1: 2, 5-14.
Sinor, Denis. 1999. "The Mongols in the West. *Journal of Asian History* 33:2, pp. 1-44.
Smith, John Masson. December, 1984. "Ayn Jalut: Mamluk Success or Mongol Failure." *Harvard Journal of Asiatic Studies* 44: 2, 307-45.
Spuler, Bertold. Helga and Stuart Drummond, trans. 1972. *History of the Mongols Based on Eastern and Western Accounts of the Thirteenth and Fourteenth Centuries.* Berkeley: University of California Press.
Vernadsky, George, 1938. "The Scope and Contents of Chingis Khan's *Yasa.*" Harvard Journal of Asiatic Studies 3: 337-60.
Vladimirtsov, Boris Prince Mirsky, trans. 1969. *The Life of Chingis-Khan.* New York: Benjamin Blom.
Weatherford, Jack. 2017. *Genghis Khan and The Quest for God.* New York: Viking.
_____, 2005. *Genghis Khan and the Making of the Modern World.* New York: Broadway Books (Reprint).
Yule, Henry, trans. Henri Cordier, revision. 1903. *The Book of Ser Marco Polo, the Venetian, Concerning the Kingdoms and Marvels of the East 2vols. 3rd ed.* London: John Murray.

Made in the USA
Columbia, SC
26 May 2023